When the Wolf Dreams

Madeleine series
Book 5

by Sadie Conall

Special thanks to selfpubbookcovers.com/woofie_2015 for my great cover

Sadie Conall's website
www.sadieconall.com

Books by Sadie Conall

Madeleine (seven-part series)
historical romance fantasy
When the Wolf Loves *(Ryder: a boy alone now a free short story added to When the Wolf Loves)*
When the Wolf Hunts *(previously published as When the Wolf Bites: Part I)*
When the Wolf Bites *(previously published as When the Wolf Bites: Part II)*
When the Wolf Dreams
When the Wolf Breathes

Escape west by wagon train (two-part series)
historical western romance adventure set around mid-1840's
Ella
Ruby

This book is dedicated to

Frank (Joe) and Mona (Noni)

for everything

Contents

This book is dedicated to 5

Author's Note 10

Alexandra, Virginia: early July 1804 ....*13*

St Louis: early July 1804 ....*15*

St Louis: mid July 1804 ....*49*

in the wild: early August 1804 ....*60*

Atlantic Ocean: early August 1804 ....*101*

in the wild: late-August 1804 ....*103*

Atlantic Ocean: early September 1804 ....*113*

in the wild: early September 1804 ....*116*

New Orleans: mid-September 1804 ....*130*

in the wild: mid-September 1804 ....*134*

in the wild: October 1804 ....*161*

Corrigan ranch, St Louis: October 1804 ....*166*

in the wild: early October 1804 ....*170*

St Louis: mid October 1804 ....*175*

in the wild: mid-October 1804 ....*188*

St Louis: mid October 1804 ....*193*

in the wild: mid October 1804 ....*208*

St Louis: mid October 1804 ....*213*

in the wild: mid October 1804 ....*223*

St Louis: mid October 1804 ....*238 in the wild: November 1804* *242*

Omaha territory, December 1804 ....*250*

in the wild: January 1805 ....*258*

Omaha territory: early February 1805 ....*267*

Translation of tribal dialects

ainqa-haih - red crow *(Bannock)*

aishi-waahni' - silver fox *(Shoshone)*

atsa-wannge'e - red fox *(Bannock)*

baagwana – wild peppermint *(Bannock)*

bannaite' – Bannock people, language *(Bannock)*

bia'isa-bihyi - wolf heart *(Shoshone)*

bia-wihi - big knife *(Shoshone)*

bitehwai-dainah - white man limping *(Shoshone)*

chahn-yah'-hoo – cottonwood tree *(Lakota Sioux)*

deaipede'tuine – baby boy *(Shoshone)*

deide'dee-daga' - little friend *(Shoshone)*

deinde'-paggwe - little fish *(Shoshone)*

deide'wesa – little bear *(Bannock)*

esa – wolf *(Shoshone)*

esa-mogo'ne - wolf woman *(Bannock)*

ese-ggwe'na'a - grey eagle *(Shoshone)*

gi'zica – brown squirrel *(Mandan)*

hanyewi'winyan – moon woman *(Sioux)*

hůŋkpapȟa – Hunkpapa people, language *(Sioux)*

huu'aidi - hunting bow *(Bannock)*

Itázipčho – Sans Arc people *(Lakota Sioux)*

kokon - old snake *(Shoshone)*

kimana – butterfly *(Bannock)*

kwipuntsi - little scorpion *(Shoshone)*

lakhóta – Hunkpapa dialect *(Lakota Sioux)*

loĉhín'míla – hungry knife *(Mandan Sioux)*

mogo'ne' – woman *(Bannock)*

mukua'hainji - friend of the spirit world or spirit guide *(Bannock)*

núnpa'sunka' – two dogs *(Lakota Sioux)*

nu'p'minaki – two suns *(Sioux)*

paddake'e - raccoon *(Shoshone)*

poongatse - little mouse *(Bannock)*

saca-tzah-we-yaa - boat launcher *(Shoshone)*

sa'zuzeca – red snake *(Mandan Sioux)*
sunka'winyan – dog woman *(Mandan Sioux)*
tahkawütik – rising sun *(Skiri Pawnee)*
Tsêhéstáno - Cheyenne nation *(Cheyenne)*
te'tukhe - yellow buffalo *(Ugákhpa)*
wakanta – man of thunder *(Wazhazhe)*
wannge'e – fox *(Bannock)*
wazhingka - little bird *(Ugákhpa)*
wesa-shangke - snake dog *(Ugákhpa)*
zintkala - brown bird *(Sioux)*

Author's Note

Like the other books in this series of *Madeleine*, I have spent countless hours of research for this story, making sure I have all the details correct, out of respect for the tribes who are mentioned here. The state of Arkansas was named after the Kansa. They were also known as Kaw and closely related to the Omaha, Ponca, Ugákhpa and Wazhazhe. These five tribes were also affiliated to the Sioux nations of the Great Plains and spoke the language of the Dhegiha Sioux.

From the early 1700's European diseases had a devastating effect on Native Americans, because of their lack of immunity to fight them. Some historians suggest hundreds of thousands died from smallpox alone, while others suggest millions perished from smallpox, typhus, diphtheria and other diseases.

The Missouria mentioned in this story once thrived in huge communities from the Great Lakes to the mouth of the Missouri and Mississippi Rivers, yet by 1829, less than 100 were still alive, ravaged by fighting with other tribes, smallpox and other European diseases. The state of Missouri and the Missouri River are named after them.

The Wazhazhe people, the village where Ryder, Wesa'shangke and Te'tukhe were born, lost a third of their nation from smallpox, as already mentioned in this series, in the early 1800's.

In 1804, crossing the Mississippi and Missouri rivers was a feat by anyone's standards and in all my research it seems the only way to cross at that time in history was either by canoe, keelboat or by lashing pirogues together, creating a flat surface to carry horses and even wagons across. The earliest reference I could find to any kind of ferry on those rivers was a flatboat, built sometime between 1820 and 1830, almost thirty years after Madeleine and her small party made their crossing.

I have taken some liberties in Madeleine owning sawn-off muskets, but in my research I discovered that one of the men in the Lewis and Clark Expedition did in fact own a sawn-off musket.

While on a road trip some years ago from New York to LA, somewhere in the west, close to Yellowstone National Park but many miles south of the Snake River mentioned in these stories, we came across a wide deep trench that looked like any other shallow valley. It was in fact a well signposted historic trail, telling of the millions of buffalo that came through that way in years long past, on their migratory paths south. Some said it took days for just one herd to pass through a valley. Like everyone else who stood on the edge of that wide deep trench, close to a tourist venue selling souvenirs and refreshments, I was in awe, that these extraordinary creatures once existed in such vast numbers to leave such a path behind them. I can only imagine the sight of them, along with the smell and noise of such a herd and the men who hunted them.

I want to thank my readers for all your encouragement, your patience (for this book broke all my deadlines, not once, but twice) and that you love Ryder and Madeleine's story as much as I do.
Sadie

Continued on from *When the Wolf Bites*, the third book in the Madeleine series.

Madeleine has arrived in St Louis, but after receiving news from London shattering all her hopes of finding Ryder alive, she decides to leave St Louis and head out into the wild, hoping to reach the Bannock before winter.

Alexandra, Virginia: early July 1804

"Pass it on without delay. It must reach St Louis with the utmost urgency."

The English captain of the Benedict clipper which had just berthed in Alexandria passed the letter over to the American, a stranger, captain of an American ship about to set sail for New Orleans.

The American glanced down at the document, which was clearly a letter wrapped in parchment to protect it from its perilous journey across the world, although it was already battered and stained. He was obligated to take it, as this was often the only way that deliveries were made to settlers in the wild, if they were not lost or stolen along the way.

But still, the American paused before agreeing to take possession of it. The letter held no value to him and despite the official looking seal of melted wax on the back, it didn't interest him. Aware that the English captain was waiting on his reply, he finally reached out to take it.

"Yes, of course. I'll pass it on to someone heading up the Mississippi as soon as we reach New Orleans," he replied, then reached out to shake the English captain's hand.

The men parted company and the American put the letter in his coat pocket. He planned to be in New Orleans soon enough, but first he had an important stop along the way.

A large consignment of home brewed whisky was waiting to be collected at a pre-arranged destination a little further south, along the coast of South Carolina. The whisky came from one of his well-connected suppliers and he dared not miss that pickup, as his buyers in New Orleans would not be happy. The stop might delay his arrival in New Orleans for a day or two, but no more, therefore he saw no reason to mention it to the English captain.

St Louis: early July 1804

One

The arrival of a letter from Sir George Ashbury in
early July changed all of Madeleine's plans. By the
time she'd finished reading it, she felt as if she'd
woken from a dream and understood at last that
she'd been waiting on a letter such as this from
London in the hope of receiving news of Ryder.

But this letter bore no such news.

Madeleine retired to her bedroom suite to read it
again in private, but as she sat on her bed, her hands
trembling as she held the fragile paper, she felt the
crushing weight of Ash's words.

He wrote of his continuing good health, which
was due in no small part to his semi-retirement. He
wrote of the success of Stretton Court, that Diccon
House and Millbryne Park were running as well as
they ever did, that Rupert and Charlotte's family were
thriving. But then he penned the words which broke
her heart.

*We've heard nothing more on Ryder's whereabouts,
although Rupert pushes the Constabulary weekly to do more.
Yet it seems, as before, they face a losing battle for there are no
clues or leads, as if Ryder has fallen off the very face of the
earth.*

*I write the Admiralty often to enquire if they have further
news, but they have so little information to share with me, it
often feels pointless to keep bothering them.*

*So my dear, for the meantime, it seems all we can do is wait
and pray that Ryder is still alive, somewhere in the world.*

Ash finished the letter by saying that they all

missed her and Harry, despite it being only two months since they set sail from England.

He wrote that Rupert, Charlotte and Bernard Fahey had also sent letters which he hoped she'd receive without too long a delay. He mentioned they might all return to Millbryne Park for Christmas, to carry on the tradition begun by Ryder, yet nothing had been confirmed.

I don't think anyone's heart is truly in it, not without your own good self being there, along with Ryder and Harry. But we shall see. I think it will be a spur of the moment thing, if we all do manage to get down there.

Madeleine looked at the first page of the letter and saw that Ash had dated it just two weeks before Christmas. He'd written this seven months ago.

She put the letter aside, feeling desolate. She'd lingered here for four months in the hope of receiving news that Ryder had been found alive. But this letter dashed all her hopes.

She'd been a fool. She'd left England to return to the Bannock yet had stayed on here, waiting for some tidbit of information, because once she left St Louis for the wild there would be no contact from anyone for at least four years. By waiting, by delaying her journey, she'd lost weeks of good travelling during the summer months.

She should have arrived at the Wazhazhe village three months ago and by now, be well on her way north to the Omaha.

She picked the letter up and reread it, allowing the bitter tears of disappointment to fall, understanding at last that the waiting was over. It was time to move on.

She put the letter aside and walked across to the sideboard to the washing bowl and jug of fresh water. She poured water into the bowl and splashed her face.

Two weeks, but no more than that! Within two weeks she must be gone from here, which would give her enough time to organize herself and Harry.

Madeleine dried her face and tidied her hair. She would tell Julia of her plans after dinner tonight, although Julia had made it quite clear that she would prefer Madeleine and her little family stay on the ranch.

"I've said it before and I'll say it again," she'd said only a few days ago, "You'd all be better off here for as the good Lord knows, in my mind, going off into that wilderness is the quickest way to getting yourselves all scalped."

Madeleine glanced across at her supplies, stacked in the corner of the bedroom.

There were half a dozen woolen blankets she'd bought from a reputable store in New Orleans.

Next to them were eight beautifully cured furs, six knee-length fur coats and six pairs of knee-high fur moccasins.

Close to the furs, wrapped in two large leather sheaths were a dozen muskets.

Alongside them was a well strung bow and a hide sheath full of arrows, purchased for her own use.

Beside them in their own leather sheaths, were three good quality knives. But after Madeleine lost her best knife trading for Poongatse and Wannge'e's freedom, she'd purchased another two in St Louis.

She'd also purchased another two bows and two

more sheaths of arrows, all of which she'd gifted to Poongatse and Wannge'e.

The muskets, fur coats, blankets and three good knives had all been purchased in New Orleans.

The furs, moccasins, bows and arrows had been traded with the Missouria, a local tribe, with some of Madeleine's French francs and American dollars. The money gave the tribe buying power in the stores of St Louis, or with French-Canadian fur trappers. Like everyone else, all they wanted were good muskets and knives.

The bows and arrows had been beautifully crafted, but Madeleine considered them a necessity on her journey north. They would allow her and the Bannock girls to hunt without using their muskets and precious supplies of powder and shot.

Poongatse and Wannge'e had been overwhelmed with the gifts, but Madeleine wanted them well dressed for the bitterly cold months ahead and well-armed and confident in using the muskets, bows and arrows. Not just to kill game, but for their own protection, as they'd be passing through territory held by enemies of the Bannock before they reached the Mandan.

But if the girls had been successful in learning how to handle the bows, arrows and muskets, they had struggled living in the big house. They had found the house claustrophobic, especially at night when the windows were closed, along with the constant comings and goings of Julia and her household staff. It didn't help that they couldn't speak English or French and when Madeleine wasn't there to interpret, it became frustrating for them. They also preferred to be outdoors, to keep busy, they didn't like sitting at tables and waiting for their food or for someone to cook for them.

When Madeleine came across the empty cabin up in the woods, she'd asked Julia if the girls could use it for their own. Julia had seen no reason why not and Poongatse and Wannge'e had been happy to move in.

Every day Madeleine rode up to see them, taking a basket of food from the kitchen and making sure they were alright. Unless it were raining, she always found them sitting cross-legged outside by a small fire, curing the hides of some small creature they'd caught in their snares, or roasting a wild turkey or rabbit on ironwood above the flames.

Madeleine knew the girls would be relieved to hear of her plans to leave within the next two weeks, as they'd been ready to move on since they'd arrived here in March. But at least these past months had given them time to rest and heal and they'd had time to get used to the ponies Madeleine had purchased for each girl. They'd been taken from Julia's herd of sturdy mustangs and with some tuition from herself and Bryn, the girls had turned into fine riders.

Although Madeleine wasn't so confident in Monique and Josette's abilities to ride, or use firearms. They didn't seem interested when Madeleine spoke of leaving, nor were they bothered overly much in learning about muskets or knives.

Monique saw no point in wearing moccasins. She didn't understand them. She wanted to wear the leather heeled boots Madeleine had bought for her in London.

Nor had they shown any particular liking for horses, even though Madeleine has insisted both girls learn to ride. When Madeleine pushed them to continue with the lessons, Monique had told her in no uncertain terms that she didn't want to leave the ranch and head out into the wild.

At first, Madeleine thought the teenage girl just repeating Julia's views on the subject, because the two had become close in the past four months. But when she found Monique crying one day, a girl who was a hard, stubborn child, well used to the mean streets of Paris, Madeleine had been shocked.

"I thought we were happy here," the girl replied when Madeleine asked her what was wrong. "I thought you'd changed your mind, as we've been here so long and there's been little talk of leaving. I don't understand why we have to go."

She'd run off then, unwilling to talk about it, leaving Madeleine distressed. Because this was a girl who faced the world with her fist curled, ready for any fight.

Well, she'd have no choice now, Madeleine thought, as she turned towards a small trunk she'd brought with her from New Orleans. They would all leave in two weeks, whether they wanted to or not.

She opened the trunk and carefully lifted out the dozens of small leather bags full of crystal beads and buttons, the mirrors, the threads of silk and wool, the bolts of material and expensive tools, all of them gifts for Paddake'e and Ese-ggwe'na'a.

But there was another gift hidden beneath a piece of cloth and as Madeleine pushed the cloth aside, she reached out and lifted a stunning box, secured with a gold clasp. It had been carved from a single piece of walnut by a skilled craftsman. She opened it, to reveal red velvet lining the inside. Nestled within the velvet was a set of single shot flintlock dueling pistols, fashioned in silver with gold inlay. The box also held a flask for gunpowder, a rod for cleaning the barrel and loading the shot, a bullet mold and extra flints.

The beauty of it was breathtaking and although it had cost her a small fortune, Madeleine thought it worth every American dollar she'd paid for it, as this had been purchased as a gift for Ese-ggwe'na'a. Except he'd never get to see it.

Madeleine regretted that, but she thought Ese-ggwe'na'a would approve the other purpose she now had for it. Because these dueling pistols, her only thing of real value, would be used as a trade to secure the release of Deinde'-paggwe and her daughter from the Mandan, Ese-ggwe'na'a's daughter and grand-daughter.

She closed the lid and secured the gold clasp and put the box back inside the trunk, before covering it with the piece of cloth.

When she'd closed the trunk she sat back and looked at the pile of belongings. It was a lot to take north with her but they'd need every bit of it, so she had no choice but to take two packhorses with her.

She reached across to lift one of the muskets, examining it, when a sudden memory came to her. She had been in St Charles saying goodbye to Jimmy, when one of the men from the Lewis and Clark Expedition had lifted a musket to clean it. It had been a fleeting moment, but Madeleine clearly remembered the musket had been shorter, as though hacked off by a saw.

If a blacksmith in St Louis could do the same to these muskets, by sawing off the end of each weapon to make them shorter, that would make it easier for her to carry them across country. But would they fire as well?

She decided to find out. On the morrow, she would ride into St Louis and ask a blacksmith herself. He'd know if it were possible and what impact it would have on firing.

She glanced around the room. Other than these things, they would take little else. There would be no fanciful things, just the bare minimum, which was warm clothing and good weapons. They could gather herbs along the trail, fill waterskins when they came to streams and river and hunt for food. They should want for nothing.

Madeleine glanced back at the letter lying on the bed. She didn't read it again, but folded it and put it away. She would reply to it before she left, but it could wait until then.

Two

My decision to leave by the end of the month didn't surprise Julia, indeed, she took my decision with good grace. Although she continued to caution me about the wisdom of taking five children into the wild.

"You know I think of you as I do Ryder, as if each and every one of you are my own family," she said, as we sat together on the porch one hot afternoon, sharing a coffee. "But those four girls are blossoming here and I see no point in dragging them away to only God knows where. You know well enough that Monique follows me around like my own shadow, and that Josette would go and live with Jeremiah and Esmeralda in a heartbeat, if she was given half a chance. As for those two Bannock girls, well, I see them riding around this ranch on those two ponies you bought for them as if they were born here," she paused, but before I could answer, she carried on.

"So must you really go?" she asked. "Oh, I know you have family living out west, but how am I expected to sleep at night knowing you're travelling alone out there in that wild country with five children. I'll tell you now Madeleine, try as I might, I can't make sense of you going out there by yourself. Can you not let a few of my hands accompany you? Or could your family not come to St Louis? Could you not write and ask them?"

I shook my head, trying to keep my patience.

"No Julia, I cannot, for you ask the impossible. And no, I don't need any of your men to accompany us. I'll take my chances alone, but you know me well enough I hope, to know I wouldn't go if I didn't feel confident.

Julia frowned. "Oh, I don't doubt you Madeleine. It's others I'm fearful of. I know you plan to pass by the village of those Bannock girls and in my mind that's dangerous enough! Besides, they seem happy and well-settled up there in that cabin," she paused and sighed deeply. "I just wish you could let things be, that's all, but of course it's your decision and I know I can't change your mind, but just so you know, I'd be happy to have any one of those children stay on with me."

I glanced across at her, biting my tongue, careful of my answer as I didn't want to offend her as she'd been so good to us. But I wasn't ready to have another discussion about it, having just returned from a round trip into St Louis where I'd received positive news from a blacksmith about sawing down my muskets.

He saw no reason why it couldn't be done. But he agreed to do one for me to see how it fired and if he were pleased with it, he'd do the others for very little cost. Feeling confident with him, I'd left all the muskets in his livery which I'd collect next week when I rode out of St Louis for the Wazhazhe village.

"And don't you go forgetting that Monique is a young woman now and Josette's not far behind her," Julia continued. "I don't know about those Bannock girls, but I'd guess they'd be the same. Although I grant you Monique looks older than her fourteen years, but in most ways she's still a child."

I felt Julia look over at me, but I said nothing. I'd no desire to begin another debate about the value of letting Monique and Josette stay on here. But my silence only gave her approval to carry on.

"As for Josette, you say she's about twelve? Well, I think her younger than that. But what do I know of children, having none of my own?" she sighed and sat back in her chair, closing her eyes against the heat of the day.

"Anyways, let me take some time to thank you for bringing them all here, including your own dear sweet boy. Those children have filled this big old house with a joy it hasn't known since I lost my Albert. So I'll be the first to admit I'll miss them when they're gone," she opened her eyes and looked out over the ranch and didn't speak for a few moments, but when she did, her voice was lower, as though speaking in confidence.

"I've seen enough of the world, good and bad, to know that those four girls have seen the hardness of life," she paused, but she didn't look at me.

"I don't want to know what happened to them because it ain't none of my business, but I just wanted you to know that. Lord knows we've all got our crosses to bear, but while they're here, at least they're safe."

She did turn to me then and I met her gaze head-on, preparing myself for more of the argument. Because I'd come to understand over the past few months that besides being stubborn, Julia owned an absolute belief in herself that her way was without doubt, the best way. Except her strong opinions weren't always appreciated by me. I'd been through enough without her constantly challenging me. Her strength of character was admirable, indeed, she couldn't have achieved what she'd done had she not been strong, but I was strong as well, and knew what I wanted. And I didn't want to leave Josette and

Monique behind, here at the ranch. And most definitely not the Bannock girls.

"Don't think for one moment that I'm doubting their loyalty to you, because I'm not. Any fool can see they all look on you as their family, but I'm just saying, if they want to stay, then they're welcome. If they do, I'll make sure they get some schooling, you can be sure of that."

I almost smiled, because I knew that Julia was an ex-schoolteacher. Along with her long dead husband Albert, also a schoolteacher, they'd spent a year teaching Ryder the ways of the English when he came to live here as an eight year old, after leaving the Wazhazhe village. So I knew she'd be committed if the girls stayed here, but I was also tired of the continual battle over my decision to take the children west with me.

"But I can see there's no way I can change your mind, so I think we'd best agree that enough has been said on the matter. I just want you to know the offer's there although the truth of it is, I could also use their help. I'm not getting any younger and this place sure isn't getting any smaller."

I took hold of the change of subject like a lifeline and turned to her. "So you've decided to accept Gideon's offer?"

Julia nodded. "I'd be a fool not to. Gideon's coming up to seventy years of age and he's just plain wore himself out working that spread all by himself, all these years. He's no longer got the love for it and when that happens, it's time to move on. Although he's put some restrictions on the sale, but I can't see much harm in agreeing to them," she paused and looked at me.

"He wants to stay living in his old cabin for as long as he's able, but I'm not really interested in the building or his few acres of scrubby land. He knows what I want. It's access to his water. That natural spring on his property is worth gold to me and if any one of those big ranchers on either side of me gets their hands on it, I might as well sell up now because everyone knows they'll squeeze me out," she paused and looked out over her land.

"I'm riding over there the day after next to take a look at the place and Monique has asked if she can come too, which surprised me. But that girl seems to have a hunger for the land and I won't be the one to stop her if she has."

I said nothing, but thought back to the first time I'd seen Monique. An angry, malnourished twelve-year-old girl, standing at the top of the stairs in Jarryth's townhouse in Paris, her little body poised ready to fight even as she shielded Josette who cowered behind her. Monique had reminded me of myself when I first went to live with the Bannock, when I was just a few years older than her, so she'd tugged at my heart the moment I saw her. I looked back at Julia, surprised to find her watching me but I chose to ignore her last comment.

"Well, whatever happens, I leave here next week so perhaps would be a good time to thank you for everything you've done for us."

Julia nodded. "You know full well you've paid me handsomely for the months you've been here, but you also know I've loved every minute of it and that's the truth."

She reached out to take my hand, surprising me by her emotion. But she'd gone out of her way to accommodate all of us and that couldn't have been easy.

"Who would have thought after all the trouble and heartbreak Albert and I went to over the years to have children of our own that I'd be lucky enough, certainly at this time in my life, to be surrounded by so many young ones, with another to be born this Christmas!"

I saw the genuine delight in her face and perhaps because of it, I finally agreed to meet her halfway.

"Julia, I promise I'll talk to Monique and Josette. If they decide they'd rather stay here, I'll respect their wishes."

I was startled when Julia gently squeezed my hand. "That's all I ask," she said softly.

Three

Madeleine had a chance to be alone with Monique and Josette the following afternoon, as they picked herbs from the back garden behind the main house. They joined her on a bench and Madeleine wondered not for the first time how they'd cope in the wild. She'd always imagined they'd love it because she'd loved it, but what if she'd got this wrong and Julia were right about them staying here?

She paused before she spoke, acutely aware of the smells and sounds of the ranch all around them. Of the cattle out in the fields, the horses down in the corrals near the bunkhouse, a dog barking somewhere just behind the main house and the faint sound of someone playing a fiddle. Somewhere else, a man sung in a deep baritone. All were the sounds and smells of comfort, of ease, of home.

As she looked at each girl, Madeleine knew in that moment what their choice would be, if she were to give them one. She'd known it for a while but had chosen to ignore it, unable to face it or discuss it, because she hadn't wanted to lose them as she'd lost Ryder. And Julia, in all her wisdom had seen it and understood it and finally forced the issue. Although Madeleine wasn't entirely sure she was grateful to her for it.

She turned as she heard Esmeralda and Jeremiah laugh, the sound coming from the kitchen at the rear of the house. The couple would soon be making their way home, back to their cottage on the other side of the main house, accompanied by their children, nine-year-old Joshua and six-year-old Ellie. Both children had been born on this ranch.

Madeleine glanced down at Josette, at the tight

dark curls framing her beautiful face and her large luminous eyes and felt her heart lurch with love for her as she recognized the longing on the child's face. Josette had grown to love being around Jeremiah and Esmeralda and their young family, spending all her free time with them. Yet Madeleine understood the little girl's need, because her own need to be with the Bannock was pushing her to risk everything, including the life of her own son and these two girls.

She turned to look at Monique. The girl was no longer a child but a young woman of almost fifteen and would soon be looking at boys and falling in love. Yet Madeleine often wondered how her past with Jarryth might affect that, as well as Josette, but in the few years the girls had been living with her, she'd never seen any signs that Josette or Monique were troubled from that encounter. No doubt they were, but for now, those scars seemed well hidden.

But Madeleine also knew she'd carried scars from her encounter with a monster she'd met when she'd been Monique's age. Ryder had helped heal those scars, but they would always be there, a part of her past and who she was and nothing could erase that.

Monique turned to her and smiled. She wasn't a beauty like Josette, but there was something about her that drew you in. Madeleine had seen enough young men who worked on the ranch, glancing Monique's way, all of them born in this territory and raised within the strong French community that was St Louis.

Madeleine reached out and put an arm about each girl, pulling them close, aware they never spoke of their time with Jarryth or mentioned Paris, but Madeleine had no intention of ever telling it. Only two other people knew about their lives in France. One of them was Jarryth and he was dead. The other was Ryder and he would only learn the truth of it if he found the letter Madeleine had left for him in the secret drawer at Millbryne Park.

But Madeleine didn't want to speak of it for another reason. She sought to protect the girls at all cost, but she also wanted to protect Ryder. To speak of Jarryth and the vile role he'd played in the young lives of these two girls was to defile the Benedict name and Ryder deserved so much more than that. Just like these girls deserved a new beginning.

Julia has asked Madeleine once about the girls' families and she spoke the truth when she replied that she knew nothing about them.

Monique meet her gaze with an honest curiosity but the girl already knew most of what was happening on the ranch, not by anyone telling her, just by watching and listening. Her hazel green eyes seemed to miss nothing, but Madeleine wondered sometimes if Monique were always waiting for that first strike, the raised fist, the demands for her young body.

She bent down and kissed Monique, before turning to Josette, a child who'd been taken from her family somewhere off the coast of Africa and somehow ended up in Jarryth's Paris townhouse. It had been Monique who named her Josette, because no-one had any idea of who the little girl was, for she'd also lost her own language.

But where Monique sat back and watched, careful of showing her feelings, Josette was a child who gave her love freely. She loved Madeleine, Harry and Monique with a passion, but now she also cared for

Jeremiah, Esmeralda and their young family.

Madeleine didn't know why Josette idolized Jeremiah, but the attraction had happened at their first meeting back in March. At six feet six inches, Jeremiah was a giant of a man, taller even than Ryder, with huge shoulders, thighs and hands. Yet beneath that exterior he was as gentle as a lamb and sometimes Madeleine wondered if that was what drew Josette to him. She felt safe with him and his young family.

Madeleine took a deep breath of the sweet scent of honeysuckle and jasmine, along with the rich smell of earth and animals. She wondered where to begin, as she looked down at both girls.

*

They listened in silence as Madeleine spoke of life in the wild. She spoke of the nights they would camp outdoors, of cooking over open fires, of the furs which would be their beds, of the rivers and streams they would bathe in. She stopped, when Josette began to cry.

Madeleine said nothing more, understanding at once how this would end. Yet she felt her heart break as Monique reached out to put a hand on her arm.

"Must we go, *Madame*?" the girl asked softly. "We would rather stay here if we can, in our warm beds with good food in our bellies. I don't want to sleep on the hard ground. I don't want to wash in the rivers," she paused to look over at Josette as the little girl wiped her eyes.

"We're grateful for everything you've done for us

and we were content in England. Now, we are content here. I like Julia. Josette likes Jeremiah and Esmeralda. The only reason she's crying now, is because she's afraid. Is there contentment in this new place *madame*, as there is here, as there was in England? And will you be sad to leave here, as you were in England? For that reason, Josette and I think we should stay here, where you are happy."

Madeleine stared at her in bewilderment. She had never thought of herself as being so transparent. Monique stood up and moved to sit with Josette, putting an arm about the girl's shoulders, protecting her as she always had.

Madeleine watched them, seeing the bond they'd always had. She was confident she could teach them how to survive in the wild, but she couldn't guarantee their happiness.

Perhaps this child of Africa and this street smart girl from Paris would find the emptiness and rawness of the wild as terrifying and claustrophobic as the Bannock girls had found living within the walls of Julia's big house. But then another thought struck her with brutal force.

What if the Bannock and Shoshone no longer made the Snake River Plain their winter camp, after that tragedy in the spring of 1800?

What if Paddake'e and Ese-ggwe'na'a were changed because of it? Would they even be alive, after five years?

She thought on it for some minutes, then she dared to ask the question, although she already knew the answer.

"I cannot stay Monique. I must go, but I'll be back here in five years, before I head on back to

England. But if you and Josette had a choice, would you prefer to stay here with Julia? Until Harry and I return?"

Josette lifted her face and looked at Madeleine incredulous, then nodded. Monique said nothing, unwilling to put into words how she felt, unwilling to hurt Madeleine. So Madeleine did it for her.

"Julia is happy for you both to stay, if that's what you want. But you must understand that once I leave here with Harry and the Bannock girls, I won't be back for a long time. Until then, this would be your home. But if that's what you want, then you shall have it."

Josette leaned into Madeleine, with something like hope flaring in her lovely dark eyes. "Can I stay with Jeremiah and Esmeralda? They have asked me to. I would very much like to."

Madeleine was startled by this, as she turned to Monique. "And you? Do you wish to stay?"

Monique nodded. "Oui, *yes*. Very much, *Madame*."

Yes, Madeleine had known, but had chosen to ignore it. Because not once in all the years she'd known them, since she first met them in Paris, had she ever considered leaving them behind. Now she must.

"Then you shall," she said softly and held out her arms. Both girls went to her, as always, yet Madeleine felt her heart lurch with sorrow. She had never expected to be parted from them, but they had just broken the bonds which bound them. She had a feeling they might never be repaired.

*

Madeleine was sitting in the dining room the following morning, finally replying to Sir George Ashbury's letter when Lily knocked on the door.

"If you don't mind ma'am, I've got Esmeralda here. She'd like a word with you, if she can."

Madeleine nodded and Lily stepped back to allow Esmeralda to come forward. Madeleine asked her to sit down, but the woman continued to stand nervously in front of her.

"I know why you're here," Madeleine said softly, speaking in English as she was unfamiliar with the Creole French spoken between Esmeralda, Jeremiah and their children. Creole was influenced by English, Spanish and Portuguese, along with West African languages and Madeleine found it almost impossible to follow.

She again asked Esmeralda to take a seat and the older woman finally sat down opposite her. Yet she sat poised on the edge of the chair as though ready to take flight. Madeleine smiled and leaned towards her, in awe of the woman's beauty. Her skin was flawless, her features perfect, her eyes like the color of emeralds which seemed to glitter with unshed tears.

"Indeed, I was coming to see you and Jeremiah this evening, to discuss Josette. You know already how much I love her, but it seems she and Monique want to stay here. They have no interest in heading west with me," Madeleine paused, choosing her words carefully.

"I'm aware of the fondness Josette has for you and your family and how desperately she wants to be a part of it. So if you're willing to take care of her, until I get back in a five years, then I won't stand in your way. Although you're under no obligation, indeed, had I my way, she'd come west with me. But I won't force her, or Monique, when both of them clearly want to stay here," she paused, then added softly. "I'm afraid I can tell you almost nothing of her past, other than that she had it hard. When I found her, she had no family or language of her own."

Esmeralda nodded and finally spoke. "I always had a feeling there was more to that child than she's willing to tell. Or remember. But I can recognize the signs and like me, I know she's been through things that no girl her age has a right to go through," she paused licking her lips, but she didn't mention her own past, that she'd be a courtesan in a private brothel when she was Josette's age. She looked at Madeleine and smiled.

"As for Jeremiah, well, he knows enough about women to understand that Josette's no innocent flower, but our own pasts aren't pretty, so we don't judge any-one. But that child is easy to love, as you well know. Everyone loves her and we've got no complaints about her living with us, none at all," she paused, clasping her hands nervously.

"Josette's told us a little of her life in England with you, but she knows we can't give her a big house with servants running after her. But we do have plenty of love to share and if she wants to move in with us, then she's welcome. Although I wanted you to know that when she returns to England with you, we won't hold her back. I just wanted you to know that."

Madeleine nodded, feeling emotional, but this was what the girls wanted and she wouldn't hold them back. She stood up as Esmeralda stood up, patting down her skirt.

"I'll go tell Jeremiah, he'll be pleased to know she's staying with us."

She turned to leave, but Madeleine reached out to stop her. "Esmeralda, I'll be leaving some money behind with Julia for the care of both girls. You and Jeremiah will receive some of it. It'll help towards whatever Josette might need over the next few years," she paused as Esmeralda began to protest. "Please allow me to do this. Indeed, I won't take no for an answer."

Esmeralda nodded, overwhelmed. "I thank you, ma'am," she said then turned and left the room.

Madeleine sat down, glancing at the letter she'd started writing to Ash and thought how ironic it was that the last of Jarryth's money would be going to Josette and Monique. She smiled at the thought of it.

Four

A week later I went in search of Lily and Bryn. I found them sitting on the porch of their cottage, just after dusk, drinking a glass of Julia's homemade brandy wine.

They didn't see me at first and I paused, unsure whether to break the moment of intimacy between them. They were sitting close, talking softly as lovers do, but what I had to say to them had to be said tonight so I stepped into the light of their lamp, startling them as they saw me come out from the edge of darkness. But as Lily's eyes met mine, she knew why I'd come. She knew I'd come to say goodbye.

Like Jimmy Morven, Lily and Bryn had been a big part of my life over the past three and half years, especially in those dreadful weeks after Ryder went missing. Like Jimmy, I now thought of this couple as my friends, not my servants.

Unfortunately, they didn't think of me in the same way despite everything we'd shared, because they just couldn't step over that chasm of class which divided us from mistress and servant. They would always see me as Countess Benedict, wife to Ryder, 8th Earl Benedict.

They both stood up, at once respectful and ready to fulfill any request I might have of them, just as they'd always done. I saw Lily flick out her muslin dress in an automatic response to curtsey to me, even though I'd asked her and Bryn not to treat me with such formality here. Perhaps when I returned in five years' time, I might find that formality finally worn off a little. I hoped so.

I lifted my own muslin dress to climb the stairs

towards them and thought of the buckskin clothing I'd bought for us while in New Orleans. Except my servants had never taken to the clothing, preferring instead to wear wool or muslin, although I understood Lily's preference for wearing a dress in the muggy heat of summer, as she needed no other undergarments other than a chemise and short stay.

I smiled at them as they stood waiting for me and although that formality was still there, I also thought them changed. Lily no longer dressed in the formal, heavy dresses required of her as part of my senior household staff in England, nor did she bother wearing heavy leather boots. Instead, she wore these simple muslin dresses and light satin slippers and her hair was now worn in a soft bun, like most of the other women on the ranch, including Julia. She no longer bore that pale luminous complexion so common among the English, but a skin turned bronze by the sun. She had also put on some weight, due mostly to her pregnancy, but she looked well and happy.

Bryn had also changed. From the shattered teenage boy I'd first met at Millbryne Park, who had just found his stepfather, Michael Woodley, beaten to death in the woods up near the Chapel, to the man who now stood before me, were like two different people.

I saw the love he shared with Lily, a love that had begun as a slow burning romance around the time that Ryder disappeared, developing into this full-blown thing, something that would simmer and blaze for the rest of their lives if they cared for it.

I nodded formally as Bryn bowed slightly and Lily did a shallow curtsey. It was nothing compared to the formality they had shown me in England, but it was enough. It was more than I wanted, but I knew they'd never behave any differently towards me.

I had never visited them at their home before and they were clearly flustered by my sudden appearance. I glanced at the drink in Bryn's hand.

"May I have one? If you don't mind my joining you?" I asked, giving him something to do in an attempt to ease the tension.

"Aye, m'lady," he said and disappeared inside the cottage.

I glanced at Lily who stood awkwardly. "Shall I?" I asked, indicating Bryn's vacant chair and she nodded.

I sat down, even as she continued to stand a moment longer, unsure, then followed my lead and sat down. Again, I felt sad that she didn't treat me as a friend, for I badly needed one. She still came to my room every morning to help dress me and do my hair and help with Harry, so we had a formal, yet easy relationship. Yet here, in her own home, she seemed shy and ill at ease.

She took a sip of her drink and I noticed she had already begun to swell with child, the babe some four months along yet she looked beautiful, her face owning a radiance to it.

The scent of summer flowers near the porch filled the night air and I glanced up at the two-story cottage which loomed above us. It was a miniature version of Julia's home, with two good sized bedrooms upstairs. Downstairs, through the door which Bryn had left open, I could see homespun rugs on scrubbed wooden floors, a bench before the hearth and a pine table and four chairs.

I looked back at Lily and saw her glance shyly at me. I knew she was thinking of the Benedict properties I'd lived in, both at Millbryne Park and Diccon House, but none of that mattered to me. I wondered what she'd think if she saw the cave where I'd lived with *esa*.

"You look well, Lily," I said and she nodded, her face blushing with pleasure.

"Aye, m'lady, I am,' she answered. "Bryn and I have found some good friends here and Esmeralda's said I can ask her anything about the babe. She birthed both her bubs and said she'll help me when the time comes. Although Julia mentioned a week or so ago that she would have her doctor attend me, so I can't ask for more than that," she paused and glanced into the house.

"Bryn loves it here. He talks all the time about one day owning a ranch of our own. Can you believe it? Even to talk of such a thing astonishes me! But none of this would have happened if it hadn't been for you, taking a chance on us. I know Jimmy felt the same."

"Well, that's kind of you to say that," I said, then wondered as I often did if I might see Jimmy on our journey north to the Bannock.

I wasn't sure how I felt about that. Although I knew if he ever came to me in the years ahead needing help, I wouldn't hesitate, for he'd been there for me, without question, when I'd been in such desperate need.

"But I think eventually you would have all found a way to come out here on your own."

Bryn appeared at that moment with my glass of brandy wine and I took it with gratitude. It was sweet with a potent kick to it and I felt my head and belly fill with fire. He leaned up against the porch railing as I'd taken his chair, but he wasn't bothered by it.

"I just heard what Lily said and I agree with her," he said, looking at me. "Because even if we'd somehow found the money for passage to come out here on our own, we wouldn't have come to this ranch, so we have you to thank for that," he paused to glance up at the cottage behind us. "I have to pinch myself sometimes that we have the use of this place all to ourselves. It doesn't seem right somehow, as it's far too big for just the two of us, but we're both aware that if we'd stayed in England we'd still be working in service and a house such as this would be beyond our dreams. But Lily and I are determined to make something of ourselves and one day, we might be able to afford a ranch of our own."

I smiled. "Do you not miss England and your families?"

Lily nodded, glancing shyly at Bryn. "Yes, I do miss Perri and Dad. But like Bryn says, they've got their own lives now. Besides, they might follow us out here one day. I hope they do."

I didn't say anything, but I didn't believe for one moment that Mourie and Angie would ever leave England, or Millbryne Park for that matter.

But Perri might be persuaded to leave her teaching duties at Stretton Court and come to America, as might Alick Woodley. Both were young and ambitious enough.

"I'm glad to hear you're both happy, for I couldn't have borne it had you been otherwise," I paused, before adding softly. "You know I'm leaving early tomorrow morning, but I wanted to come and say goodbye and wish you all the best. And perhaps offer you some advice," I said, as Lily dropped her head.

She had begun to cry, but I already knew she didn't want me to go. She had said as much last week, when I told her I was making plans to leave. In that moment, as I leaned forward to take her hand in my own, I felt infinitely older than the seven years which separated us.

"Lily, dearest girl, do take heart. I'll be back before you know it and with your babe due at Christmas, you'll be so busy you won't even know I'm gone."

She wiped her face with a bit of soft cloth she had in her pocket and looked at me. "Oh yes m'lady, I know all that, but I do worry for you and little Harry. We hear the stories some folks tell and we're terrified for you. Oh Lord, I couldn't bear it if I were to lose you both. Sometimes I can't sleep at night, just thinking on it," she said softly, a sob catching in the back of her throat.

I looked up at Bryn, yet he looked pale as he watched me.

"Please don't believe everything you hear. I can tell you now that some of the most blood-thirsty stories told are usually falsehoods. I've lived in the west for many years and if I didn't feel perfectly at ease I wouldn't be taking my son out there," I said, although I felt a sudden quiver of fear as I heard myself say the words.

"Please don't worry about us," I said, looking back at Lily. "I want you to think only of yourselves and build a happy life here and be ready for the changes that will come to this territory in the next few years as the Americans turn their attention west. If you have any doubts about anything, ask Julia's opinion on it. She hasn't survived all these years alone without being tough and she'll help you in any way she can, you have only to ask," I watched Lily as she wiped her eyes.

"If I can give you any advice, just be there for each other when things go wrong, or when one of you feels the pull of England at your heart. The bad days might seem to last forever, but they do pass," I paused, before revealing the other reason why I came here.

"I plan to leave some funds behind in Julia's care for you, so if you do decide to return to England for whatever reason, I want you to have the means to get back."

Lily began to cry again as Bryn reached out to put his hand on her shoulder, but I could see the emotion cross his own face.

"That's most generous of you, m'lady. It's something Lily's been worried about, having no way to get home if we want to, so we thank you," he said softly. "I can't promise you we'll be here when you get back, but I can promise you we'll make a good go of it. I give you my word on that."

I nodded, feeling myself get emotional, so I reached into the pocket of my skirt and pulled out a small black pouch. Inside were several gold coins amounting to, fifty American dollars which was a fortune. Along with that was some of the money Ash had given me for this journey, taken from Ryder's estate. He had given me enough funds to last me five years, although I wouldn't spend even half of it. In truth, I'd made use of the American dollars I'd found in Jarryth's townhouse in Bankside more than two years ago.

I handed the pouch to Lily but as she reached out to take it from me I put my hand over her fingers, so she couldn't pull the silk cords and open it. She looked at me in bewilderment for it was obvious it held something of value because of its weight.

"This is a little something extra for you both, but please open it later, after I've gone," I said. "I wanted to say thank you for the loyalty you've shown me and my son. Although there is a condition attached to the gift," I said, before releasing Lily's hand.

"I ask only that you speak of this to no-one, including Julia, and that you use it wisely. If you do decide to return to England in the next few years, I want you to know there'll be a home waiting for you at Millbryne Park. Before I left, I asked Sully to make a cottage available for your use, if that's what you want, if that's where you decide to settle."

I saw the astonishment on Bryn's face, but he'd been born and raised on the Millbryne Park estate, as had his parents and grandparents before him and I knew he thought of it as home.

I drank the last of my brandy wine then put aside the glass and stood up as Lily stood up, holding the pouch tight in her hand. I reached out to embrace her as she cried softly, even as Bryn stepped forward to put an arm about her shoulders.

"I'm sorry for getting upset," she said, "but you know full well I just wish you and the young Viscount were staying. Although it give me comfort to know that funds are there if we need them, but how do we go on without you, m'lady? You take care of us, you know you do, and we've probably relied on you far too much, but you always make things right. Oh, I cannot bear to think that you won't be here. And now you give us this?" she cried, holding the pouch.

"Hush now Lily. You'll see me again in a few years and the time will be gone before you know it. You won't be alone. Julia will help you in whatever way she can, but keep this gift I've just given you to yourselves. You must tell no-one of it. It's for you alone."

Bryn nodded, pulling Lily towards him, his own voice breaking. "If there's anything we can do for you or the young Viscount, you have only to ask."

"You already did it," I said softly, reaching out to hug them, then I left them alone. As I hurried back to the house, I let the tears fall, sad I was leaving them behind, remembering everything they'd done for me and Harry in those awful months after Ryder first disappeared. I suppose I was also grieving for a part of my life that was now over, that had been unbearably hard.

Five

Matt and Jeremiah sat patiently on the wagon's buckboard as Madeleine said her final farewells. Harry, Poongatse and Wannge'e were ready to go, sitting in the back of the wagon near several muslin bags of smoked beef strips, smoked bacon, fresh vegetables, bags of corn and coffee, several loaves of freshly baked bread and a waterskin filled not with water, but with fresh milk for Harry. These were all parting gifts from Julia.

"There's nothing fancy in there, but it will keep you going for a few days," she'd said earlier that morning. "Until you find your family my dear, you're going to need all the sustenance you can get."

Madeleine was grateful for the food, as it meant she didn't have to hunt for a few days at least.

Lily and Bryn stood beside Esmeralda and Hetty, Monique and Josette. The two young girls were crying as Madeleine reached out to hug them.

"I'll be back soon enough," she said softly in French. "You'll be alright, for I have every faith in each of you. Just make sure you do as Julia and Esmeralda tell you, do your lessons and learn all you can. I'll want to hear all about it on my return."

The girls nodded as Madeleine bent down to kiss them goodbye, then Esmeralda stepped forward to take Josette's hand and pull her back. Lily moved to put an arm about Monique's shoulders, as Julia mounted her horse.

Bryn gave Madeleine a leg up and she sat easily astride the horse's blanket, for she didn't want a saddle. She would be taking this journey west at a walk, with Harry tied to her for most of it and a saddle would be more of a nuisance than anything, just something else to organize.

Jeremiah flicked the reins and the two big road horses moved off, pulling the wagon behind them. Tied behind the wagon were the Bannock girl's ponies, along with two packhorses. The small group turned to follow the long dusty road to St Louis, as the calls of farewell drifted behind them.

Madeleine turned once to look back and wave. Then she kicked her horse on, not daring to stop and think for one moment that what she was doing was foolhardy, because there was no turning back now.

St Louis: mid July 1804

As they rode down the main street of St Louis, Jeremiah struggled to keep the wagon wheels from sinking in the deep ruts left by other heavy wagons, the streets having turned to a muddy slush after two days of heavy rain. Although it wasn't cold, just a light mist drifting above the town and the forest beyond it, as well as settling above the muddy waters of the Mississippi River.

The frontier town was already busy, with shopkeepers, ranchers, fur traders and housewives going about their business, alongside men and women from local tribes carrying furs and beaded goods to trade.

Madeleine rode alongside Julia, just in front of the wagon, to avoid the worst of the mud splatters thrown up by the wheels as they headed for the largest general store in town. The owners were a couple from Scotland and good friends with Julia. If Angus and Letty Stewart didn't have what someone wanted, they placed an order for it on the next keelboat heading down to New Orleans.

Jeremiah brought the wagon to a stop outside the store as Julia and Madeleine dismounted. Matt stayed with the wagon and horses, his musket primed, a deterrent for any thieves, while Jeremiah accompanied the women, Harry and the girls into the store.

Letty welcomed Julia warmly and took her out back where her monthly order was waiting for collection. Madeleine's order lay next to it.

A half-dozen sheets of buckskin, a small cooking pot, half a dozen wooden spoons and wooden mugs and just outside the door, hanging under the shade of the porch in the fresh air, were several pieces of sailcloth, some six feet square. They had been soaked in linseed oil to harden the material to make them waterproof, which had been Angus' suggestion.

"My own good father sailed on clippers most of his life off the coast of Scotland and this was all they used to keep them dry in those bitter northern storms."

Madeleine had ordered eight of them.

As Jeremiah began carrying the goods out to the wagon, Madeleine and Julia paid at the counter. But as they turned to leave, they noticed the Bannock girls and Harry trying on an assortment of narrow rimmed bowler hats at the front of the store. Madeleine turned back to Letty.

"Can I also take four hats? Whatever the girls want, they can have. But I'll take two of those beaver hats, one for myself and one for Harry."

Poongatse and Wannge'e wanted the bowler hats, even though Madeleine tried to discourage them. "They aren't practical, they won't keep the sun or rain off your face, nor will they keep you warm. I suggest you get one of these," she said, holding up the two hats she'd just purchased for her and Harry. Made of beaver fur, the hats had long flaps on three sides to keep the ears and neck warm. She took the bowler hat off Harry and put the fur one on instead.

"No, Mama," he said, pulling it off with some impatience, but Madeleine shook her head.

"This hat," she said, "or none at all."

The child wasn't happy about her choice and made it clear he wanted one of the bowler hats favored by Poongatse and Wannge'e. When the girls told Harry they would share their hats with him, Madeleine relented and paid for them.

Jeremiah helped the girls up into the wagon as Madeleine lifted her son, squeezing him in between boxes and parcels to settle for the short ride to the blacksmiths. Once Julia remounted her horse and Jeremiah gave Madeleine a leg up, the wagon rolled out, once again following behind Madeleine and Julia as they kicked their horses on down the main street. But as they went to turn off down a side road towards the back of town, another rancher and half a dozen of his men rode towards them, the riders taking up more than half the street as they rode abreast.

Matt called out to them, swearing at them to move over as Jeremiah reined the horses in to let them pass, when a window opened above them. Madeleine glanced up as a bleary-eyed saloon girl, about seventeen years of age, pushed aside the curtains to see what all the shouting was about. The rouge and powder she wore on her face was smudged from the night before, her mouth bruised and swollen looking, her hair a mass of untidy curls. She glanced down at Madeleine, but only for a moment before withdrawing back into the room, closing the window and curtains behind her.

Madeleine kicked her horse on, as the rancher and his men passed them by. Then Jeremiah flicked the reins and urged the horses on, the wagon lurching behind them.

As they pulled up outside the blacksmith's shop, a group of ten men from a local tribe rode out of the woods less than a mile away. They were dressed in buckskin, the edge of their leggings fringed, along with the arms on their buckskin jackets. They wore their hair long, yet they appeared to own little jewelry, nor did their clothing have any decorative beading.

Madeleine knew who these men were. They were Missouria, because she'd purchased her furs, moccasins, bows and arrows off them weeks ago. The men didn't look at her or anyone else in town as they rode on past, heading west, armed with muskets and good quality knives that lay sheathed on their waists. They looked intimidating, barely glancing at the townspeople who paused to watch them. They seemed disinterested, as if unaware of the town or even the people around them, yet Madeleine knew from her years with the Bannock that those ten men would be acutely aware of every noise, every smell, every person they passed and what weapon each carried.

She glanced across the street and saw a Spanish soldier come out of what appeared to be a boarding house to watch them. His face was hideously scarred down the left side with what looked like a deep burn. Madeleine saw him touch the sword worn in a scabbard on his hip, but only for a moment, for he seemed to think better of it before he turned and disappeared back inside the building. The ten men rode on, grim and silent.

Julia and Madeleine dismounted as Jeremiah and Matt jumped down from the buckboard and turned to help the girls and Harry out from the back of the wagon, just as a man appeared at the doors of the blacksmith shop. It was Jack Loudain, an American from New York who had only recently settled here.

"Hello Jack," Julia called to him. "Did you manage it alright?"

The man nodded. "Never done one myself before, but they look like some others I saw once, back east. I reckon they'll be easier to carry now, that's for damn sure," he said.

As Matt and Jeremiah began to lift Madeleine's belongings out of the wagon, helped by the girls, Jack took Madeleine and Julia inside the back of his workshop and pulled aside a great rawhide sheet to reveal a dozen muskets. They were much shorter than they had been, the tip of the muzzle sawn off by a good six inches. Madeleine picked up one of the guns, feeling the lighter weight and balance of it in her hands.

"Have you tested all of them?" she asked.

"Sure have, ma'am. Fired them all and they worked just fine," he said.

They worked to separate the muskets into four piles of three, wrapping each bundle in a sheet of buckskin and then a sailcloth.

"I reckon that will keep them dry enough," Jack said, standing back as Madeleine bent down to pick up one of the bundles.

It was heavy, but she could manage it well enough and once packed away on the back of her packhorse, no-one would know she carried muskets. She turned to Loudain and nodded, pleased with what he'd done.

"Are we going yet, Mama?" Harry asked, turning as Jeremiah and Matt brought her five horses inside.

"Soon enough. Say goodbye to everyone," she said, as Julia bent down to swing the child up into her arms.

"Oh, you're getting to be a big boy," she said, kissing him. "When you come back to see me, I'll have a new pony waiting for you. Now, let me give these girls a hug goodbye, then I must be off." She put the little boy down then turned to embrace Wannge'e and Poongatse, before turning to Madeleine. "Take care, my dear," Julia said softly, hugging her. "I'll miss you all, but you know that already. I just can't wait for the day when I see you ride down that road to my ranch. But enough of that. Just don't forget to mention my name to the ferry men, for they know me well enough and they'll treat you right."

She embraced Madeleine once more then turned to Matt and Jeremiah. "Come, come, let's get moving. I've got a ranch to run and a wagon load of supplies to get home."

Madeleine picked Harry up and walked outside to say goodbye, along with Poongatse and Wannge'e. Matt and Jeremiah said goodbye, then climbed up onto the buckboard of the wagon as Julia mounted her horse, called farewell, then kicked the animal on. Jeremiah flicked the reins and then they were leaving. As Madeleine watched them go, she felt a sudden wretchedness. Then someone took her hand. It was Wannge'e. The girl smiled up at her, just as Harry called out in French.

"Are we going yet *Mama?*" he yelled, eager to get moving, to get back on the horse.

Madeleine laughed and picked him up to kiss him. "As soon as the horses are loaded up, we'll be off."

The muskets were loaded first, the four bundles of three tied down on each side of the packhorses. The furs and blankets were packed over them to conceal them, followed by the leather bags of gifts and finally Julia's bags of food. The rest of the sailcloths were laid over them to try and keep everything waterproof.

All their other belongings were packed behind them on their own horses. Finally, it was done.

After she paid Jack, Madeleine was left with some money in her pouch, both French francs and American dollars. She hid the money within her belongings. Perhaps it could be used to trade for something in the months ahead. But if nothing else, it gave her some bargaining power if she ever needed it. The bulk of the money which Ash had given her out of Ryder's estate, was locked away in Julia's safe at the ranch. Julia had access to it to pay for Monique and Josette's living expenses, although Madeleine would also need it when she returned to St Louis, in order to pay for passage back to England.

"You sure you don't want no saddles?" Jack asked, but Madeleine shook her head. Like her, Poongatse and Wannge'e preferred to ride bareback and she had no plans to ride hard and fast, not with Harry riding in front of her.

She thanked Jack again then lifted Harry up onto her horse before jumping up behind him. She secured the child to her by a long muslin cloth, having no care to see the boy fall off. She glanced back at Wannge'e and Poongatse as they mounted their own horses. Then Jack secured the long reins of the two packhorses to the rawhide rope looped around the neck of Madeleine's horse then said goodbye, wishing her luck. She'd told him weeks ago that she was meeting her husband and his party on the other side of the Missouri River. She thought of it now as she waved goodbye and as she kicked her horse on, riding away from St Louis through the back streets, away from curious eyes, she wished with all her heart it were true.

Harry kicked his legs, eager for the horse to go faster and Madeleine put a hand around his belly, to settle him back against her. Poongatse and Wannge'e rode just behind the packhorses, keeping an eye on all their belongings. One year, Madeleine thought. One year of slow travelling before they arrived at the Snake River Plain. Until then, she had a whole lot of land to cross and enemy territory to get through. She felt the warmth of Harry as the child relaxed against her and the tug of the two packhorses coming up behind her. She glanced back at Poongatse and Wannge'e and was suddenly grateful for their company. They weren't children, they were experienced in the wild and they would work with her to get through this.

The wooden buildings and muddy streets of St Louis slowly fell away and as they neared the river, Madeleine saw a group of fur trappers, at least half a dozen of them, coming up on her right less than a mile away. They were coming from the west and heading into town. The men glanced back at her and the Bannock girls, but Madeleine turned away, eager not to attract attention for these men rode alone and she didn't trust men who rode without women. But they had no reason to bother her. What they wanted was in St Louis. Madeleine thought of the young girl she'd seen looking out from the saloon window. She would be busy soon enough with men such as these coming into town after months in the wild.

She once more glanced back at the girls and saw their excitement as they headed out of town. They rode with confidence in their new buckskin clothing and their little bowler hats. But Madeleine had also purchased woolen vests and sweaters for them, ready for the bitter winter which lay months ahead of them, along with the fur coats and boots. The woolen garments had been woven and knitted by three women in St Louis. But as the small group of riders neared the river, as St Louis disappeared behind them in that damp misty morning, Madeleine wished in that moment she'd bought more of everything. But it was too late now.

*

It took three trips and the better part of the day to cross the Missouri. Four men, four poles and four pirogues, a wooden platform lashed across each boat took the horses across. Wannge'e was the first to cross with two of the horses. Then Madeleine went next with Harry and her own horse.

"You've come at the right time, that's for sure," one of the men said to Madeleine, a tall stocky black man in his early forties, his buckskin clothing stained, his long grey hair tied back in a thick plait and his grey beard streaked with tobacco juice. He wore a large leather hat secured by a rawhide string tied under his chin, a grey muslin shirt and buckskin pants held up with a piece of rawhide leather. His three partners, two of whom were French, the other American, were dressed in a similar fashion and although they looked rough and raw, these men made a good living from this ferry service.

"You know, there's some folks who risk swimming their horses across but with these young 'uns an' all your belongings, I reckon y'all don't want to be doing that," he said in a strong southern accent mixed with the Creole that Jeremiah and Esmeralda spoke. "But the river ain't flooded yet thank the Lord, for we don't take the raft across when it's flooded, althou' she be running pretty fast today so we might just drift a bit with the current. But don't worry none ma'am, we'll get y'all across safe an' sound," he paused to take a breath, pushing the pole in deep, his body sweating from the effort as the water swirled fast and dangerous around the raft. Madeleine held on to the collar of Harry's shirt with one hand and the reins of her horse with the other.

"At least y'all ain't crossing the old muddy. You know it was the Chippewa who called that old river *misi-ziibi*? Most folks don't know that, but it's a fact an' I reckon it's as good a name as any," the man said, pushing his pole deep within the river as his partner grunted from the effort on the other side of him.

Madeleine glanced across to the opposite bank. The first raft had reached the shore and she saw Wannge'e lead the two horses off the wooden platform and up the far bank. Although Madeleine also noticed that her own raft was drifting a little downriver, but she wasn't too worried about it. As long as they reached the far bank safely because she couldn't afford to lose anything, not now. The men on the first raft were already pushing away from the far bank, to head back across the river to where Poongatse waited nervously. Madeleine turned back to look at the girl and suddenly wished she'd let Poongatse go second.

"*Mama*, shall we go for a swim?" Harry asked Madeleine in French, pointing at the swirling currents which teased the edges of the raft.

"No son, you don't want to go swimming here,"

the Frenchman said, turning to glance over at Harry as he replied in the same language. "He'll drag you down and then spit you out somewhere downriver in the Mississippi. You don't ever want to do that, unless you be a damn good swimmer."

But Harry moved to dip his moccasin boot in the water which swirled just a couple of feet beneath the wooden platform and Madeleine twisted her fingers within his collar, pulling him gently back towards her.

"Over winter we get ice floating down here," the Frenchman continued. "But today it's real fine travelling conditions. No need for you to be concerned about anything. We'll get you across to your menfolk real quick."

By the time they reached the northern bank, the raft had drifted someway downriver. Madeleine was glad to get off. She picked Harry up and carried him ashore as the Frenchman took the reins and led the horse off. As soon as she set Harry down he took off, running along the riverbank towards Wannge'e, who was riding towards them with one of the packhorses. Then the ferrymen were waving goodbye and wishing her luck before heading back across the river. As Madeleine waited for Poongatse to came across, she secured the reins of the second packhorse to her own mount while Harry ran wild with excitement. He'd tire himself out soon enough, she hoped he'd even sleep a little, because they had a good ride ahead of them before stopping somewhere safe to set up camp for the night.

in the wild: early August 1804

One

Madeleine woke in fear. She scrambled to her feet and reached for her knife, her heart beating in terror. It was pitch black, but she dared not light a fire, not out here on this exposed hill where they'd camped last night, desperate with exhaustion.

She glanced across at Harry and the girls, but they were still fast asleep. Whatever it was hadn't woken them, so Madeleine left them where they slept and stepped out into the dark. She prowled around the camp for some minutes, seeking answers as to why she'd woken so abruptly. Yet, there was no danger here. No scent of men, nor any other animals other than their horses.

She crouched there for long minutes, aware of every sound and every smell, but there was nothing other than the five horses stamping their hooves and blowing in the cool breeze of the early morning, although it was hours yet till dawn. Whatever had woken her had been nothing more than a bad dream.

They were miles away from St Louis now and by Madeleine's reckoning they should be arriving at the Wazhazhe village within the month, if not sooner, although she'd already discovered that travelling with a child and two teenage girls unused to riding for hours was slow, hard work.

She took one last look around but as she returned to their camp, she suddenly sensed something strange, something powerful. Then she had a clear, stunning image of Ryder and felt goose bumps tickle every surface of her body. Yet he looked so different to the image she'd had of him more than two years ago, lying hunched and broken in a dark, foul place. Now he looked strong and virile and as she sat on her blankets, looking out into the night and the vast empty darkness of the wild, at the countless stars above her in a cloudless sky, every instinct she owned told her he was coming. Somehow, Ryder had found his way home and was following her.

Two

The thought of Ryder following us was so profound I could think of nothing else for days, yet after the initial euphoria the reality of the situation slowly crept in. I knew it had probably been nothing more than wishful thinking after a bad dream, because he'd been missing for more than two years, without a word from him in all that time.

Yet I couldn't let go of that feeling, not after so many years of despair wondering where he was and if he was alive. But the thought of him following us had me wrapped so tight in a cocoon of hope, that I knew its fragile threads holding me within their grasp might snap at any moment, dropping me back into reality. Because the fact was, he had disappeared more than two years ago into some black hole where Jarryth had wanted him to suffer.

I didn't tell any of this to Poongatse or Wannge'e, although I knew they'd consider my feelings a good sign, because like me they held a deep belief in the spirit world and the supernatural. Instead, I concentrated on getting us through each day, making sure we were all well-nourished and happy and settled within a safe camp before night fell. And for now, that was enough.

*

I thought Ryder would be proud of his son, as the child seemed to have inherited his love of adventure, along with my own. When I first thought of travelling back to the Bannock while still living in England, I'd accepted that travelling alone with an almost three-year old would be slow and hard and although we had our moments, Harry was mostly a happy child, eager to face the days ahead, whatever they may bring.

But it was Poongatse and Wannge'e who made things easy for me and it wasn't just their company which I valued, but their knowledge of life in the wild. I realized the worth of these two capable teenage girls only days after we left St Louis and I thanked God for the gift of them, as they turned into the most wonderful travelling companions.

Unlike me, they had grown up in the wild and their skills in foraging and gathering root vegetables, nuts, seeds and berries as well as setting snares enabled us to have a rich varied diet, with very little work for me.

They also helped with Harry, looking after him while I went off to hunt or scout the territory ahead. Poongatse was especially good with him and on the rare evening when we set up camp too late and the child was overtired and grumpy, it was Poongatse who always managed to settle him. Because of this, we settled into a routine where Poongatse cared for him while Wannge'e and I hobbled the horses and unpacked them, before preparing an evening meal.

It was on one of these evenings when Harry grizzled with hunger and fatigue that Poongatse called him *deide'wesa*, which meant *little bear* in their own Bannock dialect. It made us all laugh, because it suited him so perfectly.

But there were many other ways in which I found the girls helpful. Often I'd look back to find one or both of them had dismounted to dig up root vegetables we'd passed. I hadn't seen them, but they had. When we stopped near streams or rivers, before they did anything else, they filled our waterskins, knowing we needed water out here in this big open country more than we needed anything else. They also had a habit of collecting fuel along the way, bits of dry tinder which made good kindling along with bigger, solid pieces of wood.

I suppose I was surprised by just how well they travelled, although in hindsight, I should have known. For the past four years they had become used to moving camp and travelling long distances, first with the Hidatsa and then with the Mandan on their trading journeys. The girls had learned to be organized when unpacking belongings, in case they needed to leave camp in a hurry.

Their ability in the wild along with their skill in setting up camp made my life so much easier and within a week of leaving the Missouri River behind, we'd fallen into an easy routine. I rarely had to ask them for help. They knew what needed to be done, the same duties taught to them as children by their mothers and later by the Hidatsa and Mandan.

They set snares around our camp each night and nearly always caught a hare or night bird. We also killed rabbits or a prairie chicken during the day with our bows and arrows and the girls were so skilled at butchering these small creatures they needed no help from me.

They could also sense rain when it was coming, like I could. They could smell the scent of edible wildflowers, berries or nuts and they listened always for the sound of water.

I found them cautious and careful in all they did and within a week of travelling with them, I wondered what on earth I would have done without them.

I was also grateful that Harry enjoyed an easy relationship with them and as the days passed, he grew to love them as much as I did. They spoke to him only in *bannaite'*, and because I'd begun to teach him my beloved Bannock dialect back in England, he could speak it well enough, if not fluently. But he had a whole year to learn it, before we reached the Bannock.

*

The grasses and plants of the vast, lush prairie lands often grew as high as the bellies of our horses, with some plants even exceeding that. Within those grasses lived a multitude of wildlife and along with prairie chickens and rabbits we feasted on big fat ground squirrels, gophers and voles, all creatures which were easy prey in our snares. We nibbled on enormous berries rich in juice and found eggs in prairie bird nests. We caught bass and bream in rivers and streams which were all headed south to join the Missouri, before flowing into the Mississippi.

But that vast open country, although full of bounty, offered little security. We didn't dare light a fire within those vast dry prairie grasses, nor could we escape the heat of the day. At night we camped in hollows and when we eventually left the grasslands and found woodlands where we could light a fire, we stayed there for days, not only to rest, but to replenish our supplies. We gathered fresh herbs and smoked the meat we'd caught in our snares, so we never went hungry.

But one of my pleasures during those early days

crossing the prairie was to look at the night sky when clear of clouds and take in the stars, an infinite glittering spectacle that left me in awe. I'd almost forgotten how grand it was after my years of living indoors in England, but out here, living under that endless sky with no-one around for miles, I rediscovered the beauty of those magical nights.

Another joy was to hunt the big herds of wild deer, great healthy beasts that lived in every wood and forest we passed through. We feasted on smoked venison, the meat sweet and rich, the deer having fed on the grass roots and wildflowers that abounded near these vast prairie lands.

But the woods and forests we travelled through were also home to coyotes, bears and brown timber wolves. Sometimes the coyotes followed us, animals which made a strange *yap yap yap* bark which was so different to the haunting howl of wolves I was so familiar with, that it made me uneasy. At night, to protect ourselves from predators, we gathered wood and encircled our camp with fire and the girls and I would take turns to keep watch, making sure the flames never died out. I trusted those two girls so completely, I always sleep well when I wasn't on guard and not once did they ever let me down.

Three

They came out of deep woods and into a wide open clearing. Madeleine rode up behind Poongatse and Wannge'e, even as she heard their gasp of surprise. She reined her horse in beside Poongatse and looked beyond the clearing.

The land dropped away some two hundred feet or more into a wide deep valley and in the center of that valley was a massive wooden fort. By its well weathered look, it had been there for decades.

Madeleine was surprised to see a Spanish flag flying high from a central post, suggesting the fort was still under the control of Spain, even though Spain and its military interests in this territory were now redundant. With the signing of the Louisiana Purchase, the Americans now held the power in this territory, not the Spanish, nor the French under Napoleon Bonaparte.

Madeleine stared at the flag, feeling uneasy as she watched it fly in the slight breeze, even as she remembered the thriving Spanish and French settlements they'd passed through since leaving St Louis, along with a smaller French fort. Although that fort had been nothing more than a trading post, unlike the building which dominated the landscape below, suggesting the power Spain had once claimed in this territory.

She wondered how many Spanish soldiers might be still stationed down there. Men who were battle hardened and still loyal to Spain, ready to defend the Spanish King's last remaining interests in the New World. Perhaps only a handful, along with one or two officers, men employed to stay back and officially wind things down before they relinquished the fort to the Americans.

Harry stirred with impatience against her and Madeleine moved to undo the muslin cloth which bound them. Poongatse and Wannge'e dismounted to help her and as Poongatse lifted Harry down and chased after him as he sprinted away, Wannge'e looked up at Madeleine.

"Are we going there?" the girl asked, nodding towards the fort.

Madeleine dismounted, aware of the wariness in the girl's face. She shook her head and smiled. "No, we're not."

They hobbled the horses as Poongatse chased Harry around the trees, helping the little boy burn off some energy while Wannge'e pulled cold meat from their bags, along with their waterskins. Madeleine glanced back at the fort, squinting in the glare of the day and saw some sudden movement within the high wooden watch towers at each corner of the building. She watched a moment longer, then realized it was soldiers changing guard.

More than a handful of soldiers were stationed down there then, and more than one or two officers. Which was a good enough reason to avoid the place. Madeleine had no desire to feel obliged to accept an invitation to stay for a few days and dine with lonely officers in a fading, remote outpost.

Then another thought struck her. Those men, unused to female company out here in the wild, might see a young woman travelling alone with a small boy, two teenage girls and five horses loaded down with belongings as fair game.

She glanced over as Poongatse playfully chased Harry back towards their camp. Wannge'e laughed, holding out a strip of cold meat to the child and Madeleine knew that none of them were safe if they came into contact with hardened men, bitter about coming to the end of their days serving their Spanish King and country in territory now belonging to America.

She joined the girls and Harry under the shade of a maple tree to escape the heat of the mid-day sun and shared the cold smoked meat and chokeberry cakes. Yet she continued to watch the fort. A river lay some fifteen miles to the west of it, the hot sun glittering off its surface, although it was nothing like the Missouri or Mississippi rivers.

"If you decide to go down there," Wannge'e said, looking over at her. "Poongatse and I could take the packhorses and ride south under shelter of the trees, before turning west. Look, do you see that waterfall? We could all meet there."

Madeleine moved to kneel, shading her eyes as she looked down on the woods far below them. She could make out the fine layer of mist rising above the dense foliage of trees and as she glanced back at Wannge'e, she realized not for the first time that the girl had exceptional eyesight.

"No wonder you aim true when using a musket or bows and arrows," she said smiling, even as Poongatse frowned, gazing out over the woods, having more trouble seeing the fine layer of mist.

Madeleine smiled, for even though Poongatse was the more confident of the two girls, with an easy, gentle manner around Harry, it was Wannge'e who was the leader of the two. She was quieter, with a quick, efficient way about her and Poongatse followed her lead without question.

Madeleine looked back at the fort. If the girls took the packhorses and rode under cover of the woods towards that waterfall, avoiding the fort completely, it would add another two or three days to their travels which they couldn't afford. Did she want two teenage girls looking after four horses, all of them loaded down with possessions, just so she could visit the fort and find out what was happening in the territory? Four horses wouldn't be easy to hide. Not with Spanish militia riding through this country.

"No," she said, pushing herself to her feet. "There's no reason for me to go down there."

She looked out across the valley. If they left now they could put in some decent miles between them and that fort, before they set up camp for the night. Harry had had a run around and some food in his belly so he might sleep for a little while.

"Let's get moving," she said, scooping her son into her arms, even as the little boy laughed with delight.

Four

He was pressing the warm, hard bulk of his body up against my back, his hand on my waist, the familiar scent of him pleasing to me. The softness of the bed beneath us, a combination of duck feathers and straw made me feel weightless, so different to lying on furs on the hard ground.

"My love," I whispered in *bannaite'*, feeling the heat of him, the hunger and ache for his maleness sweeping through my body, the force of it taking me by surprise as I turned to him, wanting his embrace more than anything I'd wanted in my life when a small hand touched my face.

"*Mama*," a child spoke softly. I came awake instantly and in the light of the full moon saw my son looking down at me, realizing in that awful moment that my being with Ryder had been nothing but a dream.

"What is it, Harry?" I whispered, so as not to wake the girls, the desolation of my lover's loss filling me to my core.

I sat up, trying to shake off my fatigue, trying not to think of the dream even as I remembered with a crushing weight of horror that Ryder was still missing. I pushed aside the furs as Harry came into my arms.

"I cannot sleep, *Mama*," he said softly, speaking in French.

I quietened him, holding him in my arms as I gently rocked him, yet it wasn't often now that Harry woke in the night. "What woke you, sweetheart," I asked, even as Harry yawned and fell against the warmth of me.

"Le chien, *the dog*," he whispered, for even at his

young age I'd begun to teach him to keep his silence in the wild. He pointed into the pitch black of the night. "Can I play with him tomorrow, *Mama*?"

"What dog, darling? Did it come into our camp?" I asked, as I reached for my knife which always lay beside me.

"He was a nice dog *Mama*, you would have liked him very much," he said yawning, his eyes closed, almost asleep.

I looked out into the dark, suddenly aware of how deathly quiet it was. I couldn't even hear the usual rustlings of small night creatures which forage on the forest floor and that alone sent shivers up my spine.

We'd found the sheltered camp within some boulders on a steeply sloping hill deep within the woods, well north of the fort. We were completely hidden from sight here, for the trees were tall and dense, not even allowing us a view of the valley far behind us. Indeed, I'd felt so safe here I'd been oblivious to everything, falling asleep as soon as I closed my eyes.

"Did the dog growl at you? Where did it go, darling," I asked Harry, as he clumsily lifted an arm and pointed to the trees off to my right.

Immediately I moved, placing Harry gently on my furs so he wouldn't get frightened as I reached for my musket. Then I crawled towards the pile of dry tinder and wood we'd left in the center of our camp, just as we always did, in case we needed a fire. I thought we needed one now, for the hackles had risen on the back of my neck but I paused before striking my flint, unwilling to make our camp site known, for I knew if there were dogs here, then we weren't alone.

Many tribes, along with fur trappers, kept dogs. Most of them were almost wild, bred from domesticated dogs and wolves, creating an animal with long legs and a face similar to that of a wolf. Yet these creatures were far deadlier than a wolf. A wolf, like my own *esa*, would rarely seek out human company, not even in a pack, because by nature wolves are secretive creatures. But all dogs, even wild ones, are curious beings and will always seek out humans.

Harry rolled over and looked at me, half asleep. "He was a nice doggy, *Mama*. He came and licked my face. He was big and white and had eyes the color of Aunt Julia's hair."

I felt my blood run cold at his words. And now I did reach for my flint and struck it to light the kindling. The heat and flames woke the girls and they sat up, terrified, knowing I'd only light a fire if there was trouble nearby.

But there was no physical danger here, although there was something else.

For now more than ever, I was aware of the stillness of the place, the eeriness, that hadn't been here before.

I couldn't tell the girls of my fear of nightwalkers because of their own strong belief in the afterlife and I knew if they lost confidence in me, if they saw my own terror, they would never again sleep in the darkness of night without the comfort of a fire. I couldn't afford to have them lose confidence in me because our lives depended on it. But nor could I tell them that Harry may have experienced something not of this world, a supernatural being.

I trembled from the sudden icy coldness and

spookiness of this place and wondered if the ancient one had really come to my son in the spirit of my wolf. The thought of it terrified me, for I remembered only too well the times I'd seen *esa's* spirit in England, just before the evil that had been Jarryth and Thorne Benedict shattered our lives.

I settled the girls and Harry by boiling some water and giving them each a herbal drink of chamomile to soothe their nerves and help them sleep. But Harry thought it great fun we were now all awake and went to Poongatse, climbing into bed with her, before telling us in detail of his contact with the dog.

"He was bigger than me, *Mama*," he said, as he cuddled into her arms.

It appeared he had woken and stumbled off into the trees to do his *toilette*, as I had taught him to do, although never alone and never in the depths of night. But while in the trees he had seen the dog and when Harry went over to it, the dog had led him back to camp, licking his face. "He stood next to you *Mama*, until I woke you."

I scolded Harry for going off alone which upset him, but I couldn't afford to have him wander off by himself. Not during the day, and never at night.

But from that moment I vowed to keep Harry on a lead, always attached to me during the night. Never again would he wander off while I slept from exhaustion, on those rare occasions when I fell into the deepest of sleeps.

Although I thought it strange I hadn't woken when Harry left his bed. Being a child, he wouldn't have been quiet about it, yet I had slept on. Had the ancient one wanted to be alone with Harry? Although that thought unsettled me even more and once the girls and Harry were settled back under their furs I reached for my musket and left the comfort of our camp and turned for the boulders behind us.

I moved with caution, although our little fire gave enough light for me to see easily enough. I searched the area where Harry had seen the dog but I found nothing. No scent, no spoor, nothing. After some time prowling around I returned to my bed but I lay awake until dawn, my musket and knife within easy reach.

Five

They came upon a small column of soldiers two days later and everything Madeleine had wanted to avoid, took place in that one encounter.

They had just left the forest to cross a narrow ridge, less than a mile long, before once again joining that vast wilderness which swept away to the west and the waterfall which Wannge'e had seen three days earlier, when the riders appeared out of the trees ahead of them.

Madeleine heard the beat of their horses' hooves well before they appeared but was helpless to do anything. They couldn't turn back, nor was there anywhere to hide on that barren piece of rock. Besides, they had no hope of outrunning the men coming towards them.

There were fifteen of them, with the man in front of the column wearing the uniform and insignia of an officer in the Spanish militia.

Madeleine reined her horse in, urging Wannge'e and Poongatse to be still as they rode up behind her. But the girls understood well enough that they had no hope of avoiding these riders.

Madeleine quickly glanced back at the two packhorses behind her, but the muskets were well covered by furs and blankets.

"Be a good boy for *Mama*, Harry," she said urgently to her son. "I don't want you to utter one word, do you understand? Even if the man talks to you, I want you to keep quiet. Do you hear me?"

The child nodded, but Madeleine need have no fear of Harry talking. The little boy was trembling as he watched, wide-eyed, as the riders approached and quickly surrounded them. The man in front addressed her, with some courtesy.

"Capitán Arrondo, at your service *Madame*!" he said in Spanish, tipping his hat towards Madeleine although he barely glanced at the two Bannock girls or Harry. "May I ask what your business is here and why are you travelling alone?"

Madeleine didn't mention that she thought him wrong, that this was no longer his territory to guard. Instead, she bowed her head slightly to acknowledge him formally, before speaking in high Spanish, revealing she was an educated woman.

Spanish had been just one of the languages Madeleine had learned as a child, in the classroom at her father's family home in Paris. A palace, which had once showcased centuries of his family's wealth and royal connections to the Bourbon Kings of Europe, it had burned to the ground more than sixteen years ago.

"We are travelling to meet my husband and his party just north of here," she said, thinking quickly, hoping to sound more confident than she felt.

"We hope to meet him tomorrow morning. Unfortunately we became separated due to ill health, for the pox came to a small Creole settlement we visited not five days east of here."

Every man heard her words and she saw their fear. She was glad that neither Harry nor Poongatse and Wannge'e understood Spanish. That might have saved her some awkwardness because it was an outright lie. No-one they'd come upon had suffered from smallpox.

"The pox you say?" Capitán Arrondo asked in horror. "Are you and your servants' unwell *Madame*?"

Madeleine shook her head. "No, we are quite well."

"This is most extraordinary," the Capitán said, glancing at Harry as the little boy stared back at him, his big blue eyes round with excitement at this sudden, unexpected change to their usual routine.

"Well then, I insist you accompany me back to the fort, *Madame*. Our physician will want to examine you all. We cannot afford to have smallpox sweep through this territory again, not after losing all those thousands four years ago."

Madeleine looked at him in surprise. She hadn't heard about a smallpox outbreak four years ago. Julia hadn't mentioned it, nor had anyone in St Louis.

"I don't understand your meaning sir?" she said, her voice low with fear. "What does this mean, losing thousands?"

Capitán Arrondo sighed, now irritated by her and her party. They were just another problem for him. There were never enough men to patrol this huge territory, there was never enough food to satisfy the men's tastes and since the Americans claimed ownership of this territory, wages were always slow to arrive causing ill feeling among the men.

To add to his troubles, there had been a nasty incident between some Kiowa and Pawnee just days ago and the last thing he needed was another flare up between tribes.

Now this woman, riding out alone with a young boy and two teenage girls. He thought her mind possibly turned, so he decided to humor her.

"Four years ago, smallpox swept through this area killing untold thousands, most of them from local tribes. Some blamed it on putrid blankets brought into this territory from villages already infected with the disease while others blamed it on us and other settlers bringing it into the region. I'm sure you'll understand *Madame*, we cannot afford another outbreak, so I insist you and your party accompany us back to the fort to be examined by our physician."

Madeleine paused, trying not to show her fear, but she knew she had to make a stand now or they were lost.

"No, Capitán. I thank you for your hospitality, but I cannot. I must away to join my husband. Perhaps I should explain he is Colonel of an American regiment of several hundred troops, sent this way to set up a fort. He has gone on ahead of me, as I explained, with a small contingent of men, but the rest of his troops follow in a week or so. No doubt you'll meet them soon enough."

Madeleine saw the bewilderment then rage briefly cross the man's face and saw at once his bitterness that Spain no longer held any rights here. He would be transferred eventually, along with his men, because west of the Louisiana Purchase, Spain still claimed vast tracks of land that stretched all the way to the Pacific Coast, along with almost all of central Mexico and a huge peninsula of land they were calling Florida. Spain also controlled large parts of the Caribbean and East Indies.

But in this territory, that privilege now belonged to the Americans.

"Very well, *Madame*," he said, deciding in that moment that Madeleine and her small group were one problem he didn't have to deal with. If they wanted to ride out here alone, let them be left to their own fate. "I wish you well on your travels."

He swung his horse around and rode past her, back towards the fort.

Madeleine said nothing but sat very still and watched them leave, acutely aware of every man's eyes on her and the girls.

When they had gone, Madeleine turned to Poongatse and Wannge'e, who were both pale with fear. "Let's get out of here," she said

.

Six

I lay on my stomach looking out into the dark as it was my turn to keep watch. We'd left the deep woods behind yesterday and now travelled once again through open flat country and although I wished for the comfort of a fire, I dared not light one. Not because it was cold, although the air was damp, promising rain, but because someone had camped not five miles east from our own campsite. As I watched in the dark, I could see the glow and flicker of their fire. I had no idea who it was. Perhaps men from a local tribe out hunting. Perhaps those fur trappers I'd seen in St Louis more than a week ago. Or even one or two of those soldiers from the Spanish fort.

But whoever it was, I had no wish to light a fire and let them know where we were. It only needed one man to ride the few miles that separated us, to see it was one woman travelling alone with teenage girls and a little boy. I wished suddenly for the comfort of my pipe but dared not strike a flint, so I lay there and watched and listened to the night all around us and sometimes heard the faint sound of men laughing.

I shivered when I heard this, as it sounded so unnatural in the dark. I wondered suddenly if I should wake the girls and Harry and push on through the night. Or wait until morning and take the chance these men were heading somewhere else, other than west. I thought on it until finally dismissing the idea. It would be a struggle packing the horses in the dark and besides, the noise would carry across to those men. Harry only needed to start crying and that high pitched sound would carry for miles in this flat open country. No, better to stay and take our chances here.

I rolled over onto my back just in time to see a shooting star. It was gone so quickly, yet it reminded me of my mother. She had always thought of shooting stars as good luck, a good omen, so I made a wish as I lay there in the dark, that Ryder was safe and somehow he would find us.

I glanced across at Harry as he turned in his sleep where he lay between Poongatse and Wannge'e and I crawled over to pull the woolen blanket up around his shoulders. My mother would have loved this child, her only grandson, and I think she would have loved Ryder. But she would never have understood my longing to return to the wild. Had the Terror not happened in France, my life would have become a replica of her own, a life of privilege, of wealth and a life spent in the royal court of King Louis XVI.

But I had no regrets. Unlike my dear friend François, the Marquis d'Auvergne, who would do anything to restore the monarchy to France. All I wanted, all my heart desired, was for my beloved to find his way back to me. Sometimes it seemed as if Ryder had disappeared into a great dark hole, invisible to all who searched for him. In two and a half years, a lifetime to be apart, there had been not one word from him. Yet I refused to give up hope. One day he'd find that trail of lavender ribbons I'd left for him in his library at Millbryne Park, ribbons that led to a secret drawer and the treasure hidden within, all of which explained his past. Ryder deserved that, at the very least, for I knew better than anyone just how many years he'd spent trying to unravel the mystery which had blurred his childhood.

I closed my eyes, thinking of the wish I'd made on the shooting star and hoped that wherever Ryder was in the world, that he sometimes thought of me and Harry. I hoped he hadn't forgotten us, that he still loved us. Then I remembered the dream I'd had that he was coming and I held onto it like a lifeline, grasping it close to me with all the courage I owned.

Harry settled once more into deep sleep and I smiled with love for the little boy. I'd tried tying him to me at night, using a thin rawhide rope to stop him ever walking off into the woods again by himself, but he hadn't liked that idea at all and the compromise had been to let him sleep between Poongatse and Wannge'e. Although the compromise had pleased me, because it gave me freedom to get up during the night if I needed to, like tonight, and scout around if I couldn't sleep. I turned to glance back towards the distant horizon and despite our own isolation here, the fire of that other campsite still burned. It made me deeply uneasy. Agitated, I sat up and reached for the waterskin and took a long sip. My mouth felt dry, but I knew it was from the supply of smoked, salted beef which Julia had given us, which Harry and I had finished only yesterday.

Poongatse and Wannge'e hadn't taken a liking to Julia's food, thinking the meat unnatural with its salty taste and the bread and biscuits far too sweet. So they'd continued to dig up edible root vegetables and catch fat prairie chickens in their snares. If we were lucky enough to snare some fish, we covered them in clay and cooked them in hot coals, often with wild mushrooms. Fish was now Harry's favorite meal and whenever we camped near a river or stream, one of our first chores was to set snares in the water.

I put away the waterskin then sat back to watch that campfire way in the distance. We would have to light fires of our own soon, because autumn was only a breath away. Yet the thought of someone watching our campsite, as I was watching someone's now, filled me with dread. Again, the sound of men's laughter drifted across to me. Clearly there were more than two of them and they were not afraid to be heard. Which hinted at their arrogance. I decided they weren't men from a local tribe. Men who had been born in this land, who had spent their whole lives here, would sit quietly around a fire at night listening as I did, like the Bannock men did.

I closed my eyes, desperately wanting to sleep yet unable to, as again I heard those faint shouts of laughter. To calm my mind I thought of Ryder and all the nights we'd lain together like this in the wild.

"I feel like I've come home when I'm with you," he said to me once, as we lay together in our furs, the heavens dark and glittering above us.

"Me also, halfbreed," I'd whispered, moving closer to him, curling around his male strength and hardness, finding such comfort in his large body.

As I thought of that now, I imagined I could feel Ryder's arm about my waist.

"Be safe, my love," I said softly, sending the words out across the world, hoping against hope that he might hear them, or feel the love within them. "Wherever you are, be safe."

Seven

They came around mid-day three days later. But Madeleine already knew they were coming and had prepared Harry and the girls for the inevitable attack.

For three nights she had watched the men's camp. For two nights she'd endured their laughter, but last night the coarse shouting had begun. Crude words drifting across the dark, spoken in a mixture of English, Spanish and French, their purpose to intimidate and cause fear.

For Harry's sake, Madeleine tried to avoid the conflict that loomed by setting a faster pace each day to try and get away from the men. But she quickly came to understand that they were playing a game, lingering behind them, taunting them, just biding their time before they attacked.

When the shouting started last night, she'd left the girls with Harry then quickly backtracked, running through the night towards the men's camp to see who these ghosts were, who trailed behind them, who laughed in the night. She came within fifty feet of their camp, easily seen by the light of their fire, when she heard the smash of broken glass along with foul words spoken. It was then that Madeleine understood who these men were and what they wanted.

She felt sickened by what she heard. The men were already celebrating their success, enjoying their prolonged stalking on what they saw as three vulnerable young women and a child. They thought that by the time they did attack, Madeleine and her small party would be so worn down with fatigue and terror they would be compliant and easy.

But Madeleine hadn't been compliant and easy

since she was fifteen years old, when she'd known real fear. She learned at that young age, after weeks of horrific abuse, that it was better to die fighting than be a plaything for bullies.

By the time she'd returned to her own camp to try and get a few hours' sleep, she had a plan.

They rose at dawn the following morning but instead of heading west, they turned north, towards a forest some miles off to their right. When they entered the trees in the early afternoon, Madeleine started looking for a place to hide, to hunker down, somewhere that would offer them shelter. When they stopped by a stream to fill their waterskins, it was Harry who found it. A large pine tree growing over a high bank, leaving its roots exposed to create a massive chamber beneath. As soon as she saw it, Madeleine began to put her battle plan together.

She told the girls what she wanted from them, she told Harry what part he would play in the game ahead then they spent the remainder of that day building a large bivouac within the roots of that giant pine.

Towards dusk they unpacked all their belongings, placing them at the rear of the chamber before barricading the front of it with more branches, until those great roots and everything behind it were completely hidden.

Madeleine left the girls and Harry hiding inside it as the night began to settle, then took the five horses into the woods a good half mile away. She hobbled them and left them to graze, then ran back, crawling into the shelter herself to begin priming and loading six of the muskets. Two for herself and two each for Poongatse and Wannge'e. Then they ate a meal of cold meat and piñon nut bread, wild carrots and berries.

When it was full dark, Madeleine once again crawled from the shelter to backtrack, seeing the flames of the men's fire just a mile away. She heard their angry words, arguing with each other about leaving it too late to follow the tracks. Madeleine almost smiled. They clearly didn't know where she and the girls and Harry had camped, but at least that ensured them all a good night's sleep within the darkness of their shelter.

She stayed watching them for hours, well past midnight, and when confident they wouldn't come any further into the woods to search for them, she retreated to their shelter, curled up within her furs and fell into a deep sleep of exhaustion.

*

She woke just before dawn. The forest was silent, but the men would come today, she was sure of it. She woke the girls and Harry and while they quietly ate a meal of cold meat, Madeleine run back to the men's camp. They were all still sleeping, the fumes of whisky rising from empty bottles smashed near the firepit.

Madeleine raced back to camp and carried Harry away to a thicket of wild blackberry bushes she'd seen yesterday near where their horses grazed. She sat him down in the long grass and told him they were now going to play the game, but he had to be very quiet. When Poongatse came hurrying towards them, carrying two of the shortened muskets already to fire, the girl looked terrified.

"You have to be strong," Madeleine said softly, as

the girl sat down beside them. "I'm trusting you with his life. If they come, you aim to kill."

"Who's coming, *Mama*?" Harry asked.

"Some bad men. They want to play that rough game with us, but I don't want to play. So you must be a good strong boy for *Mama* and do whatever Poongatse tells you. If you see or hear those men, you must crawl under the bushes and keep very still and hide. Do you understand?"

The little boy nodded, his eyes wide with fear. But it was good he knew fear. It would make him careful and watchful, which might just save his life.

Madeleine hugged them, not bothering to give Poongatse any more powder or shot, because if the girl had to use those two muskets against that pack of wild dogs, she wouldn't have a chance to reload. Madeleine ran back to where she'd left Wannge'e hiding within some ferns. When she saw Madeleine, the girl crawled out into that dull gloom of early morning, then joined Madeleine in laying down some tracks, their moccasins scuffing the ground and leaving a decent trail which could easily be followed, all of them leading from the ridge above them to a clearing, less than a hundred feet from their shelter. Then they waited.

*

They came just before midday, their horses' hooves echoing on the hard rock of the ridge. They rode at a walk, following the trail laid down by Madeleine and Wannge'e earlier, but there was nothing urgent about them. They thought they had all the time in the world, they thought three young women and a child were easy targets.

As the horses left the ridge and started down the bank straight towards the clearing, Madeleine turned to Wannge'e. The girl was pale and trembling with fear.

"When you fire, you aim to kill," Madeleine said softly. "It's your life, or their life. Do you understand?"

Wannge'e nodded. "I shall think of the Hidatsa. How I wish I could have fired on them that day," she whispered, before bending down to pick up one of the two shortened muskets at her feet, both ready to fire.

Madeleine held another of the shortened muskets, all meant as gifts for Ese-ggwe'na'a, except now they were being used against the worst of predators. She touched the loaded pistol which lay wedged within the belt tied around her waist, then prayed the blacksmith in St Louis had done his job and that all these shortened muskets fired well.

"Have you killed before, Esa-mogo'ne'?" Wannge'e asked, surprising Madeleine by the question.

She paused for a moment before answering, then she nodded. "Yes, I have killed. But it was my life, or theirs and I desperately wanted to live."

Wannge'e nodded, taking comfort in that, even as the men came towards the clearing. They weren't stealthy like most killers. Indeed, they were in high spirits, come to take pleasure and to steal whatever was on the back of the two packhorses. The sheer arrogance of them, that they thought themselves entitled to something that didn't belong to them, angered Madeleine. When they rode into the clearing, she saw there were three of them. They rode with no packhorses, which was rare out here in the wild.

Madeleine recognized only one of the men. He had been riding at the back of the Spanish militia which had stopped Madeleine and her small party on a narrow ridge just west of the Spanish fort. She didn't recognize the others. They had to be deserters, leaving their post for what they thought was a bigger prize. The worst kind of men. As they came further into the clearing, Madeleine became aware of the ripe smell of raw alcohol which drifted off the men. She glanced over at Wannge'e and saw the fear on the girl's face, along with rage. When one of the man threw back his head and laughed, his teeth yellow and black with disease, Wannge'e raised her musket and aimed it at him, while Madeleine aimed her musket at the man behind him, an older man, an unkempt sadistic looking creature with few teeth.

Madeleine pulled her trigger first. She felt the power of the musket as the sawn-off weapon recoiled in her hands, making her fall back even as she heard Wannge'e fire her own musket. For a moment there was only silence, as though the world had stopped, then the stench of gunpowder drifted up into the trees followed by the scream of frightened horses and cries of agony.

Madeleine didn't stop to look, but reached for her other musket, but as she swung it up and back, aiming at the third man, she saw that only one of the men had fallen.

Her shot had badly wounded the first man, leaving his shoulder a mangled bloody mess. If he weren't dead already, he soon would be. Wannge'e had shot the second man's horse out from beneath him and he barely had time to jump clear and roll away before the horse fell dead beside him. He crawled back behind a tree, screaming at the third man to get the hell behind the trees, but he was too late.

Like Madeleine, Wannge'e had already reached for her second musket and fired it, shooting the younger man in the back as he spun around on his horse, panicking, not sure where the musket fire was coming from. The shot jettisoned him forward, as though someone had punched him hard. He fell over the neck of his horse for a moment, then fell silently to the forest floor as blood pumped from a terrible wound in his lower back.

Madeleine's second shot just missed the older man as he crawled behind the tree. She cursed softly, instinctively reaching for her powder and shot to prime and reload when she saw Wannge'e reaching for her bow and arrows. The Bannock girl knew she would be too slow to prime and load another musket, so she didn't bother. She put the arrow to the bow and held the weapon to her eye, looking at the trees. Like Madeleine, she could hear the man screaming something, but she didn't understand Spanish.

"By God, I'll kill you all with my bare hands, including that little bastard. Show yourselves goddamit!"

And then all was still. Madeleine finished ramming the powder and shot and piece of cloth down the muzzle then turned to Wannge'e.

"Where is he?" the girl whispered, but Madeleine shook her head, aware that she was trembling. But Wannge'e was worse off, for her bow and the arrow were shaking badly in her hands.

"Stay here," Madeleine whispered then crept away, carrying the musket, knowing she only had one precious shot. She paused to touch the pistol in her belt. It was loaded, but if she missed, she only had Wannge'e to rely on. She circled around the wood, crouching low, yet she could hear nothing but silence and knew then that this last man had been the killer out of the three. The other two had sought only pleasure and stolen goods.

Then she heard Wannge'e scream. Just one long terrified scream and then nothing. Madeleine took off at a run between the trees, seeking cover, her musket out before her.

She found the Bannock girl lying unconscious on the ground, knocked out by a vicious punch to the head. The left side of her face was already raw and swelling, with blood oozing from her nose and mouth. Madeleine pushed herself away from the tree, reaching to turn Wannge'e over so she didn't choke on her own blood when she smelt the stench of him behind her. She turned as he rushed at her from deep ferns, his breath labored and foul and in a desperate attempt to get clear of him, Madeleine twisted her body just in time to avoid the worst of his weight as he fell on her.

But as she rolled away he reached for her plait, using it to wrench her back towards him. Madeleine grunted in pain and dropped the musket as he shoved her with such force she fell face down in the dirt, his knee digging painfully into her lower back.

"By God, you'll pay for what you've done here girl."

He grabbed the pistol out of her belt and threw it aside then grabbed the rawhide belt she wore around her waist and pulled her so viciously with it, that it cut into her belly. She cried aloud from the pain even as he swung her over and put his knee across her thighs, so she lay helpless on her back. Panting, trying to gain control, she was aware of him pulling desperately at her buckskin pants, ripping them with such force that the material pulled away from the sinew stitching, leaving her half naked beneath him. He was panting now, his breath rancid, his sweat dripping onto her face as she willed herself not to lose consciousness, but as she tried to get away, struggling against him, he reached out and with the back of his hand swept it with force across her face.

She felt her teeth and jaw smack together, creating a terrible jarring within her head, unlike anything she'd ever known. Then he was spreading her legs, crazed with rage and hate and lust and therefore so much stronger than her. He touched her with his filthy fingers and disgusted by him, Madeleine suddenly saw the image of another man's face loom before her.

Another monster she'd been unable to fight.

The memory of him and what he did to her when she was barely fifteen years old brought such a rage to the surface, a rage that had been simmering and burning for more than fourteen years, that with the last of her strength, Madeleine lifted her right leg high and wide, hearing this man's laugh of triumph as he looked down at her nakedness. But with a rage she'd never known before, not even with Jarryth, Madeleine pulled the butcher knife from her boot, her fingers trembling badly but she gripped it tight, knowing she was lost if she dropped it.

The man moved to kiss her mouth, one of his

hands fumbling to free his own clothes even as Madeleine pulled her hand back and with every bit of strength she owned, she shoved the knife into the side of his neck.

He was so thick with lust he never saw it coming. But Madeleine heard and felt the knife slice into him, she felt the hotness of his blood as it covered her, the blood of life leaving his body with such force it was a terrible thing.

It was impossible to move out from under him until he reared backwards, his face twisted in horror as he held both hands to his neck in a desperate attempt to stop that precious flow. But Madeleine wanted desperately to be free of him and she lifted both her legs then shoved them in his chest, the kick pitching him backwards so he lay twisting on the ground before her, moaning desperately as his life slowly left him.

She turned away and rolled over, pushing herself to her knees, not wanting to see the shadows come for him in death. She crawled toward Wannge'e, breathing heavily, spitting blood from her mouth.

Wannge'e was alive, but moaning softly in pain.

"Oh, dearest girl," Madeleine whispered, putting a hand gently on the girl's back before falling beside her, just as an awful buzzing started in her ears, then everything went black.

*

It was the sensation of something cool and soothing on her face which woke Madeleine. She opened her eyes to find Poongatse leaning over her, wiping her face with a damp cloth.

"Where's Deide'wesa?" she asked, her voice sounding thick and heavy for her mouth and tongue felt swollen and sore, the side of her face thudding with dull pain where he'd hit her.

Poongatse nodded back towards the hill. "Hiding under the berries. He won't come unless I call him."

"*Aishenda'qa,*" Madeleine said, thanking her, as she reached up to touch her jaw. Such pain, but he hadn't broken anything, she could be grateful for that at least. She pushed herself to sit up, to look over at Wannge'e. The girl still lay unconscious.

Madeleine turned and reached for Poongatse's hand. "Could you help me? Could you run back to our shelter and bring me a blanket? As quick as you can? We've got so much to do before we get Deide'wesa," she said, aware of her nakedness and his foul blood all over her.

Poongatse nodded, but before she left she glanced back at Wannge'e. "They came to hurt us, didn't they?" she said, looking pale and frightened.

Madeleine nodded. "Yes," she replied. "They would have used us very badly, including Deide'wesa," she looked up at the girl. "Don't call him yet. Wait until I've cleaned myself. I don't want him to see Wannge'e and me like this."

Once Poongatse was gone Madeleine pushed herself to her feet, feeling muscles and tendons pull as she made her way slowly to that stream near their camp. She took her moccasins off and walked into the water fully clothed, before lying down and floating on the shallow surface, allowing the water to soak through her clothes and her hair and over her face and between her legs where he'd touched her. The water turned red from his blood, but it also cleansed her.

When Poongatse returned she helped Madeleine out of her clothes and spent precious minutes helping to scrub her clean with herbs, removing his blood from her hair, her fingernails and even out of her ears. And all the time they spoke of what herbs they could use to help Wannge'e. Then wrapped in a blanket, leaving her clothing behind in the stream weighed down with rocks in an attempt to get the stain out of them, Madeleine walked back with Poongatse to where Wannge'e lay. It took all their strength to carry the girl back to their shelter, away from that place of death. Then Madeleine asked Poongatse to get the horses.

As she raced off, Madeleine bent down and touched Wannge'e. The girl was still unconscious and bore a nasty bruise on one side of her face. Madeleine touched the girl's neck and jaw but could feel no broken bones. Then she gently opened the girl's mouth, and saw a tooth lying on her tongue. That at least, explained the blood.

"I'll help you soon enough, dearest girl," Madeleine whispered then turned to quickly dig a firepit and get a fire going before returning to their shelter and pulling out another set of buckskin clothing. Other than this, she had one buckskin shift to wear, which gave her no choice but to repair the clothing in the stream. She grimaced at the thought of it, trying to ignore the dull ache in her body from the beating he'd given her as she slowly dressed.

It took long minutes for Madeleine to unpack all their furs and blankets, their wooden mugs, their bags of herbs, her bag of tobacco and pipes and a rawhide rope from the shelter and settle them back near the firepit. Then she set up a soft bed for Wannge'e before gently rolling her onto it. By the time she'd filled the cooking pot with water from the stream and set it close to the fire to heat, she'd decided which herbs she would use as a poultice and which ones to use as a potion.

Sundrops, which the English called evening primrose, used with the leaves and bark of willow would make a poultice to help reduce the swelling and bruising on Wannge'e's face. A tea of snakeroot and catswort would ease the pain in her mouth and help with any inflammation as well as numb her gums.

As she put the herbs in a mug, Poongatse came through the trees on horseback, with the other four horses behind her. She dismounted and Madeleine helped her hobble them, except for her own. Poongatse knew why, but said nothing. The bodies couldn't be left anywhere near their camp, because night predators would be drawn to the scent of blood and death.

Madeleine left Poongatse to make the poultice then picked up the rawhide rope and walked across to her horse. She rode back into the woods where the dead men lay and quickly tied one end of the rope around her horse's neck, the other to one of the men's ankles. Then she rode away, not bothering to look back as the man was dragged behind her.

She rode for more than a mile until she found a narrow gorge, the steep bank falling away into such dense brush and trees she couldn't see the bottom of it. She took the rope off the man's leg but unwilling to touch him, she used a branch to push him over the edge. She heard branches and shrubs break under the weight of him as he dropped below.

She did this twice more, not thinking about what she was doing, aware only of that simmering rage, that these monsters would dare to hurt two young innocent girls and a little boy.

Then one last thing remained to do. All trace of these men being here had to be removed, just in case the Spanish militia came looking for them. They were deserters as well as horse thieves, because Madeleine saw that each one of their horses carried a special brand.

She attached the reins of the three horses to the rawhide rope then mounted her horse and rode out, the three horses running behind her. When she came to the gorge she dismounted and removed the men's saddles and all their belongings and threw them into the gorge. Then she rode another mile or more downhill towards a narrow valley with a river running through it. She dismounted, removing the bridles from each horse before slapping each animal on its flank. They took off in terror, heading for the valley.

Madeleine watched until they disappeared under a stand of cottonwoods which lined the riverbank. They would eventually be found by someone, either men passing through here from a local tribe or fur trappers, but until then they could run wild.

She mounted her own horse and headed back towards the gorge, throwing the bridles over the edge to rot away within that dense vegetation far below. Then she rode hard for the blackberry bush where her son was hiding.

Less than an hour had passed since the attack, but Madeleine knew the little boy would be frightened because he would have heard the musket fire and the

screams. She pushed the horse into
the little boy hadn't wandered off.

*

Madeleine made Harry a potion of ch ...omile to
calm him when they returned to camp, to sedate him
a little, because the child was in deep shock. He had
no understanding of what had happened, yet he'd
heard it all. Madeleine found him cowering under the
blackberries, crying softly, but he came to her when
she called and he'd barely left her side since.

When Madeleine and Harry returned to camp,
Wannge'e had regained consciousness. But she'd
continued to lie quietly by the fire, unable to speak,
the left side of her face almost unrecognizable within
a mass of purple and red bruising. Her left eye was
so swollen she couldn't open it.

Poongatse also made her a potion of stoneseed,
known for its sedative effects, although Madeleine
knew the herb could also act as a contraceptive.
Poongatse also found some sumac leaves in the
woods and Wannge'e took them with gratitude,
chewing them slowly, as the leaves were a natural
antiseptic and would not only help ease the pain in
her mouth but stop any infection. Later, when
Wannge'e could bear it, Poongatse made her an
astringent, steeping the sumac roots in hot water so
Wannge'e could rinse her mouth out with more of
the antiseptic herb.

Wannge'e had taken the full force of the man's
closed fist but thought herself fortunate that he
hadn't broken her jaw. Or her cheek, or eye socket.

Towards dusk, as Madeleine changed the poultice

the girl's face, Wannge'e reached up to grasp her hand.

"*Aishe*," she whispered, thanking her.

Madeleine bent down and kissed her on the forehead. "It is I who should be thanking you, darling girl. You saved us. Had you not fired those two muskets, we would have been lost. Try and rest. If you need anything, you have only to ask."

Wannge'e tried to smile but groaned instead and turned to spit more blood from her mouth. As she closed her eyes to sleep, Poongatse began to cry softly. Madeleine went to her, taking her in her arms.

"We'll be alright now, there's nothing here to frighten us," she said softly. "Come, let's take Harry into the woods and check the snares we laid down last night."

But as Madeleine took Harry by the hand and led him away into the trees, as Poongatse picked up her bow and sheaths of arrows and followed them, Madeleine made a silent vow that this would never happen again. She could have killed those men while they slept, lost within the fumes of their alcohol fueled dreams. They wouldn't have known a thing about it. Nor would these precious young women who travelled with her, along with her son. She felt the butcher knife within its sheath on her belt. Next time she'd make sure she did it.

Atlantic Ocean: early August 1804

The rain and high waves lashed the ship, the wooden vessel's masts and spars groaning in defiance as another monstrous wave smashed against its hull, the bow dipping dangerously below another onslaught of water. Ryder sat in the Captain's cabin, frustrated at not being able to go up on deck. He'd been sent below on the Captain's orders as the crew struggled to keep the ship afloat in the storm.

"You can't help us, my Lord," the captain yelled above the wind, rain and high surf. "I'd rather you go below deck and keep out of the way of my men. Knowing you're safe down there gives me one less thing to worry about. I don't want to think of you being swept overboard and having to explain how that happened to your family."

So Ryder did as he was bid and went down to his cabin. Or rather, the Captain's cabin, for as owner of this clipper, Ryder had taken possession of the quarters for the duration of the voyage, as he and Madeleine had done on their passage to England four years earlier. To keep his mind off the storm and the queasy feeling in his belly, he began to write letters to Ash and Rupert, but found it impossible as the ship rolled in the swell of the raging seas. He gave up and put away his small writing box containing paper, quills, sharpener and pot of ink as a small candle set under a glass dome began to flicker as the ship rolled. Yet Ryder was loath to extinguish it, even as his stomach heaved again with the rolling of the vessel. He'd rather be able to see if the cabin began taking on water than wait for it in the dark, because he knew from his months aboard Saldivar's clipper what they were facing up on deck.

He paced the cabin in frustration like a caged beast, thinking of a letter he'd written to Madeleine last May. He'd sent it to Julia Corrigan's ranch, hoping the letter would reach Madeleine before she left for the Wazhazhe village. Indeed, Ryder had given instructions to the Captain of a Benedict clipper bound for Alexandria to pass it on without delay, to the first ship leaving Alexandria for New Orleans. From New Orleans, the letter must then travel by keelboat for a month up the Mississippi River to St Louis. Although Ryder knew in his heart that the letter would never have reached Madeleine in time. It took two months, sometimes longer, depending on the winds and tides and storms such as this, for a ship to sail from London to America. He should have sent the letter no later than April, but he'd been too angry with her for leaving England with his son and disappointed she hadn't trusted him enough to stay, to write to her sooner, to let her know he was alive. Realistically, the only chance the letter had of reaching her was if she were still at Julia's ranch. But Ryder doubted that. Madeleine wouldn't waste time and valuable summer days sitting around waiting on news of him. She would have left St Louis weeks ago, if not months. He cursed softly, but all he could hope for now was that this storm pushed the ship closer to the Virginian coast and not completely off course. Or worse.

in the wild: late-August 1804

Madeleine lay beside Harry watching him as he slept, taking pleasure in it, for he was so like his father even in sleep. The child's hair was worn long now, well past his shoulders, and sometimes a wayward curl would fall across his forehead just like it had with his father and Harry would brush it aside with impatience, also just like his father.

She moved to lie on her stomach and looked down the vale. They were camped in a sheltered grove of pine, beech and cedar, away from any wind and out of the sun's heat. Just above them was a sloping bank and less than a quarter mile away a small waterfall fell from the bank and met up with a shallow stream which meandered all the way down to another valley below them. Across the stream a thick wood swept away for miles before reaching rolling hills way in the distance.

They had been here for two days, taking advantage of the good weather, the fresh water and the forest, from which they could replenish their supplies before moving on. Poongatse and Wannge'e had left earlier that morning to check and reset their snares in both the woods and further downstream, leaving Harry and Madeleine to rest.

The girls had had some luck yesterday, catching six good sized rabbits and two wild turkeys. They had roasted two of the rabbits last night over a frame of ironwood above a fire for their supper while the rest of the meat was being smoked today, the hickory wood giving the long strips of meat a lovely flavor.

Away from the smoke, up near the bank, were several more willow frames and across these were stretched the fur of each rabbit, adding to the pile the girls had already cured and collected since arriving at Julia's last March. Madeleine thought the furs a good enough dowry when they eventually returned to the Bannock village.

Just behind the fire were two bivouacs Madeleine and the girls had built when they arrived here two days ago. One was bigger than the other but here Madeleine had stored all her belongings and where she slept with Harry. Poongatse and Wannge'e shared the smaller shelter. They had laid the large buckskin sheets on the floor of each bivouac then placed the sailcloths over the wooden frames to keep the shelters warm and waterproof. Over this they had added branches from the forest and mud from the stream.

She turned as a bee flew close to Harry's face and as she lifted her hand to wave it away she heard the faint whicker of a horse. She moved instinctively, not even thinking about it, and reached for her musket which lay beside her. Yet as she crouched beside Harry she couldn't see anyone, not in the woods across the stream, nor the woods behind them where her five horses were hobbled, grazing on rich summer grass.

Then she heard the sound again and swung around. It came from the bank above her.

Moving quickly, she laid the musket on the ground then swept the sleeping child into her arms, her shoulder taking the weight of the boy as she reached down to grab the gun. Then she rushed for the cover of the trees behind their bivouacs, stepping behind a great pine before lying Harry gently on the ground. By the time she looked up again, a horse and rider had appeared above her on the other side of the falls.

She watched as he glanced down the sloping vale, following the path of the stream. Then he turned and saw the camp below him. He reacted immediately, reaching for the bow over his shoulder before pulling several arrows from the sheath on his back, placing one of the arrows within the taut sinew string even as he kicked his horse away from the edge of the falls to disappear among the trees.

Harry stirred behind her, irritated at having been woken. Madeleine bent down and pulled the child to her, urging him to silence. Harry immediately felt her sense of urgency and put a finger to his own lips, copying her, before she turned back, looking up into the forest in search of the rider.

He appeared some minutes later on the other side of the stream opposite their camp, having used the same route that Madeleine, the girls and Harry had used to get here two days ago. But as he reined the horse in and stared at their camp, Harry uttered a soft cry of horror.

"*Mama!*" the child whimpered, clutching at Madeleine.

She held him, hushing him to be silent although there was a good enough reason for the child to be distressed. The man and his horse were a startling sight.

The horse was enormous. Madeleine knew it's kind to be a warhorse, an animal not usually seen this far west, because a horse such as this was more suited to a battlefield, or pulling a great wagon or plow on a ranch.

The man seemed a giant, for he was broader and

taller than even Ryder. He also rode with a saddle which was unusual, because from the style of his clothing and the way he wore his hair Madeleine thought him Pawnee and that alone was enough to strike fear in her heart as she knew that tribe could be vicious. They were feared in battle because they were such ferocious fighters but worst of all, they were enemies of both Bannock and Shoshone.

She glanced down at Harry as the child clung to her, trembling, staring in terror at the man standing on the other side of the stream. But Harry hadn't yet met a man painted in grief, like this man was.

His hair had been cropped close to his scalp on both sides, yet the hair on top of his head was secured in a scalp lock, similar to how Te'tukhe and Wesa'shangke had worn their hair. Several silver hoops were worn in pierced ears and above his leather vest he wore an elaborate necklace of bone, rawhide and feathers, an exquisite thing which fell almost to his waist, something only a Chief would wear because of its craftsmanship and beauty. Buckskin leggings were tucked into knee high moccasins and both were decorated with feathers, fur, European buttons and dyed seed beads.

He and his horse were an impressive sight, but it was the paint he wore which was truly startling. His face and neck bore long narrow strips of black dye, taken from fire ash, or perhaps even charcoal or wild grapes and mixed with grease. The black strips, smeared with careful strokes across each cheek and his forehead were there to intimidate, marking him as a man in grief.

His magnificent horse, with its unusually long mane and tail, with long fine hair draped over its massive hooves had not escaped the painting. The animal's face and neck also bore long strips of black dye, along with red handprints across each flank.

The man dismounted, appearing to stumble as his feet touched the earth then he stepped forward to kneel at the edge of the stream. But before he filled his waterskin and drunk his fill, he turned once more to look behind him, then back at the camp site. Satisfied he was alone, he put down his bow, resheathed his arrows and filled his waterskin before cupping his hands and drinking. Yet as he moved, his leather vest parted to reveal fearsome looking handprints laid across his belly and chest, all painted red, the dye taken from cherries, grapes or berries, mixed with grease.

Everything about the man and horse signified death.

Yet they weren't dead. They weren't ghosts. These two were very much alive. But the man's movements were awkward, as though he were in pain and when he stood, he almost fell against his horse, clutching at the saddle as though gathering his strength.

He didn't carry a musket. His only weapons were the bow and arrows and a knife within a sheath tied around his waist. That the man didn't own a musket surprised Madeleine, as most tribes this close to the Missouri and Mississippi rivers had been trading for decades with the French and Spanish for muskets and knives.

He turned and looked back towards the camp and Madeleine lowered her musket as she saw fresh blood on his leather vest. This man was not only grieving, but he was injured.

He didn't try to mount the horse using the stirrups, but walked the horse to a fallen log, then he took a moment to gather his strength before climbing awkwardly up the log to mount the horse that way. He pulled himself awkwardly into the saddle and Madeleine saw the grimace of agony cross his face and heard his low grunt of pain. He sat there for a few minutes, staring at the camp opposite him, then he kicked his horse across the stream, those great hooves crushing everything beneath them, before climbing up the bank and heading straight towards Madeleine and Harry.

She hissed at Harry to stay where he was then stepped out from behind the tree, the musket up against her shoulder, the barrel sighted along her eye, her finger on the trigger. The man reined the horse in and looked at her in surprise. Yet beyond those terrible strips of black paint which adorned his face, Madeleine saw the rings of darkness around his eyes suggesting terrible stress and felt the extraordinary sadness which seemed to pulsate from him, along with a murderous rage.

He looked behind her at Harry, who peered out from behind the tree, before returning his gaze to Madeleine. He raised his right hand in a sign of friendship and called out to her, his voice raspy and deep, yet Madeleine didn't understand his dialect.

"Do you have Spanish or French? Or the English?" she called out to him in French. "Who are you? What do you want here?"

The man paused for a moment then nodded, replying in crude French. "I am Tahkawiitik of the Skiri Pawnee," he said, glancing once more at Harry who had come out from behind the tree but remained leaning against its trunk as though it offered him some protection. The Pawnee looked back at Madeleine. "I saw the smoke from your fire. But where are your men, woman? I have urgent need to speak to them. I ask of them a trade."

Madeleine paused before she answered him, glancing back towards the waterfall to make sure he was alone, that no more riders followed him. For now, it seemed he rode alone. She gripped the musket, her knuckles white, trying to hide from him how afraid she was.

"Our men are hunting close by in the woods. As to where they are, I cannot tell you."

She felt his rage then, a potent thing of raw anger.

"Then woman, I ask it of you. I have need of a musket, but I am willing to trade for it," he paused to reach behind his saddle, emitting another low grunt of pain as he twisted. He grabbed a long leather sheath then threw it on the ground. It was about eighteen inches long and from the ornate handle looked like a miniature sword or dagger.

"It is yours, if I may have the musket," the giant said, then nodded towards the weapon on the ground. "I took it from a man who no longer had need of it, although I had no hand in his killing," he said, glancing at the weapon in distaste. "Will you trade for it? I must have a musket."

Madeleine said nothing, wondering how best to win against such a man, but she knew her chances unlikely. Unless of course she killed him. He wouldn't have time to reach for his knife or bow before she pulled the trigger. But as if reading her mind, the man smiled, yet his face seemed twisted from the effort and only then, among the long strips of black dye down each side of his face, did she see the cruel knife wound at the corner of his mouth.

"I will not harm you or the boy," he said, glancing at Harry who suddenly pushed away from the tree and ran to Madeleine, gripping her buckskin pants.

She couldn't push him away, she didn't dare release her grip on the musket, but Harry had unfortunately hindered her, as his tight grip on her clothing preventing her from moving. She couldn't fight while a small child clung to her.

"I give you my word, I will not harm you or the boy," the man said again. "I have no taste for another man's woman or child, unlike the four men I hunt. They ambushed us when we were hunting. They killed two of my brothers and left me for dead. They took our muskets, then returned to our camp and took our women and children. Now I seek to honor my brothers' deaths. I ask only for your musket, so I may seek revenge and follow them north. So, woman, I ask again. Will you trade your musket for the big knife?"

Madeleine looked at the ugly gash on his face and aware of it, he opened his vest to reveal three more ghastly knife wounds, one in his shoulder and another two deep slashes across his belly. All were packed with herbs, yet Madeleine knew they must be causing him considerable pain. Indeed, it was a wonder he was still upright. He would have lost a lot of blood from such deep cuts.

But as she watched him, feeling the sadness and rage and hopelessness pulse from him like a heartbeat, she thought of the dozen other sawn-off muskets she had stashed behind her in the bivouac. She had no desire to lose any one of them, nor the one she held. And certainly not in exchange for a dagger! Indeed, it was a poor trade, because a dagger held no value to her.

But this was a fight she could not win. This man was deep in grief, willing to embrace death in his vow for vengeance and neither she nor Harry would stand in his way. He would take the musket, one way or another.

Harry was still clinging tightly to her so Madeleine lowered the musket and turned, pushing the child gently away before walking across to the rider. Her eyes never left his own, but she saw no deceit there, only pain.

She bent down and reached for the leather scabbard lying on the ground. It was a thing of beauty, with metal studs pierced down the center and detailed filigree up the sides. She pulled the dagger free of the scabbard and stared at it in astonishment.

It had been made by a craftsman. The blade itself was a good eleven inches long, the hilt and pommel another five inches. She turned the pommel in her hand, recognizing immediately the *fleur-de-lis* which had been chiseled within the metal, as were the hilt and steel guard. The grip had been made of twisted iron wire wrap, and the blade so sharp it would slice through parchment like butter.

This weapon had been crafted in Europe and commissioned by a wealthy man, a French noble, for the *fleur-de-lis* revealed his aristocratic links to the dynastic house of the European line of Bourbon Kings.

Madeleine felt her hand tremble, understanding at once that the man who had once owned this weapon had been related to her father's own aristocratic line.

Although the owner was long dead, for the dagger was old fashioned and had been crafted decades ago, possibly even hundreds of years. Madeleine resheathed it. It held little value to her, but it appeared fate insisted she have it.

"You shall have your trade," she said. "Indeed, I wish you every success in your hunt." She lifted the musket and held it out to him. He took it with care, then checked the weapon with familiarity. Then he looked down at her, his face a grimace from that awful wound.

"I offer you some advice, woman, for what it's worth. Trust no-one, for the sickness of the skin sweeps across the land. Many tribes have suffered from it, including my own," he glanced at Harry before turning back to Madeleine. "Protect the boy, for this pox does not care who it takes. For your generosity, I ask that the Great Spirit keep you and your family safe."

Then he turned and kicked that giant horse back across the stream, the massive hooves leaving great imprints behind in the crushed earth. Within minutes they'd disappeared into the woods and only then did Madeleine turn and run back towards the bivouac Poongatse and Wannge'e shared. She took one of their muskets they'd left behind and quickly primed it with shot and powder then knelt within the trees with Harry, watching the woods across the stream.

She didn't relax until she saw the horse and rider leave the trees on the far side of the forest, heading for the distant hills, both no more than a dark smudge on the far horizon. Yet she kept watching long after they'd gone.

Atlantic Ocean: early September 1804

The clipper drifted slowly towards land, its sails flapping in the fickle breeze, the coast of Virginia just a blur in the distance. Ryder stood on the foredeck looking out at that formidable coastline that stretched away into the distance, both north and south, as far as the eye could see. It seemed impossibly close, yet he knew it would be another day before they dropped anchor. Three other ships passed them, their sails also struggling to catch the wind as they headed north, possibly to Europe or even further up the coast to Boston or New York.

After two months at sea, Ryder longed to put his feet on dry land. He'd spent enough time aboard ships over the past few years that he had no care to linger aboard this one now, even though it was part of the Benedict line.

They had been pushed off course by the storm, which had hindered their arrival in Alexandria by almost a week. Which in itself was little to complain about as no lives were lost and the ship had suffered little damage, but it had upset Ryder's carefully planned schedule.

He had originally planned to spend a few days in Alexandria, while the clipper unloaded its holds of wool from London, before heading to New Orleans with a new cargo of tobacco and coffee.

But Ryder no longer had the luxury of spending days here, although he was committed to meeting up with his business partners, which had been organized by Bernard Fahey. Ryder was now hopeful the meetings could be cut short. He hoped to avoid any social invitation extended to him by paying for passage on the first ship sailing for New Orleans.

Thinking on it, Ryder decided to get Fahey more involved in any future dealings here. After twenty-six years, it was time that Fahey made another trip to America. While Ryder was away for the next four years, Fahey could lead the business from this end.

Although realistically, Ryder didn't think for one moment that Fahey would leave his life in Westminster, not for any enticement, certainly not for a long sea voyage. But Alick Woodley might do it. The young man was ambitious and loyal, he was smart enough for Ryder to trust him in any future dealings with the Americans and Ryder knew his old friend Michael Woodley would be well pleased with the idea.

He turned as the sailors on deck called to one another, hoisting sails to try and catch more breeze, reminding Ryder of his days aboard Tomás Saldivar's clipper. He knew every rope, every stay, the name of every piece of equipment, along with every man's role aboard this ship. But he didn't envy them. He had spent more than enough time aboard the *Zeferino* to know that his life was fated to be on land.

Ryder often thought of Saldivar, for the man had played a pivotal role in his life. The Spaniard would be sailing down the coast of Portugal this month, with two important scheduled stops along the way. One would be at a small village just north of Areosa where Viktor and Luisa Cardozo lived, where Ryder had been shipwrecked. The bag of gold he'd asked Saldivar to deliver to them would go some way to repay them for saving his life.

The second stop was at Viana do Castelo, a town just south from Areosa where Mateo Branco and his family lived. Like Viktor and Luisa Cardozo, the bag of gold would repay them for giving Ryder a job along with a place to stay, when everyone else thought him a criminal.

Ryder knew Saldivar would deliver the gold. Because that rugged, hard Spaniard had given his word and Saldivar's word and his handshake were as good as a legally bound document signed before a Judge in a court of law.

He smiled, thinking of his Spanish friend, as an early morning haze drifted slowly down the coast of America. It was only an hour or so past dawn, yet it promised to be another hot day. He glanced up as one of the sails snapped above him, catching the longed for breeze and as he turned to look back at the land way in the distance he felt his spirits soar, for somewhere out there, somewhere on that land, a thousand or more miles away, were his wife and son.

in the wild: early September 1804

One

Harry was sleeping, yet it wasn't a peaceful slumber as his little body burned with fever.

Poongatse sat with him, wiping his hot little body with a damp cloth to try and bring down his temperature while Wannge'e sat by the fire, waiting impatiently for the pot of water to boil.

I sorted through our herbs again in a desperate bid to find something that would help my son, as nothing we'd used so far seemed to be working.

Without showing it, I was quietly panicking, even as I saw my own fear reflected on the faces of both Poongatse and Wannge'e.

The sickness had taken hold in Harry's lungs, causing his breathing to be labored and full of phlegm. That scared us more than anything, for we'd seen many children die from fevers such as this.

I turned to watch his small sweaty body struggling to breathe, his belly heaving from the effort and wondered again how this had happened so quickly. He had started to cough only yesterday, but he'd been lethargic and grumpy for the past three days and I should have known then that my child was ill because he was usually such a sociable, happy little boy.

The girls had taken it in turns with me last night to watch over him, waking him every few hours to give him a potion of willow bark, wild onion and chokecherry berries. When he began to fret and cry with distress in the early hours of the morning, Poongatse urged me to add stoneseed to the potion, to help sedate him.

Which made me think of Ryder, when I'd sedated him during those weeks he lay injured in my cave, almost five years ago.

My babe stirred in his sleep and coughed, his three-year old body struggling from the effort and I looked down at my herbs and decided to try something else. I picked out some milkvetch, which would help with the infection in his lungs and aid his immune system. I also decided on wind root, which would help get rid of that phlegm.

When Poongatse suggested we make him a poultice of saltbrush leaves and wild onion for his chest, I agreed, willing to do anything to draw out that infection in his lungs.

I glanced across at Wannge'e and recognized the fear on her lovely face, the bruising and swollen eye long since recovered from the beating she took, although she still grieved for the missing tooth.

But I knew she was afraid for Harry, along with our dwindling supply of herbs and wood, both of which were getting dangerously low.

I tried to smile, to reassure her, but could not.

Poongatse continued to gently wipe down Harry's arms and legs with the damp cloth, even as she glanced at me. "Only his chest and throat hold the sickness. It doesn't linger in his limbs for they flow with good health so once the sickness leaves your son, he will be stronger than he was before."

I reached for the girl's hand and held it within my own, so grateful that I had her and Wannge'e with me.

Yet I wanted Ryder so badly in that moment that I felt his loss like a physical pain.

I didn't trust myself to answer her as my own

throat was suddenly tight with unshed tears, so I simply nodded. I prayed she was right.

We'd been caught in a thunderstorm several days earlier and although we'd found shelter and made a bivouac, the storm raged on for two more days, leaving Harry with a chill.

When we left our primitive shelter and continued west, Harry's health began to deteriorate, leaving us no choice but to stop and let the child rest.

Because of it, our camp site was chosen out of desperation, not safety. It lay nestled in a hollow, set within endless rolling hills and the only thing which offered us any shelter from the winds and occasional rain showers were several massive boulders around us, wedged into the earth like great balls set down eons ago.

But there was almost no wood to gather here to light a fire or construct a bivouac, which left our camp vulnerable to the elements and any creatures that passed by in the night.

To keep safe we'd built a crude shelter using our sailcloths, spreading them over the boulders around us and anchoring the ends of them with rocks and our own belongings.

It wasn't ideal, but at least it gave us some protection from the weather and night-time predators.

I turned away from Poongatse and glanced out over the rolling hills, but there was nothing to see but lush grass.

There were no trees, no brush, no scrub, nothing except for a bluff rising out of the prairie several miles away to the northeast.

The bluff looked absurd rearing out of that vast

rolling hill country as it swept away to the north, with several stands of trees on its promontory.

Although we did have something to be grateful for.

Less than a mile below us was a river. The deepest part of it reached to my thighs while at its widest point it stretched out for a good quarter of a mile. It drifted southeast, which suggested it was a major tributary coming down from the north to empty its load into the Mississippi.

Poongatse and Wannge'e had laid down snares last night in the hope of catching some fish. They had also put down snares in the grasslands yet strangely, the land appeared to be eerily empty of life for they had checked the snares only that morning to find them empty.

These hills were nothing like the rich prairie grasses we'd crossed before, which had teemed with wildlife.

It seemed like a lifetime since we'd left St Louis, although we'd been travelling for less than a month. It seemed so much longer than that and far slower than my expectations. But the attack by those soldiers had held us up for over a week and then we'd been caught in bad weather, forcing us to seek shelter until it passed.

I'd also had to put my son's needs before my own, along with those of the girls, by making sure he was well fed and settled before nightfall, which took more hours out of my day. Had I been travelling alone, I would have kept riding regardless of the weather, regardless of whether I was hungry or tired.

There were also times when Harry refused to ride, wanting to run and stretch his legs. I learned it was easier to let him have his way, because travelling with a happy child was far less stressful than with a grumpy, frustrated child.

Now we were held up again.

I could feel the weeks slipping by and I was not only fearful for my son's health, but our plans to reach the Omaha before winter.

My schedule suddenly seemed unrealistic and as Harry stirred to cough again, I wondered if I'd got this horribly wrong.

Two

Madeleine wondered later how very strange it was that Harry's fever broke so suddenly the following evening. It was as if his illness, coming on so suddenly and leaving just as quickly, had deliberately made them stop and linger in that hollow. Because his illness changed everything.

He woke towards dusk almost twenty-four hours later, crying with hunger and although still damp to the touch, his labored breathing had settled. He managed to take several mouthfuls of broth which Madeleine had made from the last of their supplies, but whatever strange thing was at play during those few days of Harry's illness, it was Harry who ended up saving their lives.

The morning after his fever broke, the child woke as though someone called him. He pushed aside his furs and sat up, glancing at his sleeping mother and the two Bannock girls, all of them exhausted after the long days and nights watching over him. The boy smiled and looked out across the hills.

He couldn't see them, nor could he hear the soft thunder of hooves, because the beasts were still many miles to the north. He shook his head and smiled again, as though playing a game, then stepped away from the camp site and headed down the slope towards the river. Only then did he laugh aloud as though being stubbornly disobedient, but it was his laugh which woke Madeleine.

She sat up, pushing aside her own furs, feeling a terrible sense of urgency. When she saw her son's empty bed her heart lurched with fear. She raced out of their shelter and saw Harry running towards the river, even as she became aware of their smell, followed by the sound of hooves on hard ground. She uttered a soft cry of terror, waking Poongatse and Wannge'e and as the girls stumbled outside, they saw what Madeleine saw.

The little boy running towards the river, his arms up to balance himself as he ran downhill, his childish shrieks of delight echoing up towards them. But behind him, way in the distance, the rolling hills were no longer green, but brown, as a moving mass of buffalo headed this way, straight towards the water.

"No wonder no other creature lives here," Madeleine cried in dismay. "We've camped right in the middle of their migratory path! Once they reach the river, the ones coming up behind will push the ones in front on, straight towards us," she swung around to the girls.

"Grab anything you can and pack it quickly. What we don't have time to take with us, we leave behind," then she turned and looked down at Harry.

"Come back to *Mama*, quickly now baby, we're leaving," she called, knowing she risked everything by raising her voice, because the last thing she wanted was to cause a stampede.

The urgency in her voice made Harry stop. He turned back to her and laughed before turning to point to the buffalo. Madeleine called again, and now the child could hear the fear in her voice and he turned and began to walk back towards their camp, unaware of the danger behind him. Madeleine barely took her eyes off him as she grabbed the bundles of rifles and ran for one of the packhorses.

She swung them over the back of the animal, her hands trembling as she tightened the rawhide strap beneath its belly then returned for the others, tying them down on the other horse, keeping an eye on Harry the whole time. Yet even the horses could smell the buffalo now and stamped their hooves in panic.

Poongatse helped Madeleine tie down furs, hides and blankets along with canvas sheeting to cover the muskets, while Wannge'e filled buckskin bags with the rest of their belongings. Madeleine talked to them the whole time, encouraging them, keeping them calm.

"Don't wait for me," she said, "but ride for that bluff in the distance. Don't stop to look back, whatever happens, just keep going."

The last things she packed away were the musket which had been lying beside her, along with her knives and the dagger. She tied them all to her horse with terrible panic, all the time watching her son and that brown mass moving closer to the river which was the only thing separating them from the small boy.

Madeleine threw the contents of the cooking pot over the fire before throwing dirt on the last of the hot coals, aware of the smell as hundreds of thousands of hooves churned up the earth, along with the scent of fresh manure. The sound of their bellowing now filled the valley, echoing out across the hills and as Madeleine secured the cooling pot to the back of the other packhorse, she urged Poongatse and Wannge'e to flee.

"Don't worry about anything else," she called, mounting her horse, eager to get her son. "Just get moving. Let's get to the safety of that bluff!"

She kicked the animal into a walk, terrified of scaring the first of the buffalo which were now almost at the river. She wanted to ride low and fast, to grab the child and get out of there, but she forced down her panic and continued at a walk, down the hill, towards the small boy.

But with the innocence of a child Harry laughed aloud with delight when he saw his mother riding towards him, then turned to point at the masses of bison heading straight towards him. He began to chatter away, to tell his mother about this curious looking beast with its great shaggy head and small horns, its wide humped shoulder which tapered down to a narrow rump and short tail. But even as the child laughed, the buffalo kept coming. They now covered every bit of land as far as Madeleine could see, a species that had dominated this country for centuries.

The first of them stepped into the shallows of the river to drink and Madeleine felt a moment of awe for the men who hunted these powerful creatures. Men like Ryder and Ese-ggwe'na'a.

She dared to glance back at the camp site and saw Poongatse and Wannge'e packing away the last of their belongings. She wanted to scream at them to ride, to forget about anything else and just get to safety, but she dared not. If the buffalo began to stampede, they were lost.

By the time she reached Harry the first of the bison had entered the river, pushed forward by the ones behind. It would only take a few precious minutes before they reached the other side, not even fifty feet away from where Harry stood. Madeleine dared not dismount. She called to the boy softly, as though playing a game. The child grinned at her.

"*Mama!*" he said, pointing to the bison, just as the

first of the buffalo were pushed violently into the river by the animals behind, impatient to drink.

Madeleine knew she couldn't pick Harry up without dismounting, but she had another idea. She rode behind him, so he stood above her on the hill. The she leaned over and with all the strength she owned, her legs gripping the belly of her horse, she grabbed the collar of Harry's buckskin shirt and pulled him up to sit before her.

The child suddenly screamed, not wanting to leave, but as Madeleine turned the horse, one hand on the reins, her other arm wrapped tightly around her son, she kicked the horse forward. But as she urged the horse back up the hill, she became aware of the low bellowing behind her along with the thrash of water. The child's screams were sending the buffalo into a frenzy of panic.

Madeleine saw Poongatse and Wannge'e looking down at her and Harry. They knew as Madeleine did, it was only a matter of time before the buffalo started to run. Madeleine wanted to scream at the Bannock girls to ride, but she didn't have the voice for it. She was breathing too hard, terrified, pushing the horse into a gallop as she held the screaming child tight against her.

Harry's small hands now gripped her arm in terror, hurting her as he pinched, but she didn't care about that. She saw the girls pull themselves up on the backs of their horses and holding the reins of the packhorses behind them, kicked their horses into a gallop, turning east, heading back the way they'd come.

Madeleine followed them, passing their campsite, noticing the girls had left nothing behind. She rode on, not daring to look back, because she could now hear the thunder of hooves as the bison began to run. They were so close she could smell them, a scent as ripe and fertile as the earth itself.

*

As they raced across that open country and headed towards the bluff, it seemed an impossibly long way off. Harry now instinctively leaned back against his mother's body, clinging to her arm with all his strength and although Madeleine could hear his soft whimpers, she could do nothing to help him.

The buffalo coming up behind her were now so close she could hear them snorting. She urged the horse on and by the time they reached the bluff, she knew more of the buffalo had begun to stampede. The noise was deafening as they pushed their horses up the steep slope of the bluff.

Poongatse reached the trees first, followed by Wannge'e. As Madeleine came up behind them, she saw the other side of the bluff sloped gently away to another valley and a river, which joined up with the river they'd just left behind. It was inevitable the buffalo would head that way, towards the water.

The trees offered some shelter and as Poongatse reined her horse in, followed by Wannge'e, Madeleine turned to look behind her. Most of the bison had continued running on down the slope towards the river, with just a few bothering to follow them into the trees. But like the horses, they were tiring and they quickly turned and followed the rest of the herd down the slope.

"Keep going," Madeleine called to Poongatse and

the girl kicked her horse on.

They rode along the narrow bluff for another half a mile, leaving the trees behind to come to a high wall of rock. A steep drop lay on either side and it was here they finally stopped. Poongatse dismounted, passing her reins to Wannge'e so she could reach up and take Harry. The child went into her arms, sobbing with fright. Trembling, Madeleine dismounted and helped Wannge'e settle the horses, for they were badly spooked. Then she fell to her knees beside Harry and Poongatse, even as she felt Wannge'e's hand on her back, a thing of comfort.

They were on the narrowest part of the bluff, not even half a mile wide, with a steep drop on either side. Below them, as far as they could see in all directions, were bison. Too many to count, an impossible number. As Harry's cries subsided, he left Poongatse and went into Madeleine's arms, but she couldn't scold him. Had he not woken they would have been trapped in their vulnerable campsite, unable to get food or reach the river. They might even have been crushed.

She gently bent her head on the child's dark curls, wondering at how well he looked after so many days with a high temperature. She closed her eyes in gratitude that he was alright, that he was unhurt although like Madeleine and the girls, the child was trembling with shock. But he'd get over it soon enough. It was another lesson for the boy to learn.

"We can't go east, we can't go back," Madeleine said softly, a hopelessness to her voice. "But nor can we head west or south, not until the bison leave and they might be here for weeks," she paused to look down on the never ending stream of animals coming to drink at the river. "It's got to be more than one herd," she said in dismay. "They must come this way to migrate south, to breed, yet how long will they stay? We've already lost so much time, we can't afford to stay here one more night, let alone a week, or more."

The girls said nothing so Madeleine picked Harry up and carried him on her hip to the rock wall. She stepped behind it and saw the bluff carried on for miles, nothing more than a narrow ridge but wide enough for them to take the horses across. She turned as Poongatse and Wannge'e came up behind her.

"This seems the only way we can go," she said, "but it heads north."

Even as she said it, Madeleine knew her plans to go to the Wazhazhe village and introduce her son to Ryder's people, were over. That promise she'd silently made to him, to introduce Harry to Te'tukhe and Wesa'shangke, was nothing now but empty words.

She had let him down. A man she loved with all her heart, she'd let him down.

But they couldn't go back. Time was of the essence now. She had to get these girls and her son settled before winter and their only choice now was to continue north to the Omaha.

"They might not be there," Wannge'e said softly and Madeleine turned to look at her, taken aback by the girl's comment.

She was right, of course. Madeleine had always known Te'tukhe and Wesa'shangke might not be at the Wazhazhe village, but she'd been prepared to take that chance for Ryder, because he'd been unable to.

"I know," she whispered, seeing the truth of it.

Well, she couldn't go there now, but perhaps on the way back to England in four years, she and Harry could make that trip to the village where Ryder had spent his childhood.

"I know," she said again. "But the decision has been taken out of my hands. The buffalo have turned us north, so north we shall go."

*

They rode their horses at a walk past that wall of stone, then on across the top of the bluff. But it turned out to be an easy ride, with the ridge being flat enough in some places that it came close to thirty feet wide. Way in the distance, just a hazy blur from this height, was a forest. Madeleine hoped they'd reach it by dusk, as she had no desire to camp on this bluff, not with a sheer drop off on each side.

They stopped briefly at mid-day to share some dried meat and some berries and the last of the bread which Madeleine had made the evening before. Then they carried on riding at a slow walk, finally leaving that massive herd of buffalo behind as they rode closer to that distant forest.

New Orleans: mid-September 1804

Ryder drew the razor over his chin, the blade scraping across his whiskers. Although the harsh brittle sound of it was lost among the other sounds coming in through the open window beside him, along with the smells of the harbor and the street below. Smells of salt and sea, of spicy cooking from the Creoles, the sweetness of French pastries and broths, of ale and wine from the tavern downstairs along with horses and manure and sewage.

New Orleans was a busy port town, not only from the river trade, but with ships arriving from Europe, along with those from towns along the American eastern seaboard and the West Indies.

The Mississippi River was a major water highway through this part of the country, with keelboats, canoes and pirogues arriving daily from the north, either dropping off passengers or coming to trade.

As Ryder scaped the blade across his jaw, he could hear the dominant languages of French and Creole, but he could also hear Americans along with the English, Scots and Irish. Alongside them were voices from Europe, from Poland, Germany, Holland and Russia and many others.

He paused as he heard someone curse loudly and leaned forward to peer out the window. A man was driving a wagon full of muslin sacks of tobacco towards the wharf, urging another driver to get out of his way. The other man swore in frustration but urged his dray horses on, using his whip on a couple of dogs following his wagon which was carrying barrels of salted pork. A landau weaved around them, the thoroughbred throwing back its head as the coachman flicked the reins, although the window of the landau was shaded, allowing the person within it privacy.

Ryder turned as he heard the cry of a child from a nearby house and the laughter of two men on the other side of the street who flirted loudly with a saloon girl, even as people walked around them. Down the far side of town, close to the wharf, he could hear the distinct clank of chains as slaves gathered in a small private square, taking water from a horse trough.

It was the sound of the chains which irritated Ryder the most, because he knew how those chains felt around a man's wrists.

As he went to turn away, he heard the call of sailors shouting to one another and looked back towards the wharf. Men were rolling great barrels of produce down the planks of ships. He watched another ship pull anchor, its great sails snapping in the wind as the sheets caught the breeze and he could even hear the call of the Captain as the ship turned, taking advantage of the morning tide and the currents as it swung away from shore and headed out towards open sea. Ryder paused for only a moment, wondering about those men aboard that ship and where it was heading, before he returned to the job of shaving.

He'd hired this room for one night only and although it didn't offer peace and quiet, he didn't particularly care, for it was right by the wharves and he had paid passage on a keelboat leaving for St Louis just after dawn the following morning. One month and some seven hundred miles upriver before he reached St Louis. Longer if the keelboat stopped over at settlements or trading posts along the way.

Ryder turned back to the bed where his clothes of pants, shirt, waistcoat and jacket were laid out. He quickly dressed, then picked up the wallet containing American dollars and French francs and turned for the door, glancing briefly at the broadsheet, or newspaper as the Americans had begun to call them, he'd left lying on the bed.

Napoleon Bonaparte was to be crowned Emperor of France by year's end, despite the failed assassination attempt on his life. The threat had come from Bourbon aristocrats, men directly related to the doomed King of France. When he read this, Ryder thought of Madeleine's friend, François, the Marquis d'Auvergne and thought it more than likely he'd been caught up in the scandal, as he'd been plotting for years to overthrow Bonaparte and restore King Louis XVI's heir apparent to the French throne. For the Marquis' sake, Ryder hoped he was safe, that he was unharmed, although the chances of ever hearing from him again were unlikely.

He also read of the war which continued between France and England, as well as other conflicts in Europe brought about by Bonaparte.

He read of the smallpox outbreaks that had once again flared up in settlements along the Missouri and Mississippi Rivers. It seemed no-one was safe from this ghastly disease, especially people from tribes living close to the affected areas. According to men reporting on the phenomenon, it appeared that native peoples lacked any kind of immunity against European diseases such as smallpox, cholera, typhus and many others. These men wrote that the fatality rates within some tribes had been more than fifty percent. One reporter quoted a loss of hundreds of thousands over the past twenty years alone, even leaving some tribes extinct, their people and language lost forever.

Reading this had made Ryder feel physically ill, not only for the people who lived along those natural water highways like his own people, the Ugákhpa and the Wazhazhe, but for his wife and son who were travelling through that country. As he closed and locked the door behind him, he swore softly.

He hurried along the boardwalk, his thoughts on that newspaper article and Madeleine and Harry, oblivious to the admiring glances of women and covetous glances of men, who glanced at his fashionable London clothes while they still dressed in hose and breeches. But Ryder would have given them all away, in exchange for someone telling him where he'd find his wife and son.

in the wild: mid-September 1804

One

It was too early for birds or any other creature that lived in the light of day as Madeleine stood alone on the edge of the lake, savoring the silence. In that grey-black light of pre-dawn, as the moon fell away and the sun began to rise, the mist over the lake slowly rose then faded away, creating something quite lovely, although eerie.

They had come across this lake around midday yesterday and it was so lovely they had decided to stay a few days to give them all a chance to rest. Harry was as boisterous as ever, but Madeleine was worried about his pale complexion and black circles under his eyes, although he seemed to have recovered well enough from the sickness.

They had built one large bivouac for them to sleep in when they settled here yesterday, as Madeleine had found a better hiding place for the muskets and her other gifts. It was a deep cleft between rocks less than one hundred yards from their camp. After Madeleine's experience with the Pawnee, she now kept everything they didn't need in a separate place away from their camping area, if they were going to stay somewhere for more than one night.

Thinking of the muskets, she turned away from the lake edge and headed in that direction to check on them. But she felt confident in leaving their camp for a little while, even though the girls and Harry were still asleep, because she only planned to be gone a little while. She quickly ran through the trees and found the hiding place easily enough. The weapons were still wrapped in their hides, along with the smaller parcels which held the gifts for Paddake'e. She stood back, well pleased with her hiding place, as everything would stay dry there until they left on the morrow.

She walked back to the edge of the lake, finding herself drawn to the beauty of it. She couldn't see the end because the lake was so vast, but the opposite bank was at least a mile away. Deep forests of pine, cedar and oak bordered the shore, alongside deciduous trees of maple and aspen, their leaves already starting to turn and all of it lay reflected off the water, creating an illusion of utter beauty, despite the rising mist at this early hour.

A fish jumped, breaking the surface of the lake, startling her, leaving a ripple effect on the water and Madeleine instinctively moved back to stand behind a massive oak. She glanced back through the trees but from here, their campsite was well hidden.

They had camped under a high bank a quarter mile or so from the lake edge, shielded by a thicket of cottonwood. Except for the fire they had lit last night to protect themselves against bears or moose which might come here to forage and drink, their shelter was well hidden. Even their campfire was invisible because other than the smell of the wood smoke, it mingled with the early morning mist.

Madeleine had been relieved and more than happy to settle in this lovely place for a few days to rest and replenish their supplies. Last night they had happily feasted on roasted prairie birds along with wild onions, mushrooms and some eggs Poongatse had found in nests around the lake. When Wannge'e and Harry discovered some chokeberries, Poongatse made them cakes.

But that sense of relief and contentment had changed during the night, when Madeleine woke to the strong scent of blood, that hot, sickly sweet smell that was impossible to mistake. She had crawled from the bivouac to look out into the pitch dark of the night, because that smell meant they were no longer alone.

Yet she'd found nothing threatening near their camp, although the scent lingered. Just before dawn, she'd once more crawled from her warm furs to check on their belongings and their horses. Then she decided to try and find the source of the scent. But before leaving their campsite she'd turned back, wondering if she dare leave Harry and the girls alone, sleeping. But she'd felt no sense of danger there and thought them quite safe.

She glanced back once more at their camp, hidden beyond the trees, then turned and headed west, running at a fast jog around the lake but keeping to the shelter of the trees, following that sweet cloying smell. She had covered only a few miles before she began to smell wood smoke. It carried the scent of hickory wood. She ran on for another mile, an easy run for Madeleine, her moccasins silent on the soft fertile soil, as silent as any creature that lived in the woods, listening for the slightest sound, looking for what may have been slaughtered here, when suddenly it was right there before her.

A huge beast, a buffalo carcass, or rather it's hide, recently removed from the beast and now hanging between great frames of dogwood. The hide hadn't yet been cured and hung in all its raw, bloody state. Just behind it was a massive fire pit and here, sometime during the night, great logs had been set alight, although now they were nothing more than red-hot coals yet the heat coming off them was still searingly hot. Behind the firepit stood eleven teepees.

Madeleine stopped in bewilderment. These people were hunters and their own great fire explained why they had been unaware of Madeleine's camp smoke from the other side of the lake. The carcass suggested it had been butchered here last night, so whoever these people were, they had come here to work. There would be no drums, nor chanting, for this small village was a temporary camp, set up for hunters.

Not far from the huge central firepit were several smaller fires, with frames of ironwood built over them. Hanging from the frames were strips of buffalo meat, the fires beneath kept low, allowing the smoke from the hickory wood to preserve and add flavor to the meat.

Madeleine crept around the other side of the village, bewildered as to why these people had no-one on watch, for wolves and bears would be attracted to that scent of blood. But then she heard the snort of a horse, followed by another one blowing and then the soft plod of hooves on sandy ground coming towards her. She crouched low behind some ferns just as two youths appeared on the far side of the village, both riding bareback with a dozen horses following behind them. Madeleine watched as the youths dismounted and quickly hobbled the horses.

The boys were no more than fifteen or sixteen years of age. They wore buckskin pants and a loincloth around their waists with knee high moccasins. They wore no vests or shirts and seemed oblivious to the chill of the autumn morning. Both wore their hair long, with rawhide strips threaded through their hair. Neither owned tattoos nor jewelry, yet it was obvious they were affiliated to a local tribe for they clearly felt at home here, as if they knew this place well.

The youths talked quietly among themselves then one of them whistled softly and Madeleine heard a cry, followed by others and felt her blood turn to ice. She knew well enough what was coming and in a heartbeat understood why this village had no need for guards to stand watch over that meat.

She spun on her heels and raced off through the trees, back towards the lake. When she reached the water's edge she paused long enough to pull off her moccasins before entering the water, gasping at the icy coldness of it before running along the shore as fast as she could, the water up to her ankles, already numb from the cold. Then she heard their excited cries and howls as they found her scent in the ferns where she'd been hiding, followed by a startled shout from one of the youths.

Madeleine saw a steep cliff ahead of her and raced for it, pushing herself to sprint faster, for they'd be behind her soon enough. As she reached the cliff she put her moccasins in her mouth, holding them with her teeth as she pulled herself up, searching for rocky handholds, moving as fast as she could, her feet seeking purchase in the sandy soil and just as she made it to the top and rolled herself over to hide, the creatures came racing out of the trees, following her scent to the lake shore. She crawled back to the edge of the cliff and saw the youths come running out of the woods, yet too far behind to stop the attack which would have happened had she not run.

Dogs. These hunters had dogs. Madeleine cursed softly as she watched the animals run back and forth along the water's edge, sniffing the ground and whining with frustration at having lost her scent.

But Madeleine knew well enough that these creatures weren't anything like domesticated pets such as Bootie, the little black Labrador she'd left behind at Millbryne Park.

These dogs were usually reared half-wild and bred to attack.

Madeleine watched their dark shapes in the pre-dawn light and counted six of them. They had only to run to the cliff face and they'd find her scent, yet they hung back, nearly a mile away, running in a frenzy along the lake's edge sniffing desperately, when two older men came racing out of the trees and called the dogs to heel. They carried similar muskets to what she owned, suggesting these people were well used to trading with the French and Spanish fur trappers who travelled this route between St Louis and Lower Canada.

She watched as the youths gestured towards the lake. They thought the intruder had slipped away by canoe because the dogs had lost the trail at the water.

Well, it didn't matter what they believed, because Madeleine knew that soon enough their scouts would be sent out to search this entire area. Which meant it was inevitable they find her camp.

She reckoned an hour, but no more. Which didn't give her enough time to run back to camp, wake the girls and Harry and pack up. Besides, their five horses were all loaded down, leaving a good trail behind them, which these men would find easily enough because their survival depended on their tracking skills, taught to them as babes in arms.

Madeleine felt a desperate sense of urgency as she thought of her sleeping son and the Bannock girls. She moved quickly, dusting off her feet before pulling on her moccasins and sprinting away as silently as she could. Her feet felt numb from the icy water as she fled but she ran as fast as she could, knowing they didn't have time to flee, so once again they must fight.

Two

By the time I made it back to camp the only plan I had was to keep Harry and the girls safe. I woke them and hurried them away, urging them to hide in the woods with four of our horses. The girls took their weapons along with their woolen blankets and furs, leaving me with the bare minimum of our belongings, the rest hidden away in that cleft of rock.

"Stay close so you can see what happens and only come if I call for you. But come unarmed. Leave your muskets in the woods, hidden well."

I watched as they rode away with the two packhorses behind them, my belly gripped with fear as Harry glanced back at me, his eyes wide with terror. But I knew he'd settle soon enough with Poongatse.

I turned back to the fire and checked my own musket, making sure it was primed, then I waited.

I didn't have to wait long. I heard their horses down by the lake followed by men calling to each other. I stood up, holding my musket in front of me and moved to stand beside my bivouac. Within moments I saw a blur of movement through the trees followed by the soft thud of hooves on sandy soil and then they were there, reining their horses in on the edge of our camp.

Eight men, all riding bareback and all armed with knives and muskets. An older man, well into his winter years appeared to be the leader. Behind him were five men about Ryder's age and bringing up the rear were the two youths I'd seen earlier. Running alongside the horses were the dogs, all growling and baring their teeth as they recognized my scent. The man in front yelled at them to heel, never taking his eyes off our camp, like the men behind him. Then he lifted his head and let out a high shrill call and within moments six more riders came thundering through the trees, riding hard.

The older man kicked his horse forward, even as I raised my musket and aimed it at him. Well into his fifties, his face and body worn and lined from a lifetime of living outdoors, there was something about him that reminded me of Ese-ggwe'na'a. He seemed to own a quiet strength, yet I also knew he could be ruthless and even cruel.

I did my best to hide my fear, because I could feel the raw anger emanating from these men. Although I understood well enough the reason for it. They were outraged that someone had entered their village unannounced while they slept, after working half the night to butcher the bison carcass.

But I knew from my years of living with the Bannock that they had good reason to be angry, because any village or community anywhere in the world would track down an uninvited intruder.

The men were dressed simply, like the youths. They wore buckskin pants under a loincloth and no shirts. Not one of them owned a tattoo, nor did they wear jewelry. Their hair was worn long and loose, although some of the men wore a rawhide band around their foreheads.

As I watched the man in front, who was obviously the most senior member of their camp, he surprised me by lifting his arm, motioning his men to lower their muskets. They did as he asked and then he surprised me further by lifting a hand in welcome.

"One of your people came to our camp this morning. For what purpose did you seek us out?" he asked. He was clearly angry yet also curious, even as I found it intimidating to have fourteen men on horseback staring at me. Although I shouldn't have been surprised. I was a young white woman, far from European settlements and apparently alone. I also knew they wouldn't believe for one moment that I was the one who had entered their camp uninvited.

I lowered my musket and raised my own hand in a formal greeting because astonishingly, I understood the man's every word.

*

He was speaking in the same dialect as Ryder's own people, which meant these men were from one of the five tribes owning familial connections to the Ugákhpa. Indeed, I could hear Ryder's voice echoing down the years, when he first told me about these tribes during those weeks we lived in my cave.

Wazhazhe, Kansa, Ponca, Omaha and Ugákhpa, all are affiliated to the Dhegiha Sioux

I'd learned the Dhegiha Sioux dialect from Ryder and his Ugákhpa brothers, Te'tukhe and Wesa'shangke, during our journey south to St Louis more than four years ago. Yet even though I understood what the man on horseback was saying, I paused before answering him, aware of his unease, along with the men around him as they looked at the trees, suspicious to find me alone, wondering where my menfolk were.

But he took my silence as not being able to understand him and with some impatience lifted his arm and urged one of the younger men to come forward. They spoke rapidly for a moment then the younger kicked his horse towards me. "Do you have French?" he asked.

I nodded and he looked relieved. "We want to know what you're doing here," he asked. He spoke French reasonably well, not like the guttural *patois* a lot of the tribes here knew. "Someone came to our camp this morning. We want to know why."

My instincts warned me not to give them the truth of it, so I gave him the answer they most expected. But I didn't reply to him in French. I answered in Ryder's own dialect.

"We are on our way to the Omaha, to winter over there. My husband taught me his dialect, which of course is your own. He grew up in the Wazhazhe village although he is half English, half Ugákhpa. He goes by the name Mi'wasa."

The men were startled by my knowing their language, but I used it as a matter of survival. If they knew I was wife to a man who belonged to the powerful southern Sioux nation, they might let us go on our way with little trouble. Because I knew they'd find out the truth of our situation easily enough, as they had only to track us for a day, no more, to discover I travelled alone with two teenage girls and a little boy, so there was little point in lies.

They exchanged glances and that silent communication between them suggested they were a tight group, well used to each other, possibly even family. The older man kicked his horse towards me. "Who lives here with you?" he asked.

"I travel with my three-year old son and two teenage girls from the Bannock nation. When we leave the Omaha in the spring, we head north to their village in the far northwest territories."

It was obvious they didn't believe me, for it was inconceivable that a white woman far from her own settlements would travel in the wild alone with a child and two girls. The leader once again looked about our camp, basic compared to their own, yet obviously set up for a small group. He looked back at me, his eyes dark and intimidating.

"Who came to our village at dawn?" he asked softly, yet his voice was brittle with menace. The pleasantries were over. They thought me a liar.

I put a hand on my heart, to show him I was speaking the truth. "I was your intruder, yet I meant no harm," I replied. "I woke in the night and smelled blood and wanted to know the reason for it," I paused, realizing too late what I'd said as the men were all looking at me in disbelief, for no human can smell blood from such a distance. Our camps were too far apart. I carried on, eager to explain myself.

"The scent of blood drifted in on the stillness of the night and I couldn't mistake it. I came simply to find out what caused it and if we should ride on. I was happy to see you were hunters of buffalo. Had I not heard the dogs I would have stepped forward to introduce myself, but I thought them vicious brutes."

I nodded towards the dogs, half wolf, half dog, but the leader dismissed me, his voice hard with distrust. Again he looked towards the woods, expecting to see men appear, ready to attack. "Where are those you travel with?"

I paused before answering him, because now it was my turn to ask something of him. "Do I have your word we are safe? Otherwise I will not call them."

He looked at me for a long moment, then nodded.

"Call them. You have my word."

I turned and called for Poongatse and Wannge'e to come with Harry. I spoke in the Ugákhpa dialect so there would be no misunderstanding between me and the men. The Bannock girls knew enough of that dialect after hearing me speak to Harry that they'd understand me.

My voice seemed to echo in the stillness of those woods and as I glanced back at the men I felt their unease. Clearly they expected an ambush.

But they had only to wait a few minutes before the Bannock girls appeared, with Harry hiding behind Poongatse as she held his hand. When he saw me, he ran to me, clutching at my legs.

"It's alright, baby," I said, continuing to speak in the Ugákhpa dialect so the men could understand me. "Come to Mama, you'll be alright."

Poongatse and Wannge'e came and stood beside me, unarmed, as I had asked. I was glad of it, because I didn't want to lose those weapons and I didn't yet know the character of these men. They looked at Harry and the girls with curiosity mixed with disbelief, then the leader leaned towards Harry.

"Who else travels with you, boy," he asked.

The question took all of us by surprise, but they didn't trust me. I watched Harry as he looked up at the man in bewilderment.

"No-one but us," he said, answering in the same language.

The man sat back on his horse, frowning, before once more leaning towards Harry.

"Who is your father, child?"

As I glanced down at Harry, for the first time since I held him as a newborn in our bedroom at

Millbryne Park, I saw the future man in my son. He stepped away from my shadow, stood up straight and tall, looking older than his three years, then spoke clearly in Ryder's dialect.

"My father is named Mi'wasa. He has Ugákhpa blood. His mama lived with the Wazhazhe, in the village where my papa was born. My Bannock name is Deide'wesa', but the Wazhazhe have yet to name me. We would be there now, but the buffalo came and turned us north. Now we head to the Omaha people."

"The buffalo turned you? What does this mean?" The man on horseback asked, turning to look at me.

I stepped forward in front of Harry, protecting him. "We were camped south of here some weeks ago, heading west to the Wazhazhe when my son woke one morning to see buffalo, too many to count, heading straight for our camp. In getting away, we started a stampede. We escaped by heading for a bluff, which took us north."

He nodded slowly. "We did not see these buffalo you speak of, but we have been hunting another large herd just a few miles west of here. We come here several times a year to hunt them, before returning to our village," he said, glancing down at Harry and then the girls, before looking back at me.

"You are welcome to come and stay at our village. You will be quite safe as we travel with our families." He waited only a moment, then swung his horse away from us and headed back to the lake. All the men, except one, followed him, along with the dogs. The man who remained had been the one who spoke to me in French. When he turned to follow the other riders, I called to him.

"Who are you? Who are your people?"

"We are Kaw," he said, in his own dialect. "Although most know us as Kansa. I am called Mi'nanpanta and our village is many days' ride southwest of here, but this is our hunting territory for buffalo," he glanced at Poongatse and Wannge'e then nodded towards Harry. "You will be safer at our camp then here. Our women and children travel with us and my own son is about the same age as your boy. Think on it. It will be to your advantage."

I glanced over at the girls and they smiled at me and nodded. Yet it was their desire for buffalo meat that drew them. I turned back to Mi'nanpanta and nodded. "Very well, we accept your offer."

He smiled, then turned away. "You know the way," he said, then he was gone among the trees.

Three

The four days they spent with the Kansa were the happiest Poongatse and Wannge'e had known since they were taken from their Bannock village over four years earlier. They feasted on buffalo meat. They slept under cover of a hide teepee at night and had the company of women and children around a campfire. The Kansa spoke of their ancestors, the old ones, who had come to this place by the lake to hunt buffalo for as long as anyone could remember. It was part of their story telling.

Madeleine was surprised that the hunters' women and children accompanied them. When the Bannock men went out hunting buffalo, they went alone. But these families were kept busy, not only preparing meals, but with the butchering.

There were forty men in the temporary village, along with thirty women and fifteen children. During the four days that Madeleine, the girls and Harry lived with them, in return for their hospitality they helped in any way they could.

Every day more buffalo carcasses were brought in. Nothing was wasted. Fires were lit to smoke and preserve the meat, sinew was saved to be used for sewing, bones were sharpened for tools, horns were cleaned and used as vessels for drinking and eating, hooves, claws and foot bones boiled for glue, or used for spoons and even toys for babes. The man who felled a beast, kept the teeth as a necklace. Once the meat was smoked, it was wrapped in hides then loaded onto the back of packhorses. Young men then rode out with it, back to the Kansa village.

The Kansa people were also farmers and in exchange for some of the small furs Madeleine and the girls had cured over the past two months, they traded some of their corn and squash along with buffalo meat.

They also gave Madeleine the use of one of their smaller, older teepees. When they appeared eager to trade for it, Madeleine offered them the French dagger. But they had no care for such a weapon. When Madeleine thought of the bitterly cold winter months ahead of them and this teepee giving them shelter, she offered them a musket, one of the sawn-off weapons she'd purchased for Ese-ggwe'na'a. The Kansa accepted and although Madeleine wasn't happy with the loss of the musket, the teepee was worth it.

*

Poongatse and Wannge'e sometimes struggled with the Dhegiha Sioux dialect during those days with the Kansa, even though they'd learned enough from listening to the conversations between Madeleine and Harry to get by.

But Harry turned feral, running around in just a loincloth on those lovely autumn days with Mi'nanpanta's four-year old son. Watching him swim naked in the lake or sit astride a horse while being led around at a walk by one of the village youths gave Madeleine hours of pleasure. But as he and other young boys did battle with sticks, or made toys out of twigs with the help of Mi'nanpanta, she couldn't help but think of Ryder. He was missing out on all this, watching his son grow up, becoming less of a toddler and more of a little boy. The last time he'd seen Harry, the child had been six months old.

She thought of Ryder as a little boy in the Wazhazhe village running wild with Te'tukhe after their mother died in childbirth with Wesa'shangke. He'd only spoken a little of that time in his life, but Madeleine knew enough to know those days had been hard for Ryder.

Perhaps because she missed him so much, or perhaps because Harry reminded her of what Ryder might have been like as a child that she allowed Harry too much freedom. But she saw no harm in it, because the little boy was desperate for the company of men and other boys.

One morning when he came running to tell her of the snares he'd been setting with other boys down by the lake, Madeleine thought her heart might break anew as he smiled at her. He owned so much of his father, from that smile to the blue eyes and long hair inclined to curl, to the easy charm and stubbornness. When the little boy hurled himself into her arms, laughing with the joy of life, Madeleine remembered all those other times, the special times, she'd known in her son's life.

From the newborn lying in her arms at Millbryne Park, to the days when she took Harry out riding with her around the estate. She remembered the child sleeping beside her in the stables at Diccon House, as they waited on news from Jimmy. The little boy aboard a ship bound for America and now here, running wild in a Kansa hunting camp. He was a child eager for adventure, growing up fast, yet Ryder was missing all of it.

*

On their last day in the village, as Madeleine made plans to leave at dawn the following morning, some of the Kansa women helped her and the Bannock girls build a travois to carry the hides that made up their teepee. It was hard work cutting the strips of wood with small axes and binding them together with rawhide strips.

They left just after dawn amid cries of farewell and good luck. But before they turned north, they rode around the lake and back to their old camp to retrieve their belongings still hidden in the cleft of rock.

Then at last they turned north, taking the shortcut the Kansa suggested which would take them a little east but would avoid passing through the hunting grounds and territory of the Pawnee. Madeleine gladly took the advice, eager to avoid that tribe.

Four

I knew he was there, before I fully woke. I had felt his presence in the deepest of my sleeps, as though he were calling to me, his purpose to wake me, so I would go to him.

I pushed myself out of my warm furs as if in a dream, although I was awake enough to feel the chill of the night air.

I didn't see him at first. The night was too dark. Then I saw him less than twenty feet away, illuminated by the light of the coals burning low in our fire. He stood in silence as I approached, leaning on his staff, which was nothing more than a well-used branch, long since honed to a smooth ivory finish over the long years.

He indicated I sit before him. Again, I felt like I was dreaming, as if I were in another world, somewhere far away to where my son lay sleeping between the Bannock girls.

I barely remembered sitting down as my legs seemed like liquid as they folded beneath me, as I sat in a cross-legged position at his feet. Then he was seated before me, his aged arthritic limbs as nimble as my son's young legs, although I'd never seen him move.

I wasn't aware of anything, but him. I didn't feel the cold, or my fatigue, or that Harry and the girls slept alone behind me. I also knew on some instinctive level that they wouldn't wake, for they lay in the deepest of slumbers while the ancient one visited me.

He had come to me before, three times in fact, but in London. The first occasion had been in the kitchen at Millbryne Park. The second had been on the steps of Thorne's home in Mayfair. The third had been in the Chapel at Millbryne Park when I faced Jarryth. Each time he'd come, he'd taken the form of my wolf *esa*, so that I would trust him, so I would understand he was there to protect me, to help fight against the evil that was Lisbeth, Thorne and Jarryth.

I had met this ancient one more than fifteen years earlier and despite the passing of time, he looked now as he had then. As old as time, his body withered and worn, his skin like leather after a lifetime on earth spent living outdoors, his limbs thin and well used, his white hair still worn long, well past his waist.

But I also knew he was ageless, for he was my protector, my guardian. His dark all-knowing eyes watched me, as they had watched me all those years ago when I had woken to find him sitting opposite me. I had been close to death then, starved and dehydrated, a bruised and battered fourteen-year old girl used to a life of wealth and privilege now lost and alone in the wilderness of the New World.

I had been terrified when I first saw him, thinking him an old man lost in the wild as I was, for he'd been achingly thin and all alone, with no weapons or a horse. Of course, I came to know him as so much more after he saved my life not once, but five times.

The first time, without speaking one word to me, he'd shown me where to find water, what berries and nuts to eat, what edible roots I could dig up.

The second time he'd urged me to hide just before a large group of hunters appeared, riding down the same valley where I'd been only moments before.

The third time he'd showed me a cave where we

sought shelter from a violent storm. It was there, in that cave, where I tried to leave that he grabbed my wrist in a bid to make me stay, leaving his mark on me, a branding I'd never be able to erase, which I'd carry to my grave.

The fourth and fifth times were my fights with Thorne and Jarryth Benedict. Had this ancient one not come to help me in the form of *esa*, I wouldn't have survived.

It had been the Bannock who explained that the mark on my wrist had come from my spirit guide, my *mukua'hainji,* and that it would mark me forever as one who had walked with the dead. Because of it, even after some ten years of living with the Bannock, some of them were still wary of me.

I touched the mark on my wrist now as I looked at him. He saw me do it and smiled, then nodded slowly, for that mark, his touch, had left me with some of his own extraordinary gifts.

I can see almost as well as a cat in the dark. I can hear a whisper across a room. I can sense intuitively when danger is near. I can run for long distances without fatigue and jump from certain heights without breaking a limb. I can scent a human or animal and can tell their intent by their smell, their body language, the look in their eye. All instincts owned by an animal, yet I also own them, because of this ancient one.

I looked at his lean body, at the loincloth held in place by a strip of rawhide around his hips and the robe of fur worn around his shoulders which fell almost to his knees. The robe was stunningly decorated with eagle and hawk feathers, dyed seed beads and quills from a porcupine.

I knew when I saw that robe, even as I'd known it all those years before, that this man had once held a position of power within his tribe.

I blinked, aware of a soft white light which seemed to pulse gently around us, giving me the feeling that we were floating, that we were no longer sitting on the ground. Then he clasped his hands in his lap and I saw his fingers and joints swollen with arthritis, although I doubt he'd been bothered by pain for a long time. Not since he'd joined this afterlife in which he now lived.

His eyes held me and drew me in, making me aware of nothing else but those deep calm pools of black, which pulsed with love and knowledge. When he spoke to me, astonishingly, I could understand every word and for the first time I realized he'd come from one of the many Plains' tribes, for his dialect was similar to Ryder's own people.

But when he lived, all those long years ago, his people would have known a vastly different time to the one he saw now. Years past, maybe even centuries, his tribe would have been wealthy, producing farmed goods such as maize, squash and beans. Like every other Plains' tribe, they would have hunted buffalo and deer, gathered fruits and vegetables and traded with others who lived close to their territory.

Their enemies had been other tribes, not Europeans. They had not yet seen muskets or good quality knives, nor felt the curse of European diseases such as smallpox, cholera or typhus. I doubt they'd even seen horses, for the horses came later, with the Spanish.

His voice was hoarse with age, yet there was

gentleness there, underlying an absolute power.

"I chose well," he said slowly. "You have not disappointed me, Esa-mogo'ne'. Or shall I call you Madeleine, as the whites know you," he smiled again, his eyes never leaving my own.

"You might think it was I who gave you courage when I found you, but I did not, for I could see you already owned it. I watched you for days astride that horse as you rode aimlessly north and although it was obvious you were quite alone in the world, not once did you give up. You should have died, yet you had a fierce desire to live. You should know that others, like me, watched you. But I think you know already that there are others like me who walk these lands, both in the day and in the dark of night. Yet only I thought you worth saving. I am glad I did. You have pleased me, Esa-mogo'ne'."

I wanted to reach out and touch him, to draw him to me, to feel his strength and power, but I dared not.

"You have helped many people and righted many wrongs. I have seen you stand against evil, where others would not."

"But you were there," I managed to whisper. "You were always there."

He smiled. "Perhaps you think this, but I haven't always been there, not for you at least. Perhaps had I been, I may have stopped you crossing an ocean too soon because it was not your time to return here, not yet," he said softly, then shook his head. "But once the decision was made, I could do nothing, as you have free will as does everyone else so although your destiny lies in this country, it was not your time to come. Because of it, you have known more sorrow. But take heart Esa-mogo'ne', for others have been saved because of your decision to come."

I thought then of Poongatse and Wannge'e, of Jimmy, Bryn and Lily, of Josette and Monique. But had I done so much to help them?

Perhaps. But they had also done much to help me.

"There will be others," he continued, "but that is in the future and must not be spoken of here. You will know when the time comes. So! I leave you with the instincts I gave you, for I trust you to use them well," he paused, smiling. "I shall tell you now, that she will also have them, as does your son. But that will be for you to discover later, in the years ahead. Now you must rest Esa-mogo'ne', because the days before you will seem like a storm but take heart, you will not be alone," he smiled again and the love he felt for me in that moment smothered me like a wave of bright light.

I felt it reach into every cell and nerve ending in my body, making me feel more alive than I'd ever known, as though I could see a blade of grass in the most infinite detail, the depths of the heavens above and of worlds unimaginable, of smells that assailed my senses, of a lightness that made me feel so powerful I felt as if I could fly.

Then it was over.

Whatever he'd allowed me to see and feel and know for one precious moment was gone, leaving me feeling utterly exhausted, with a fatigue that reached down into the deepest part of my limbs like a monstrous weight. I could feel myself falling asleep, as I must have fallen asleep in the crypt after Jarryth died, when this ancient one revealed himself, rising from *esa's* body. A fatigue where I'd had no memory of climbing the stone steps out of the crypt, or of falling asleep on that pew in the back of the Chapel.

"You have pleased me, Esa-mogo'ne'," I heard his voice from a long way away, as I closed my eyes to that paralyzing fatigue. "I am glad I met you."

Then I felt the comfort of my furs, yet I didn't remember walking back to my bed. I just felt their warmth enclosing me like an embrace as I settled into deep sleep but before I lost myself to that darkness, I heard the ancient one's voice, low and urgent and full of love.

"You know he lives. Wait for him at the Omaha, Esa-mogo'ne'." Then I heard nothing more.

*

I woke the following morning well before dawn and lay utterly still in my furs, enjoying the heat from the fire, for the coals still burned warm. Yet I felt more alive and at peace than I had since Ryder disappeared that awful day in February, more than two and a half years ago. The children were still asleep and I was loathe to wake them so I lay there, trying to remember everything from the night before. Some of it was hazy and lacked any kind of depth, like a dream. Other things were clear and sharp and vibrated with urgency.

you know he lives. wait for him at the Omaha, Esa-mogo'ne'

These words filled me with hope and a restless energy. That Ryder might come for me at the Omaha filled my heart to overflowing, yet when? I hardly dared believe it would be in the next few months, that he might already be in this country, on his way north even now. The thought of it moved me to push aside my furs and I walked across to the small stream near our camp and washed my face and filled the cooking pot with water when I remembered something else the ancient one had said.

the days before you will seem like a storm

These words, unlike the others, filled me with fear. What else had I to endure? Had I not been through enough? Then I remembered the worst of what he told me.

your destiny lies in this country, but it was not your time to come. because of it, you have known more sorrow

Had I forced the hand of fate by making the decision to return to the Bannock? Yet I'd been overwhelmed by loneliness, terrible grief and the war between England and France. To think that I should have stayed in England brought with it a whole new heartache and for my own sanity, I turned my thoughts away from that.

I walked back to camp and stirred the coals, adding more wood to heat the pot of water even as the girls began to stir. But of one thing I was certain. Ryder was alive and on his way north to the Omaha.

in the wild: October 1804

"Pull up, pull up," the older man hissed in French, glancing at the five men riding behind him.

They reined their horses in and sat quietly in the dusky light of sunset, staring down into the undulating valley below them, at the small village of teepees. Close to the teepees were several dozen horses grazing on the lush prairie grass.

"Who are they, do you recognize them?" the older man asked, turning to speak softly to the younger man on his left.

In his early thirties, the man was the youngest in the group and as he squinted in the shadows of dusk, he shook his head, also speaking in French.

"It's impossible to see anything in this light. They might be passing through, just like we are."

He glanced at his five companions who all owned French-Canadian lineage. He'd been living and working alongside these men for almost eighteen months, trapping in rivers to the west of this territory for beaver, mink, ermine and otter and now their packhorses and travois carried a fortune in furs. His own investment in the furs meant new weapons, which he planned to buy in St Louis before heading home.

He glanced back at the small village of teepees below them, then leaned forward, before swearing softly in French.

"They're buffalo hunters! Look at the dozens of travois in the center of the village loaded with buffalo hides!"

Another of the men nodded. "Which means they'll have plenty of freshly smoked meat."

The older man in the group pulled a spyglass from a brown leather bag tied behind his saddle and turned the thick three-stacked lenses to focus on the group below.

"They've got a fortune in buffalo hides down there alright, along with horses," he said, then whistled softly. "They've also got women and children with them."

"They got muskets?" another of the men asked.

The older man nodded. "Yes, enough to put up a good fight," he replied, his voice hard.

Another of the men leaned over to spit out a mouthful of tobacco, before continuing to chew the wad in his mouth, his teeth stained from the use of it

"Well, I reckon we ride on," he said, his accent from the French-Canadian provinces way to the north. "We don't want trouble with these folks and I'm darn sure they don't want trouble from us, especially since they got women and young ones with them. I reckon we keep riding for St Louis like we planned."

"But they've got fresh buffalo meat," another man said. "I've got no problem trading a couple of my pelts for some smoked meat. I've got a real taste for it."

There was silence as the men thought on this when a fierce barking came from the direction of the village, followed by a man's shrill cry.

Then everything turned to noise and chaos as men raced for weapons and horses while women urgently gathered children close.

"The dogs caught our scent," the older man said, swearing softly. "Well, I guess we've got no choice now but to go on down and introduce ourselves.

Because I've got no desire to have my belly all shot up, or one of their dogs taking a chunk out of my leg."

He snapped the spyglass shut and once again turned to the youngest man, who knew the question was coming before it was asked.

"You're more likely to know their dialect than we are, so you go on down and meet them. Might stop them firing at us. But ask them to heel in their dogs! And maybe let them know we've got a few pelts to trade for a bit of meat."

The younger man didn't bother replying. He was too busy watching the men below riding at a hard gallop, their muskets held high as they uttered shrill cries. He was also thinking on the benefits of a good fire and a full belly, so without looking back at his companions, he kicked his horse on, riding across the darkening landscape towards the men coming straight towards him.

*

As the riders surrounded him, their horses blowing and snorting in the cool evening air, their hooves churning the earth beneath them, he raised his hand in a sign of friendship that all Plains tribes knew, indicating he held no weapon.

Then he quickly introduced himself, speaking in his own dialect, relieved when the riders lowered their muskets and called back their dogs.

He glanced back at the five men on the hill, who were watching in silence.

"We're loaded down with furs, beaver, ermine and mink, after a year of trapping in the wild. We head to

St Louis to sell them, so mean you no harm."

They spoke for a little while, then the leader of the group invited him and his five friends to share their camp for the night.

The young man called for his friends to ride down and join him, then he turned back to the men on horseback and asked for their name.

"We are Kansa," the man in front replied.

*

It was close to midnight and he was almost asleep when he heard the muted tones of a conversation spoken in French just across from him. It was between one of the Kansa men and another of the fur trappers. The Kansa man was talking about a woman they had met almost a month ago.

He tried to ignore the conversation, wanting nothing more than to go to sleep, but then he came fully awake, not quite believing what he was hearing.

"They camped with us for several days. The woman was French, but she could speak our dialect fluently," he paused, aware of the younger man listening, although it didn't bother him. By all accounts, it was a good story.

"You say she was French?" the other man asked.

The Kansa nodded. "Yes, she was. And young enough, travelling with a small boy and two girls from a tribe called the Bannock. She said her man was Ugákhpa, although he was born in the Wazhazhe village. She had planned to take her son there to meet his Wazhazhe family, but was now heading north to spend the winter with the Omaha."

The man pushed aside his furs and sat up,

reaching for his waterskin which lay beside him, aware that his hands were trembling as he took a long sip from it.

As he drunk his fill, he took the opportunity to watch the Kansa man as he spoke, yet could find nothing deceitful about his manner.

He put aside his waterskin and leaned forward to speak to him. "This woman, what name did she go by?"

The Kansa paused for only a moment before replying. "Esa-mogo'ne'."

Corrigan ranch, St Louis: October 1804

The wagon pulled into the yard and the men on the buckboard dismounted. Julia and Jeremiah stepped out of the front door and onto the porch, both carrying muskets, watching as one of the men took the horses to drink from a trough of water by the wooden railings. Just beyond the railings lay the bunkhouses of the ranch hands.

The other man turned and smiled, yet Julia thought it closer to a smirk. As he stepped forward and headed towards them, Julia saw the arrogant swagger of him. Well, to hell with him.

"Sorry to come uninvited like this ma'am," he said. "We were in town this morning picking up supplies and Letty Stewart asked if we'd drop some mail off to you. Arrived on a keelboat first thing this morning. Letty knew we'd be passing by this way and we got no problem at all in dropping it off," he paused, licking his lips, aware of their muskets as he glanced up at Jeremiah who towered beside Julia. Then he pulled a letter from his shirt pocket and made a play of reading the address.

But Julia already knew the character of this uninvited visitor and expected nothing less. She almost dared to glance at Jeremiah but stopped herself, unwilling to show this man how nervous she was, but she took comfort in Jeremiah's presence as she was all alone this morning, the ranch hands having left to see to the cattle.

"Just leave it on the stairs, if you please," Julia said softly.

The man smiled again, that same self-satisfied

smirk, but Julia ignored it. He was nothing to her, despite being the right hand man to one of St Louis' biggest ranchers, who owned the big spread west of Julia's property.

The man raised one of his hands. "We don't want no trouble ma'am. Only came by to deliver this. Saves it sitting in town for a couple more weeks until you next go in." He stepped forward and dropped the letter on the bottom step, even as Jeremiah raised his musket.

The letter was a stained, battered parcel wrapped in parchment. The address written on the front had been written in a good, strong hand.

Julia looked across at the horses drinking from her wooden trough, then turned to Jeremiah.

"Go get a pitcher of water for these men and something for them to eat," she said, her voice hard. As Jeremiah left, Julia turned back to the man, lowering her musket. "I thank you for bringing the letter, but you know full well why I won't invite you into the house. You can go wait by your wagon for your refreshments, but once done, I want you to leave. You can tell your boss I'm still waiting on him to come see me about his cattle coming onto my land. Every time I call on him, he's not available to talk, so you tell him the invitation to talk is getting urgent."

The man nodded. "Sure thing, ma'am. Thank you for your hospitality."

Julia watched as he turned and walked back to the wagon. He thought she held no threat to him and his boss. A woman alone, they thought she'd be a pushover. But she'd known this land and this territory and the people in it for a long time, better than these newcomers with all their money. That letter had been delivered, not by a friendly neighbor, but as an excuse to spy on her.

She ran down the stairs and picked the letter up, turning it over. She recognized the seal at once, stamped within the wax which secured the parcel.

It was Ryder Benedict's personal seal, the same seal his father had used when sending mail to Albert all those years ago.

She felt ill on seeing it, for it could mean only one thing. The letter had been addressed to Madeleine, although Julia would open it as Madeleine had given her permission to do so.

But she wouldn't open it now. She didn't think she could bear to read the news it held, not while those two men remained on her property.

She stood on the porch, watching as Jeremiah took water and slices of apple cake to the men. Then he joined her at the top of the stairs and they stayed there, holding their muskets, until the two men climbed back aboard their wagon and rolled out of the yard and back down the dirt road. Only then did Julia step back inside the house.

*

She pulled gently at the seal, feeling the wax break beneath her fingers. Then she tore away the stained and battered parchment with some impatience to get at the letter within, aware that her hands were shaking, dreading the news it must contain.

But she'd only read a few words before she sat down in astonishment. The handwriting was Ryder's own. He'd sent the letter from London in May, some five months ago.

The letter was short and had clearly been written in haste. Ryder wrote that he had a man waiting to take the letter with all urgency to a Benedict clipper sailing that very morning from London. He wrote that he was very much alive and in good health and would shortly be leaving for America with the hope that Madeleine and Harry might still be in St Louis.

Julia finished the letter and looked out of the window but she didn't see the fields and outhouses before her. Instead, she saw only those words of anguish written on that paper along with Ryder's hope that Madeleine and Harry would still be here, safe with her on the ranch.

She vividly remembered how Madeleine had looked when she'd left here almost ten weeks ago, a young woman thin with grief, who had never once given up hope, even after more than two years, that Ryder was still alive.

Julia bowed her head, feeling wretchedly helpless and sad. Because other than Harry, the one person who Madeleine loved most in the world was alive and coming for her, yet there was no way Julia could let her know.

in the wild: early October 1804

Madeleine sat just beyond the teepee, the fur coat she'd purchased in St Louis wrapped around her for warmth, although she still shivered from the cold. But there would be no warmth of a fire for her out here tonight and as she pushed herself to her feet, handling with care the sawn-off musket which was fully primed and ready to fire, she walked silently about their camp, not only to keep warm but to keep watch.

She glanced often at the teepee where Harry and the girls slept. They trusted her completely to take care of them in this wide open country in which they had camped, for there wasn't a tree or shrub as far as the eye could see in any direction. The teepee lay in complete darkness, for there was no flicker of flame from a fire inside, not tonight. Although Madeleine wouldn't have a choice whether to light a fire or not in the days ahead, for it was getting too cold now to sleep without one. Every day, the further north they travelled, the colder it became, with the temperatures dropping every day.

By Madeleine's reckoning, they had another month before they reached the Omaha. Had she been travelling alone, she would have made it in a matter of weeks. But travelling with a child, two teenage girls, five horses and the travois was slow hard work and she had no choice but to keep the horses at a steady walk. Unpacking five horses and raising the teepee each night also took time, although Madeleine would never have done it without the Bannock girls.

She glanced up at the stars, making sure as she

always did that she was on the right path north. But even as she stood there in the complete and utter blackness of the night, she felt it again. She turned slowly to look out into the dark, aware of that strange sensation. It was nothing more than a shift in the wind, a smell, but all her instincts warned her that they were being followed. Although she had nothing to prove it. Not so much as a cloud of dust. Nor had she seen anyone, but she knew that someone was tracking them. She'd thought of everyone they'd met since they left Julia's ranch and dismissed them all, except one.

The giant painted man, the Pawnee, who had traded his dagger for her musket. He was the only one who had anything to gain by catching up to them. Indeed, they offered him everything he had lost.

Madeleine thought of the dagger. She had wrapped it away with the muskets, as she had little use for it. If anything it was a nuisance, because it was heavy and cumbersome, although for some reason she couldn't throw it away, even though Wannge'e and Poongatse had urged her to do so.

She walked once more around their camp and after checking on the horses she made her way back to the teepee. She crawled inside the unsecured flap and was surprised to find Wannge'e awake. The girl pushed aside her furs and sat up.

"You need to sleep," she said in a whisper, so as not to wake Harry and Poongatse.

Madeleine smiled. Wannge'e was strong-willed and there was little point in telling her to go back to sleep. Besides, she'd be taking over Madeleine's watch soon enough. The girl moved to kneel, leaning towards Madeleine, her voice low. "I know you feel it, for I feel it too. Did you see anything?"

Madeleine shook her head, but shuddered with fear. She'd always loathed the nights in this big open country. It was the reason she used to barricade herself into her cave at night. Not only to protect herself from wild predators, but from the nightwalkers.

It was the Bannock who taught her about nightwalkers, for they were a part of their story telling. Ghosts, people long dead, who lingered between this world and the next, who continued to walk the earth. Some nights when Madeleine couldn't sleep she thought of Jarryth, or Thorne and even Lisbeth and the power they might wield in the afterlife. She had never seen them, or felt threatened by them, but when she felt like this, uneasy and even frightened, she wished for the light of morning.

"Try and sleep, I'll wake you in a couple of hours," she said, putting a hand on Wannge'e's shoulder. "I'm just going to take one more look around."

Wannge'e nodded and slipped back under her furs, although Madeleine knew the girl would lie awake, waiting for her. She might not yet be fifteen years old, but she was more mature than some of the young women Madeleine had met in London who'd been ten years older. She quickly glanced over at Poongatse and Harry but they were fast asleep. Then she turned and crawled back out into the night.

*

There was nothing to see in that vast empty darkness

and Madeleine felt the blackness of the night surround her like a cloak. Except for a few stars glittering above her through a cloudy sky and her own ability to see in the dark, the country around her was nothing but a black, desolate emptiness. No animals passed through here but buffalo and another massive herd had passed through here recently for the land was trampled, laid open like a raw wound. But something was out there in that pitch darkness. Madeleine could feel it and as she walked around their camp a third time, she turned to look back the way they'd come earlier that day.

Would she chance it? Would she chance leaving Harry and the girls alone, just for an hour, no more, to backtrack a few miles. She paused for a moment to glance back at the teepee, wondering if she should get Wannge'e up after all. In the end she decided against it, before turning south and running slow, just an easy jog, careful of the uneven ground churned up by countless buffalo hooves.

She remembered a slight rise in the land they'd passed about four miles south of their campsite and it was to this landmark that she now headed. When it rose before her, nothing more than a shadow against the cloudy night sky, she felt the land beneath her moccasins change as she began to climb and within minutes she was at the top of the rise. She bent low to catch her breath then looked back the way she'd come. She couldn't even see the teepee from here. It was lost within the dark, some four miles behind her. She turned and looked back across the valley where they'd travelled earlier that day. There was nothing to see. It was just darkness everywhere. A thick velvet curtain of pitch black. She crouched down, her forearms resting on her knees, the musket in her hands as she looked out across that invisible landscape, then closed her eyes, remembering what Ese-ggwe'na'a had taught her all those years ago, of how to see in the dark.

Listen to its sounds and be aware of its scents. Feel and understand why your body reacts, for your instincts will warn you if you are in danger, not your mind, for your mind will argue with how you feel, what you hear and smell. Be aware of the smallest prickle on your skin, of the hair rising on the back of your neck, of your feet urging you to flee, of your hands clawed, ready to fight. This is what you must trust, not your mind.

So she listened now. For any little thing, no matter how subtle, which might suggest who or what was following them. Yet, she was met with only silence. Deep, utter silence. But something was out there. She knew it with every instinct she owned. For long minutes she continued to crouch, watching and listening, until finally she stood up and turned away to go back down the hill when something way to the west caught her eye.

And there it was. The flicker of a fire. It was way, way in the distance and she realized as she watched it, that she'd been wrong. She'd thought someone was following them from the south. But this person was coming from the west. She crouched down again and watched for long minutes, but could see or hear nothing, not the drift of muted conversation, nor laughter, nor the smell of a beast roasting over a fire which might suggest there was more than one person there. There was just silence.

St Louis: mid October 1804

One

Ryder stepped off the keelboat and onto the wharf of St Louis, feeling grubby and tired, yet utterly relieved to finally be here.

It was late in the afternoon and he hoped to hire a carriage to take him out to the Corrigan ranch, because he'd no plans to stay overnight in town.

Julia wouldn't be expecting him, despite a letter he'd sent from New Orleans advising her of his plans, because his arrival here was almost two weeks later than he'd originally planned.

He'd hoped to be in St Louis in early October but the trip up the Mississippi River had taken just over a month, mostly because of bad weather. They'd also stopped more than once to drop off produce and parcels at new settlements, built since he was last here, alongside old French and Spanish settlements.

He thought of the letter he'd sent from London last May, addressed to Madeleine. If she received it, she'd be waiting for him at the Corrigan ranch. If the letter had been delayed, which Ryder expected more than likely, she'd now be somewhere between the Wazhazhe village and the Omaha.

Although Ryder hoped she was still at the Wazhazhe, choosing to winter over there with his brothers, because that's where he was headed in the next few days.

He left the wharf, leaving his belongings with the keelboat until he could collect them later. Then he walked through town, astonished by its growth and the number of new stores, saloons and whorehouses along with the American voices that now mingled with the Spanish, French-Canadian and European accents.

He remembered coming to this town in the summer of 1797, more than seven years ago, looking for answers to his past. St Louis had been nothing more than a few wooden buildings back then, just a small French settlement.

But the town was quite different now. The Spanish Governor and his aides had left, making way for the Americans.

Ryder had heard rumors in New Orleans that the American Congress wanted this town and its surrounding settlements, which included St Charles and St Genevieve, a small settlement just downriver from St Louis, to be known as the District of St Louis, although it wouldn't be governed from here. That would be done across the river, in a territory they were calling Indiana.

Although Ryder was shocked by how quickly the Americans had moved. They had claimed ownership of this land a little over a year ago so if nothing else, all these signs of growth revealed their ambitions for this territory.

He chose a livery on the main street and hired a horse and buggy cheaply enough, then headed back to the wharf to collect his belongings.

Then he turned south and took the old road out to the Corrigan ranch. Yet even here he saw changes. The old, rutted track he remembered from when he was a child was gone, replaced by a wide, well-travelled road.

Acres of forests which had once hugged the edge of that old, rutted track had been felled, making way for several big ranches where herds of cattle now grazed.

Several wagons and another buggy passed him, along with ranch hands, all heading to St Louis to do business.

A little further on Ryder heard someone call his name, yet astonishingly, they used his English title. Startled to hear his Benedict title so far from home, Ryder reined in the horse and pulled on the buggy's brake before reaching for the pistol he'd left on the seat beside him.

As he turned to look behind him, he saw a rider galloping down the hill towards him, waving his arm in greeting. Ryder uttered an oath of astonishment.

"Lord Benedict!" the rider called again, leaving the fields and kicking the horse into a run along the dirt road, coming up fast behind the buggy. "Lord Almighty! It's really you! I can hardly believe it!"

Ryder jumped off the buckboard to stand in the road as the man pushed his wide brimmed hat back off his face and dismounted.

"Bryn Harlan!" Ryder said in disbelief as the younger man hurried towards him.

"Miss Julia told us some weeks ago she'd received a letter from you and you were on your way to America! We couldn't believe you were alive after all this time, not after everything that happened. Yet here you are! God above, I swear I can't believe it!"

Bryn was crying, even as he laughed in delight, wiping his tears away on his sleeve. "Forgive me m'lord, but it's such a shock. Here you are, standing before me after all these years. Wait 'til I tell Lily. She'll have the babe right there in front of me, I swear it."

Ryder knew from the letters Madeleine had left

him at Millbryne Park that Jimmy, Bryn and Lily had come with her to America. So he was prepared to find all three living at Julia's ranch.

He wasn't prepared for how much Bryn had changed since he saw him last, some three years ago. He was no longer the thin, pale teenage boy Ryder remembered who'd been grieving for Michael Woodley, his step-father, but a grown man, dressed in muslin shirt, leather vest and pants. He seemed taller, his body strong and healthy, bronzed from the hot St Louis sun, his face mature and showing all the experience of a man well used to the ways of the world and women.

But as if Bryn suddenly remembered who Ryder was and his own position in life, that he and his family had been former servants to this man, he stepped back, his body rigid with formality. Ryder felt it and smiled, stepping forward to embrace him.

"It's damn good to see you again Bryn. I can't tell you how good it is," he said. "My wife wrote and told me that you and Lily had accompanied her out here. She also mentioned the babe. Can I just say how happy I am for you both?"

He stepped back, feeling the emotion of the reunion, of the years behind them and their shared connection to Michael Woodley. "Look, why don't you tie your reins to the back of the buggy and come sit up front with me? Then you can fill me in on what's been happening,"

He paused, then dared to ask it. "My wife and son? Are they still here? Or have they left already?"

Bryn nodded in dismay. "They left here almost three months ago, m'lord."

Ryder understood at once that Madeleine had

missed his letter. Well, nothing could be done about it now. The sooner he saw Julia, arranged horses and supplies, the sooner he could be on his way and follow them.

Yet as he climbed up onto the buckboard, as Bryn tied his reins to the back of the buggy, the crushing disappointment that they'd gone threatened to overwhelm him and Ryder felt the sudden, unwelcome bone weary fatigue of months of travel hit him. He'd been pushing himself for months to get here as soon as he could, but he knew better than anyone that he'd left London too late. He turned as Bryn climbed up to sit beside him and forced himself to listen, to hear his news.

Bryn spoke of his marriage to Lily and his impending fatherhood, along with his love of living here. Then he spoke of those dire weeks after Ryder disappeared. He paused, unsure whether to speak of it, but Ryder encouraged him to tell it, needing to hear it, wanting to forget his fatigue and the bitter news that Madeleine and Harry were gone.

"I know some of it," he said softly. "Sir George Ashbury and my cousin Lord Petherington told me what they knew, along with Sully."

"They was hard times, m'lord. That week after you went missing, we still don't know where her ladyship went that week, but wherever it was, she returned with two young French girls. Then we all left for Millbryne Park in the dead of night, as if the hounds of hell themselves were upon us. She left Will and about a dozen other men behind to guard Diccon House and then once we reached Millbryne, her Ladyship had the estate locked down," he shook his head, frowning as he remembered those days.

"Sully and the men on watch found two men breaking into the big house in the early hours of the morning. They were chased off, but they were found dead the next day up by the Chapel, their throats torn out by some wild dog. After that, people stopped going anywhere near those woods."

"Did you see my wife that night," Ryder asked, thinking of all he knew from the letters Madeleine had left him in the secret drawer at Millbryne Park.

Bryn nodded. "She gave the young Viscount to Missy to look after, along with Monique and Josette. I was one of those who stood guard around Sully's cottage and I saw her the next morning. She was splattered with blood and looked as pale as a ghost," he paused and glanced at Ryder. "She said she'd had a tumble from her horse. But over the next few weeks no-one saw much of her and she got thin as a bird. Lily said she hardly ate anything, but it was around that time that Lily and me got together."

Ryder knew all this and more from Madeleine's letters. So many people had suffered during that time, but nothing could be done to undo the heartache. The past could not be changed.

"Are you happy here, Bryn? No regrets?"

Bryn smiled. "I love it m'lord. I can't imagine ever going back. Not sure I can say the same for Lily. I know she misses Perri sometimes, along with Mourie. Sometimes I think her heart is back in London at Diccon House, or down at Millbryne Park. But she's promised me she'll give it a go out here, because I don't want to go back. There is no going back, because if I save enough money I could buy my own ranch one day and I know I'd never have that chance in England."

"Well, I'm pleased for you," Ryder said softly, as they headed towards Julia's ranch.

He agreed with Bryn. Because he also knew there could be no going back, but still, he wished with all his heart he could change the past few years.

Two

Ryder woke early the following morning and made his way downstairs to the kitchen. He accepted a large cup of black coffee from Esmeralda then stepped out onto the porch, feeling the bite of the cool autumn morning.

It was only an hour or so past dawn but already the household staff and ranch hands were up and about. He could hear men down at the corrals saddling their mounts and getting ready to ride out.

The occasional sound of laughter drifted up to him along with the lowing of cattle out in the fields, the *yap* and growl of working dogs, the smells of earth and dew on the ground, hay and horses, chickens, pigs and manure. From the back of the house, from the kitchen, came the sweet smells of someone baking biscuits along with fried eggs and ham.

Ryder was surprised by the changes Julia had made to the ranch since his last visit here with Madeleine over four years earlier. Another barn and bunk house had been built, two more wells had been dug, the kitchen had been extended out the back and a dining hall added where all the indoor staff could eat.

He was astonished to discover Julia had recently purchased another ranch and although it was nothing more than a small holding south of her own extensive land, it held valuable water rights.

Ryder suddenly wondered what his father would think of the ranch. How different it must look to when Torrance brought his young bride Wazhingka here some thirty five years ago.

In 1769, Torrance had bought twenty acres of

mostly untamed land, with just a few acres cleared for farming along with a small basic cabin. Thick forest would have stood where the main house and outbuildings now were, along with those green rolling hills on which cattle now grazed.

Julia had clearly prospered here but Ryder was pleased for her, because he knew how hard she'd worked to make a go of it after Albert died. It would have been easy for her to leave and get a teaching job back east, but quitting had never been what Julia was about. Nor had it been Albert's. Had they been quitters, they would have sent that rebellious little half-breed Ugákhpa boy back to the Wazhazhe within days of Hubert Lemoine dropping him off here all those years ago.

Ryder smiled at the memory. What would his life be like now, had they done just that? Although he was quite sure that one way or the other Torrance would have found a way to get him to England, because Torrance had never been a quitter either.

He tried to imagine his teenage mother Wazhingka living with Torrance in that small cabin up in the woods, but found it impossible, because the image was so different to how Ryder remembered his father. Yet according to the diaries which Torrance had kept and Ryder had read, this ranch was where his father had been the happiest.

He wondered what his mother had thought of this place. She would have been just sixteen years old and already pregnant with him when she first came to live here. A lifetime ago. Almost thirty-five years. Yet knowing she'd been here, that she'd walked this very ground, gave Ryder unexpected joy.

She was often in his thoughts these days because

he now knew so much more about her, thanks to what Madeleine had found and left for him in the secret drawer at Millbryne. Perhaps like Lily, Wazhingka would also have stayed here and made a go of it, had Torrance not felt compelled to return to England and his duties as 7th Earl Benedict.

Although Ryder would bet a large wager that Torrance would have eventually become bored living here, perhaps even with the company of his young wife. He thought it inevitable that Torrance would have found a way to return to England and the wealthy, privileged society into which he'd been born.

Although, perhaps he was wrong in that. Because Torrance never sought a dissolution of his marriage to Wazhingka and he could have done it easily enough. He'd had unlimited funds to make anything disappear.

Ryder shook away the negative thoughts. He knew better than anyone that there was little point in second guessing the past. No-one could change it. What was done, was done.

He was grateful that Julia knew nothing of his past. Only Albert had shared that information with Torrance. The two men had made a deal. In exchange for ownership of the ranch, Albert would make it available for Wazhingka if she ever had need of a sanctuary for herself and her halfblood son, heir to an English title and prodigious fortune, a child she'd named Mi'wasa.

But she never did return to the ranch. When Torrance left to return to England, she returned to the Wazhazhe people where she gave birth to Ryder. It was also where she'd fallen in love with Hubert Lemoine and devoted the rest of her short life to him and their two sons, Te'tukhe and Wesa'shangke.

But if Torrance had been happy here, Ryder had no such memories of the place. This ranch represented to him the beginning of his father's control and the responsibilities which lay ahead of him within the Benedict family.

He thought back to that lost, lonely year he'd spent here as a troubled eight-year old boy and knew from those secret documents he'd read in the library at Millbryne Park, that even if Julia had secretly wanted him gone, Albert would have done everything in his power to keep Ryder here. The incentive, of course, was ownership of the ranch, gifted to him years earlier by Torrance, on the condition the ranch always be there for Wazhingka and her half English son.

Ryder glanced up towards the hills where he could see some of Julia's cattle grazing. Unlike the stone fences back in England, these big ranches out here had no physical fences to keep stock in, or out, other than ancient stands of trees.

He had spoken to Julia about it last night over dinner because the lack of fencing was becoming a problem. Thick forests and woods which had once bordered her property were slowly being cut down, the trees cleared by wealthy men who could afford to buy that land and clear it. But big ranches carrying big herds of cattle needed a lot of water and some of these ranches didn't have access to such reserves.

But Julia did. A stream ran right through her property and although one of her neighbors benefitted from that water, others did not.

She also had access to an underground river and had sunk five deep wells on her ranch over the years, guaranteeing healthy animals and crops. But without adequate fencing, neighbors were sending their cattle to graze on Julia's rich grassland, which was causing tension.

Ryder knew she couldn't afford to put railings up to protect her boundaries. He knew she'd never recover financially from the cost of it. The best she could do was send her ranch hands out every day to check on her cattle and scatter those not carrying her brand. Until a cheaper way to close off her property became available, she had very little control over her neighbor's stock.

Although Ryder might be able to help her out with that problem. The cost of putting railings up all around her ranch would be prohibitive, but railings could be put up where her property bordered the easiest access to her neighbors. He must write to Fahey and organize some funds for it.

He finished his coffee and allowed his thoughts to return to Madeleine, his son and the Bannock girls. Julia told him last night of the attack on the Bannock village four years earlier and of Poongatse and Wannge'e taken as slaves and sold to the Mandan.

"That's all I know. Madeleine only spoke briefly of the tragedy they suffered. She said you both passed through their village some years ago, so knew the girls rather well. That's why she insisted on taking the girls home, back to their village. I do admire her for it, although it's obvious she shares a close bond with them. It's a shame they didn't care too much for living here in the house, but they settled well enough living in that old cabin up in the woods."

Ryder asked nothing more on the subject, but he

thought it fitting somehow that the Bannock girls felt at home in a cabin where a young woman of Ugákhpa blood, just a little older than themselves, had also made it her home.

He was thinking of his mother when Julia stepped out on the porch and approached him. The breakfast they would share together was ready, but as Ryder turned to escort her into the dining room, he was already thinking on how soon he could leave.

in the wild: mid-October 1804

One

Madeleine let go of the reins to pull the sailcloth further over herself and Harry to try and protect them from the rain even as the child lay back against her, sharing her body heat, for the rain held an icy chill to it. She glanced over at Poongatse and Wannge'e as the girls huddled beneath their own sailcloths, looking as miserable as she and Harry.

They had been riding along the banks of the river for an hour or more in the hope of finding a place to cross. But as the rain continued to fall, the overflow from the hills all around had found its way down here and the river was now a raging torrent, with white water rushing over submerged rocks.

Madeleine knew it was madness to carry on. The weather was deteriorating, promising thunderstorms and it was already late in the afternoon. As she looked ahead through the misty fall of rain, she saw a large group of boulders less than a half mile away and a good mile or so back from the river. She glanced back at Poongatse and Wannge'e and pointed towards them. The girls nodded and kicked their horses on, following Madeleine and the travois, a sailcloth over the teepee and furs and buckskin sheets in an effort to keep everything dry.

They found a large clearing between the boulders which mercifully offered some shelter from the wind and driving rain. Madeleine quickly untied the muslin cloth which bound her to Harry, allowing Poongatse to take the child in her arms. As Madeleine dismounted, she helped Poongatse place one of the sailcloths over the little boy, before settling him under an overhang of rock to keep him out of the way. Then Madeleine and the girls quickly worked together, hobbling the horses, clearing the ground of leaves and debris, before erecting the teepee. Like most women, they could do it in less than an hour, but the driving rain and wind made it a slow hard process. When it was finally up they spread three of the sailcloths on the wet ground inside, before placing the buckskin sheets over them. Then they unpacked their belongings off the horses and what remained on the travois.

Poongatse crawled inside with Harry, not only to get the child out of the rain but to begin making a fire pit. She dug a hole in the wet earth and surrounded it with river stones while Wannge'e and Madeleine sought out firewood. Although they always had a store of it, picking wood and kindling up as they travelled each day, making sure they never ran out. But in this sheltered spot they found deep bundles of rotten wood around the boulders, brought up here by the river and high winds over the years.

When a shaft of lightning lit the sky overhead followed by a roll of thunder, Madeleine urged Wannge'e to get inside the teepee. She encouraged the shivering girls to get out of their wet clothing and wrap themselves in woolen blankets while Madeleine undressed Harry and wrapping him in a blanket. The little boy was trembling from the cold.

As they huddled around the fire, waiting for the wood to take hold, Madeleine offered them leftover smoked meat and chokeberry cakes which Poongatse had made only that morning.

Madeleine forced herself to eat, even though she had no appetite. She sat quietly, watching as the flames begun to lick at the wood and felt a moment of dread as smoke began to rise and drift upward towards the hole at the very top of the teepee. It could be mistaken for mist or fog. But no-one could mistake the scent of wood smoke.

She reached for her musket, making sure it was primed with shot and powder but as she went to crawl outside and back into the rain, she glanced briefly at Poongatse and Wannge'e. She saw the knowing in their eyes, but they said nothing. They knew as well as Madeleine, they were being followed.

Two

I'd left my sailcloth outside the teepee but now pulled it over me, not only to protect myself from the rain, but my musket. Then I began to climb the boulders, feeling my moccasins slip on their wet surface. When I reached the highest point I lay down, pulling the sailcloth right over me so that the musket and I were almost hidden. I positioned the weapon so that I had a good sightline right along the riverbank, back the way we had come, then I lay still and watched.

There was nothing out there. Not yet. But he would come, because he hadn't let up in days. At least it was only one man who followed us and I knew that because I'd backtracked again that morning, leaving the girls and Harry to ride on alone with the packhorses and travois.

When I finally got a glimpse of our pursuer he'd been some way behind us, way in the distance. A few hours away, but I knew he'd catch us tonight. Yet why would a solitary man follow us? What reason did he have? I felt uneasy about his motives, yet clearly he was an expert tracker because no matter how hard we'd tried to lose him, he never once faltered in following our trail. Today, he'd seemed determined to close the gap between us, even though we'd pushed hard all day to try and get ahead of him.

As I lay on top of that boulder covered with a sailcloth, I cursed the weather. The rain might hide our tracks, but he only had to see our smoke. Tonight we couldn't hide in the dark. We needed that fire because I had to get Harry and the girls warm, I couldn't risk them getting fevers. Because of that, I had no choice but to remain here until he came.

I knew it wasn't my beloved. I had known from the beginning that this man wasn't Ryder. I would know if it were him.

Nor was it the Pawnee chief. This man wasn't a giant, nor did he ride a massive warhorse.

As I waited, I thought again of everyone we had met since we left St Louis. I knew that the Kansa wouldn't bother following us because we held no value to them. They saw no wealth in slaves, nor did they desire our possessions because they already owned muskets, powder, shot and good knives.

A burst of lightning way off to the east lit the darkening afternoon followed by a burst of thunder, a shattering noise out here, for it seemed to echo across the land, rolling on for long minutes.

I settled down to wait. He would come, I knew that, but I'd be here for him, no matter how long it took.

St Louis: mid October 1804

One

Ryder stepped out of the general store and onto the boardwalk, but paused before he turned and headed for the hotel where he planned to meet Julia and Monique for lunch.

He'd rode into town with them, alongside their buggy, but they had parted ways on arriving in St Louis to attend to business of their own. Although Ryder was glad of it, because he'd no desire to accompany two women into dress shops or help choose rolls of fabric for dresses. Instead, he'd headed for the general store where he'd ordered supplies to take with him when he rode out.

He'd already purchased muskets and several good quality knives in both Alexandria and New Orleans along with powder and shot, all of which he planned to give away as gifts to Te'tukhe, Wesa'shangke and Ese-ggwe'na'a. For Paddake'e, he'd purchased pretty necklaces, mirrors, beaded jewelry, good woolen cloth, scarves and blankets. For himself, he'd purchased several good quality woolen blankets along with some thick cured furs to sleep on, as well as a new fur coat. The coat had been made of beaver and ermine skins, with a hood sewn into the back of it. Ryder hoped the coat would get him through the brutal northern winter.

He was thinking on all this when he heard raucous laughter coming from across the street. He turned to see five men being pushed in good humor out of a saloon by two working girls. The women were encouraging the men to take baths.

Fur trappers, Ryder thought. Men who had been

in the wild for some time by the looks of them. Their buffalo robes were filthy, their buckskin and fur boots worn and ragged. Three of the men wore fur hats roughly sewn with sinew. The other two men wore leather hats, one of which had three raven feathers sewn into the back of it while the other had porcupine quills pushed through the left brim.

Ryder recognized these men as halfbloods like himself and wondered what tribe they were from, even as they laughed again at the girls' insistence they take a bath. They all spoke French, as did the girls, but as Ryder turned away and crossed the street at a less muddy patch of road, aware he was now late for his lunch with Julia and Monique, he saw the men turn and head for the bath houses at the far end of town.

He turned his attention back to the lunch ahead of him, even though food was the last thing on Ryder's mind. He'd rather forego the lunch and make a start on following Madeleine and Harry, but that was impossible until he'd collected supplies and they wouldn't be ready for him until tomorrow. He'd no choice but stay at Julia's one more night, so he might as well try and enjoy the lunch.

*

They were sitting at a table near the open fire drinking hot chocolate. On a chair beside Julia were several large parcels, including the material she'd ordered from New Orleans several months ago to make dresses. It seemed Lily, Monique and Josette all needed new clothes, but Ryder wasn't really interested in the womanly purchases. Although he did notice the smaller package beside them and wondered if it were a gift for Lily's unborn babe.

Ryder had caught up with Lily the day before and although swollen with child and keeping well, he thought her aged since he saw her last. She spoke to him briefly of how happy she was, of Bryn's ambitions to one day own a ranch of his own, yet Ryder suspected Lily was homesick. She asked after Mourie and Perri, desperate for news of her father and younger sister and admitted to missing them, along with Madeleine and Harry. She also spoke of the money Madeleine had left for her and Bryn, if they ever decided to return to England.

Ryder made no judgment on Madeleine's generosity, although he'd been surprised by it. Perhaps she knew, as Ryder knew, that Lily might one day persuade Bryn to return to England.

He settled at the dining room table after kissing Julia on the cheek and nodding politely to Monique. He'd only met the girl yesterday, along with Josette, and although he liked them both well enough, indeed, he thought Josette a delight and well settled within Jeremiah and Esmeralda's household, Monique seemed far too worldly for a young girl.

He had no way of knowing of course, just how curious Monique and Josette had been to finally meet him, this man whom Madeleine had longed for, for so many years.

Julia felt Ryder's agitation as he ordered a coffee although she was taken aback, as she had been when he arrived at her ranch two days ago, by the sheer size of him. He had always been taller than most men, but Ryder was more muscular now than she remembered. Perhaps it was nothing more than her memories of him as a child of eight, compared to this powerfully built man who now sat before her. He looked well, but despite Ryder's obvious good health he had also aged in the past four years. Grey now licked at his temples and there were deeper lines around his eyes and mouth. Yet there was something in his eyes that made her uncomfortable. It was as if this tall, handsome, well-educated aristocratic who had always owned a resolute determination which one might call reckless, now seemed quieter, as though he were filled with such a deep sadness that his whole being pulsed with it.

He spoke of his purchases at the general store which would be ready for collection on the morrow, revealing his plans to ride out after breakfast the following morning.

Julia nodded, but didn't bother voicing her opinion on the matter because like Madeleine, she knew Ryder wouldn't listen. All she knew was that once he left, she wouldn't see him again for years and that was only if he were very lucky and didn't succumb to the savages and join his wife and son in having their scalps taken.

Two

He'd said his goodbyes the previous night, although Julia was still up at dawn to wish him well. She offered him biscuits, cured bacon, salted meat and corn picked from her fields, all wrapped in muslin cloths to take with him. While he carried them down to the stables to saddle his horse and pack everything onto his two packhorses, Julia insisted on making him a fresh pot of coffee.

As Ryder entered the stables, he was surprised to find a lantern glowing in the far stall. He was even more surprised to find his horse already saddled. He approached the horses cautiously, then saw Bryn putting bridles on the two packhorses. He turned as Ryder approached, then smiled.

"Couldn't let you do it alone, m'lord," he said softly, then turned back to run his hand over one of the horses. "You've got three of Julia's best mustangs here. They're good hardy animals, so they'll do you well enough out there in the wild."

Ryder was overwhelmed that Bryn was here, that he'd bothered to come and see him off. He knew well enough that the younger man had a busy working day on the ranch, so for him to come and be Ryder's groom one last time meant a lot.

But the two men also shared a bond that could never be erased and that was their love for Michael Woodley.

Bryn helped pack both packhorses. The muskets were placed to balance the weight, even though the weapons were well wrapped and tied securely in buckskin. As the men finished packing, Julia arrived with a tray of coffee and a few savory pies. As she set the tray down, Bryn excused himself.

"I'd best get moving. The lads in the bunkhouse will be up soon enough and they'll be wondering where I am," he said, but suddenly felt awkward as he stepped away, unsure whether to shake Ryder's hand. "I wish you all the best, m'lord."

Ryder felt Bryn's unease and stepped forward to embrace him. "I wish you and Lily the best as well," he said, his voice soft with emotion.

Bryn nodded, feeling his own emotions at this farewell. "Thank you, m'lord. I can't ask more than that, other than you keep safe," he paused, aware of how different Ryder was here, than he'd been in England.

Bryn was used to seeing Ryder dressed in the most fashionably tailored European clothes.

He knew him as Lord Benedict, 8th Earl Benedict, with all the privileges and wealth that went with being a member of the powerful Benedict family and an English aristocrat.

Ryder's friends and family were of the same social background, along with most of his business partners. He'd owned the best of everything, including horses, carriages and homes, filled with exquisite furnishings. He'd employed hundreds of staff to run his homes and businesses.

Yet he now stood before Bryn dressed in buckskin and knee high moccasins, his hair worn longer and a morning shadow on his strong jaw because he hadn't bothered to shave. And somehow, dressed like that, Ryder seemed more formidable than he'd been in London, surrounded by all the trappings of his wealth. There was now a dangerous rawness to him, as if this were his true self.

"Good luck, m'lord," Bryn said softly, then he

stepped away, nodding politely towards Julia before leaving.

Ryder felt an emotional pull as he watched the young man leave, as he remembered Bryn's stepfather, a man Ryder had loved like a brother.

He shook himself free of the memories then turned to Julia. She was watching him with some curiosity, thinking he owned a dark radiance now, a man in his mid-thirties, secure in his world. She wondered suddenly what his life might have been like, even if he'd still be alive, if Albert had returned him to the Wazhazhe village all those years ago. He'd run away from them so many times, and here he was, a grown man, heading out into the wild again. She smiled as she poured him a coffee, then nodded towards the food parcels.

"They'll keep you going for a little while," she said, as Ryder took mug of coffee from her with gratitude, even though Julia could see he was eager to get moving.

Aware of the big man's restless energy, she sipped her own cup of coffee, glancing at the buckskin leggings Ryder wore, along with the buckskin jacket and vest. Beneath these, Julia knew he would be wearing woolen undergarments to keep himself warm, as did most men.

By his saddle were two leather sheaths, one carrying his musket, the other his horse pistol. A leather sheath also hung from the leather belt around his waist and within it was a large butcher knife. He wore thick fur boots that reached to his knees and on the outside of both boots were more sheaths, holding more knives.

"Do take care," she said softly. "I told your wife I

thought her quite mad going off alone with Harry and two teenage girls, asking for nothing more than to get themselves scalped. Now here you are with every intention of doing the same."

Ryder laughed. "Rest assured I have no plans to get myself scalped," he said, putting the coffee cup aside to reach out to hug her. "Thank you for everything. I'll see you in a few years, I expect."

Julia kissed him on the cheek, standing on her toes to reach him, for he towered above her.

"I'll hold you to that," she said, then stood back as he took the reins and led the horses out of the stables. She walked with him to the barn doors then Ryder once more hugged her goodbye before swinging up into the saddle. Then he was kicking his horse on, the two packhorses behind him and was soon lost in the early morning shadows.

Three

By the time he'd reached the bustling frontier town of St Louis, the sun had already started to rise, the dawn sky marked with vivid streaks of yellows and reds. Off to his right lay the Mississippi River, with keelboats, pirogues and canoes berthed on its banks.

Several campfires lay nearby, most of them belonging to the men who owned the pirogues and canoes, but Ryder also recognized two men who'd brought him upriver from New Orleans. No doubt their keelboat would be leaving soon and making that journey back down the river, but he was glad he wouldn't be on it. He was happy to be heading into the wild, back to his roots, back to where he belonged.

As the wooden buildings of St Louis reared before him, Ryder recognized this was stunning country, yet so primitive, with most of it still in wilderness. But he knew that would change, not only because the Americans now claimed ownership of it, but because of their ambitious President.

The ink had barely dried on the Louisiana Purchase documentation before Jefferson organized an expedition force be sent across country, to find a passage through to the Pacific coast.

Ryder wondered how the President's men would get on when they came upon that vast wall of mountains which Madeleine called home. They were unlikely to find a way through, unless they had help from local tribes.

He thought suddenly of Jimmy Morven, one of his grooms at Diccon House. He didn't know Jimmy very well, he'd been a youth of nineteen when Ryder last spoke to him. But after reading the letters and documents in that secret drawer at Millbryne, Ryder knew that Jimmy had become close to Madeleine in those weeks after he'd gone missing. He'd come to America with her and Harry, along with Lily and Bryn. Now he was a member of that discovery expedition, heading into the vast Pacific Northwest, trying to find a way west on orders from the American President.

Sometimes Ryder felt a moment of resentment when he thought of Jimmy. Only because Jimmy had been there for Madeleine and Harry, when he could not. He trusted Madeleine enough to know she would never have taken Jimmy as a lover, not one of his servants, but the fact remained, whenever he thought of Madeleine and Jimmy together, it unsettled Ryder.

Jealousy perhaps? Of course it was. But until she could tell him about it, such thoughts lingered and often turned to anger.

Yet that anger was directed to one person only and that person was his brother.

No, not his brother, his cousin.

Jarryth Benedict. Damn him to hell.

*

Ryder left his horses and belongings at the livery, unwilling to leave his packhorses unattended outside the general store, even though it was just past dawn and the town lay quiet and empty. But it would raise itself soon enough and Ryder trusted no-one.

A few stores were just beginning to open for business, including a few eating places, but nothing else. Certainly not the whorehouses, saloons or bathhouses. They would open much later in the day.

He stepped towards Stewart's, hoping to be the first person there, as they were one of the biggest general stores to open early, which was the only reason Ryder had ordered his supplies from there. But as he pushed open the door, he was surprised to find eight people already inside. Two women stood at the long wooden counter and were being served by Letty Stewart, an attractive woman in her early fifties. She looked up as the door opened and smiled when she recognized Ryder.

"Angus is just out the back," she called in her soft Scottish lilt. "He won't be long."

Ryder nodded and glanced at the five other customers waiting on the far side of the room. A group of men, yet they looked vaguely familiar. Then he turned as Angus staggered through the back door carrying a large sack of beans.

"You're lucky to get this," he said in his broad Scottish brogue to the five men waiting for him. "It's the last of the stock until the keelboat arrives from New Orleans next week."

As he placed the sack on the counter he looked over and saw Ryder. "Won't be long," he called out. "I have everything you asked for."

Ryder nodded, just as the two women at the counter turned to look at him.

"Why Lord Benedict, how lovely to see you again," the older of the women said. "I do hope Julia is in town with you? Although perhaps not, for this is an ungodly hour, is it not? We're setting off for New Orleans this morning and have passage on a keelboat leaving within the hour. Perhaps on our return in the summer, you would do us the honor of dining with us."

Ryder knew who she was of course. He'd met her briefly when he was in town yesterday with Julia and Monique. But he was surprised to hear his title spoken aloud, as Julia hadn't used it when introducing him. Ryder bowed his head, formally acknowledging the woman, but also to hide his annoyance. Why would she use his title in such a public place? It wasn't necessary.

"Unfortunately I cannot, for I am also leaving this morning to follow my wife and son west. Perhaps when I am next in town," he said, aware of the woman's barely suppressed disappointment.

Ryder glanced at her younger companion and saw the older woman's likeness there and understood at once that this was mother and daughter. But he was well used to this.

He'd had years of dealing with ambitious women from his bachelor days in London, long before he met Madeleine. He'd always done his best to avoid them, although ambitious mothers always managed to seek him out.

"Well, we shall look forward to it, Lord Benedict. Please allow me to wish you all the best on your travels," she said.

Ryder bowed his head again, politely, before the woman and daughter returned to their business with Letty. But the encounter left Ryder wondering how they'd come to know about his title. It wouldn't have come from Julia, as she understood only too well his desire for anonymity.

Perhaps one of her ranch hands had heard Bryn or Lily address him formally.

Ryder shrugged his annoyance off, yet he felt his

aristocratic lineage served no purpose out here and if anything, attracted unwanted attention. Indeed, he saw it now, in the curious glances of the five men on the other side of the room. Ryder ignored them and headed to the open fire to warm himself when he suddenly remembered where he'd seen them before.

Those five men were the fur trappers he'd seen yesterday, being evicted from a saloon by two whores. They had been in desperate need of a bath then. Now they looked quite different. Their filthy clothing and moccasins had been replaced with new buckskin and fur boots, similar to what he was wearing. Their faces no longer bore a layer of grime and their hair had been cut and their faces freshly shaven.

He leaned against the chimney breast and dismissed the men from his mind, thinking instead of the journey ahead of him and the woman and small boy who held his heart so securely when someone spoke to him, interrupting his thoughts.

"Excuse me, Mr Benedict?" a man asked in guttural, heavily accented English, his voice low and husky with age.

Ryder turned and found a man looking at him intently, a tall man well into his seventies from the withered, aged look of him. Ryder said nothing, just returned his gaze, recognizing him as one of the five men.

"My apologies for interrupting you, but am I indeed speaking to Ryder Benedict, lately of London?"

Ryder was momentarily startled by this, but then, gossip travelled fast in these parts.

"What business do you claim with him, sir?" he

asked, as the man's four companions strolled across to join him.

Ryder glanced at their weapons, but their muskets were secure within buckskin sheaths held across their shoulders and their knives held in sheaths attached to their belts. These men were not killers. They were hunters, trappers of fur.

"Again, my apologies for disturbing you," the old man said in heavily accented English. Then he shook his head in frustration before switching to speak in French. "May we talk in French? My English is so poor."

Ryder shrugged. "What's this about? Do I know you?"

The old man looked over at his companions, before turning back to Ryder. "Well, that is yet to be seen, however, I believe you will be glad of this most opportune meeting."

He paused at the look of irritation that passed over Ryder's face and said nothing for a moment, then he smiled and spoke in rapid French.

"You're an arrogant young pup I must say, so different to how I imagined you. But know this *monsieur*, it's in your best interests to hear what I have to say, as we share a mutual acquaintance," he paused at the sudden stillness of Ryder, then laughed softly. "If I tell you that our acquaintance knows you as Mi'wasa, would I have your attention?"

Ryder looked at him in astonishment. "What is this?" he asked slowly, replying in French, feeling a knot of fear in his belly. "Who are you?"

"Who we are," the old man replied, "is perhaps not as important as who we know. However, you may regard us as friends *monsieur,* for we mean you no harm. Indeed, we have news regarding that mutual acquaintance which I think will greatly please you."

"What the hell are you talking about," Ryder asked, his voice low and threatening as he lost his patience, having no time for riddles with strangers.

The man laughed again and as Ryder glanced across at his companions, he was surprised to find the four men looking at him with something like astonishment.

"What I'm talking about," the old man said, "is news concerning the whereabouts of your wife and son."

in the wild: mid October 1804

The lightning flashed overhead, lighting the gloomy afternoon as though it were dawn, followed by the *boom* of thunder, the ground seeming to vibrate as the sound echoed out across the darkening landscape.

I lowered my head instinctively, even as I heard the horses below me, distressed and unsettled, but at least they were hobbled and safe and had some shelter between the walls of rock.

Harry and the girls would also be frightened as the storm raged above us, but I took comfort in knowing they were warm and dry in the teepee.

As for myself, I was safe enough for now and grateful for the sailcloth as I lay concealed beneath it. I pulled it further over my head to keep my face and musket dry, although my clothes were already saturated.

I looked out into that darkening gloom and watched as another flash of lightning streaked across the sky, illuminating everything around me. I closed my eyes instinctively against that white hot light, but not before I saw his shadow less than half a mile away from where I lay.

A rider, with a packhorse trailing behind him, was making his way slowly along the riverbank and in that extraordinary flash of lighting, I'd seen him lean over to look at the wet earth.

Of course, I knew what he was doing. He was following our tracks. But they were easy enough to find, even in this storm, because the hooves of our five horses left great gaping holes in the soft wet sand of the riverbank.

But as I watched, I felt a real, terrible fear. This

man had followed us relentlessly for several days for reasons known only to him, with skills that matched my own. He was someone to be feared and while I waited to see the face of this enemy, I thought of what Ese-ggwe'na'a had said to me once, about hunting and protecting myself in the wild.

better to face your enemy Esa-mogo'ne', then be hunted in fear. But when you face your hunter, be prepared to kill

Oh, I was prepared to kill. I was tired of this game, of little sleep, of continuously watching our backs, of trying to think why this man followed us.

Another streak of lighting followed by another *boom* of thunder and I saw his horse rear in terror. But the man was a good rider because he held on, bringing the animal under control before kicking the horse on. Then he turned and rode straight towards the boulders. Straight towards me

I could see him clearly now. His long dark hair was plastered down his back from the rain, yet he wore a turban on his head. I recognized it as a ceremonial headdress, for I'd seen such hats before on my trip to St Louis with Ryder all those years ago. They were usually worn by the Potawatomi, Pawnee and Wazhazhe. Round objects, not unlike Poongatse and Wannge'e's bowler hats, these turbans were made of pure otter fur and usually decorated with dyed seed beads or eagle feathers, the animal's tail left to hang down the back. Although this man's hat bore no such decoration. Not even the otter tail remained. Instead, he'd fastened a wide leather belt around the hat, a massive silver buckle worn in the front of it.

I thought him arrogant that he would wear such a hat, unless of course, he was a Chief. That he was travelling alone was also unusual, as it was rare to see anyone alone out here in this country.

As he came closer, as he rode towards the boulders, I became aware of his energy, a lethal powerful thing and knew this man was a loner. He needed no-one to compliment him, nor keep him company.

When he rode within twenty feet of me, another shaft of lightning lit the evening sky as though it were day and I saw his buckskin clothing was well worn, as were his knee high moccasins. On his back he carried a sheath of arrows and attached to his saddle was a bow. Beside the bow were two sheaths. One held a musket, the other a horse pistol.

I was surprised to see he rode astride a saddle. Not bareback then, which suggested he owned European connections. A halfbreed perhaps, able to live between two cultures, two worlds, a man who owned two destinies, like Ryder.

As though aware he was being watched, the man suddenly reined in his horse and looked up towards the boulder where I lay. He was astute enough to know that someone would be waiting for him and my boulder was the highest vantage point from which to see the country below. Yet strangely, he didn't move to arm himself. Instead he turned the horse to look behind him to make quite sure he was alone and as he did so, I saw the glint of a blade. I also saw two other buckskin sheaths attached to the belt worn around his waist and a sheath sewn to the outside of each of his moccasins. Three of the sheaths held knives. He carried the fourth knife in his right hand.

I felt the adrenaline flood through my body as I watched him and knew this man to be a killer. He lifted his face within that murky mist as though smelling the air. But I knew he'd already smelled our woodsmoke. The scent was drawing him straight towards our camp.

He kicked his horse on but I dared not move, not yet, not until he came closer.

But that's when I noticed it.

There was something achingly familiar about him.

It was there in the shape of his shoulders, in his powerful body, in the way he rode the horse, in the way he moved. Yet there was also something terrifying about him as well and I suddenly thought of Harry and the two Bannock girls just below me in the teepee and realized our vulnerability.

When he was almost beneath me I finally moved, pushing aside the sailcloth to jump to a boulder directly below me with the quickness of a cat before jumping to another one, until I stood just above him.

He reined in his horse and even in that gloomy afternoon I saw that he was indeed a halfbreed. He owned the dark stain of tattoos on his face, but he also wore European clothes along with his buckskin. A blue linen shirt, a muslin scarf draped around his neck, heavy silver jewelry around his wrists and within each pierced ear. All these things had been traded with the Spanish or French, or taken from dead men.

I aimed my musket at him as he sat astride his horse. But as he looked up at me, as he raised his hands to reveal the knife and show he was no threat to me, I slowly lowered my musket, staring at him in astonishment. Because under the turban I saw a handsome face, indeed, a well-loved face and then he was grinning at me before bowing his head, formally acknowledging me.

"You have become lazy since I saw you last, Esa-mogo'ne'," he called out in French, his voice a deep, pleasant baritone, not unlike Ryder's.

Then he laughed aloud and threw his right leg over the saddle and jumped easily to the ground, his eyes never leaving my face as he placed the knife back in the sheath on his right boot. For a big man, he moved with an easy grace.

"I've been tracking you for days," he said, taking a step towards me. "And luckily for me, unlike the old days, you don't appear too concerned about covering your tracks," he laughed again then raised his eyebrows as I continued to stand and stare at him in bewilderment.

"Oh come, Esa-mogo'ne'," he said in good humor. "This is a fine welcome for your brother-in-law!"

Then I laughed with absolute delight as I looked down into the handsome face of Ryder's Ugákhpa half-brother, Te'tukhe.

St Louis: mid October 1804

They sat at one of the rough sawn tables at the rear of the room near the fire. The building was a single story wooden cabin and was part saloon, part restaurant, and had just opened to serve breakfast.

It was also one of the less desirable places in town, but the only one to serve a drink this early in the day. For the moment, Ryder and the five men were the only customers, except for the owner who stood behind the long wooden plank that made up the bar, washing glasses in a bucket of soapy water.

A small tumbler of raw, eye watering whisky sat before each man. But Ryder ignored it, preferring to watch the men who sat opposite him, wanting a clear head for what they had to say.

When a young girl appeared from a door at the back of the room and approached them, encouraged by the man behind the bar to offer them a service other than whisky, Ryder was surprised when the men declined.

At least they shared the same morals. Like Ryder, they had no care to share a bed with the girl as she looked ill, her face and body puffy and swollen with disease. In any case, she didn't seem too bothered by their rejection and wandered away, back through the door, no doubt to seek rest where she could find it. As the door closed behind her, Ryder returned his gaze to the five men, who in turn watched him.

Two of them were about his age. Two others were in their forties. The fifth, the old man, was easily in his early seventies. He was wizened with age, his face, neck and hands burned like leather from a lifetime of being outdoors.

"So! What's this news you have regarding my wife and son?" Ryder asked impatiently in French, allowing his voice and manner to reveal his feelings.

Clearly he thought these men nothing more than opportunists. But against his better judgment, he felt compelled to stay in this filthy place and hear what they had to say, because he was desperate for any news regarding Madeleine and Harry. Still, he glanced behind him and around the empty room expecting thugs to appear to rob him, acquaintances of these men. But they were all alone, other than the man behind the bar.

The old man took a sip from his tumbler, almost choking as the raw liquor hit the back of his throat then he set the small glass down, wiping the back of his hand across his mouth and looked at Ryder for a long moment.

Ryder frowned and pushed aside his own tumbler, unwilling to drink it's dubious contents.

"Please speak plainly *monsieur*, for I'm at a loss to understand any of this."

The older man nodded, then sat back in his chair. "Of course," he said slowly, also speaking in French.

"But perhaps it's best we introduce ourselves first. Then you will better understand the reasons why we sought you out. Indeed, we have much to thank that woman in the store who spoke your name aloud *monsieur*, for had she not, alas, we would have gone our separate ways and you would have been none the wiser."

He turned to the two older men sitting on his left. "Allow me to introduce my sons, Didier-Édouard and Armand-Baptiste. They are my sons from my first marriage. Their mother and my wife, Angèle,

214

passed away many years ago."

He paused before turning to the man sitting on Ryder's left. "This is Chahn-yah'-hoo, my son from my second marriage. His mother is Ska'zica, a woman from the Lakota Sioux. She's waiting for us in the north, near the Lakota village, where I've made my home for the past thirty-five years."

He turned towards the fifth man who sat on the other side of Ryder. "And this is Wakanta."

Ryder looked at each man, yet they were strangers to him. He turned back to the old man who shrugged in typically Gaelic fashion as though he were disappointed.

"Well, some years have passed after all, so I can understand you not recognizing him. Well, no matter," he said, aware of Ryder's irritation.

"But perhaps I'll have your interest if you know we ride to the Wazhazhe village from here. I thought it opportune to pay a visit to those good people since our business brought us this far south. Although in all truth I admit it's been a lifetime since I was there, indeed, Hubert Lemoine was still alive when last I visited the Wazhazhe people," he paused at the look of bewilderment which passed over Ryder's face.

"Ah, at last, a name you recognize. I'm grateful for it *monsieur*, for it means neither of us need waste precious time explaining familial connections. So, please, allow me to introduce myself," he leaned towards Ryder, putting his elbows on the table.

"I am Allard Lemoine, first cousin to Hubert and Sébastien Lemoine," he smiled as Ryder looked at him incredulous.

"I see from your reaction that Hubert never spoke of me. Well, no matter. You were a boy of eight when you saw Hubert last," he smiled, even as Ryder searched his face, looking for features that claimed some resemblance to his beloved Hubert.

"But know this, Mi'wasa. My father was brother to Hubert and Sébastien's father. I was raised with Hubert and Sébastien from the time we were infants at our mothers' breasts," he paused, then nodded towards Wakanta.

"You do not recognize Hubert's youngest son, born to a young Wazhazhe woman not long after your own mother's death. But understandable I think, for you were but a child yourself. When you left the Wazhazhe to go and live at the Corrigan ranch, Wakanta wasn't even a year old."

Ryder turned to look at the man beside him. This was the child born to the young girl Hubert took as wife, after Ryder's own mother died in childbirth with Wesa'shangke.

Allard sat back in his chair. "When Wakanta's mother died a few years later, long after you'd left for England, Hubert brought his three sons north to live with me. When he eventually decided to return to the Wazhazhe, Te'tukhe and Wesa'shangke left with him, but Wakanta remained with me. My wife was happy to care for him as he was just a child, younger than you were when you left the Wazhazhe for the Corrigan's ranch. Because of it, I've always thought of him as my own."

Ryder thought the young man a tall, moody looking character and try as he might, he could see nothing of Hubert in him. Everything he owned came from his Wazhazhe mother for he had her coal black eyes, her high cheekbones and generous mouth.

He was dressed similarly to the other halfblood,

the Lakota Sioux named Chahn-yah'-hoo. Both wore beautifully beaded necklaces and plaited rawhide bracelets around their wrists. Their hair was long, almost to their waists, yet on the left side of their heads both wore a thick braid. Their ears were pierced with a piece of silver wire and from this, dangling almost to their shoulders, were several exquisite feathers of vibrant reds, blues and greens.

By comparison, the two French-Canadians were dressed plainly with little jewelry, no tattoos or piercings, their hair worn short, having been cut yesterday before their enforced bath by the saloon girls.

Ryder reached for the glass of whisky. He no longer cared whether the glass was clean, or if the whisky was pure, because all these memories were flooding back. Memories he'd repressed as a child in order to cope with his new life in England and his emotionally cold father, Torrance Benedict.

But now he remembered a young girl, who could have been no older than sixteen or seventeen, who Hubert took as wife after Wazhingka died. She'd been so young and so overwhelmed in caring for newborn Wesa'shangke, as well as four-year old Te'tukhe and six-year old Ryder that she'd let the two older boys run wild. She'd had no authority over them, especially when Hubert left for months at a time to trap for furs, leaving Ryder and Te'tukhe to fend for themselves.

But there was something else that Ryder remembered. Something raw, even after all these years.

It was that all too familiar lurch in his belly as he remembered Hubert riding away, leaving him alone at the Corrigan ranch. This from a man who'd been a father figure to him for more than six years, a man whom Ryder had loved with a passion, a great bear of a man whom Ryder had wanted so desperately to be his own father.

"He often spoke of you," Allard said, as if he knew what Ryder was thinking. "I know of the battle he fought with your English father, to keep you at the Wazhazhe village," he paused as Ryder took another gulp of the whisky and Allard was surprised to see that the big man's hands were trembling.

When Ryder set the tumbler back on the table, he nodded slowly.

"Yet, he betrayed me," he said. "He left me at that ranch like he was dropping off a piece of garbage. He knew I loved him, yet I never saw him again."

There was an awkward silence around the table, then Allard leaned forward, aggressively.

"Know this Mi'wasa, my cousin loved you like his own son. When he left you at the Corrigan ranch he was a broken man, but Hubert wasn't someone who easily showed his feelings and certainly not to a child he loved," he paused, leaning back.

"Shall I tell you the reason you never saw him again? Why he never returned to the Corrigan ranch? Because he was with me, in the north. He was so stricken at having lost the battle to keep you, a battle he'd waged for almost two years with Torrance Benedict, that he didn't return to the Wazhazhe people for over a year," he shook his head in grief.

"He may have left you behind at the Corrigan ranch but he also left Te'tukhe, Wesa'shangke and Wakanta behind as well, in the care of his young wife and her family," he paused at the look of surprise on Ryder's face.

"Ah, I see you didn't know that. Well, my cousin had his faults Mi'wasa, but he loved his family. He loved his four sons. He loved your mother. He loved Wakanta's mother. But know this for a fact, because if he abandoned you at the Corrigan ranch, then he also abandoned the rest of his family. Although I doubt Te'tukhe, Wesa'shangke or Wakanta remember it because they were so young, just little boys, as indeed you were," he shook his head, looking at Ryder in despair.

"Hubert fought a war with your English father, who the Wazhazhe called Mi'khidh, for over two years. It almost destroyed him, because he knew that Torrance Benedict was always going to win. Not only because he was your biological father, but because he had the money to fight it in court. But for two years Hubert managed to keep you in the Wazhazhe village, until the day came when he couldn't. But he always loved you, which I would have thought obvious. Indeed, I'm surprised you ever doubted it."

There was silence for a long moment, then Ryder shook his head. "No, it wasn't obvious to me. What did I know of men and their feelings? I was a child of eight. All I knew was that I waited for Hubert every day for over a year, right up until the day I left for England," he felt the pain of that day again, as he left the ranch in the company of his father's man, Bernard Fahey.

"I had no way of knowing he went north. As for his family, I only knew of Sébastien," he shook his head, as though clearing it of memories.

"Yet why are you here, when your home is in the north? And who is this person who knows the whereabouts of my wife and son?"

Allard smiled. "Ah, now we come to it at last. In answer to your first question, we are here to trade our furs for gold, because gold lasts a lot longer than French francs or American dollars. Indeed, we came here on the advice of friends who sell their furs in New Orleans. They get a better price for them down there, but we've no plans to travel that far south," he paused and took a sip of his whisky, watching Ryder with those intense dark eyes, as though intrigued by him.

"As for your wife and son, in all truth we never met them, but we heard of them through our mutual acquaintance. That woman in the store, by mentioning your name, has saved you a great deal of unnecessary travel. If I heard right, you told her you were heading west. I take it you were planning on heading to the Wazhazhe village? Well, if I tell you there's few people left there that you know, I might persuade you to head north instead, because the Wazhazhe lost hundreds in an outbreak of pox four years ago," he paused at the look of distress on Ryder's face.

"Have no fear, your brothers are alive and well, but like Wakanta, they no longer live with the Wazhazhe. Wesa'shangke chooses to live with the Comanche, with Sébastien's family. As for Te'tukhe, well he goes where he pleases, but he's a man who'll never settle," Allard sat back and smiled.

"Perhaps I should mention that we stayed with a band of Kansa on our way south several weeks ago," he said, slowly.

"One of them spoke of a young French woman they'd met, who was travelling with a small boy and two teenage girls. Most astonishingly, this young woman spoke their dialect and told them she was heading to the Omaha to winter over there. She spoke of meeting her husband there, a halfblood, whose mother had been a full blooded Ugákhpa, his father English, although he'd grown up with the Wazhazhe people," he paused again as Ryder stared at him in bewilderment, his face suddenly pale.

"I take it that halfblood is you Mi'wasa and this woman is your wife," Allard said softly.

"Although we only know that because there was another man travelling with us who overheard the conversation and who bothered to ask the woman's name. Tell me, does the name Esa-mogo'ne' mean anything to you?"

Ryder nodded, feeling physically ill, thinking of Madeleine somewhere well north of here, traveling all alone with his son and two teenage girls.

"Esa-mogo'ne' is the name the Bannock gave my wife," he said very quietly.

Allard nodded. "Well, shall I tell you that on hearing that name our mutual acquaintance left his share of the furs with us and headed north the very next morning to follow your wife to the Omaha?" he paused at the look of astonishment that passed over Ryder's face.

"It seems he has some loyalty towards her Mi'wasa, because he couldn't bear to think of her out there in the wild alone. He also wanted to find out why you weren't with her and perhaps it was that, more than anything else, which drove him north, making him leave behind everything he'd worked so hard for, for over a year."

Ryder sat back in his chair, aware of the other four men watching him.

But he knew what Allard was going to say.

He could have said it for him.

"You know, of course, who I speak of. Because there's only one man alive who is that reckless and that loyal," Allard said softly.

Ryder nodded, his voice barely a whisper as he replied. "My brother, Te'tukhe."

in the wild: mid October 1804

Madeleine jumped off the boulders to land easily on the damp ground below, to where Te'tukhe stood watching her.

"How is this possible?" she cried in astonishment, shouting to be heard above the wind and rain. "That you are here? That you knew I was back in this country?"

Te'tukhe looked at her as the rain battered her lovely face. She was as beautiful as he remembered, yet now there was a maturity to her, along with a haunting stillness. She was also too thin, with dark shadows circling her eyes.

"I think fate, or destiny, has played a stronger hand in this Esa-mogo'ne', than either you or I will understand," he said, leaning towards her. "But come, where is your camp? Let us take shelter from this foul weather and talk around the warmth of a fire. I know you have a teepee because the Kansa told me they traded one with you."

"The Kansa?" Madeleine asked in bewilderment. "But what have they to do with this?"

"Everything," Te'tukhe said. "Do we have far to go? Do you want to ride with me?"

Madeleine shook her head. "Our camp is sheltered within these boulders. You have but a short walk."

Te'tukhe turned back to his horse and reached for three rabbit carcasses tied behind his saddle. He held them out to Madeleine. "They will get us through the night I think, but on the morrow, I will go hunting."

Madeleine took the rabbits with gratitude but as

she turned away, she was suddenly aware of Te'tukhe's hesitation and wasn't surprised when he reached out to stop her, even as another shaft of lightning burst across the sky.

"I need to know if he lives, Esa-mogo'ne'," he said, his voice full of anguish. "The Kansa said you hoped to meet him at the Omaha, but I know that's not true. I know what he thought of you, how much he loved you and never would he have allowed you to ride out alone in this country, not with two teenage girls and a little boy who I believe must be his son. So, tell me the truth of it. Does he still live?"

Madeleine closed her eyes then nodded, her voice hoarse with longing and fatigue. "With all my heart, I believe he lives, just as I believe I shall see him at the Omaha village," she paused and looked at a man she loved like a brother. "Indeed, I pray he comes Te'tukhe, because I don't think I can leave the Omaha without him. Sometimes I feel my strength running out, my body sick from not being with him. I thought myself stronger than this, but if he does not come, I know I will be lost, as I was lost in England."

Te'tukhe said nothing for a moment then he moved to take her in his arms. And in that embrace, which was so like Ryder's, yet also nothing like it, Madeleine felt herself collapse into his hard male strength, the only man in all these years since Ryder disappeared that she'd been able to share her grief.

But Te'tukhe understood her pain, because he and Ryder also loved each other. They'd been childhood allies, helping to keep each other alive after their mother's death. So for those few precious minutes, as Te'tukhe held her, Madeleine gave herself up to her grief, allowing her tears to mingle with the rain.

*

Harry was fast asleep in Poongatse's arms when Madeleine and Te'tukhe crawled into the teepee. Wannge'e looked up in astonishment, while Poongatse let out a soft cry of surprise.

It had been five years since Te'tukhe and Wesa'shangke were guests of the Shoshone and Bannock in their winter village on the Snake River Plain. With their scalp locks, piercings and tattoos, no-one could ignore the two Wazhazhe brothers during that bitterly cold winter of 1799-1800.

Te'tukhe didn't remember the girls. They had been children then, no more than nine and ten years old.

But both girls remembered him.

Madeleine introduced them, before turning to Harry. "Mi'wasa's son. He's our only child."

Te'tukhe knelt on the buckskin sheets and took off his turban, allowing his wet hair to fall about his shoulders.

Madeleine thought he'd changed little in four years. He was still an extraordinary looking man, with many similarities shared with Ryder. But with each man having the same mother, they both owned that dark rugged look of the Ugákhpa people.

Yet at thirty-two years of age, just two years younger than Ryder, Madeleine also saw that Te'tukhe still owned that restless energy. This was a man who would bow to no man, who preferred to ride alone, who had been taking care of himself since he was four years old.

He peered down at the sleeping child. "He's a fine boy, Esa-mogo'ne'," he said, speaking in the dialect of the Dhegiha Sioux. "I can see he's my brother's child, indeed, he's Mi'wasa's double." His voice was soft with wonder. "How old is he?"

"He was three years old in August," she replied in the same language, although she was startled by Te'tukhe's compliment, because he rarely gave them.

"He's tall for his age, but then you and Mi'wasa are tall," he said.

Madeleine looked down at her sleeping son. Harry was tall for a three year old, but his little body was strong and well defined. She'd let his hair grow since they left Julia's, so now it hung long, just past his shoulders. With his skin burned olive brown from the summer sun, he looked like any other child born in the wild.

"What do you call him?" Te'tukhe asked.

"His English name is Harris, but everyone calls him Harry. The girls have given him a Bannock name. They call him *deide'wesa*."

Te'tukhe smiled. "*Little Bear*," he said in French. "It's a good name."

He glanced over at Wannge'e and Poongatse, unaware until then that both girls were staring openly at him. But on meeting his lovely black eyes they lowered their gaze, but not before Madeleine saw their admiration for this handsome halfbreed.

"Does the boy speak the dialect of the Dhegiha Sioux?" he asked, before nodding towards the girls. "Do they?"

Madeleine nodded. "They know enough, as I've been teaching Harry his father's dialect for some time, along with *bannaite'*. The girls have picked up some of it, but they're not fluent."

Te'tukhe nodded. "Then we shall speak in their own dialect. I remember the *bannaite'* well enough."

She smiled, suddenly remembering how she and Te'tukhe used to loathe each other. He'd thought she was dangerous, that Ryder should stay away from her. She'd thought him arrogant and hard. But once they'd got to know each other, they'd enjoyed a warm friendship. Indeed, Te'tukhe wasn't all arrogance and hardness, he did own some of Ryder's easy charm. But one thing these Ugákhpa brothers all shared was that same self-assuredness. She thought perhaps that came from their childhood, from losing their mother at such a young age, by learning to be totally self-reliant.

Madeleine watched as Te'tukhe looked back at the girls, seeing him take in their youth and character in one easy glance. It made Madeleine think of Ryder. She'd seen him look that way at people many times but just thinking on it, remembering the easy beauty of him, was like a knife through her heart.

Unsettled by the memory, she moved to throw more kindling on the fire just as another boom of thunder burst overhead followed by the terrified screams of the horses outside.

"I'll go check on them," Te'tukhe said, putting his turban back over his wet hair. But before he left, he picked up the rabbit carcasses to take them outside to butcher. Then he was gone, back out into the rain.

"It was Te'tukhe following us?" Wanngc'c asked in surprise.

Madeleine nodded. "I don't understand it myself yet, but let's get into dry clothes before he gets back."

When Te'tukhe returned, he passed the chunks of

meat to Madeleine who had a pot of water boiling near the fire. She added herbs and root vegetables and as the girls joined her in preparing the meal, Te'tukhe pulled off his wet clothes, standing naked with his back to them, taking the dry blanket Madeleine offered him with gratitude, leaving his clothes and other belongings to dry by the fire.

He was intrigued by the sailcloths, how the material had hardened with linseed oil and its success in keeping her belongings mostly dry. As he settled by the fire to warm himself, as the girls moved back to sit beside Harry who still slept soundly, Madeleine reached for her bag of pipes. She offered him one of her spares, three of which she had purchased in London before she left, but Te'tukhe declined her offer, choosing instead his own pipe, along with a pouch of his own tobacco.

"I find the tobacco sold by Europeans not to my liking," he said, stuffing the bowl full of the herb. "Although I'm surprised you still have a love for it," he said, smiling. "I thought the civilized world which my brother swept you away to might have cured you of the habit."

Madeleine laughed. "I'm afraid the taste I acquired for it while living with the Bannock will never leave me. Besides, it brings me comfort and reminds me of happier times."

Te'tukhe nodded as he took a brand from the fire and lit the tobacco in the bowl of his pipe. Then he turned to her, his coal black eyes intense and asked her what she'd been dreading.

"Where is he, Esa-mogo'ne'? Why isn't he here with you?"

*

Heavy rain battered the sides of the teepee as Madeleine wondered how best to answer him. She glanced across at Poongatse and Wannge'e as they discreetly turned away to work quietly, sorting through their provisions of food to see what they needed. She knew the girls weren't bothered about joining them to smoke pipes, because they'd never acquired a taste for tobacco. Nor were they bothered about sharing a conversation between Madeleine and her brother-in-law, because clearly they'd be discussing Ryder.

Madeleine looked back at Te'tukhe, finding his gaze on her, and thought his dark brooding eyes like the glitter of dark obsidian in the light of the fire. She found him intimidating in that moment, like a hawk flying over prey, or one of the big cats that roamed the high mountain country, all sharp claws and fangs, waiting, ready to pounce in all their quickness. He wanted the truth and would settle for nothing less, but how did she tell him she didn't know where Ryder was.

Te'tukhe was well travelled and a man experienced in life, but he'd never been to New Orleans, let alone London. How did she explain it?

Madeleine also knew that Te'tukhe rarely trusted people, so the last thing she needed now was for him to think she was holding something back, or worse, that she was lying. Yet as she held his gaze, she saw so much of Ryder's honesty and stubbornness in his face that for the second time that night, she thought her heart might break. Then the answer came to her. Te'tukhe was half Ugákhpa, yet he'd been raised with the Wazhazhe people, giving him a double understanding of the afterlife and the spirit world. If nothing else, Madeleine knew Te'tukhe would understand the evil that had been Jarryth Benedict.

But would Ryder want her discussing his English family? Perhaps not, but Te'tukhe deserved something of the truth. He deserved that much at least, after coming so far to find her.

"I'm not sure where to start, or how to tell it," she said, suddenly switching to speak in French as she once again met Te'tukhe's dark eyes. "However, shall we continue in French, or your own Dhegiha Sioux? Either way, this conversation remains private between you and me and no-one else need know of it, but you."

Te'tukhe nodded. "We shall speak in French, if you desire it," he said softly.

"Well then," Madeleine began. "In answer to your question brother, I don't truly know where he is. He was taken from me more than two years ago and although I did everything I could to find him, as did his family and friends, it came to nothing because in all that time, we've heard not one word from him."

She began to tell him a little of Jarryth, a man filled with bitterness and hatred, bred into him by parents seeking revenge. She spoke of the note which arrived that fateful morning and of Ryder leaving the house, thinking he was going to meet his cousin, Rupert Petherington, but meeting the brutality of Jarryth and his men instead.

"We never saw him again. All we know for certain is that he was put aboard a ship, bound for only God knows where. It's as if he disappeared off the very face of the earth but wherever he is in the world, I know he still lives. I believe that with every breathe I own."

Te'tukhe said nothing for a long moment, then nodded slowly. "This news distresses me Esa-mogo'ne', but I take comfort in knowing you think him still alive."

"The loss of him almost broke me, indeed, sometimes I cannot bear to face the dawn each day, not knowing where he is or what has happened to him. But after two years of waiting I needed to come home, to return to the Bannock and try and heal, yet I take comfort in knowing I'll see him one day. I believe that with all my heart."

Te'tukhe said nothing more but as Madeleine watched him, she saw the grief in his face. She leaned towards him.

"Yet how is it that you're here, Te'tukhe? How did you find me?"

He took several puffs of the pipe then turned to watch the white smoke drift upwards, towards the hole in the top of the teepee. A draft of wind blew in, along with a few drops of rain, yet the chamber was warm from the heat of the fire.

"As I said to you before, Esa-mogo'ne'," he said, looking back at her. "I think some strange hand of fate has brought us together. But first let me explain the part I've played in all of this, although you will not like some of it," he paused to cross his legs, before he carried on.

"Four years ago, just months after you and Mi'wasa left Wesa'shangke and I at the Wazhazhe on your way east to St Louis, smallpox came to our village. We were a tribe of some six thousand people, but when the pox was done with us, more than two thousand lay dead. It spared no-one. Newborns lay dead alongside the elderly. Families were destroyed. Friends and lovers were lost and among them were those whom Mi'wasa, Wesa'shangke and I grew up with. So many perished."

He paused to take another puff on his pipe, his head lowered, but Madeleine offered him no pity, nor sympathy, for she knew he would welcome neither.

"To escape such despair, Wesa'shangke and I rode west to the Comanche. We lived with them for over a year, until my brother decided to make his life there with Sébastien Lemoine and his family. Sébastien has many grandchildren now and even great-grandchildren, although his mind is lost in the past," he shrugged as he met her gaze.

"I had no desire to settle, so I headed north to see my father's cousin, Allard Lemoine. Like my own good father and Sébastien, Allard has spent most of his life in the wild trapping furs, but unlike Sébastien and Hubert, he prefers the colder climates of the north. He has a home up in the hills some miles east of the Hŭŋkpapȟa, one of the seven tribes which make up the Lakota Sioux," he glanced back at Madeleine.

"But there was another reason why I rode to the Lakota Sioux. It was to meet another man. You may have heard Mi'wasa speak of him. He goes by the name of Wakanta."

Madeleine shook her head. "I've never heard that name."

Te'tukhe shrugged. "Well no matter, for in fact Ryder and Wakanta barely knew each other and share not one drop of familial blood. Indeed, Wakanta was younger than your son when Mi'wasa saw him last," he saw the look of bewilderment on Madeleine's face and smiled.

"Wakanta is my younger brother. We share the same father, but different mothers. When his Wazhazhe mother died, Hubert took us all north to visit with Allard. Wakanta stayed there, rather than return with us to our own lands and the Wazhazhe. Because of it, he is almost a stranger to me. But I wanted to meet him again, to see what kind of man he has become."

He paused again, then shrugged. "I liked him well enough. He is a man of twenty-seven years now. We spent the past year together, trapping beaver in the wild, along with Allard and two of his sons. On our way south to St Louis to trade our furs for gold and weapons, we ran into the Kansa."

He stopped and looked at Madeleine and smiled at the look of surprise on her face.

"I see you know them also. You'll be amused, I think, to hear we shared their camp for a night. It was there that I overhead one of their young men talking of having met a young French woman, travelling north with a little boy and two teenage girls. When I asked the Kansa the name of this woman, they said she went by the name of Esa-mogo'ne'."

Madeleine uttered a gasp of astonishment, even as Te'tukhe nodded.

"I was astonished to hear this. I hardly dared to believe it was true, that you were back in this country after all these years. But I was puzzled as to why you were travelling alone and knew that something must have happened to Mi'wasa, so I left my furs with my cousin and followed you north."

He paused, frowning, looking across at her. "You

know me well enough Esa-mogo'ne' to know my skills in tracking, so you know I found your tracks and campfires easily enough. Yet in one camp I found signs of a brutal fight, along with tracks that led to a steep ravine. I went down there, to see if you had fallen, but found instead the bodies of three men. Do you know what happened? I saw your tracks leave that place, so I know you were there."

Madeleine glanced at Wannge'e then nodded. "We had a hand in their deaths, yes. But they had been tracking us for days, tormenting us, camping close enough so we understood their intentions were to hurt us. Had that young girl not had the courage to fight alongside me, we would have perished."

Te'tukhe looked surprised and glanced over at Wannge'e who turned to look at him, aware they were talking about her, although she had no understanding of French.

Madeleine was startled when the girl held Te'tukhe's gaze, boldly, as though challenging him, before lowering her eyes.

Madeleine said nothing, but understood well enough the look which had just passed between the girl and the man. Wannge'e was a clever girl, that was without doubt. She also owned more than her share of courage, but in society, she was timid. So to see her boldly meet this man's gaze, a hard man like Te'tukhe, was astonishingly. Yet in those few precious moments, Madeleine had felt something between them, like an invisible thread that reached out and connected them, creating a palpable beat, something pure and deep.

She shivered as Wannge'e looked away and for a moment all was silent as Te'tukhe continued to look at the girl, as taken aback by Madeleine by what had just taken place. Then a log crackled in the heat of the flames and threw sparks into the air, distracting him.

Such strangeness, Madeleine thought.

When Te'tukhe looked back at her, she saw the question in his eyes. Then he asked it. "Why are they here, Esa-mogo'ne'? So far from their village?"

She told him about the Hidatsa attack on their village some five years ago. "It happened just weeks after we left them in the spring of 1800. The Hidatsa sold them to the Mandan. By pure chance I saw them with the Mandan in St Louis a year ago and traded for their freedom. Now we head for the Omaha to winter over there, before turning north to the Mandan."

Te'tukhe looked at her in surprise. "The Mandan? Yet if the girls lived there as slaves, what madness takes you back there Esa-mogo'ne'? Surely you know you'll not leave their village alive if you go back there? These girls will be punished for leaving and your son will be raised Mandan."

"I have no choice," Madeleine said, her voice hard. "Because another Bannock girl still lives there, taken from the Snake River Plain at the same time as these girls, and others like them," she paused, seeing the bewilderment in the man's face.

"You know her well, Te'tukhe. It is Deinde'-paggwe, daughter of Paddake'e and Ese-ggwe'na'a. I could not look at either of them and tell them I did nothing, when I'll pass so close to their village. Not when I know she's living there as a slave, along with a child she bore to the son of the Mandan chief," she paused again, before adding softly. "I hope to trade for her freedom. I want to take her home with us, along with her daughter."

Te'tukhe frowned. "Yet you know full well that country is also held by the northern Sioux, by Blackfeet, Hidatsa and Kiowa. You step into that territory and none of you will come out alive. You know what I speak of, Esa-mogo'ne'. You'll be taken as slaves, or worse."

"What you say is the truth, brother," Madeleine said, her voice slightly raised. "Yet I cannot abandon this girl. I loved her as if she were my own. I cannot leave her there. I will not."

Te'tukhe uttered a low soft curse, as Madeleine leaned towards him.

"There is hope, because I'm not so foolish that I'd put my life in peril. Nor that of my son or these girls. But I had a dream Te'tukhe, a dream so real I know it's a sign."

She did not speak of the ancient one, that was her secret to keep. But she spoke of Ryder, that he was alive and that she must wait for him at the Omaha village.

Te'tukhe didn't say anything for a long moment, then he nodded. "So, it is decided then," he said, his beautiful face set as in stone, his coal black eyes looking at her with such intensity that he frightened Madeleine in that moment.

"I knew as soon as I heard your name spoken by the Kansa that my destiny lay with you in the north, even though I had no desire to return after spending a year or more up there with Allard and his family," he frowned, putting aside his pipe.

"Yet it seems that someone, or something bigger than either you or I, has had a hand in this. I cannot explain our both meeting the Kansa. That in itself is extraordinary. But I must tell you something else."

He leaned towards her, his voice soft and urgent. "On my ride north, there were many times I felt an overwhelming urgency to keep moving, even when I was so tired I could barely go on. But on more than one occasion I felt as if my horse was being led by someone, or something, invisible to my eyes. Even now I can't explain it, but I know that some days, even some nights, something was travelling alongside me," he stopped, seeing the sudden fear on Madeleine's face.

"You know what I speak of. You understand this Esa-mogo'ne' so I don't mind admitting it to you. But I've travelled alone in this wilderness for much of my adult life and have seen many strange things I cannot explain. I don't dwell on them, as I've heard other men who travel alone talk of things they see and hear that have no reality, that have no meaning to life as we know it. Yet what I felt when this thing was with me, was very different," he shook his head and once more leaned towards her.

"I felt no danger from it, yet I was afraid. So, what lies ahead for us Esa-mogo'ne', for a spirit being to ride alongside me?"

Madeleine suddenly remembered something the ancient one had said to her.

the days ahead will be like a storm. But I promise, you will not be alone, so take heart from that

"I have no understanding of such things," Te'tukhe continued. "But it seems I have been chosen to ride with you, although I have no objection. My heart is happy to see you and my nephew and if we are to be reunited with my brother at the Omaha, then I embrace the months ahead. So! Will you take me on as your companion Esa-mogo'ne'? For it appears I must accompany you north to the Omaha."

St Louis: mid October 1804

Another set of tumblers full of whisky was placed before them and as the men reached for them, Ryder sat back in his chair in disbelief.

"Te'tukhe? Yet how can this be? And how do I begin to repay him for what he's done! Along with your own good selves!"

Allard laughed. "There's no need to repay anyone Mi'wasa, but you might well do us a favor."

"Anything," Ryder answered, leaning forward. "Name it and it is yours."

Again, Allard laughed. "We ask nothing for ourselves, as we have everything we need and more. But I would ask a favor on behalf of Te'tukhe. If you could deliver to him the weapons which he hoped to buy with his share of the furs, I'd appreciate it. We took it upon ourselves to choose a musket for him, along with a couple of good knives. I think he will be well pleased with our choice."

Ryder nodded. "Of course," he said, as Allard set his empty tumbler down then pushed his chair back and stood up, followed by his sons and Wakanta.

Struggling to absorb everything he'd been told, for in less than an hour all his plans had changed, Ryder reached for his glass and threw the whisky down his throat, feeling the raw liquor burn all the way down, before pushing himself to his feet.

He walked with the men back to Stewart's general store where they collected the last of their supplies.

He waited while they pulled the musket and knives they had purchased for Te'tukhe free of their own belongings and he saw at once that they had purchased only the best.

"We wish you well," Allard said, as they stood on the boardwalk outside the store. "Perhaps you will visit us one day. The Hŭŋkpapȟa know where we live. You would be most welcome."

Ryder nodded and reached out to hug the men goodbye. "Oh, I gladly accept your invitation," he said.

"Then I'll look forward to the visit," Allard said.

He stood with Ryder and watched Wakanta and his sons mount their horses and turn west, heading for the Wazhazhe village. Then he turned to Ryder, a sense of urgency about him.

"I urge you take care, Mi'wasa. Ride hard and fast before winter sets in. Follow the Missouri River all the way, keep it in sight as it'll take you directly to the Omaha village," he reached out and grasped Ryder's arm, gripping the younger man with a strength that belied his age.

"I met your mother once," he said, his voice low. "I thought her a beauty, yet so young. When I think on it now, all these years later, I know I was envious of the relationship Hubert shared with her. I also thought her overly protective of you, for she seemed afraid to let you out of her sight."

Allard paused and when he spoke again his words were chosen with care, so as not to cause offence.

"Hubert spoke to me at length of your father, Torrance Benedict, and his hatred of him. Yet in all truth I think Hubert was a little jealous of him, because your father held a part of your mother's heart that Hubert could never touch," he paused, frowning.

"When Torrance returned to England, your mother remained true to him for some two years after you were born. I think she was besotted with Torrance Benedict and it was only when she realized he was never coming back, sometime after you turned two years old, that she accepted Hubert. He'd always loved her, you see. From the moment Hubert first met her, he'd loved her. It's a tragedy she died in childbirth with Wesa'shangke, not only for you and Te'tukhe and Wesa'shangke, but for Hubert. He almost lost his mind in grief, but I think he blamed himself for her death," he sighed and looked towards his sons, who were almost at the end of the street.

"But now you know why Hubert left you at the Corrigan ranch without another word. It was because he'd lost the war with your father. It was because his heart was broken. He didn't dare let you see his grief. Because by losing you, he lost another piece of her, your mother. I think he grieved for Wazhingka until the day he died."

Ryder didn't have the words to answer him so he just held out his hand to shake Allard's own. Then at last, he said the only words he could.

"I owe you a debt of gratitude I can never repay."

Allard shook his head. "And I'll say to you again, you owe me nothing," the old man said, then turned to mount his horse.

He pulled on the reins to follow his sons west, but stopped and looked back at Ryder.

"I do wish my cousin were alive, so he could see the boy grown into a man. I think he would be well pleased."

Then he kicked his horse on and rode away, leaving Ryder standing alone on the boardwalk.

He felt it slowly, like something small that suddenly seemed to blossom within him and perhaps for the first time in his life, other than when Madeleine fell in love with him, Ryder didn't feel alone.

He felt loved.

He felt as if hands from the past were upon him, holding him close.

He'd never experienced such an extraordinary feeling.

in the wild: November 1804

Ryder reached the top of the hill and reined his horses in to look out over the land before him. A vast prairie, reaching to the horizon and beyond, usually covered in lush green grass waist deep in places. But it wasn't like that now. Because just below him lay a vast deep trench ploughed through by hundreds of thousands of buffalo hooves. Ryder knew it was buffalo, because nothing but a massive herd could have laid waste to the grasslands like this. The land lay raw and open like a wound.

He dismounted and opened his saddle bag to pull out his spyglass. It was of the highest quality, purchased in London, and as he pulled the four cylinders free and held the spyglass to his eye, he spotted them on the third sweep around that vast prairie.

But not buffalo. The buffalo had long since moved on. What Ryder saw were men.

He'd first seen them not even an hour ago and had been careful to keep south of them and out of sight. But now the spyglass picked them out in more detail. There were more than two dozen of them, all heading west and they were clearly hunters, because their packhorses and travois were loaded down with buffalo hides, with buckskin parcels full of smoked meat. They rode bareback, with each man dressed in buckskin with a thick buffalo robe about their shoulders, their hair worn long and loose to their waists. Some of them carried muskets which suggested they had been in contact with French Canadian fur trappers, or Spanish, although most of the men also carried a sheath of arrows on their backs along with a bow.

Ryder wondered who they were. They looked confident, at ease in their world, used to winning battles. Perhaps Kiowa, or Arapaho, or Crow. Ryder was glad to see them heading away from him, because tied down on the two packhorses behind him were more than a dozen muskets, including the one for Te'tukhe. He wondered sometimes if he should have waited a few more days and had the blacksmith in St Louis saw the ends off the muzzles, as Julia had mentioned Madeleine had done. But in the end, he had been too eager to get moving and had no alternative now but to hide them as best he could.

He sat and watched the men until they disappeared way in the distance, wondering if their lives would change now that President Jefferson had claimed ownership of this territory for the Americans. He was quite sure that Jefferson would seek to colonize it, as the Americans had done in the east, although Ryder hoped not to see it in his lifetime, nor in Harry's.

He kicked his horse on, feeling the pull of the two packhorses behind him and shivered as another blast of cold wind came rolling down the prairie. Winter was licking at his heels and although he was pushing himself hard, he knew he had no hope of reaching the Omaha until February. Which meant another two months of hard riding, but with luck the snow would hold off for a few more weeks.

He didn't dare think he might miss her. He couldn't bear to think on that.

*

The river came sweeping out of the trees on his left, the force of water coming from a gorge, some five miles west. Ryder had seen the gorge way in the distance when he'd sat above this valley a couple of hours ago. From up there it had seemed a pleasant ride, a short cut, but now he wasn't so sure. It was gloomy down here, with the forest deeply overgrown and reaching almost to the river's banks. Although in some places, grey rock and shingle took precedence, spread some twenty feet or more back from the river, brought here by the sheer volume of water which came racing down through the canyon walls when it flooded.

It had seemed a good place to set up camp when he sat on that hill looking down on it, but now Ryder had no care to spend the night here. The forest was too dense on either side, suggesting a haven for bears, moose and timber wolves to come here and drink, along with herds of deer.

He rode on, along the mossy banks just above the water when a mile or so later, the river took a sudden turn to the right before disappearing deep into the forest. But some fifteen feet or more above that bend in the river was a ledge. It was sheltered on two sides by a deep wood of great pines and fir trees. It was also high enough to keep dry if a flash flood come roaring down that gorge.

It was still a couple of hours away until dusk but Ryder thought to hell with it. He was cold and hungry and desperate to get warm. That ledge would not only offer him shelter against the wind, but offer protection against any creature that might wander out of the forest in the dead of night to drink at the river.

He reined his horses in at the water's edge and dismounted, taking his time to fill all three of his waterskins before taking a mouthful and spitting it out, rinsing his mouth free of dust.

He had been riding since dawn with shorts breaks and was eager now to rest up. A good night's sleep, a full belly and he could be gone from this place at first light. The decision made and his waterskins full, he remounted his horse and kicked the animal on, the two packhorses coming up behind him as he rode away from the shingle bank and climbed up towards the ledge. It was an easy ride through the trees and when he saw the ledge he was well pleased with it. At least thirty feet wide, allowing him more than enough room to build a crude shelter and keep the horses close.

He dismounted and hobbled the horses under the trees, allowing them to graze while he unpacked his belongings then made a crude bivouac out of kindling and wood he found lying about the forest floor. He then lit a fire, roasting a couple of prairie chickens he'd caught that morning and wrapping some wild carrots in leaves and placing them in the hot coals.

He ate the birds hungrily, his thoughts lingering on the silver canister of brandy he'd purchased in Alexandria, hidden in one of his saddle bags. He was tempted to take it out and drink from it, but he'd bought it for something special, so instead he reached for one of his waterskins to quell his thirst before eating a handful of berries he'd saved, along with the roasted carrots.

His belly full, he lay with some contentment

within his furs inside the bivouac, not bothering to wash or shave for such things were for civilized men. But as the afternoon deepened into evening, as he watched black clouds gather overhead, bringing with them a deadly chill, he began to feel a deep sense of unease. He tried to ignore it, thinking himself overreacting for it was a gloomy place. But as the shadows lengthened and the forest and river slowly disappeared into the darkness of night, he felt an urgency to extinguish the fire and trusting his instincts, he pushed aside his furs and moved to scoop some dirt in his hands, throwing it on the flames to extinguish them so they wouldn't smoke. Then he grabbed his furs and went and sat behind the wooden shelter he'd made, his back against the stone wall behind him, holding his primed musket, his pistol and knives beside him, his furs pulled close, not only for warmth but also to hide within them.

As complete darkness settled on that place, Ryder couldn't see his hand before his face, blind to everything, yet unwilling to light a fire. He could hear the river rushing below him, he could smell the pine trees and the dampness of the riverbank and even mold within the deep reaches of the forest where the warmth of the sun never reached and wished he'd never come here.

He woke some hours later, so exhausted he hadn't been aware of closing his eyes, to find the dense black clouds had drifted apart to reveal a few stars and a quarter moon, allowing him some precious light. Yet everything around him lay in deep shadow, or pitch blackness. Off to his left he could hear the occasional snort from one of his horses and the restless stamp of hooves. Satisfied he was alone, he moved back into his bivouac and settled within his furs, his weapons beside him, before once more falling into a deep sleep.

*

It was the soft whicker of one of his horses that woke him. Ryder moved quickly, coming awake in an instant, his heart racing as he pushed aside his furs and climbed from the bivouac. He could see a little from that sliver of moon and those few stars high above him when again, came that soft whicker.

Ryder grabbed his weapons and in a low crouch ran for the trees where the horses were hobbled. He crouched behind a fir, allowing his eyes to get used to the dim light amongst the trees, but everything was just shadows within shadows. But something was here, moving silently in the woods, enough to spook the horses.

He became aware of the utter silence, other than the sound of the river. No sound of night creatures rustling within the forest, not even the hoot of an owl. He reached up to touch the horses to settle them, yet felt them shiver in terror beneath his hands. When he glanced back towards his bivouac, he caught a sudden inexplicable movement down by the river and stared in astonishment as several shadowy figures stepped out of the trees to stand on the shingle bank opposite him.

They gathered together, as if talking, a dozen or more men, yet Ryder heard not one sound come from them. Then one of them pointed north and they turned, as if in agreement.

They seemed oblivious to the cold as they wore

no warm clothing, just simple loincloths tied around their waists and crude moccasins made of thin hide material, with plaited rawhide strips wrapped around their feet and legs to hold the material in place. Nothing appeared to be sewn together using bone needles and sinew.

Each man held what appeared to be a musket, until Ryder realized they weren't guns at all, but long bows. Then he saw the thin, rawhide sheaths on their backs and the arrows held within them. Finally they moved, breaking into an easy run along the shingle bank, oblivious to the uneven surface of stones and rocks when the last man in the group suddenly stopped and turned back, looking straight up to where Ryder watched them. He took a step forward, then stopped when another man called him.

Ryder heard not one word leave their lips. The man glanced back once more to where Ryder stood by the horses, then he turned and ran after his companions. Within moments they had disappeared back into the forest, although Ryder knew that was impossible. No man alive, not even Madeleine with her gifted sight could enter those trees without a light.

But he already understood that these men were not of the living.

He reached out to the horses again, taking comfort in touching them, while he continued to watch the river. But whatever had been there, was gone. He spent the rest of the night huddled behind his bivouac, sitting up against the stone wall. He didn't think he'd sleep, but he drifted off with exhaustion a few hours before dawn only to wake to the sound of the river.

Yet there was no birdsong in this strange place, although he hadn't noticed that yesterday. He wondered if some tribe from centuries past had once made this place their home, their village built on that place where the forest now grew thick and dense. Perhaps some tragedy had taken place here and the souls had never moved on. He would never know of course, but he decided not to linger here.

He quickly packed up his belongings but before he rode out of there he demolished the bivouac and scattered the cold remains of his fire. He wanted no trace of his ever having been there, he wanted to leave no trail of his presence, because he wanted nothing following him in the dark. He'd heard enough stories from Madeleine about nightwalkers to know full well they existed.

Omaha territory, December 1804

One

The village of the Omaha people lay sprawled along the banks of the Missouri River and from her vantage point on the hill, just over a mile away, Madeleine could just make out the dozens of round earth lodges.

They all faced east to catch the first light and warmth of the dawn sun and were built around the Huthuga, a massive, beautifully carved pole which sat in the very center of the village.

Madeleine knew this to be the spiritual center of the Omaha, as these people shared the same beliefs in the spirit world as the Ugákhpa and Wazhazhe for these three tribes, along with the Kansa and Ponca, all owned familial and linguistic ties to the Dhegiha Sioux.

More than four years ago, in the summer of 1800, Madeleine had met the Omaha people for the first time. Along with Ryder, Te'tukhe and Wesa'shangke she had spent several days here, resting after their long journey south from the Snake River Plain. One of the chiefs had welcomed them to share his lodge, a massive building dug into the earth, some sixty square feet, able to shelter several families.

The Omaha left these warm, underground sanctuaries to live in teepees during the heat of summer, but summer was long over and Madeleine could see smoke curling from the top of each lodge as this tribe hunkered down during these freezing days of winter.

As she stood on the hill next to Te'tukhe looking down on the village, she glanced at Harry who ran off, leaving Poongatse to chase after him.

But Madeleine let him go. The little boy needed to burn off some energy before they reached the village below.

Wannge'e came to stand beside her, but as Madeleine glanced at the girl, she saw the fear on her face as she looked down on the village.

"You'll be safe there," she said softly, reaching out to put an arm about the girl's shoulders.

"I know, it just looks so much like the Mandan village. They also have earth lodges."

Te'tukhe glanced at her, even as Madeleine had a sudden memory of Ryder, remembering how soundly they'd slept in those warm earthen lodges. Although Madeleine had no plans to sleep in one of them during this visit. She intended to make use of the teepee, to give her and the girls some privacy.

Te'tukhe stepped away from them, closer to the edge of the hill, his face hard as he watched men on horseback way in the distance moving among a herd of horses. A few women worked at the water's edge, filling waterskins and washing soiled furs and skins, but they didn't linger long because the water was freezing.

It was also too cold for Te'tukhe to sleep outdoors now, even though he preferred to sleep around an open fire. But he'd shared Madeleine's teepee on those few nights it had rained, although he was like a caged beast indoors, anxious and restless, always ready to move on. At least here he had the choice of sharing Madeleine's teepee, or sleeping inside one of those lodges.

"Are we ready?" he asked, turning back to her.

Madeleine nodded, glancing over at the

packhorses. They carried their most basic of belongings now, as they'd hidden the muskets and everything else away in a small cave they'd found, rolling boulders across the entrance to keep them safe over winter from predators and winter storms.

Te'tukhe hadn't understood her logic in hiding everything away. But Madeleine couldn't risk losing the muskets, or anything else, during her two month stay here. In the end, Te'tukhe agreed to help her.

She looked over at the river, the Missouri, which wound its way past the village. She could see great chunks of ice floating downstream and Madeleine shivered, eager now to get Harry and the girls settled and out of these bitter temperatures.

As if feeling his mother's urgency, Harry turned and ran towards her, squealing with delight. Madeleine reached down and scooped him into her arms, kissing him as he laughed.

"I hope they remember us," Madeleine said, glancing at Te'tukhe.

He shrugged and turned for his horse. "We'll find out soon enough. Let's get moving."

He reached for the reins of his packhorses then swung himself up onto the back of his horse as Poongatse helped Madeleine secure Harry to her.

Then the girls mounted their own horses, pulling the packhorses behind them.

Madeleine could sense Te'tukhe's frustration but the journey north had taken longer than he'd expected, not only because the load on thc packhorses had slowed them down, but the demands of travelling with a small child.

Te'tukhe had often allowed Harry to ride with him to keep the little boy content, talking to him in a mix of English, French and his own Ugákhpa dialect.

The child was kicking his little legs now, eager for the horse to run, just as a high-pitched warning cry came from the village below them.

Within minutes, a large group of horsemen come galloping towards them, holding muskets.

Two

I lay watching my son, listening to the sweet baby sounds of him deep in sleep and the soft slow breathing of the girls asleep beside him. The village lay quiet beyond the teepee, with everyone long since retired for the night.

I turned and rolled over, feeling physically exhausted yet unable to sleep. My mind was a turmoil of emotions, of excitement that we were finally here, relief that we'd arrived safely, along with wonder that Te'tukhe was with us.

In the weeks we'd travelled north together, I'd come to understand just how alike he was to his father, Hubert Lemoine. Hubert had found a home with the Wazhazhe, along with two women who'd loved him and given him sons, yet he'd only ever managed to stay with them for months at a time before heading back into the wild to trap furs. Te'tukhe owned that same restlessness.

He'd made no mention of accompanying us to the Mandan. He'd made a commitment to come north with us to the Omaha, so I expected him to leave here before winter and head south for the Wazhazhe village. Perhaps he'd go on to visit the Comanche and see Wesa'shangke and his cousins, Aishi-waahni' and Ainqa-izhape', Sébastien Lemoine's Comanche sons.

I couldn't blame him for leaving us. He'd come north to find me, and to accompany me to the Omaha. Now he'd done that, he was free to leave.

I watched the smoke from our fire drift up towards the outlet in the top of the teepee, but felt too agitated to lie there. I pushed aside my furs and sat up, glancing back at Harry and the girls. They all slept deeply, but the girls were as exhausted as I was. They had helped me every step of the way since we'd left Julia's and I knew I could never have coped as well without their help.

After the Omaha people had welcomed us, while Te'tukhe accepted an invitation to smoke a pipe with the Chief, the girls and I had raised the teepee with the help from some of the women in the village, as this was seen as women's work.

Then we unpacked our belongings, hobbled the horses nearby, set snares in the nearby woods and river and built a firepit inside the teepee. The last thing I wanted now was to wake them. As quietly as I could, I rose from my bed, pulled on my fur coat and moccasins then crawled outside.

The village lay in silence, the earth lodges covered in a fine layer of snow and ice, although the occupants inside would be warm from their fires. There were only a few men on guard. I glanced across to where Te'tukhe had set up his own camp a few feet from our teepee, but the cold had forced him indoors and now he slept within a lodge of one of the Chiefs.

We had set up camp less than a quarter mile west of the village near a thick stand of beech trees, their branches already bare of leaves. And although there were several thousand people living here, my teepee was the only one raised.

I felt better outside, breathing in the cold, fresh air and I stood for a while and looked out across that cold, white world, which was utterly silent except for the river and the sound of horses. The Omaha let their horses graze on open land just beyond their village, leaving the long rawhide bridles attached and trailing behind each animal, allowing for easy capture.

I put my hands within my coat to keep them warm and glanced over at a man on watch who came towards me. But he didn't bother me. He nodded, then walked on, as amiable as the rest of the Omaha people who had been more then generous since our arrival, just as they had been on my last visit to this village all those years ago. But when we were offered shelter within their earth lodges I'd declined, even as Te'tukhe accepted.

I turned and headed for the small wood behind the teepee where we'd hobbled all our horses. But the animals were fine, standing close together to share each other's warmth as they sheltered within the small grove. Then I walked slowly back to camp, feeling suddenly at ease with the world, something I hadn't known for a long time.

When I crawled into the teepee, the heat from the fire was almost overwhelming after the cold outside and as I took off my coat and moccasins and snuggled within my blankets and furs, I thought again of the words the ancient one had spoken to me all those weeks ago.

You know he lives. Wait for him at the Omaha, Esa-mogo'ne'

Even as I thought on them, I knew it was those words which were unsettling me. What did they mean? Would Ryder be here before I left in March? Or was I meant to wait here, beyond March?

Yet the sheer joy and excitement of seeing him again after all this time, also brought fear. Because after so many years apart, would he still love me?

I'd changed since he disappeared from our lives almost three years ago. Lines of worry and grief now showed on my face and I'd lost a lot of weight. I was no longer that wild, arrogant girl he'd fallen in love with in the wild five years ago. I was a woman now, fast approaching thirty, responsible for a child and two teenage girls.

When I'd collapsed in Te'tukhe's arms, when I'd told him I'd felt my strength running out, I meant every word. I felt deathly tired. But during the two months we'd winter over in this village I'd have time to gather my strength, before we pushed north to the Mandan. Not only would I rest, but with the help of Poongatse and Wannge'e I'd replenish our supplies and decide how I'd go about trading for Deinde'-paggwe and her daughter.

And when Ryder came, I'd be ready for him.

I closed my eyes, hearing the hiss and crackle of wood burning a few feet away and as I finally drifted off to sleep, I whispered a prayer to him.

"Hurry, my love, please hurry, wherever you may be."

in the wild: January 1805

Ryder stood for a moment by the lake, looking at the clear, icy water before him. He was cold, despite the beautiful, blue sky day. He glanced back at his camp, at the fire he'd lit and his shaving blade waiting by the flames, then he took a deep breath and pulled off his clothes followed by his moccasins and plunged into the lake.

He knew he reeked like a bear and although he had been prepared for the coldness of the water, it was still a shock. He washed himself quickly, using his soap with care, unwillingly to see the last of it as he scoured his body and buckskin clothing before diving beneath the surface, gasping from the cold. By the time he turned and stumbled back to shore, his limbs were already numb. He paused long enough to throw his travel worn buckskin over nearby rocks to dry from the heat of the flames, before wrapping himself in several blankets, shivering violently as he put more wood on the fire. Then he skewered a couple of small wild rabbits he had killed and butchered earlier that day and placed them on ironwood stakes above the flames.

His battered cooking can, full of water and the last dregs of coffee was heating at the edge of the fire. His mouth watered from the smell of it, although Ryder was loathe to drink it as that was the last of his supplies, along with the rabbits.

He'd been focusing so hard on reaching the Omaha before the end of winter, no matter the cost to his own health, he wasn't being careful. He couldn't afford to get sick, not out here, not alone.

He searched through his belongings for clean

woolen undergarments and a fresh pair of buckskin and quickly dressed, pulling his fur moccasins on and his thick fur coat then he settled by the fire, pulling his hood up over his head.

As the day slowly settled into early afternoon, as he ate the roasted rabbit meat and finished two weak cups of coffee, the clouds returned to obscure the blue sky, even as the temperature began to drop.

Ryder reluctantly moved away from the comfort of his camp to collect more firewood, although he didn't have to look far. There was plenty of kindling and wood scattered around.

He also found evidence of someone having camped here before, and not too long ago by the looks of the fire pits and the frames which had obviously been used to smoke meat, along with the remains of a child's toy. It was the figure of a man, the twigs twisted together with thin strips of rawhide. Ryder smiled as he turned it within his fingers, thinking of his own son, and on impulse he decided to keep it.

By the time he'd collected enough fuel to see him through the night, the afternoon had settled into dusk with a light mist coming off the lake. Thick grey clouds moved in slowly overhead, promising snow later and for the first time, Ryder wished for the warmth of a teepee, instead of his crude bivouac.

As he wrapped a blanket around himself and watched the night come down, he thought again of how many more weeks he had ahead of him before he reached the Omaha.

Perhaps another month but no more, despite pushing himself to exhaustion each day. He was also struggling with the snow and the bitter cold, as were the horses. His hands and fingers were often numb from the chill winds and he wished more than once that he'd purchased a pair of fur lined mittens he'd seen some of the fur trappers wear in St Louis.

Perhaps the Omaha would make him a pair, if he traded one of the gifts he'd bought for Paddake'e. The fur hat Julia had insisted he buy, similar to those which Madeleine had purchased for herself and Harry, had been a good buy. The back and sides of it came down low and along with the hood he wore, protected his head and ears. Although in all truth he'd forgotten how damn cold it got up here in these northern territories.

He moved back under shelter of his bivouac as the first flakes of snow began to fall, as dusk turned to full dark, glad he'd moved all his belongings inside under cover, because it promised to be a miserable night.

He was almost asleep sometime later when he sat up, unsure he'd heard it at first.

But that sound had been unmistakable.

A horse and rider were coming towards his camp, just off to his right, near the edge of the lake.

With an urgency born of instinct and fear, Ryder swept aside his blankets and reached for his musket before turning and running for the cover of the trees and the safety of darkness. But as he knelt behind a massive fir, he thought of the weapons he'd left behind in the bivouac, including his knives. He'd should have secured them to the sheath on his waist and the outside of his moccasins after he'd bathed. That had been careless of him.

He cursed softly, holding the musket up to his eye, pointing the weapon towards the lake when two horses suddenly appeared out of the dark on the other side of his camp. Yet the falling snow and mist from the lake made it hard to see them until the man and horse entered his camp. He wasn't alone. Another rider and horse came up behind him.

It was obvious they'd been drawn to the light of the fire and the smell of smoke, but when a voice called out to Ryder using the Wazhazhe dialect, Ryder lowered his musket in astonishment. He came up off his knees, watching as the two men pushed aside fur hoods to reveal their faces as they looked about the camp, speaking loudly in that same dialect and laughing.

Ryder came out from behind the tree, his musket still lowered, to stare at the men in bewilderment. They didn't see him as he was still under cover of the trees but as they dismounted and stepped towards the fire, Ryder recognized the strong jaw and well-loved face of one of them, even as he glanced at the other man.

"Good Lord, I don't believe it," he said, stepping out of the trees to welcome Wesa'shangke and Aishi-waahni'.

*

"You're slowing up in your old age, brother," Wesa'shangke said as he stepped forward to embrace him. "We thought you'd be at the Omaha by now!"

"By God, what magic is this? How did you know I was here?" Ryder uttered incredulous. "I've only been in the country a few months!"

Aishi-waahni' laughed and came up to hug him. "It's not magic, old friend," the Comanche said. "But let us settle the horses, then we shall talk."

Wesa'shangke walked back to his horse and retrieved a large parcel of buckskin. He threw it at Ryder. "Some smoked meat for you," he said.

Ryder felt his stomach growl in hunger. He'd consumed the small rabbits hours ago, yet he was still hungry. "I have little to offer you," he said, as the men hobbled their horses. "I'd planned to hunt on the morrow."

Wesa'shangke laughed and pulled his belongings off the back of his horse before settling before the fire. He reached out to slap Ryder playfully on the back. "You don't look like you're starving brother! Indeed, you look bigger than I remember, how do you ever fill your belly?"

Aishi-waahni' joined them by the fire, dropping a leather bag at his feet. "Don't concern yourself overly much Mi'wasa, we have more than enough to share." He pulled several corn husks and wild carrots from the bag and wrapped them in leaves before placing them near the coals to bake. He glanced across at Wesa'shangke who was looking at Ryder's small bivouac.

"We'd best build our own cousin, before this storm gets worse."

Wesa'shangke nodded and reached for a short-handled axe from among his possessions which included a musket and horse pistol, even as Aishi-waahni' took another axe from his belongings. Ryder moved to help them, the warm glow from the fire giving them all the light they needed.

The three of them worked quickly, cutting long branches along with scrubs and ferns to create a bigger structure over the front of Ryder's bivouac, resembling a teepee.

When it was done, the men placed all their belongings in the back of it, then sat with Ryder by the fire and feasted on smoked venison, baked carrot and corn.

They spoke of the changes that had happened in their lives over the past four years. Wesa'shangke told Ryder of his decision to live with the Comanche. Ryder told them of Harry's birth and learned that Ainqa'izhape' was now a father of a two-year old girl.

"My brother will not come east again," Aishi-waahni' said. "But Wesa'shangke and I decided to make one last visit to the Wazhazhe in the hope of seeing Te'tukhe," he laughed and looked over at his cousin. "Yet here we are, well north of the Wazhazhe and heading for the Omaha!"

"Yet why is that? I don't understand why you're here. How did you know where I was?" Ryder asked, bewildered.

"Because when we arrived at the Wazhazhe we didn't find Te'tukhe, we found Allard Lemoine and his sons instead," Wesa'shangke said. "My younger brother Wakanta was also with them, who I haven't seen for many years. Allard told us of his meeting you in St Louis and of Te'tukhe's plans to ride north to follow your wife and son to the Omaha," he shook his head, looking at Ryder in wonder.

"Even now I hardly believe it's true, that you're both back in the country. Although it's a strange thing Mi'wasa," he said softly.

"Before I left the Comanche with Aishi-waahni', I had an urgent need to see Te'tukhe. I haven't seen him for some years and had hoped to find him at the Wazhazhe settled with a wife and child. Instead, here we are! How could we not follow you and Te'tukhe north, once Allard told us of it!" he laughed and leaned towards Ryder.

"What a reunion it will be, to meet again at the Omaha after all these years!"

Aishi-waahni' leaned forward. "You may wonder how we managed to track you here Mi'wasa, because in all truth we had no plans to follow you. We wanted only to find the quickest route north to the Omaha before the worst of winter set in, but we came across your tracks not two days ago. We knew it had to be you, for what other man is mad enough to travel alone in this weather?"

Ryder shook his head in astonishment. "Well, I'm grateful to see you both. Indeed, I can hardly believe you're sitting there before me."

He looked back at his brother. "Allard told me of the smallpox which devastated the Wazhazhe village four years ago. Yet how could so many perish!"

"It's the reason Te'tukhe and I left," Wesa'shangke said softly. "We'd only been back with the Wazhazhe a few short weeks when the pox came, not long after you and Esa-mogo'ne' had left for St Louis. I cannot tell you how many friends we lost. Almost one third of our people gone, in a matter of weeks. We've heard rumors it's moving along the Missouri and Mississippi rivers even now, but the new settlers bring pestilence with them brother, yet what can be done about it?"

"I don't have the answer," Ryder said, thinking of Madeleine and his son up there on the Missouri river with the Omaha.

No-one could be spared from the pox and if it were on the rise again, no-one was safe.

He looked over at Aishi-waahni'. "Allard told me that Sébastien still lives. Is your father in good health?" he asked.

Aishi-waahni' nodded. "He is well enough, except for his mind. He has returned to the days of his youth and now speaks of people and events long past. He barely recognizes us or any of his many grandchildren, but he appears content enough. Yet what of you, Mi'wasa? Allard told us something of your plans, but have you been well since we saw you last?"

"Well enough," Ryder answered, knowing he could not share with these men, despite how close they were, most of what he'd endured over the past three years. Because how did he explain the war between England and France or the months he'd spent aboard the *Zeferino*? They had no knowledge of ships or oceans, or continents at war a world away.

But he did speak a little of the brutality of Jarryth and of Madeleine leaving England to return to the Bannock.

"I must reach the Omaha before the end of winter, as Esa-mogo'ne' plans to leave for the Bannock come spring."

He told the men what little he knew of the attack on the Bannock and Shoshone village all those years ago by the Hidatsa.

"I know very little, but I understand Esa-mogo'ne' met two Bannock girls in St Louis some months ago. It seems they were taken by the Hidatsa in that attack along with others and sold to the Mandan. By a stroke of luck, the Mandan took them along with them when they went to St Louis to trade. From the little I understand, Esa-mogo'ne' traded for their freedom. They travel north with her and my son now, along with Te'tukhe."

He knew only what Julia had told him. He knew nothing of their friends' fate, not Ese-ggwe'na'a or Kokon, Kwipuntzi or even Cameahwait. He could only hope they survived the attack.

When the conversation turned to Ryder's plans to reach the Omaha in the next two months, Wesa'shangke leaned towards him.

"At least you have two more travelling companions, brother. Like I said, it will be a fine reunion meeting up with Te'tukhe and Esa-mogo'ne' again after so many years."

Ryder nodded, but wished he were there now.

Omaha territory: early February 1805

One

They heard the chanting male voices and the beat of drums long before they saw the village, as the sound rolled out across the night and the dark landscape, lit by a full moon, giving rise to shadows. When they came to the crest of a hill the three men reined their horses in, because spread out below them, although more than a mile away but seeming closer in the dark, was the flickering light from dozens of small campfires. In the center of the small fires were the flames from one huge firepit. This was the village of the Omaha people and although most of it lay in deep shadow, a few earth lodges rose in silhouette against the flames of the dozens of small campfires.

Ryder didn't dare look at his brother, or the Comanche, because he knew they'd see the fear in his eyes. Fear that she might have left already for the north and the Bannock.

"Look!" Aishi-waahni' said, pointing to a teepee perched way on the other side of the village, on its far western boundary. The soft amber light from the fire inside the teepee gave out a warm glow, along with a campfire which had been set up just a few feet away from it. "Allard said she purchased a teepee off the Kansa. It could be hers."

Ryder felt his heart lurch with anguish and longing. It had been almost three years to the day since he'd seen Madeleine and his son.

"We shall camp here tonight and ride in tomorrow," Wesa'shangke said, his voice holding a touch of warning as he watched Ryder, feeling his brother's restlessness and urgent need to get down there, to find her and the boy. "It will be too dangerous to ride in there tonight."

Ryder nodded, knowing the words were meant for him. He turned to Wesa'shangke, acknowledging his brother's concern. "You're right, of course. But I can't wait for morning. I cannot endure being this close to them after so long and not knowing if they're down there. I have to go, Wesa'shangke, I can't not go," he turned to look back at the village. "But I go alone. If the three of us ride in now, they'll likely kill us before we reach the light of their fires. If I go in alone and unarmed, I have less chance of an arrow or musket ball in my belly."

He reached out to untie his musket sheath from his saddle then passed it across to Wesa'shangke. He untied the sheaths holding his knives to his belt and moccasins and passed them to Aishi-waahni', along with his horse pistol. Ryder knew well enough the risk he was taking.

"They'll likely have guards and scouts all around the camp, so I suggest you walk in," Aishi-waahni' said, dismounting. "They'll see that as a weakness, a disadvantage to you."

Ryder nodded then glanced at Wesa'shangke. "Get a fire going, brother. Once they see it, they'll know we've made camp up here and that we've got nothing to hide."

Wesa'shangke nodded, but said nothing more. He dismounted and stood beside Aishi-waahni', watching as Ryder kicked his horse on down the hill and rode out into the dark.

*

Just over half a mile out from the village Ryder reined his horse in and dismounted. He could see the village more clearly now. He could make out the mounds of earth lodges and the great fire in the center of it and men dancing around the flames.

It seemed the Omaha people were enjoying a feast, but the sound of drums and chanting men was intimidating, the very earth seeming to vibrate with the primal noise of it.

Ryder took a step forward, leading the horse behind him, mindful of his safety, because he knew how brutal the Wazhazhe would be if someone walked into their village in the dead of night. But he couldn't bear not to. His heart was pounding, wondering what she would look like now, how she would feel about him after all these years.

A cold breeze swept across the land as Ryder hurried on, the icy chill in that breeze sweeping away the last of the clouds to reveal the new moon, which loomed large and stunningly beautiful above him to light his way. He understood then that the Omaha were likely celebrating this new moon along with the end of winter.

When he reached the first lodge he stepped into the shadows, for now he was close enough to see hundreds of people sitting in a circle around that huge fire. Off to one side a group of men beat hard and rhythmically on drums, while others danced around the fire, bare feet and moccasins stomping the earth.

Then the chanting and drums came to an abrupt stop. Had someone seen him? Yet, no cries went up in alarm. There were no men on horseback racing towards him.

When the sound of a flute rose into the night, the reed instrument's soft, sweet notes drifting up and away, Ryder heard women laughing, calling out to each other in good humor. He watched as a large group of women, fifty or more, made their way towards the fire. Some of them joined hands, others stood alone, but then almost as one they began to move, to dance slowly around the flames to the high haunting sounds of that flute. There was no battle frenzied stamping of feet like the men, instead the women moved slowly and sensuously, rising and falling in rhythm, spell binding in their beauty, as powerful as the men.

All Ryder's senses strained to hear, to see, desperate for a glimpse of her, to confirm that she was still here. He dared to take another step closer, keeping to the shadows and he didn't see her, not then, because there were so many women dancing.

But then that cold breeze came again, causing the fires to flare up and only then did Ryder catch sight of a young woman standing off to one side.

She stood with her back to him, some way from the women dancing, yet she swayed gently to the sounds of the flute, holding a child in her arms. The child's face was turned into her shoulder as though asleep and her own face was lowered to rest upon the child's head, in the typical pose of a mother trying to settle her babe. Yet it was impossible to see either of them clearly for they stood in shadows.

Ryder cursed softly in frustration when two teenage girls dressed in buckskin suddenly danced close to the woman and child, one of them reaching up to push the woman slightly, as though teasing her. Only then did the woman turn and raise her head, allowing the fires to illuminate her every feature, even as the movement woke the child. A boy, half asleep, yet in good humor he reached out to touch one of the girls, his small face soft with love.

Ryder took a sharp breath, for there could be no mistaking them. It was his Madeleine and the child in her arms was his son.

He uttered a soft cry of gratitude that they were still here. Yet in that cry came all the grief and frustration of the past three years.

She was as glorious as when he first met her all those years ago in the firelight of her cave. Her hair was loose and flowed in waves down her back. She wore a buckskin shift over buckskin pants with thick fur moccasins that reached to her knees. The child also wore thick fur moccasins and buckskin pants, but he also wore a thick woolen jumper, not a buckskin shirt.

The beauty of them took Ryder's breath away. The child was a handsome little fellow, with long hair worn past his shoulders, as black and unruly as his own. He owned chubby legs and arms and a good strong face. The child was his own image.

Ryder was incapable of moving. He felt like he was in a dream, as if everything were moving too slowly yet as he watched, the young woman suddenly turned and stared out into the dark, to the very place where he stood, although Ryder knew it wasn't possible she could see him as he remained in the shadows. Yet it seemed she was instantly alert, with something like fear in her eyes.

She kissed the child then turned and passed the boy to one of the teenage girls before moving to step away, out into the dark to where Ryder watched, when a voice suddenly rang out, high and shrill. It echoed out across the village, the sound of it slicing through the night, full of warning and fear, rising above everything else. In its wake came deathly silence. Then the murmurs of fear and bewilderment began, as everyone stood and turned to look at the fire burning brightly on the hill.

Wesa'shangke had done as Ryder asked. He had made a campfire and the Omaha had seen it.

Ryder turned back to look at Madeleine. She stood utterly still, her whole attention focused not on the fire, but where he stood, as though she knew he was there. So Ryder did the only thing he could do and stepped forward into the firelight, pulling his horse behind him, eager to be seen now.

But even as he stepped forward, he heard men shouting close to him, followed by the beat of horses' hooves as men rode out towards the hill. Then strong hands were grabbing him and pulling him towards the center of the village and that huge fire. Yet it was a relief for Ryder, because now he could see her and his son clearly, after three long years apart.

*

Everyone moved back as he was dragged before the Chiefs. Women forgot about dancing and urgently sought their children, eager to be out of the way of men. But Madeleine remained where she was, all her attention focused on Ryder as he stood not twenty feet from her.

He felt the frustration of not being able to go to her and struggled to shake himself free. But it was pointless to fight this. Had any of these men entered a village, town or city uninvited as Ryder had done, where celebrations were taking place, they would also have been treated harshly.

He took a breath to calm himself, knowing he mustn't do anything foolish, not now. He stood tall, his shoulders back, looking every bit his full six feet three inches as the head Chief approached him.

But he couldn't help but look at her, meeting her gaze and holding it, feeling his breath stop with love and desire as he looked into those extraordinary gold brown eyes. Yet in that one moment, Ryder saw all he needed to know because the look of astonishment on her lovely face slowly gave way to wonder, then love.

He watched helplessly as she began to cry, silently, the tears coursing down her face. All he wanted, all he'd ever wanted, was to go to her.

He was oblivious to the silence that had fallen over the village, oblivious to everything but her, when she suddenly fell, her legs folding beneath her as she dropped to her knees, as if her legs had given out beneath her. Ryder uttered a low cry, instinctively moving towards her when the sudden hard *thud* of a weapon rammed against his body.

The Chief stood before him, his great staff held with force, pressing into Ryder's chest, preventing him from moving. The staff was a thing of beauty, decorated with feathers, plaited rawhide and colorful beaded strips of rawhide, but it's weight and the force of it was intended as a threat of violence and Ryder became aware of his vulnerability. He turned to face the Chief, a man in his fifties, his face deeply lined and weathered, with eyes and mouth hard and uncompromising, suggesting he didn't suffer fools, a man who demanded respect. He wore a traditional buffalo horn headdress and a beautifully made buffalo robe decorated with feathers, quills and seed beads, showing his seniority within the tribe.

But as he looked at Ryder, his lip curled with distaste, he once again rammed his staff against Ryder's chest as another shrill cry came from behind them. The crowd parted as someone pushed their way through that mass of people.

Yet this cry hadn't been one of warning. This cry was one of welcome.

Ryder heard a man calling him by his Ugákhpa name and he turned and stared at the tall handsome man who pushed his way towards him, covered in facial tattoos, silver jewelry in his ears and around his wrists.

"She said you would come," Te'tukhe said, laughing, before reaching out to slap Ryder on the back, even as he turned to the Chief. "May I introduce Mi'wasa, my Ugákhpa brother. Indeed, do you not remember him? He stayed here as your guest some five years ago, along with me and his woman."

Te'tukhe glanced over at Madeleine who still knelt on the ground. Ryder and the Chief followed his gaze. She didn't bother to wipe away the tears, even though they still coursed down her face. Yet there was no sadness in her lovely face, only joy.

The Chief looked back at Ryder and held his gaze for a moment, then nodded. "Then you should know better Mi'wasa, than entering our village in the dark of night, uninvited," he turned and nodded towards the fire blazing on the hill. "Who is responsible for lighting it?"

"My two companions," Ryder said. "You know one of them, as he was also a guest here five years ago. He is my other Ugákhpa brother, who goes by the name of Wesa'shangke. The other is his cousin, a Comanche. He is called Aishi-waahni'."

Ryder turned at the cry of astonishment uttered by Te'tukhe, but before he could explain how Wesa'shangke and Aishi-waahni' came to be with him, he felt that staff *thud* into his chest again. He turned back to the Chief.

"Understand Mi'wasa, the Omaha will not tolerate those who enter our village uninvited. Had your brother not stepped forward to claim you and had I not remembered you, you would not be welcome here. However, as we are already friends, you and your companions may join us. But I shall wait for the morrow to renew my acquaintance with you all," he turned away, indicating the flute once more begin to play.

Te'tukhe reached out to grasp his shoulder. "I will also talk to you tomorrow, brother," he said, glancing at Madeleine. "I doubt I will get any sense from you until then, so I shall join my brother and cousin."

Ryder reached out to embrace him. "I can hardly believe you stand here before me Te'tukhe. But yes, go to Wesa'shangke and Aishi-waahni'. They have come all this way to see you. Tomorrow we shall talk," he paused, then reached out to put a hand on Te'tukhe's arm. "There's a weapon for you, wrapped within my own belongings, chosen for you by Allard Lemoine in St Louis. It was purchased from your share of the furs you left behind, to follow Esa-mogo'ne' north."

Te'tukhe laughed as Ryder stepped back and handed the reins of his horse to him.

"Tomorrow it is, brother! I look forward to it." Then he was gone, riding out into the night and up towards the hill and that roaring campfire.

Ryder turned to Madeleine, aware that the crowds were moving away to resume the feasting and dancing. He stepped towards her, then slowly, hesitantly, he held out his hand to her. She reached for it, taking it in her own, gripping it as though afraid to let it go and as Ryder gently pulled her to her feet, without a word, he turned and led her out into the dark, where there was privacy and silence.

Two

I knew he was there, well before he stepped into the light of the fires. It happened suddenly, almost violently, like a physical thing, like an intense vibration passing through me as though every sense I owned were suddenly alerted to his being there.

I turned in shock, in disbelief, not able to endure the disappointment if it weren't him, because there had been so many other times, so many dreams, where I'd woken to find myself alone.

But then he stepped into the light. I met his gaze and felt that physical pull towards him, even as he was dragged forward to face the Chief. I watched as he shook his handlers free. I watched as he stood proud, tall and handsome. I watched as the Chief approached him and only then did I seem to wake as if from a dream and understand that this was real. That he was here, at last. I felt myself falling, my legs suddenly having no strength in them as I knelt on the ground, unaware until later that I was crying.

I watched him as he spoke clearly and confidently and I felt myself drowning in the sound of that well-loved voice. Then Te'tukhe was there, claiming Ryder as his own.

Yet I had eyes only for my beloved. He was as I remembered him, yet he also seemed bigger and more muscular than before. I looked at him greedily, as though he were my only sustenance, as if all I needed to breathe was him. I devoured every bit of him, taking in his height, the beauty of his face, the width of his shoulders, the length of his legs, that long hair that always curled, annoying him even now as it fell across his forehead, and his eyes, so blue, like those of his son.

Then he was coming towards me, holding out his hand and I reached for him as a hungry beggar reaches for a loaf of bread and I felt the strength and the calluses in that big hand as it curled around my own. He felt warm to my touch, his eyes hungry with love and desire as they searched my face as though looking for something, as though remembering every detail. Then he was firmly but gently pulling me to my feet, leading me away from the firelight until we were out in the dark.

But again, my legs seemed unable to sustain me and aware of it, Ryder turned and lifted me, carrying me in his arms as though I weighed no more than a babe, my whole body falling against him, aware of nothing but the hard muscular strength of him and his scent as I drowned in his being, my face moving against his buckskin as though I were an animal leaving my scent, anything to touch him, to claim him as my own, as we went out into the night.

Three

Even in the dark, as Ryder led her away from the firelight, he was aware of the touch of her hand within his own, aware of the way she watched him with disbelief and an urgency that he recognized and understood. When her legs once more collapsed beneath her, as though she no longer had the strength to stand upright after three long years of waiting for him, in one easy movement Ryder swept her up and into his arms, aware of the soft whimpers coming from her throat as her body relaxed into him.

But then, like Madeleine, he felt the strength in his legs begin to fade away as if the tragedy of the past three years were also fading away, now he had her in his arms. Ryder sunk gently to the damp grass, holding her tight, the village close enough to take advantage of the firelight behind them, along with the new moon above them.

He couldn't let her go, because he was afraid to, in case he lost her again. Although she didn't move. She remained curled in his lap, looking up at him with bewilderment and joy and love, as his arms hugged her to him. She smelt of lavender and sage and honey, as though she'd just bathed. When she reached up to grasp his fur coat, as though frightened he would leave, as though he were nothing more than a vision, her fingers straining, her knuckles white with the power of her grasp, she uttered just one word.

"*Halfbreed*," she whispered urgently, her voice full of want and need and yearning.

Ryder bent to kiss her gently, on her eyes, wet and salty from her tears, on her nose, on her cheeks, on her lips. But his lips barely touched her own, because he was truly afraid to make that contact. It might be too much for him to bear, because her lips would slay him and make him lose control, sending him over the edge into helplessness. He didn't want to feel that. Not yet.

"Halfbreed," she said again, her voice as he remembered it, husky and soft. "Where have you been?"

He looked down at her, at her full mouth, her high cheekbones, the autumn colors that had always defined her hair, at her black-lashed gold brown eyes which seemed to him at that moment like fragments of glass as she wept.

"Trying to find my way back to you," he whispered, bending once more to kiss away her tears, his voice hoarse with longing and grief, closing his eyes as she reached up and gently touched his face, feeling the smoothness of newly shaven skin, smelling the freshness of newly washed clothes.

Ryder let her touch him. He barely touched her. He could not. Not here, not now. His touch for her would come later, when they came together at last. If he touched her now, he would be lost.

The tips of her fingers lingered gently on his mouth before moving down to drift across the thickness of his neck. Then further down, to his chest. And there she rested her hand, feeling the thunderous beat of his heart beneath her fingers. She bent forward to kiss him there, on his heart, at the opening of his buckskin shirt. Ryder reached up to place his hand over hers and Madeleine bowed her head, leaning into him, each aware of the other's heartbeat, each aware of the heat between them.

When Ryder began to speak, Madeleine heard the deep baritone of his voice vibrating through her very being.

"Some might say what has passed is in the past," he said softly, "but I have known bitterness over what Jarryth did to us, along with hatred. But now at least we are together and I'm just so grateful for that. We have the rest of our lives before us, with our son to share it. Later we shall talk on what happened, but not tonight. Tonight, I just want to be with you and our son," he paused then asked hesitantly. "May I know this at least, is he a worthy child?"

Madeleine nodded. "Oh yes," she said softly. "He is worthy in every way. Indeed, he is your double Ryder, but you will see that for yourself soon enough. He owns your stubbornness, he's tall for his age, he has your blue eyes and dark hair and his great love is not me, but horses, although he tolerates me well enough," she laughed softly.

"I love him more than I love my own life, as I do Poongatse and Wannge'e, two teenage girls who travel with me. You will know them from our days living with the Bannock on the Snake River Plain."

Ryder nodded. "I know all about Poongatse and Wannge'e. Julia Corrigan told me of your meeting them in St Louis back in March last year, so I know some of it, though not all of it."

"Yet I know nothing of you or what happened to you," Madeleine said softly. "Although I refused to believe you had perished at the hands of Jarryth. I never gave up hope that I would see you again."

Ryder laughed. "Well you have better instincts than me, for I often despaired of it. Indeed, I thought I might have missed you even now," he paused and added softly. "Julia told me of the attack on the Bannock village, of Poongatse and Wannge'e being taken as slaves. Yet what became of Ese-ggwe'na'a and Paddake'e? Do you know?"

Madeleine took a deep shuddering breath and shook her head. "Poongatse and Wannge'e don't remember seeing Ese-ggwe'na'a and Paddake'e that day. But both saw Huu'aidi fall to a Hidatsa axe. They said he could not have survived such a hit."

She moved in his arms to swing around so that she sat facing him, her legs stretched out on either side of his hips. She reached up and once again grasped his buckskin shirt to pull him gently towards her, her eyes consuming him, taking in every detail of that strong, rugged face. Then she pulled him towards her, desperate to feel his mouth on her own.

But as her lips touched his, Ryder gave in to his longing, his whole being thinking of nothing but her, of her taste and smell and softness and when the low moan of longing escaped the back of her throat he moved, his male instincts taking over everything else and his big hands were lifting her, swinging her up and away from him, his huge body moving as though it were a thing of fluid, not hard muscle or bone, to lay her gently on the grass beneath him.

He looked at her for a long moment, holding her gaze, aware of her trembling beneath him as her legs came up to claim him, as her hands moved to his shoulders, down his chest to his waist and then back to his face, touching him everywhere, aware but not caring that Ryder was struggling with his emotions.

He closed his eyes and moaned aloud before rolling over to drop heavily on his back to lie beside her, breathing hard, his arm over his eyes even as she moved to sit up, cross legged beside him. He moved his other arm and laid it across her legs.

"You drive me too close to the edge woman and as much as I want you, we are in full view of not only my brothers up there on the hill, but the village behind us and I would wager everything I own there are curious children about," he took a deep breath and moved to sit up. "Besides, I smell like a bobcat."

Madeleine smiled. "You know you do not. I can see well enough you have recently bathed. Besides, I don't care how you smell. I'll take you any way I can have you. I love you. I have to pinch myself to be sure this is real, that I won't wake shortly to find myself alone, not knowing where you are or what you're doing, or if you've fallen in love with another."

Ryder laughed. "Oh, how could anyone compare to the memories I have of you. Impossible! Whenever another woman came near me, I saw only you, I heard only you. No other woman has been alive to me since that moment I saw you in your cave, all those years ago."

And then unable to help himself he leaned over and kissed her, but this time the kiss was long and slow and gentle. As his hands reached out to touch the curves of her body, he became aware for the first time, of how thin she was. He moved back and only then saw the hardness of her mouth, the deep shadows around her eyes and the grief within them.

He took a deep breath, understanding in that moment a little of what she'd been through over the past three years. He'd read her letters at Millbryne, so he knew what she'd endured physically. But now he saw in her face what his disappearance had cost her.

He pulled her onto his lap and held her, aware of the pulse of life within her, her scent and heat, just as the beat of the drums once more soared out into the night, followed by men chanting, the flute finished for now. It was the drums which stirred them to move.

"Do you want to meet your son?" she asked. "You will be proud of him. He is afraid of nothing and all who know him, love him."

Ryder nodded and she climbed off his lap and reached for his hand, but as he pushed himself to his feet he seemed in that moment to tower over her and again, Madeleine was taken aback by his height and the muscular bulk of his body. She was tall, at five feet ten inches she was taller than the average woman, yet still, Ryder loomed beside her. Her memories of him had been of a tall, muscular man, broad of shoulder and ruggedly handsome. Yet now he seemed bulkier, bigger than she remembered. What could have changed him so much physically in three years? She couldn't wait to hear him tell it and she smiled as they walked back to the village to meet their son.

Four

I was aware of my heart beating too fast, my limbs still trembling from that first moment of seeing him and the heat in my woman's body proved I was ready for him, yet in so short a time! Had he not been the stronger between us, I would have allowed him to take me there in full view of so many, oblivious to anything but him. I'd felt his heart flutter beneath my fingers when we lay together on the grass, like a wild bird caught between my hands as he'd struggled to get himself under control. I admired him for it, because I could not.

Our first kiss had been slow and gentle, so unlike the first time we'd kissed all those years ago. Ryder had given me a ride back to the Bannock village with the armful of wood I'd collected. I'd ridden in front of him, yet even now I can recall the heat and muscular male strength of him behind me, his body against my own. The kiss between us when we dismounted had been almost inevitable, all heat and desire and lust.

Now our kiss was almost chaste, but I knew the lust would come and it wouldn't take much to stroke that fire, because it was still there, that spark, ready to ignite that raging heat between him and me. He was my life and nothing on this good, great earth would ever change that, not until I took my last breath.

Five

Harry was sitting in Poongatse's lap on the edge of the crowd, away from the heat of the great fire. He was leaning into the warmth of her, the little boy content to watch the men chanting and beating the drums. The child looked up with curiosity as Madeleine and Ryder came and sat down beside them.

Poongatse and Wannge'e remembered Ryder from the days when they'd all lived together on the Snake River Plain. Although they were changed from how he remembered them. They were no longer little girls, but young women in their teenage years.

He nodded politely as Madeleine introduced each girl, speaking in the dialect of the *bannaite'*. Then she turned to Harry.

"Hello," Ryder said, his voice soft as he spoke in English. "How are you?"

The child glanced at Madeleine, unsure of this stranger. She smiled and encouraged him to answer.

"Very well, thank you," the boy replied in the same language, speaking formally as Madeleine had taught him to do, as he would be expected to reply on his return to London.

Ryder was surprised by the child's voice. He didn't speak with the clipped English vowels as expected of a child of an aristocrat, but owned a slight accent. Perhaps it was due to the French influence of his mother. Or perhaps because the child could speak French and the *bannaite'* dialect fluently, along with some of Ryder's own Wazhazhe dialect. Those languages would have a bearing on his vowels. But Ryder didn't care, one way or the other. He thought the child perfect.

He held out his hand, tentatively, yet Harry immediately responded, as Madeleine had taught him. He placed his fingers within Ryder's own and for the first time since Harry was six months old, father and son were reunited.

Six

Harry felt asleep in Ryder's arms a little while later, but I had no care to move the little boy and take him back to the teepee. Let his father enjoy this moment. Besides, it was warm enough by the great fire and I was also content just sitting there with Ryder and my son together for the first time in so long, that I didn't want that moment to end. The privacy and intimacy I craved with Ryder would come later. For now, it could wait. I just wanted to look at him and be with him and watch our son with him, to hear his voice beside me and know this was real, to drown in the beauty of his eyes as he looked at me, to allow his laughter to wrap around me like something wonderful.

I couldn't take my eyes off him. When he turned to me and held my gaze I couldn't look away, because I saw my own feelings mirrored in his eyes.

He kept hold of my hand, yet I grasped his as well, unwilling to let any part of him go. When he raised his right arm to embrace me, I moved even closer to him to share his body warmth, although we sat on furs, which the girls and I had brought out from the teepee earlier, to enjoy the Omaha feast.

It was impossible to talk over the beat of the drums and the chanting of men, so we sat in silence, yet both utterly aware of the other. With Harry asleep in his arms, Ryder gradually leaned back against the slight bank behind us and despite the noise, he slowly drifted off to sleep with exhaustion. I sent Poongatse back to the teepee for a woolen blanket and when I covered Ryder and Harry with it, neither of them woke.

The feasting came to a stop just after midnight

and as people drifted off to their beds, Ryder slept on, even with the muted conversations and laughter all around us. I chose to stay where I was, right there beside them, unwilling to wake either. When Poongatse and Wannge'e left for the teepee and their beds, I took one of their blankets and covered myself in it, before curling up beside Ryder and my son. It was cold, but we sat close enough to the heat of the great fire to not feel it.

Only a handful of people remained now, mostly old men who preferred to sleep outdoors, away from their families and the broken sleep of young children.

It was a glorious night, despite the cold. The clouds had long ago been swept away, the brilliance of the stars slightly dimmed by the brightness of the huge full moon which hung above us. Before I closed my eyes to it, before I succumbed to sleep, I tried to think of the last time I'd known such joy. I didn't need to think on it long. It had been a usual morning in our dining room at Diccon House, where I'd shared breakfast with Ryder and Harry. Just before Ryder left to meet Rupert at Bankside, but where he'd met Jarryth instead. That morning was three years ago, almost to the day.

Seven

Ryder woke in the early hours of the morning, startled as to where he was at first, bewildered by the weight of something lying against him. He blinked and looked down in astonishment to find Madeleine and his son curled around him, both fast asleep. He stared at them in wonder, not daring to move in case he woke them.

Madeleine was as he remembered, although it saddened him to see the grief in her face, the same grief and hardness he'd recognized when he first met her in the cave all those years ago. But her suffering over the past three years had not diminished her beauty, although she was achingly thin.

His gaze moved to his son. The boy was a bonny lad with a strong face and good hardy limbs and sometime during the night the child's small hand had slipped up to lie against Ryder's neck. He felt the touch and heat of the boy as if it were a brand and he closed his eyes, swearing on his life that although his son was a stranger now, he had the rest of his life to build a relationship. And Ryder was damn sure it would be a better one than Torrance Benedict had bequeathed him.

*

Madeleine woke some hours before dawn to find him watching her. His eyes were red rimmed with fatigue, the dark shadows under his eyes suggesting the hard journey he'd taken to get here.

"*Behne*," he said softly in *bannaite'*, using the word of greeting.

"*Behne*," she whispered back, holding his gaze,

both of them aware of the little boy sleeping between them.

"You're as lovely as I remember," Ryder said in a soft whisper, before glancing down at the child. "And how he has grown! He is more beautiful than I could have imagined."

Madeleine said nothing, content to look at the two of them, but when Ryder reached out to pull the fur up around her shoulders she felt her body surge with desire, wanting him desperately. But not yet.

"How many years we've all lost," he said, his voice soft. "But here we are, a few months from the Bannock, almost back to where it all started," he paused and looked around the village. "Yet had Jarryth not tried to destroy me, would we be here now? I've wondered on it often, because what are the odds of us meeting like this, here in the Omaha village? You, me and Harry, along with my brothers and Aishi-waahni'."

Madeleine smiled. "I cannot explain it either halfbreed, but I agree. It's a strange thing that we should all come together, when we were all so far apart. Fate has been kind to us, I think, at last, yet I have a feeling that others more powerful than us have had a hand in this," she paused and reached out to caress his face, running a finger down his cheek, across his mouth.

"But what plans have you, my love? Now you have found us, must we all return to England? Or will you accompany us north to the Bannock? Because I've made a promise to Poongatse and Wannge'e that I'll take them home and I'd dearly love to see my Bannock family, Ryder. I cannot think I might have come this far only to turn back now."

Ryder took a deep breath before he spoke, even as the child stirred in his arms. Madeleine watched him, desperate to hear his answer, even as he paused, allowing the child to settle. When he spoke again, his voice was soft with regret.

"I didn't follow you all this way and push myself through a bitter winter to ask you to turn back. I knew from the beginning, after reading your letters in England, what your plans were and your desire to return to the Bannock. Who am I to change them? In all truth, I also want to see the Bannock, to meet again with Paddake'e and Ese-ggwe'na'a. Indeed, I think we must, before it is too late," he paused before adding with some urgency.

"I saw the changes on the American borders as I travelled up the Mississippi River from New Orleans and although it hasn't yet been two years since Bonaparte and Jefferson agreed on the sale and purchase of the Louisiana Territory, I saw and heard enough to know there are great plans ahead for this country. Indeed, if progress to the east is anything to go by, things will change rapidly in this territory and if anyone dare underestimate the ambition of the Americans, then let them be called fools," he paused, frowning.

"It's inevitable that settlers will cross the Mississippi River and head west. Although I dare not think on such things happening during our lifetimes, but I want Harry to see how we lived in the wild before it's gone forever."

Madeleine curled back around him, resting her face on his chest. "So we go west, to the Bannock," she said.

Ryder nodded. "Yes, we go west."

She moved to put her leg against his own, aware of his warmth, then raised her head to look at him. "We don't have to lie out here in the cold. I have a teepee of my own which I traded with the Kansa. If you have a care to go there now, the girls won't mind you moving in with us. In all truth, they're probably wondering where we are."

Ryder moved his arm to pull her close. "For the moment, I'm content enough here. Besides, I'm not cold. How could a man be cold with a woman such as you lying beside him and a child like this?" he smiled as Madeleine laughed. "Perhaps when he wakes we'll move, but until then, I am content."

Madeleine pulled the furs over him, making sure he was covered then said nothing more. Within minutes she heard the slow rhythmic breathing as he once more fell into deep sleep. She closed her eyes, yet her thoughts weren't on Ryder or Harry now, nor Paddake'e and Ese-ggwe'na'a, but on Deinde'-paggwe and the Mandan.

Eight

We woke around dawn. It was cold, but the coals of the great fire simmered before us, still giving off heat although some of the old men had long ago retired to their earth lodges to seek the warmth of the indoor fires. Harry lay between us on furs, where Ryder must have placed him sometime during the night, but the boy was still asleep.

I turned to find Ryder watching him, a soft look of love on his face. Then he saw I was awake and reached for my hand which still lay on his chest and brought it to his lips, his eyes meeting mine with an urgency that we both understood.

We both desperately needed to be alone, somewhere private and not only to talk of the past.

"This might be the only chance we have today to talk," he said softly. "My brothers will come soon enough, then the Chiefs will want to officially welcome us. But later, can you and I go somewhere private? I doubt we'll be assured of privacy in your teepee, without my brothers or Harry or one of the Bannock girls disturbing us, so I ask you now my love, will you come away with me for the night?"

I didn't hesitate to agree. "There is a place not five miles from here. The girls and I found it one day while out hunting, although they didn't care for it much. But we'll be quite alone, I can assure you of that."

Ryder nodded and rolled away, rubbing his hands over his face. "I'd better go and tidy myself up and get ready for the day. Shall I accompany you and Harry back to the teepee? I can carry him. You'll need a hand with these furs and blankets."

We walked back to the teepee together, with

Harry still asleep in Ryder's arms. When we crawled inside, Poongatse and Wannge'e were still asleep in their furs so once he'd settled Harry, Ryder left us alone, taking one of my horses to ride back up the hill to the camp shared by his brothers, to wash and shave.

*

It would be a day I'd never forget. To have him back with us, to look over and see him there, was nothing but a joy. It was also wonderful to see Wesa'shangke and Aishi-waahni' again and as the Omaha people opened their homes and hearts to them, Wesa'shangke and Aishi-waahni' joined Te'tukhe in one of the lodges, with Ryder moving into the teepee with me, the girls and Harry.

The men spent several hours with the Chiefs and were invited out to hunt afterwards. I didn't see Ryder again until they returned late in the afternoon. I was sitting outside our teepee with Harry and the girls preparing an evening meal when we heard their laughter and I sat back on my heels to watch them approach.

Four halfbreeds, all tall good-looking men, related to each other by Sébastien and Hubert Lemoine or Ryder's mother, Wazhingka. All owning olive skin and well-muscled bodies, they each wore buckskin and knee-high fur moccasins. Wesa'shangke no longer wore a scalp lock, but wore his hair long and loose in the Comanche way like Te'tukhe now did, although I thought the Ugákhpa brothers more handsome and less intimidating without their hair roaches.

The men were laughing at something Wesa'shangke had said but my eyes were drawn to the tallest of them, my own halfbreed. He'd been here for less than twenty-four hours, yet I found it impossible to take my eyes off him, in disbelief that he was here. As he looked at me, as those blue eyes sought my own, I felt my heart melt and after three years of heartbreak, I fell hopelessly and desperately in love with him all over again. Completely and utterly.

I was helpless in the hot wave of it and as he came towards me, along with the others, I was vaguely aware of Poongatse and Wannge'e standing up and moving away, taking Harry's hand and pulling him gently back, allowing the men to sit close to the fire.

The men didn't acknowledge the girls or take any notice of their submissive behavior except Ryder, who reached out to put a hand on my shoulder, indicating I stay where I was, so I reached for Harry and sat him on my lap, bringing him back into the circle of men. He sat in silence as he watched our visitors, his fingers in his mouth, his big blue eyes watching each of them in turn.

It was Wesa'shangke who made another firepit. It was a few feet from my own and here the men sat and smoked their pipes while the girls returned to help me roast several rabbits they'd caught earlier in their snares, along with some fish Harry and I had caught downriver that afternoon. I'd taken the boy with me, to keep him occupied, to answer any questions he might have about Ryder. But he had none, and it seemed my son had already accepted the big stranger into our small family.

*

I sat outside with the men around the firepits and smoked my pipe, long after Harry and the girls had gone to bed. We spoke of Aishi-waahni's Comanche brother, Ainqa-izhape', who had been one of Ryder's travelling companions on his journey north to the Shoshone back in 1798, some seven years ago.

"He's well settled with his young family now and has no plans to leave Comanche lands," Aishi-waahni' said. "Although, had he known we would be meeting you both, along with your son and two girls from the Bannock tribe, I think he might have been persuaded to join us one last time."

Wesa'shangke nodded. "But I also have a hunger to stay on Comanche lands. I've little love for all these new villages I see, with European settlers building everywhere. Nor do I like these strange vessels on our rivers which bring passengers and goods up from the south, including illnesses like the pox."

I listened with dismay as Wesa'shangke and Aishi-waahni' spoke of this being their last trip east, of Wesa'shangke's plans to never return to live with the Wazhazhe. He told us of the devastation his people had suffered when smallpox swept along the Missouri and Mississippi rivers some four years earlier.

"The Wazhazhe people are not rich like they once were, Mi'wasa," Wesa'shangke said softly, looking at Ryder. "The buffalo no longer come south in their huge numbers. Because of it, I've seen many villages in ruin along the Mississippi and Missouri rivers, their people starving or ruined from the pox and other diseases they've caught from European settlers," he paused and glanced across at Te'tukhe. "You know it also, brother. I see it in your face."

Te'tukhe nodded. "Every trapper I've met over the past two years spoke of the Americans claiming ownership of this land," he shook his head. "I know nothing of these people and I saw no battle where they claimed this territory. Do I believe this talk? I have my doubts, but if they come and they're willing to trade as the Spanish and French have done, all will be well. But if they continue to bring their diseases to our nations, then I hope they do not come."

I glanced at Ryder and he met my eyes, but only for a moment and I knew, like me, he dared not reveal the truth of it, of what we knew. Such talk would only bring fear and invite distrust. Best to let the future play out as it must.

"How did you know we were in the north?" I asked Wesa'shangke. "How did you know that Te'tukhe had followed me, or that Ryder was even in the country?"

He smiled as he looked at me. He still had that pleasant nature and the easy laugh. He told me of his meeting with Allard Lemoine and his sons at the Wazhazhe village.

When Ryder told of his meeting with Allard and his sons in St Louis, the men listened incredulous.

"It was the strangest thing. I could have missed them by minutes, but because of that meeting, here we all are."

"Don't forget the Kansa," Te'tukhe added, looking across at me. "Had we both not met them, I would never have known you were back in the country, nor heading north."

"And if Allard had decided not to visit the Wazhazhe one more time and say goodbye to his past, we would never have known that you and Esamogo'ne' were heading north," Wesa'shangke said, before turning to Ryder. "When Allard told us of his meeting you in St Louis, we could hardly believe it."

The men talked late into the night, mostly speaking in the dialect of the Comanche, the same dialect as the Shoshone, but sometimes they lapsed into French and even English. But that night was special to all of us, as we spoke of the past five years.

I could feel the closeness of the men, like a vibration between them, for although blood relations, these four men were bonded like brothers, sharing something unbreakable. But as I listened to the banter between them, I began to wonder about my carefully laid out plans to ride to the Mandan.

*

He didn't share my furs that night. When I left the men still talking by the fire, long after midnight, I glanced at Ryder as he looked up at me and I saw the longing on his face. I wanted him to come to me, but I knew he would not. Tonight, he would stay with his brothers, because they'd be gone soon enough. Our time would come later.

They stayed up talking into the early hours of the morning. I drifted off to sleep hearing his voice outside, that deep baritone, low and soft. Then I fell into the deepest sleep I'd known for three years.

Nine

They had a visitor early the following morning, eager to do a trade.

It was one of the chief's sons and he had an old teepee he wished to trade, for a musket.

A teepee was a valuable item for any tribe, but the Omaha only used them in the heat of summer and on hunting trips, so to trade this old one for a musket would be a profitable deal.

But neither Ryder, his brothers nor Aishi-waahni' had any intention of trading one of their muskets, not even for the luxury of a teepee.

As the negotiations came to a standstill, Madeleine thought of her own stash of muskets which were still well hidden. Ryder didn't know anything about them, as they hadn't had a chance to talk yet, but as Madeleine glanced at Te'tukhe, he caught her eye then looked away.

He would not use her weapons to barter. That must be her choice.

Madeleine thought of the long months of travelling ahead of them and decided the offer of the teepee was too good a deal to turn down. Indeed, the girls could move into it along with Deinde'-paggwe and her daughter, giving her and Ryder some privacy.

She approached Ryder and asked him to reopen the negotiations by offering the French dagger, traded with Tahkawiitik for her musket all those months ago.

The dagger was refused.

Then Wannge'e surprised everyone by stepping forward to offer her own musket for the teepee.

Madeleine looked at the girl in astonishment,

understanding at once the reason behind it. She had only just turned fifteen, but like Madeleine, she was thinking of the months ahead and like Madeleine, she desired privacy. Not just for herself however, but to be alone with Te'tukhe.

The attraction Wannge'e felt for Te'tukhe begun almost five years earlier, when he'd lived in the Shoshone village on the Snake River Plain. But those long forgotten feelings turned into something else the night Te'tukhe arrived at their camp after following them for days, wet and disheveled from the rain, his face fierce yet handsome. Later, as they travelled north to the Omaha together, Madeleine became aware of Wannge'e'e feelings.

"She was in love with him all those years ago," Poongatse teased, when Madeleine warned Wannge'e to be careful.

"You were children!" she scolded, even as Poongatse and Wannge'e laughed.

"Everyone watched those two Ugákhpa brothers when they arrived in our village, along with the two Comanche," Poongatse said. "But Wannge'e always loved Te'tukhe, right from the first moment of seeing him."

Madeleine wasn't aware of Te'tukhe's feelings. If he thought of the girl at all, he kept those thoughts well hidden, so Madeleine decided it was nothing more than a flirtation on Wannge'e's part. She was barely fifteen years old. Te'tukhe was a hardened man of thirty-two.

But as they continued north to the Omaha, Madeleine began to understand that this was no flirtation on Wannge'e's part. The girl was clearly in love with him, even if Te'tukhe largely ignored her.

Yet it was clear that if Te'tukhe ever bothered to claim the girl for his own, Madeleine knew that Wannge'e wouldn't object. Madeleine did everything she could to protect the girl, to warn her off this hard, older man because she saw nothing but heartache came of it.

Just a few days from the Omaha village, as they sat around the campfire one night, Madeleine saw Te'tukhe turn and meet Wannge'e's gaze and in that one moment it seemed he finally saw her. Madeleine felt the sudden explosive sexual tension between the pair and knew then that she could do nothing to stop what was coming. If she asked Te'tukhe to leave, or leave the girl alone, she knew he would abide with that. But Wannge'e would never forgive her for interfering.

Madeleine had no doubts about Te'tukhe's character. He made no apologies for being his own man, with morals similar to Ryder's own, so he never set out to seduce the girl or take advantage of her youth. Yet the growing attraction between the pair was obvious. By nature, Wannge'e was a quiet timid creature, yet she owned a core of steel within. She preferred to be around people, to know she was safe, whereas Te'tukhe preferred to be alone. Yet if the girl revealed a new strength and maturity around Te'tukhe, Madeleine noticed a gentleness in Te'tukhe which she'd never seen before.

By the time they arrived at the Omaha village, the frightened girl who Madeleine had rescued in St Louis all those months ago had become someone else. Wannge'e seemed to bloom under Te'tukhe's gaze. Her face took on a radiance and that quiet strength she'd owned was fashioned into a blade.

She might be fifteen, almost sixteen, but she seemed much older. She would have her way, and no-one would sway her.

Madeleine spoke to her about it almost every day, urging her to be careful, because she knew the hard side of Te'tukhe. But there was little she could do. Whatever this thing was between them, love or lust, it must take it natural course. It could not be stopped, although when Wannge'e stepped forward to offer her musket for the teepee, Madeleine wanted to deny the girl's request. She had no care to be a party to this thing between Wannge'e and Te'tukhe, even if Te'tukhe were yet unaware of how deeply Wannge'e cared for him.

"Please," Wannge'e said softly, begging Madeleine for the chance of a home of her own, as she held the musket out to her. "You must take this for the teepee."

In the end, the deal was done. It was Ryder who saw the sense in the extra teepee, whether Te'tukhe and Wannge'e became a couple or not, so the offer was made and the trade agreed. The Omaha delivered the teepee to them the following morning.

Ten

Madeleine woke early and quietly gathered her pipes and tobacco, her cooking pot, her bags of herbs along with some of her furs and blankets. Ryder helped her secure them to the back of her horse. He decided not to bother with his saddle, as Madeleine also rode bareback, but they weren't going far. Only five miles upriver, just a short ride.

She told Poongatse and Wannge'e where she was going, although the girls understood well enough her reasons for leaving for a few days.

"We'll be back tomorrow, or the day after. I know you'll be alright with Harry and he trusts you."

"Be careful there, you know how Poongatse and I feel about that place," Wannge'e said.

The words made Madeleine feel uneasy, as though they were a warning, a foreboding. "Once we shut the gates, we'll be safe enough," she said.

But Wannge'e's words lingered as they rode out around mid-morning, an hour after Te'tukhe, Wesa'shangke and Aishi-waahni' left with a small band of Omaha for a hunting trip that would take them away for most of the day.

Madeleine explained to Harry that she was also going on a hunting trip and would be back soon enough. The little boy accepted this, well used to her going off to hunt and secure in Poongatse and Wannge'e looking after him. Yet as Madeleine rode out of the village, she felt unsure about leaving him behind. It was the first time they'd been apart for over a year.

"We can go back," Ryder said, aware of her unease.

Madeleine shook her head. She needed this time

with him. Not just to be close, but to talk of what happened in the past three years and of the hand she'd played in Jarryth's death.

As they followed the river west they rode mostly in silence. What little conversation they had was of the Omaha or Harry, both of them safe things to talk on, that didn't draw on raw emotions. And they were raw. Madeleine could feel the heat and nervous energy of him from where she rode, not six feet away.

They turned away from the Missouri and followed another tributary that ran southwest. This river wasn't so wide or deep, but it was pleasant under the thick willows growing along its southern bank. Then they left behind the well-worn track made over many years by the Omaha women, who came here to wash and bathe.

As the miles fell away behind them, as the noise and smells of the village drifted away, that awkward silence once more settled between them. Madeleine watched Ryder discreetly, as he looked out to the horizon in this unknown country. She noticed his right leg which had been injured by his own hand during an altercation with *esa* over five years ago now looked strong and it was then that Madeleine noticed something different about Ryder.

He no longer limped, which he was prone to do when he was tired. Despite his exhaustion since he arrived at the Omaha village, not once had she seen him limp.

But she didn't ask him the reason why. Indeed, she said nothing as they rode on, but as she led him away from the tributary to head inland, she began to feel apprehensive and nervous, as if he was a stranger. It seemed an invisible wall had suddenly risen between them and as the silence deepened into a thing of awkwardness, she wondered if she'd made the right decision in bringing him out here. She was thinking on this when Ryder asked where they were going, interrupting her thoughts.

She turned to look at him, thinking how blue his eyes were, how full and sensuous his mouth, how sharply defined his cheekbones and how square his jaw, revealing that Benedict stubbornness.

How was it possible to love someone so much, yet feel so distant from them?

"An abandoned fort," she replied, wondering if he would have preferred to spend these last few days hunting with his brothers before they headed west, back to the Comanche.

But then he smiled. That charming smile that was so seductive. Although she knew Ryder was unaware of it because like Te'tukhe, he wasn't a vain man, nor was there anything false about him, for his truth was there for all to see in his face and in his words, which was in fact the strength of him, which drew people in.

Madeleine wasn't averse to it. She could feel herself succumbing to the beauty of him, to that indefinable force that made him who he was, and she had to turn away from him to protect herself and her heart.

She knew she loved him as much as she ever did, but did he love her the same? He spoke of there being no other woman, or women, yet he was a passionate man, there must have been someone at some time.

She frowned at the thought of it, yet Ryder saw it,

along with her withdrawal from him and mistook it for something else. The smile left his face and he turned away, feeling out of his depth with her, not knowing how to get the intimacy back that they had shared last night and as he looked out towards the beginnings of a forest a mile or so away, he decided to break this sudden awkwardness between them. He needed to speak, to say something, anything at all.

"Who built the fort?" he asked, looking across at her as she rode beside him. "Do you know?"

Madeleine shrugged, then turned to him. "The Spanish perhaps, or the French. Whoever it was, they left very little behind. According to the Omaha it's been empty for years, although it's not quite a ruin yet. But if we shut the gates, we should be safe enough. It's only about a mile or so beyond the first of those trees. You'll see it when we come to a clearing."

She was going to add, *I'm sorry I misjudged this, I'm sorry for bringing you here, away from your brothers and your son, but I want to be alone with you. I need to touch you, to hear you talk about the past three years.*

But she said nothing more and they rode on. By the time they reached the trees, thick grey clouds swirled above them, bringing chill winds and promising heavy snow. Madeleine pulled her fur hat further down her head, seeking its warmth before turning to Ryder.

"We should be there soon. Follow me," she said, then kicked her horse into a run down a wide, well-worn deer track through thick woods.

*

The fort had four square towers built above each corner, allowing two men to be stationed in each tower, so eight men could look out across the country. The fort was constructed of pine, the trunks embedded deep into the earth before rising some fifteen feet in height into axe sharpened points. On the south wall of the fortress was a double wooden gate.

Deep forest surrounded the building like a dark thing and Ryder had an ominous feeling about the place as soon as he saw it. But he said nothing, dismounting beside Madeleine and reaching for his musket as she walked across to the massive gates and pushed one of them open. It swung awkwardly, its rusted iron hinge screaming in protest as she pushed the gate all the way back. Ryder saw her enter a parade ground and he followed her, pulling the two horses behind him. Once safely inside, Madeleine pushed the gate shut then swung the great pine arm down to lock it behind her. No-one could get in now, unless they burned the place down.

They both turned at a great fluttering noise, their muskets held out before them as a flock of crows rose from the rafters on one of the buildings and swept away into the sky. Ryder turned to Madeleine and saw his own bewilderment and anxiety clearly on her face.

"Do you feel safe here?" he asked incredulous, needing to trust her instincts, for he didn't feel safe at all. It felt creepy, as though the place had been abandoned in fear.

Madeleine looked about the deserted fortress then nodded. "There's no-one here. We're quite alone."

Ryder put away his musket and came to stand

beside her. "How on earth did you find this place?"

"We found it one day by accident when we were out hunting with Harry, not long after we came to live with the Omaha. I couldn't believe it when I opened the gates and came inside. Harry and the girls wanted to leave almost straight away, but I've never felt afraid here. I don't think anyone's been here for decades," she said. "No animals can get in, not with the gates shut. I tasted the water from the well the first day we came here and it's as clear as any river we've passed."

"Good Lord," Ryder said, turning around, looking at the building. "What a place! Yet why don't any of the local tribes live here? It looks perfectly sound to me."

Madeleine shook her head and began to walk to the opposite end of the parade ground, pulling her horse behind her. "No, they won't come here, including the Omaha. They believe bad spirits live here. But I've never felt it."

They crossed the vast parade ground, once filled with men and horses and wagons. Off to one side was a deep well, a four-feet high wall of logs built around it to protect the precious supply of water and prevent any wayward man or animal falling into it. Next to it were several troughs for horses, although the water inside was now green and stagnant.

Around the perimeter of the empty square were other buildings, some of them two story. The buildings had once been staff quarters and officers' rooms, cook houses and livery stables.

Ryder wondered why the fort had been given up, as there appeared no sign of any battle having been fought here. Indeed, it just looked like an abandoned building, as if the men who lived and worked here had just packed everything on wagons, mounted up and left.

Some doors hung off hinges, many shutters had come away from window frames to leave rooms open and vulnerable to the weather, for there was no glass in any of the windows. This fort had been too isolated to bring the luxury of glass this far into the wilderness.

Madeleine pointed to one of the largest buildings on the left.

"That's the livery, so we can leave the horses in there overnight, out of the weather. Behind it is a small cabin, although you can't see it from here, which makes it the perfect hideaway," she turned to Ryder as the first snowflakes began to fall and saw him shiver with the cold.

But they had no choice but to stay here now. They wouldn't make it back to the Omaha before nightfall and they needed to get warm.

He followed her to the livery. Once again, she stepped forward to pull open a huge door and as Ryder peered into the gloomy building he saw rows of stalls, twenty or more on each side of the building allowing stalls for at least forty horses.

Madeleine pulled her horse in behind her and again, Ryder followed, pausing to close the door behind him. They quickly brushed the horses down, giving them buckets of fresh water, then once the animals were settled they took their small bags of belongings and headed out the back of the building to where a small cabin stood.

It sat within a courtyard and just behind it was the rear wall of the fort.

Madeleine stepped up and opened the cabin door, which was nothing more than one room with a fireplace. There was no furniture. One small window, shuttered against the cold, was on the far wall.

Ryder pulled open the shutters, warped with damp and saw the window overlooked the wall of the fort. A blast of icy wind came in and he quickly secured the shutters, wishing they could leave. The place gave him the creeps.

They left their cabin to explore the fort and collect water and gather wood for a fire. There was a surplus of wood, as though the previous occupants had planned to spend another winter here, before receiving their orders to leave.

They also found more buckets outside and while Madeleine cleaned them with water from the well, Ryder carried on collecting wood. He had no desire to leave the cabin in the dead of night and search for wood. Not in this place.

He made his way through dining rooms and dormitories and offices, noticing that decay had already started in many of the rooms because of missing roof shingles and shutters. Doors left open had allowed water to get in, rotting away floorboards and door frames.

It had once been an impressive building. As good as any fort he'd seen. He counted fifteen buildings, half of them two story, all opening onto a wooden boardwalk before a step down into the parade ground. From the size of the bunk rooms, the place must have housed close to a hundred men.

Madeleine had a fire going in the cabin by the time he returned. As he stepped up onto the wooden step to open the door, he glanced back behind him.

All he could see from here was the back of the livery.

There were only two ways in and out of this fort. One was the massive front gates where they had entered. But there was another single gate, big enough to ride one horse and rider through, at the rear of the fort, just behind their cabin. But no-one could get through either, because Madeleine had dropped the pine bars down, locking them in.

He shivered and opened the cabin door, just as a chill wind blew around him, covering him in fine flakes of snow. It was hours yet until dusk, yet already it was getting dark. He shivered again, eager now to get warm, but as he stepped into the room he stopped and stared in astonishment.

Madeleine was sitting on furs spread out before the fire, a blanket wrapped around her, her clothes folded in a pile by the hearth. Beside her was a bucket of warm water, heated by the flames and beside that lay a damp cloth and a precious bar of soap, the last of her supply she'd bought in St Louis. The room smelled of lavender and winter flowers.

"Halfbreed, it's cold, do shut the door and come in, my love," she said softly.

*

Ryder did as she bid and gently kicked the door shut behind him, dropping the wood by the hearth before turning back to place the wooden pine bar down across the door to lock it. Then he moved to kneel beside her.

"Now I do feel like I smell like a skunk," he said.

"And I need to shave."

Madeleine reached for the cloth and dipped it in the bucket of warm water before lathering it with soap. Then she nodded towards Ryder's clothes.

"Take them off halfbreed. Let me bathe you," she said softly.

But Ryder paused and in that moment, for just a heartbeat, Madeleine felt unsure again and suddenly regretted coming here. They were like strangers. They had been apart for too long. Three years too long.

She put aside the cloth then reached up to pull the blanket close, feeling foolish.

"We shouldn't have come here," she said softly. "I just thought, after what you said last night, about spending the night alone with me, that this was the perfect place. Yet I think I've badly misjudged what it is you wanted, so we can leave for the Omaha at first light. We can be back with your brothers and Harry by mid-day."

Ryder looked at her in bewilderment, then shook his head.

"No Madeleine, you haven't got it wrong. Indeed, I want to be alone with you so desperately that I'm afraid I'll get it wrong. I've wanted this for so long it feels unreal, as though I'm dreaming," he moved to sit beside her, taking her hands in his own.

"Yet how do I explain how I feel! If I tell you you're my life, it wouldn't come close to how I feel. You've been a part of me since the moment I met you in your cave. I remember it even now, feeling as if I'd come home after years of looking, without knowing I was," he brought her hands to his lips and kissed each palm.

"Tell me what it is you want," he said, with such a haunting look on his face that Madeleine couldn't move. "What do you want me to do? I'll do whatever you ask, because I want this to be right between us. I want you to love me again, as you once did, and not to be repulsed by what you see, because I carry more scars Madeleine, both inside and out although you'll discover them for yourself soon enough. All I ask is you understand I'm still the same man, that my love for you never once faltered. I want you to know that above all else."

Madeleine held his gaze then nodded slowly. "Then do as I ask halfbreed and take off your clothes."

Again Ryder paused, but only for a moment. Then he stood up and pulled off his fur coat, followed by his buckskin shirt. He turned his back and pulled down the sleeves of his woolen undergarment, revealing his shoulders and back and Madeleine understood at last why he'd paused, why he'd been silent for most of the ride here. It was because of his scars.

She looked at him in dismay but said not a word, just stood up and went to him, reaching out to gently touch his back and shoulders, the scars a permanent reminder of a beating that had almost claimed his life.

Ryder reared back as though he'd been touched by a hot iron, then he turned to her, his whole body rigid, the top of his woolen undergarment hanging around his waist, his pants still on, forgotten.

The bruises that had once covered his body had long ago healed, but there was an ugly welt on his belly where a vicious kick from a boot had broken two ribs, leaving a weal of scar tissue beneath the skin.

Thin white and red welts and ridges showed where he had been cut with a knife for the hell of it and marked from rings on a man's fingers as he was viciously punched.

Around his neck was a white ridged scar where a rope had been tied so tight to subdue him, that it had left a permanent mark. Thin white scars circled each wrist, revealing where manacles had cut deep.

"Dear God," she whispered. "What did they do to you?"

Ryder watched her as she traced the scars with her fingers. He had long ago got used to them, but yes, it mattered to him if she was repulsed by them.

"It doesn't matter anymore," he said softly. "They've long since healed and no longer trouble me. But Jarryth's boot delivered the worst damage of all when he kicked me here," he paused to touch the back of his head.

"Because of it, I suffered blinding headaches for many weeks. For months afterwards, I didn't know where I was or who I was."

He took her hands in his own, unwilling to have her touch those telltale marks.

"I know from your letters I found at Millbryne Park that you discovered I was put aboard a ship by Jarryth. Yet I have little memory of it, nor do I know even now where I was bound. Had the ship not become wrecked in a storm off the coast of Portugal, only God knows what would have happened to me."

Madeleine released one of her hands to touch him again, tracing her finger along a deep scar where a boot had left its mark. Ryder almost reeled from her touch.

"Yet you can't have survived these injuries alone. Who helped you?" she asked, knowing a woman had been involved with this healing.

"I know almost nothing about her, other than her name was Luisa Cardozo and she was someone's grandmother. Her husband, Viktor, saved me from drowning. He pulled me from the surf when no-one else would, as I still wore the chains that Jarryth had placed around my wrists. Everyone in that village where I was shipwrecked thought me a criminal, but this elderly couple offered me sanctuary in a crude hut they owned on the beach. For weeks, while I lived there in pain, not knowing who I was or why I wore manacles, they continued to give me fresh water and what little food they had. Had Luisa not treated my wounds I might have died. It was Viktor who freed me of the manacles."

He shook his head, looking at the marks on his wrists. "I had not one word of their language so could tell them nothing of my past, but it didn't matter anyway because every memory I had was gone, including everything I knew of you and Harry. It wasn't until months later when I met a small child in France that I began to remember things. Yet how to return to you, when France and England were at war! It took months before I managed to get across the Channel to England. By then, you'd already returned to America."

Madeleine looked at him, remembering the words of the ancient one.

Your destiny lies in this country but it was not your time to come. Because of it, you have known more sorrow

But she wouldn't think on that now because they were here together at last. She reached out to take

Ryder's hands, tracing those telltale scars on his wrists. One day he might tell her the whole of it. Until then, they had all the time in the world.

*

Ryder joined her by the hearth and reached for the leather bag he'd brought with him. He pulled out his razor and a small silver canister. Madeleine watched, curious, as he unscrewed the top of the canister and held it out to her.

"I've been saving this for a special occasion. No-one else has drunk from it. Will you share it with me?

Madeleine nodded, her fingers brushing his own as she reached to take the canister from him. "What is it?" she asked, taking a sip, even as the rich liquor left its mark on her mouth and the back of her throat.

"Brandy!" she exclaimed in delight. She smiled and dared to take another sip before offering it back to him.

Ryder took the cannister and drunk from it before moving to cross-legged beside her, even as Madeleine reached for the warm soapy cloth and moved to kneel behind him. She gently bathed his neck and shoulders, his arms and down his back.

When she leaned forward, she saw his eyes were closed, his big hands held lightly in front of him, his fingers clasped, trusting her completely, utterly vulnerable, and she felt such love for him in that moment she had to close her eyes, willing herself to breathe and carry on, or she would ruin this.

But there was nothing devious about Ryder. He was everything that was right in the world, he was honest and just and the goodness of him filled Madeleine's heart and soul. He turned her world to light.

When he stopped her to shave, unable to bear the thought of touching her without shaving, she sat and watched him. They talked a little of Harry, of his first words, his first steps, his love of horses.

After Ryder wiped his face and neck clean, Madeleine dipped the cloth back in the water then moved to kneel before him, running it over his arms, down his belly, before reaching for his hands.

She didn't look at him now, because she knew he'd opened his eyes to watch her. Gently, she washed each finger but as she held his hands within her own, she began to tremble from the power of him. He was a big man, tall and broad of shoulder but as he sat there he seemed to vibrate with a potent male energy. When she took the courage to look at him, she didn't need to speak. She understood what he wanted.

He stood up, paused for only a moment then pulled at the rawhide belt which held up the buckskin pants. He stepped out of them, his back to her, then pulled off the woolen undergarment which most men wore to keep warm. His body was well-formed, yet Madeleine thought him bigger and more muscular than she remembered, his arms and legs and belly taut with hard muscle. He turned and came back to her, holding his clothes discreetly in front of him, then he sat down, his clothes still covering his sex, his long legs stretched out before him.

Madeleine dipped the cloth in the water and once again lathered it with soap. Then she began to wash his legs, aware of his gaze as she moved past his ankles, his shins, his knees, up to his thighs. She glanced up at him, stunned by the desire she saw in his face, along with something else. It took her a moment to understand what it was and then she knew.

That vulnerability, again.

In case he got this wrong, in case she might not love him enough, in case he lost her again.

Madeleine watched as his beautiful eyes, so like his son's, searched her face, as though seeking an answer there. When she saw the flicker of fear pass over that handsome face which held such strength, it almost broke her heart.

Did *he* not yet understand?

Was he still so unsure of her and what these past three years had meant without him?

Her whole being ached to reassure him, so she moved closer to him.

"There are no words to tell you how much I love you," she said, slow and soft, so he wouldn't mistake one word of what she had to say.

"Since you were lost to me, I've waited every second of every hour of every day for you to come back. No man alive can stir my blood as you do. I only need to hear your voice, or look at you, or touch you and I'm yours. You lit a fire within me all those years ago halfbreed, when we lived with the Bannock, a fire that will last until the end of my days," she paused and shook her head.

"I learned I can live without you, yet I am not alive. I exist only for Harry. But we cannot change the past three years or undo what Jarryth did to us, so shall we let it go my love? Let us see the ugliness for what it was and be grateful for its passing and in this strange and empty place we find ourselves in tonight, shall we take a step towards a new future?"

She held the cloth in both hands, yet she saw only Ryder, watching her in silence.

"I pray you might love me again, as you once did, when we lived in those distant mountains with the Bannock and again, when we lived in England. I pray that Jarryth, Thorne and Lisbeth haven't won, that no bitterness lingers there, that you and I might find something good again and use it to build a bridge to something wonderful, a future we can share with Harry."

Ryder said nothing for a long moment, then finally he nodded.

"You need have no fear of my not loving you, nor of my holding onto the past," he said, his voice full of love. "I let all that bitterness go the moment I read those letters and diaries you left for me in the secret drawer at Millbryne Park. I was reborn that day and I have only you to thank for it. Had you not gone to France to seek Jarryth, you would never have found those documents and I would never have read them. Indeed, were I to thank you for the rest of my life, it would never be enough."

Madeleine reached up to run a finger down the side of his face, along that square jaw that was now clean shaven.

She drew a line with her finger, gently, gently, around his mouth and he allowed her to touch him, yet for the moment, he didn't respond.

"You have no reason to thank me halfbreed," she whispered. "I sought only to discover your whereabouts. Indeed, I would have gone to the end of the world, to hell itself to find you and I almost did, when I fought Jarryth in the chapel. But that is something we can talk on later. Just know that everything I found, everything I did, was all for you. But it all came to nothing, for your whereabouts remained a mystery," she said, as a single tear fell and ran slowly down her cheek.

Ryder reached up and gently wiped it away. "No need to cry, my love," he whispered.

"The time for tears, for both of us, is over. We have the rest of our lives together," he said, bending his head close to her own, closing his eyes as he took in the scent of her, that sweet smell of herbs within her hair and on her skin.

From his touch, Madeleine felt his body throb with lust and she moved to sit across his thighs, her legs on either side of him, keeping the blanket around herself before reaching up to wipe his face, because he was also crying.

Ryder closed his eyes to her touch, the heat of her almost consuming him. He was trembling as he placed his hands within the blanket and after three long years, he felt the softness of her skin.

Madeleine felt every touch of those big, callused hands as they caressed her and she collapsed on his shoulder, her breath coming in short pants of desire. Unable to help herself, she moved to kiss his shoulder, tasting and smelling the lavender from her cloth along with his own sweet smell, her lips trailing along his shoulder to his neck, pausing to kiss that white scar before moving to touch his lips with her own. His mouth was gentle at first, and for a long lingering moment their kiss was chaste.

Until Madeleine licked his lips. Ryder groaned deep in the back of his throat, the heat between them an intense, passionate thing, full of urgency. He groaned again, a deep primal sound and then his hands were pulling the blanket away, his fingers in her hair, long and loose down her back, then around her waist before reaching up to cup her breasts.

Madeleine uttered a soft cry as he looked at her, at her young body, her skin flawless and then his mouth was on her own but no longer gentle, now it was rough with a man's need, his lips seeking to devour her even as her arms went around his shoulders pulling him closer, her nails sharp as his fingers went between her legs, finding her heat. Ryder groaned again, a deep animal grunt which came from the back of his throat and after that, both were lost.

Kissing his face, her hands in his hair then everywhere, touching the hard strength of him, she felt him lift her and she willingly moved with him, her legs supporting her as she raised herself above him, oblivious to everything but him, his strength, his beauty, his smell, his lust, and slowly, slowly she moved to lower herself down on him. As her heat and sex enclosed around his own, as she began to move in that ancient rhythmic dance, as Ryder's hands came back to her hips to help her, she moved back a little, crying out his name as he caressed her.

She was lost to him, letting him do what he wanted, because after three long years, their lovemaking was all mindless, primitive lust and desperate need. They both knew the slow love would come later. After.

Eleven

I woke during the night, aware of the bitter cold outside as an icy draft came in under the door. With great care so I didn't disturb Ryder, I placed a fur against the door to keep the cold out. Then I placed more logs on the fire, although I saw logs had been placed on the hot coals not long ago. Ryder must have woken while I slept yet I didn't hear him, which showed how safe I felt with him.

I moved to sit beside him, just so I could look at him, even though he lay deep in sleep. A blanket lay across his thighs, yet his chest and arms and most of his legs lay bare. He had a beautiful body, his skin flawless except for the scars and I almost wept at what he must have endured.

The head injury he'd suffered at the hands of Jarryth had been the second in a matter of three years, the first suffered during an altercation with *esa*. I glanced down at his right lower limb and saw that scar, a legacy of that meeting with my white wolf, yet it was nothing more than a thin white line. The thick raised uneven skin which had previously marked him, showing my own desperate attempts to save his life while he battled a fever, seemed to have faded away. I wanted to touch it, to retrace that awful wound he'd suffered all those years ago.

There was a fine sheen of sweat on his skin, but it wasn't from fever. This was from the heat of our fire and our lovemaking. With the memory of what we'd done, I felt the heat rise in me, my body aching for him again yet I didn't wake him. I let him sleep on, as I could see the dark circles of fatigue under his eyes.

I moved to lie beside him, watching him, still

finding it hard to believe that he was here. He must have battled through the depths of winter to get to the Omaha, when a lesser man might not have bothered.

His arm jerked in sleep and then his hand, large and more calloused than I remembered, moved as though to grasp something. Then he was still again. I couldn't bear to think what he'd gone through over the past three years although I hoped one day he'd tell me of it. Just as I'd tell him of my life during those long years apart, although he knew some of it because of the letters I'd left for him at Millbryne Park.

He'd aged a little. He now owned some silver hair at his temples and he had deeper lines around his eyes. Yet he was still the same man. Fearless and strong, not bitter, nor full of hate, although perhaps a little towards Jarryth, but not for himself.

He was still wary of people. I saw that the moment he'd stepped into the Omaha village, although that wariness had more to do with his childhood than anything else. From a young boy he'd rarely trusted anyone and I could count on two hands the people he'd confided in, people who had never let him down, except one. That person was me.

Had I only stayed in England and recognized my loneliness, grief and homesickness for what they were, Ryder and I would have been reunited over a year ago. Had I only quietened my own impatience and my desperate need to heal, had I only believed in Ryder, that he'd eventually find his way back to me as he'd promised when we first became lovers all those years ago, we wouldn't have endured another year of suffering.

I closed my eyes, not wanting to think on it, because something deep inside me knew I'd forced my hand. Because when I made the decision to leave England, I'd known that if Ryder returned to me in whatever state after being missing for years, he would never have returned to the Bannock. Not least until Harry was an adult. Because being the man he was, he would have felt duty bound to stay in England, to make up for those lost years, to work for the Benedict estates because of his loyalty to men like Rupert, Ash and even Bernard Fahey. Once he was settled back in England I would never have left him, or Harry, to return to the Bannock alone.

But my own determination to return home, to heal, had allowed fate to play a hand in so many other lives beside our own. The Bannock girls were no longer living with the Mandan. Lily, Bryn, Jimmy, Monique and Josette were all making new lives for themselves. Te'tukhe and Wesa'shangke had been reunited after some years apart, Ryder had met with his brothers and Aishi-waahni' and had that fateful meeting with Allard Lemoine in St Louis.

No, the past could never be undone nor could we ever reclaim those lost years, but look at what we'd gained because I'd left England. Now we had a chance to rebuild our lives, to make every day ahead of us count for something and live them the best way we could. I vowed never to turn away from Ryder's embrace, but then I could deny him nothing and even as I moved to curl around his warm body, he moved beside me.

"Madeleine," he moaned softly then his arm swung over me, pulling me close, his hands touching me, gentle yet urgent and as he pulled me beneath him I moved my body to accommodate his and felt him enter me, the movements no longer hurried or desperate, but slow and gentle. He looked down at me in the soft light of the fire, his eyes holding my own, his hair tangled around him from sleep, his face soft and full of love, his body large and looming as I raised my legs to hold him, to bring him closer. I reached out and touched those scars around his neck and on his chest and belly and when the loving was done, when Ryder fell asleep in my arms, his head on my breast, I held him there, both of us unwilling to move away.

Twelve

Madeleine woke just after dawn to find Ryder gone. She stood up and opened the shutter, looking out onto a world of white, framed by a sky of the deepest blue. It had snowed heavily during the night and as she shivered from the cold she thought of Harry and the girls. She hoped she'd left enough wood to keep their fire going through the night. She closed the shutter to keep the room warm then went back to the hearth to touch the water in the bucket. It was still warm. She took the cloth and soap and quickly washed herself before dressing. When she stepped outside, it was bitterly cold. She threw the soiled water away but as she sat the bucket down by the well, she heard Ryder call out to her.

"Come on up, the view is spectacular!"

She turned to find him high up in the tower on the western wall. Laughing, she ran across the square and began to climb the wooden ladder. As she made her way through the trapdoor, Ryder held out his hand, pulling her up and into his arms.

"*Behne*," he said in the Bannock dialect and kissed her lightly on the mouth.

She smiled and returned the kiss, yet it was nothing like they had shared last night. She kissed him again then he grabbed her by the hand and pulled her across to the railing. The forest, which swept away from the fort in all directions was no longer green but white, with snow and icicles hanging off branches. Beyond the forest, way off to the east, they could see smoke rising on the far horizon.

"Look, the Omaha village," Ryder said, smiling. "And just beyond it, can you see that long wide ribbon of water? That's the Missouri stretching north as far as you could see."

Madeleine shaded her eyes with her hand against the white glare of the day and saw the tributary they had followed yesterday. To the west, way in the distance, lay an endless range of mountains which disappeared over the horizon.

"Are they your mountains, do you think?" Ryder asked. "Perhaps that is the very southern edge of them."

Madeleine turned to put her arms about his waist so she could lean into him and share his warmth. "I wish I were a bird," she suddenly said. "Seeing those mountains gives me hope that in a few more months we'll be there."

Ryder heard the longing in her voice and he leaned down to kiss her. "Do you regret it?" he asked. She looked up at him, puzzled and Ryder asked again. "The Bannock. Do you regret leaving them to come to England with me? I know how much of a wrench it was, taking you away from that life."

For a moment Madeleine didn't answer him, then she shook her head. "In all truth, I couldn't imagine living there now, not without you or *esa*. He had to return to his own kind and I remember Ese-ggwe'na'a telling me that, although it seems so long ago now. So no, I don't regret it. I miss them, because *esa* and the Bannock are my family. But you and Harry are my family too, so I must be where you are."

Ryder hugged her close. She loved the smell of him, the bigness of him, the comfort of him.

"Ash showed me the papers you signed, enrolling Harry in boarding school," he said. "You're sending him to the same school I went to, along with Torrance and Thorne and my grandfather before them. I must thank you for it, because I could not have done it, although I know it's the right thing to do," he paused as he looked out over the country below them. "But he's only three and half years old and we have at least four years ahead of us before he must be in school, so let's make the most of it Madeleine," he paused as she stepped back to look at him, curious and a little uneasy.

"What are you saying Ryder?"

He smiled and reached to take her hands in his own. "I think we should stay with the Bannock a little while, if they'll have us. By my reckoning we should arrive at the Snake River Plain this November, some eight months away, in time to settle before the worst of winter. Come spring, perhaps we could leave with them when they head to their summer hunting grounds in the north. Or we could spend the summer in your cave with Harry," he shrugged. "But whatever we decide, we have a little more than four years to make the best of it," he paused, frowning. "Before I left London I asked Ash to confirm Harry's start date at boarding school. The child is enrolled for August 1809, just after his eight birthday."

He felt Madeleine tense in his arms and knew the questions she would ask. He bent down and kissed her. "Don't worry about my responsibilities in England. I took care of them before I left. Rupert and I now own very little together and what I do own, I've left in the hands of Ash and Bernard Fahey. Indeed, their staff have been running the Benedict estates without me well enough for the past three years, so I don't think another four years will hurt. Besides, my role was always to grow the business, so in truth, I think I've spent enough years doing that. Now it's time for us, even though we both know this life can't last forever because of Harry's future in England. But for a few short years we shall have a little freedom, away from all the chains that bind me to the Benedict estates. We shall teach Harry all we know of life in the wild and by the time he returns to London in four years' time he'll be totally incapable of coping with life in an English boarding school, as indeed I was, but perfectly able to take a knife, musket or bow and arrow to anyone who dares cross him," he paused and looked at her, his voice low and soft. "So, what say you to my plans my love?"

Madeleine nodded with emotion as she leaned into him, hugging him. "Of course, you know how much I want this. But there's something you don't yet know, Ryder. Something I haven't had time to tell you."

He stood back, bewildered. "Is this going to change our plans?"

Madeleine nodded. "Just a few weeks, nothing more."

She told him then about the Bannock, about that attack on their village four years ago. She told him about Huu'aidi and everyone else she knew who had died. Then she told him about Deinde'-paggwe. "Knowing she is living as a slave with the Mandan, with a small child, keeps me awake at night. I cannot stop thinking about that beautiful little girl who loved us both so well. Nor could I look Ese-ggwe'na'a or Paddake'e in the eye and explain to them why I didn't try and rescue her, when I was so close. Had it been

Harry who was taken, I would curse the man who passed on by and did nothing to find him. Indeed, the moment I met Poongatse and Wannge'e in St Louis and learned of the attack and Deinde'-paggwe's fate, I began making plans to head to the Mandan and trade for her freedom. Te'tukhe knows of it, but he will head south to the Wazhazhe before winter's end, in the company of Wesa'shangke and Aishi-waahni'. So I ask you Mi'wasa, will you come north to the Mandan with me, to trade for that young girl's freedom, along with her small daughter?"

Ryder said nothing for a long time, he just leaned on the railing and looked out over the forest. Finally he turned back to her, frowning. "We both know it's dangerous country up there, Madeleine. We won't be safe, let alone the girls and Harry. But like you, I could not look at Ese-ggwe'na'a and know Deinde'-paggwe lives with an enemy and we did nothing to help her. So, the decision is made. We shall ride north to the Mandan. But we must have a plan. Perhaps we can hide Harry and the girls somewhere to keep them safe until we come for them."

Madeleine reached out to hug him. "I know all too well the dangers we'll face so I agree, we'll come up with a plan to keep Harry and the girls safe. But if you can teach him how to survive in the wild, then you can teach him how to cope with life in an English boarding school."

Ryder laughed and bent down to kiss her. "Oh, I'll do that alright," he said softly.

Thirteen

We stood in that high wooden tower looking out on the world until thick black clouds swept down from the north and it began to snow again. Ryder followed me down the ladder and while I returned to the cabin to throw more wood on the low coals to get the room warm, Ryder filled the bucket with clean water from the well. We sat and ate a breakfast of cold smoked meats and bread I'd baked yesterday before we left the Omaha village. While we waited to drink the herbs of peppermint I'd placed to steep in hot water, we spoke of our future. We didn't speak of our past, not then, and as the room warmed, Ryder insisted I undress so he could return the favor of yesterday and bathe me.

He was gentle at first, the warm cloth touching every surface of my body before his hands and mouth drove me to the point of madness. I became the weak one. Me, who had always been the fighter now whimpered like a child, feeling emotions that were impossible to contain after so long. The touch of him was like an unbearable heat, the ache of sexual need I felt for him became both pleasure and pain. I wondered how it was possible that he didn't succumb, that he was now the strong one and it was I who was helpless and vulnerable. But his turn came later and as he reared above me, the weight of him bearing down on me was the most wonderful thing in the world.

Fourteen

It was Ryder who began speaking of the past, long before Madeleine. They lay together by the fire covered in warm blankets when he began to talk, his voice soft and low in that gloomy early morning cabin.

"I cannot begin to tell you how I felt when I found all those letters and documents in that secret drawer at Millbryne Park. The portraits of Harry almost brought me to my knees because until that moment, I'd carried a lot of anger towards you for leaving, for not believing I'd find a way back. But how could I not follow you, after reading what you left me."

He reached out to caress her leg which lay over his. Her head rested on his shoulder and her hand moved slowly over his naked belly.

"When I received the letter you sent from St Louis, I made plans to sail from London within the week. I sent a letter to the Corrigan ranch to let you know I was coming but Julia said she never received it. For that I blame myself, because I should have sent it months earlier to let you know I was alive and well," he paused, moving a little, putting his arm behind his head.

"But luck was on my side, because I met Allard Lemoine in St Louis. Indeed, had I not spoken with him, I would have continued on to the Wazhazhe in the hope that you and Harry might still be there. I would have had to winter over there, missing you completely, unable to catch you for another year at least, not until I reached the Snake River Plain."

Madeleine turned and looked up at him. "Te'tukhe told me everything. About his familial ties to Allard and the years they spent trapping together up north. Of their meeting the Kansa and of Te'tukhe's decision to come north to try and find me. He knew something must have happened to you, because why else would I be travelling alone. So I know all that, except the part you played in it."

Ryder smiled and told her of his meeting Allard Lemoine and his sons in St Louis.

"When Allard told me that Te'tukhe had left to head north to follow you, I hardly dared believe it. As for the part the Kansa played in all of this, how do we thank them? They brought us all together, through the simple act of inviting you to stay with them. Had they not met you, Te'tukhe, Allard and his sons would never have heard of you, nor known of your plans to head north. I would have another year of travelling ahead of me. Had Allard not decided to visit the Wazhazhe people one last time with Wakanta, he would have missed Wesa'shangke and Aishi-waahni'. They would have returned to the Comanche, never knowing that Te'tukhe had gone north to meet you and Harry," Ryder paused in wonder. "So many people involved, with such critical information, all held within a breath of chance."

"I think it more than chance," Madeleine said and then told Ryder of her dream, of meeting the ancient one.

"I think it was he who turned the buffalo, because I was determined to ride to the Wazhazhe village so that Harry could meet your brothers and your people. I was also determined to ride through winter, to reach the Omaha because I knew I had to be there by early March at the latest, otherwise I wouldn't reach the Snake River Plain for another year. But the buffalo coming and turning us north, changed everything. It was one of the most terrifying moments I've ever known," she said. "Not only because Harry was running straight towards them, but if they had begun to stampede, we would have been lost," she paused as Ryder took her hand and threaded his fingers through her own.

"Yet the strangest thing of all, for several days before that, Harry had been so sick with fever we thought we might lose him. Had we not stopped to settle him, we would have continued north, completely trapped as that herd of bison headed straight towards us. That Harry rallied just as they appeared on the distant hills, was nothing but astonishing. Sometimes I think on it and wonder if the ancient one was there with us, knowing we were heading into certain death. He used Harry to make us stay in that one place, then he used Harry again to wake us when the buffalo came. Except our son decided not to wake us, he decided instead to head for the river."

She told Ryder of their desperate ride to the plateau with the bison stampeding behind them.

The story unsettled him and he rose to place more wood on the fire as Madeleine sat up, sitting cross-legged, a blanket around her. Then he reached for the canister of brandy and handed it to her. But as Madeleine took a sip then passed it back to him, Ryder asked about Jarryth, Thorne and Lisbeth Ashbury.

Madeleine told him everything. She left nothing out. For the next few hours they sat in that small cabin in the wild and spoke of what happened in those months after Ryder disappeared.

She told him of her desperate flight to France, of meeting Jarryth at Napoleon's Ball, of finding Monique and Josette and all the documents in that squalid townhouse in Paris. She spoke of Thorne and that fatal fall down his stairs and the meeting with Lisbeth in that house in Bankside. She revealed her own hand in Lisbeth's death. She spoke of the tunnels at Millbryne Park, of the role their servants had played in keeping Harry safe, of that desperate fight with Jarryth in the Chapel. Finally, she spoke of the ancient one, of seeing *esa* and the dream she'd had, when the ancient one told her that Ryder was coming.

Ryder said nothing while she spoke. When she was finished he reached for her, taking her in his arms.

"I take my courage from your own," he said, kissing her. "Had it not been for you, our son would have been lost, because I know Jarryth's hatred of us would never have stopped until he'd destroyed us all," he paused, frowning.

"When I regained my memory, I dreaded to think what I'd find on my return to England. I knew there was a chance that Jarryth and Thorne might have sold Millbryne Park along with Diccon House. But I never expected to find them dead. Nor did I ever imagine the part that Lisbeth Ashbury played in all the deceit," he paused, watching her.

"I took your advice and destroyed almost everything I found in that secret drawer. Other than a few things which Harry might like in his later years, I burned everything else."

"I'm glad of it," Madeleine said, then asked what

she'd wondered about for so long. "Do you think Ash had any idea of Lisbeth's deceit during all the years they were married?"

Ryder nodded. "He suspected some of it, like her affair with Thorne, but in the end he chose to ignore it. He knew nothing of her being Jarryth's mother," he shook his head. "I can tell you this. Ash admitted to me that he was sad at Lisbeth's passing, but there was no regret on his part about her death. When I said my goodbyes to him in London he seemed at peace with it all, indeed, I believe him happy."

Madeleine turned in his arms and ran her fingers down his arm, feeling the hard muscle there.

"I must hear of your travels now, because I've been tormented long enough as to what happened to you. By the telling of it, I think I shall also find some peace."

"You have every right to hear it," Ryder said softly. "I'll never forget the last time I saw you and Harry. You were at the front door of Diccon House and I was on my way to meet Rupert, or so I believed. I vaguely remember arriving at a squalid building somewhere in London, but that memory is mostly lost to me, along with everything else until I woke on that beach in Portugal. I have a memory like a dream, of someone laughing as they kicked me, followed by the most extraordinary pain and then the strangest sensation of being shackled. I have the scars to prove I wore manacles, yet I have little memory of them, nor of the ship I was on. I do have some thoughts of being shipwrecked, of being under water, of crawling onto a wooden beam, of drifting in the current. But my real memories started as I healed in that primitive hut on the beach in Portugal."

Ryder spoke of Viktor and Luisa Cardozo, of meeting the Branco family, of Tomás Saldivar and his clipper the *Zeferino*.

"All these people and more helped me. I owe them so much," Ryder said before telling of the gold he had entrusted to Saldivar, to be delivered to his friends in Portugal.

"Without them, I might still be somewhere in Spain or Portugal, my mind lost to me," he smiled suddenly. "The frustrating thing is, had I decided to head south to Lisbon, instead of joining Saldivar on his ship, someone in that town might have recognized me from my business dealings there and I could have caught a Benedict clipper back to the England!"

Madeleine laughed at the irony of that. She also understood at last why Ryder looked so different. Those months aboard the ship had made him more muscular, had given his body bulk. She smiled and looked up at him.

"Jarryth came so close to destroying us," she said softly. "Did you go into the crypt and see where he was buried?"

Ryder shook his head. "The wrought iron gates above the crypt were padlocked and I had no care to find the key. He caused so much unhappiness when he was alive, I had no desire to visit his grave."

"Then let us speak fondly of Ash and Rupert," Madeleine said. "They never faltered in their loyalty to you and always treated me with kindness. I admit, I trusted no-one after you disappeared, not even Rupert, because he had the most to gain from your death. But both men, including Charlotte, proved your friends. They did everything they could to help me find you."

They were silent for a little while then Madeleine asked Ryder about the war between England and France.

"Napoleon continues his threats of invading England, but to do so he must first destroy the British fleet. But his strength lies in his army, not his navy. The French are soldiers, not sailors, although there is talk of the Spanish joining him in an alliance, which would give Bonaparte access to the Spanish Armada. Which would mean England must then face two great adversaries, because the Spanish are masters on the water, just like the English," he moved to stretch his legs and watched her.

"May we speak of our son, Madeleine? By God, you have done a fine job with him. He is a beauty."

Madeleine smiled. "He is your double, a good strong boy, afraid of nothing. Te'tukhe thinks the world of him and Te'tukhe is notoriously hard to please," she paused for a long moment then added softly. "There's something else you should know Ryder. I have muskets, almost a dozen which I purchased for the Bannock, along with some gifts for Paddake'e. Te'tukhe knows of them, because he helped me hide them away until we leave the Omaha as I've no care to trade for them."

Ryder nodded. "Julia told me of your purchases. She also mentioned the sawn-off muskets. I almost did the same, as I've also purchased muskets for the Bannock, but in the end I was too impatient to follow you. Do they fire well enough?"

"Well enough to kill two men." She told him of the Spanish solders who had tracked them, teasing them for days, to intimidate and bully.

Ryder said not a word, just lifted her gently as though she weighed no more than Harry and pulled her down to lie on top of him. Her hair fell across his shoulders and he reached up to touch it, his face soft in the light of the fire behind him.

"I find myself wondering sometimes what I did to deserve you. I touch you now as I did in my dreams, but if this is another dream then I pray to God, it lasts for a while. You haunted me, tormented me. I wondered how it was possible for a simple mortal man to bear such torture. You have claimed me, all of me, my heart, my body, my soul and I pray these next few years ahead of us with the Bannock is enough for you, Madeleine. That you can leave them behind when we must, that your love for the Bannock and the mountains and even *esa*, can be put to rest for a while, until Harry is an adult at least, giving you some peace when we return to England," he paused as he watched her then when he spoke again, his voice was hoarse with emotion. "I hope it's enough Madeleine, because four years is the best I can do."

She said nothing for a long moment, then moved to lay her hands gently on either side of his face, before moving to kiss him, although her lips barely touched his own.

"I'll be happy enough with those few years Ryder. I knew before I left England that's all the time I had. I knew I had to be back in England for Harry's schooling, not only to honor you, but his Benedict heritage. But to be able to share these years together, the three of us, will be more than I ever hoped for. So if this is your dream halfbreed, then it is also mine," she whispered, bending to kiss him, wanting to stay like that forever, in his arms.

*

It stopped snowing just before mid-day, so they left the cabin to get some fresh air and take the horses out to let them graze. They took their small bags with all their belongings, ready to fill them with herbs and root vegetables if they found any.

Ryder went to get the horses, while Madeleine quickly washed, using the warm water from the bucket. Once dressed, she put another couple of logs on the fire to keep the cabin warm. Then she slung her sheath of arrows on her back before picking up her bow. As she opened the door of the cabin and stepped outside, she glanced back and other than the logs burning in the hearth, no-one would ever know they had been there.

She stepped outside, pulling her fur coat tight against the bitter cold, but before she hurried towards the parade ground to meet Ryder, she raised the pine bar on the gate just behind their cabin, leaving it unlocked as it had been when they first arrived. Ryder had already opened the two front gates to lead the horses out and he waited there for her now. She closed them behind her, then mounted her horse and followed Ryder into the trees.

*

They rode at a walk, the horses' hooves silent upon the fresh snow. When they came to a narrow, fast flowing river, the water icy cold, they set several snares.

"Shall we leave the horses here and go on ahead on foot?" Ryder suggested. "They can graze here while we hunt."

Madeleine agreed, so they hobbled the horses, allowing them to nudge aside the snow to get at the tender roots which lay beneath. Then they headed upstream. A couple of hours later Madeleine had shot three plump wild rabbits with her bow and arrows.

By midafternoon it was snowing again, the temperatures dropping to below freezing so they turned back and headed downstream to where they'd left the horses. They were almost there when Madeleine suddenly stopped, grabbing Ryder by his arm and putting a finger to her lips, pulling him back behind some thick pines. He said nothing but followed her, trusting her instincts, understanding at once that they weren't alone.

They crouched behind the trees, hidden by thick ferns and shrubs when the riders came into view. There were eight of them, their horses ridden by men who wore scalp locks, buckskin leggings, thick fur coats and knee-high moccasins. They carried only bows and arrows which was unusual, being this close to the Missouri River and the easy trade with fur trappers.

The band of men rode in silence, alert menacing as they looked out into the forest. Madeleine and Ryder dropped lower into the ferns and then the riders were gone, disappearing as quickly as they had come.

"They're wearing scalp locks," Madeleine whispered.

"Pawnee," Ryder said, feeling uneasy at these men

being so close to the fort. "Yet they're riding through Omaha country. If the Omaha find them, these Pawnee must know they'll start a war. Although I thought them young. No more than teenagers heading into manhood and not one of them carried a musket. Perhaps they rode this far east by mistake?"

Madeleine shivered from the cold, with the snow falling heavier now. She put her hands within her fur coat to get them warm.

"Come on," Ryder said. "Let's get the horses. We need to get back and get a fire going." He glanced at her. "Or would you rather ride for the Omaha? We can be back within a few hours."

Madeleine shook her head. "It'll be dark soon enough and I've no care to be riding at night in these bitter temperatures. If agreeable to you, I'd rather return to the fort."

They found their horses hobbled where they'd left them. Madeleine secured the rabbits to the back of her horse while Ryder checked the snares in the river, but they were empty.

They kept to the trees on their way back, staying away from well-worn deer paths. But less than a quarter mile from the fort, Madeleine reined her horse in. Ryder didn't need to ask why, because in that silent world of falling snow he'd heard it too. The sound of rusty hinges grinding open, the sound echoing out into the woods as someone opened the fort gates.

They dismounted to peer through the trees. The huge wooden building loomed ahead of them in the light of the gloomy afternoon, even as the group of riders dismounted, their voices low yet earnest as though they were arguing. Then one of the young men seemed to lose his patience and kicked his horse on, past the gates and into the parade ground

"You're right," Madeleine said, turning to Ryder. "They're youths, not yet out of their teenage years. Yet they must know of the fort's reputation. Everyone in the territory knows that European soldiers held this fort and no-one comes here because of the spirits who walk within."

"Which means those boys are reckless," Ryder said softly.

He glanced behind them at the fresh tracks in the snow, left by their horses then glanced at Madeleine. He saw his own fear on her face. The snow would cover those tracks soon enough but until they did, those youths were more than capable of following them, even through the night, using brands lit from a fire. Young men would think it good sport.

Ryder and Madeleine didn't talk about the hot ashes in the cabin, or the scat left by their horses in the livery. They both knew that as soon as they were found, the hunt would begin. But they couldn't outrun eight riders, not in these conditions. Young men riding in a pack, whether they were on enemy territory or not, would take risks. Ryder wondered briefly what prize these youths might claim, if they were to take him and Madeleine back to the Pawnee village as captives.

"Our fire must be almost out," he said, as Madeleine turned to him. "I can't see any smoke." He said nothing more, because the look on her face told him everything.

Madeleine was thinking of the part she might play in the night ahead, if she were taken captive. She looked away as laughter came from the fort.

"You were uneasy when we arrived here yesterday," she said. "Would you have stayed had I not been with you?"

Ryder shook his head. "No, I would not. Like our son and the Bannock girls, I found the fort too silent for my liking, too eerie, as if someone watched me from a window. However, I am most grateful for it, as it gave us precious time together."

"Then if a fire had started in one of the rooms, without a reason for it, would you have lingered here?" she asked.

Ryder looked at her in bewilderment, then shook his head. "No, I would not," he said again.

"Then if I can get to our cabin before they do and start a fire, I might scare them off," she said.

Ryder shook his head. "It's too dangerous. If they get hold of you, I wouldn't be able to fight eight of them off."

Madeleine nodded. "Then let's see what they're doing?"

They dismounted and led their horses into a deep grove of oak and elm, tying their reins securely. Then they ran back through the woods towards the fort, the worsening weather giving them cover in that gloomy light. They crouched low within some ferns, directly opposite the front gates which hung open. They could see the youths standing in the parade ground, looking about with unease at the darkening interior of the fort. Now and again one of them raised his voice and from the challenging tone, it sounded as if he were arguing with his friends about staying there.

"I don't think they came here by mistake," Ryder

said. "I think they know exactly what they're doing. But they're playing a dangerous game. I bet no-one in their village knows they're here."

"Then we should give them what they came for," Madeleine said, huddling within her fur coat. "If they've come all this way to see the dead, then perhaps we could help them," she said. "Or we could ride away and leave them to it and hope they don't come after us. We could let the Omaha know there's Pawnee prowling around their territory."

"We'll have to make a move soon, one way or the other, because this brutal cold will push them to do something," Ryder said, turning to Madeleine. "How do we go about scaring them off? If, indeed, we can? Youths like that won't scare easily."

"I need to frighten them. I need to show them they're not alone here," she turned to him, shivering now. "I left the back gate unlocked. If I can light a fire in one of the abandoned rooms and draw them away from our cabin and the livery, it might frighten them enough to leave."

A blast of icy wind came whistling through the trees, dumping snow off branches. They needed to get shelter before it got dark. He turned to her and nodded. "Very well, let's do it. But I'll follow you with my musket."

Madeleine shook her head. "I won't even take my own musket. If you wait with the horses I'll meet you back there," she reached up and kissed him on his mouth, yet his lips were cold. "You know I can run faster than you."

Fifteen

I left Ryder to find his own way back to the horses as I took off at a sprint. I ran through the trees then once I came alongside the back wall of the fort I left the woods and raced across that open ground. I dared not look up, I didn't want to see if one of the Pawnee had climbed up into the tower.

I reached the back gate and crouched low beside it, catching my breath, listening for the sound of foot falls behind that high pine wall. But there was only the sound of muted conversation as the youths in the parade ground continued to debate whether they should stay or go. I heard someone shouting, challenging his friends so I stood up and gently pushed open the gate.

I slipped inside before it swung all the way back then shut it carefully behind me, then I stood for a moment just behind the small cabin where Ryder and I had slept last night. There was no-one around.

I crept over to the shutters and opened them. They swung inwards, and I felt the heat of the cabin embrace me like a warm welcoming thing, compared to the cold outside. I grabbed hold of the windowsill and pulled myself up, easily clambering over it to climb inside the room.

Our fire was almost out, as Ryder thought it would be, yet there were enough hot coals and ashes remaining to show these boys that someone had stayed here recently. With fingers that now trembled, feeling that my time here was running out, I took one of the smallest logs which Ryder had brought in last night and dug two of the biggest coals out of the ashes with it. Then I turned and opened the door, running down the alley towards the first door that opened into the building beside our cabin. If the youths had been standing near the livery, they would have seen me, but they were still in the middle of the parade ground.

I ran inside, my moccasins silent on the old wooden floors, even as the wood in my hand began to smoke from the hot coals. I turned and ran upstairs to the first floor and as I approached the hearth, the wood in my hand burst into flame. I placed it carefully in the hearth then ran to another room, daring to stop and peer out a window.

I was dismayed to see the boys were no longer together but had spread out, obviously having made the decision to explore. I saw three of them head for the bunkrooms on the far left, away from me. Another three headed for the livery. Two more came directly towards the building where I was.

I couldn't let them get to the livery. They mustn't see the scat left by our horses. So I took off my hat, shook my hair free then reached up and tapped on the shutter beside me.

I must have looked very odd. A pale young woman, standing at the open window, no dirty pane of glass to hide me, my hair wild about my face and clearly someone with European connections. Such a woman was a rare thing out here.

The reaction was immediate. One of the youths looked up, saw me, uttered a cry and stepped back. I moved away from the window then took off, racing not for the stairs but for another room, because I knew from my own explorations of this fort when I'd come here before with Harry and the girls, that a window at the back of these rooms lay very close to the perimeter wall. I found it and raced across to open the shutters, aware of the youths yelling outside as they once again gathered in a pack, their footsteps on the boardwalk outside. I had precious minutes before they found enough courage to come into the building.

I climbed out of the window and onto the roof, closing the shutters behind me. The youths couldn't see me from where they were, as I was now in the very back of the fort, the cabin which Ryder and I had shared some fifty feet away.

I turned back and saw the first tendril of white smoke begin to drift out of the chimney from the room I'd just left. The youths would see it as well, which made my leaving here desperate now.

I crawled off the roof, careful of loose shingles, then climbed onto the fort wall, a distance of no more than a few feet, balancing between each of those upright posts with my hands and feet, aware of the sharp jagged points on either side of me. Then I jumped. It was about fifteen feet but I landed easily in the deep snow before sprinting back the way I'd come, along the northern side of the fort, across that open land and then into the safety of the trees.

If the youths stayed calm now, if they trusted their own instincts instead of the supernatural, they would find us. If they lit brands from the fire I'd lit and searched the fort, they'd find the hot ashes in our cabin as well as evidence that horses had recently been in the livery. They'd find my tracks at the back of the fort, my footprints in plain sight, heading back into the woods.

But like Ryder, I was hoping the boys would be scared witless as I would have been, because of our belief in the afterlife and the rumors in this territory about this building.

I found Ryder crouched by the horses waiting for me, a fur around his head and another around his shoulders in an attempt to keep warm. He reached out to hold me and I felt his body tense and stiff within my arms even as we heard shouting.

It took less than ten minutes before we heard the hard beat of horses' hooves on that open ground outside the fort and even though the light was now a shadowy dull grey, with full darkness already in some parts of the forest, we saw the youths ride hard through the trees, back the way they had come.

Ryder and I remained where we were, huddled together, then when all was quiet we hid most of our belongings under some rocks and hung two of the rabbit carcasses high in a tree to keep safe from predators until we could get them in the morning. We left the horses where they were, a blanket over each to get them through the night, then ran for the back gate.

Before we entered the fort we butchered the smaller of the three rabbits, leaving the remains buried deep in the snow, covering our tracks as best we could, then we returned to the cabin.

It was a risk staying there, but it was too cold not to. We needed the warmth of the fire. Besides, the boys wouldn't come back, not tonight at least. They would hunker down somewhere, light their own fires and keep warm.

We talked about sleeping in the mezzanine area above the stalls in the livery, but in the end decided not to, even though we could pull the ladder up. But if those youths dared each other to come back and they found us up there, there'd be no escape. We'd be trapped, with no windows to climb out of. Nor was there a hearth to light a fire to keep us warm, so we returned to the cabin. But there'd be no sleeping together that night. One of us must stand guard. As we quickly roasted the rabbit carcasses and ate, throwing bones and other waste into the flames so we left no evidence behind, Ryder took the first watch, leaving me to sleep. He woke me some hours after midnight, having let me sleep longer than he should have. Before I left the cabin and stepped out into the dark, he was curled within his blankets before the fire, fast asleep.

I wandered around the parade ground, my hands buried within my coat to keep warm. At least it had stopped snowing, but it was so cold.

The two main gates stood open, just as the youths had left them, although I could barely see them. The thick clouds above obscured all light from the stars and moon, promising more snow.

It was eerily quiet, but I wasn't afraid. Unlike Ryder, Harry and the girls, I felt safe in this unloved building, as if the thick pine walls offered me protection from the predators out there in the forest, both man and beast. I didn't even feel threatened when I heard the softest of footsteps in one of the rooms above me. Until then, I hadn't felt any supernatural presence here but whatever it was, it meant me no harm. Although I didn't venture inside. I remained outdoors, walking between the front gates and the back gate, envying Ryder his fire, but I let him sleep on.

Towards dawn I dared to climb one of the towers to look out over the forest. But there was no sign of life, even as the first rays of dawn broke through the dense cover of that black night.

I was still up there when I heard the cabin door open, the sound echoing in the silence of the morning. I turned towards it and noticed in the gloomy light, still full of shadows, there was no smoke coming from that part of the fort. Ryder had let the fire in the cabin die out. When he appeared on the edge of the parade ground, I climbed down the tower and hurried across to meet him. It was time to move.

Sixteen

They shut the back gate and crept away from the fort, reaching the woods safely before breaking into a run. They found their horses and belongings as they left them, including the rabbits and within minutes they were riding east, back towards the river under cover of the trees, unwilling to ride across open country.

When they reached the tributary that came off the Missouri, knowing they hadn't been followed, they finally stopped to give the horses a rest.

They spoke of the Bannock. They talked of what might lie ahead for them at the Mandan village. They also spoke of the people they'd left behind in London and those in St Louis.

When Ryder asked Madeleine about Jimmy, she didn't take offence from it, because she understood why he did.

"I didn't love him, not in that way, but I did trust him. When you disappeared, Jimmy became the friend I desperately needed, when I trusted no-one, not even Ash or Rupert. Jimmy knows some of my secrets, but I know he'll keep them safe until his dying day. He knew I went to Thorne's house the night Thorne died because he rode there with me, indeed, he showed me where to go. He took care of the leather bag of cash I took from Jarryth's house in Bankside, yet he took not one penny from it. It was Jimmy who arranged the boat to France for me, who drove me to Gravesend in the early hours of the morning and who was there to pick me up one week later. No matter what I asked of him, he never once questioned my reasons, nor my judgment. Nor did he ever make a claim on me, even though I think he was in love with me," she paused and looked at

Ryder.

"With Rupert and Ash, I had to play games with them because they saw me as a helpless woman, someone who couldn't think for herself or make decisions. Of course I don't judge Ash and Rupert for that, because we know that's the way the world sees women. But Jimmy never once treated me like that."

Madeleine paused and looked out over the river. "He was my friend, nothing more. He never saw me as a widow in mourning, as London society saw me, where I had to wear black gowns and stay at home, even though I knew you weren't dead. Jimmy never pitied me, as everyone else pitied me. When I began to make plans to return to the Bannock, Jimmy, Lily and Bryn asked if they could accompany me. At first I said no, but then I thought, why not?"

She turned to look at Ryder. "It's a decision I've never regretted but know this halfbreed, Jimmy was the one who stood alongside me in the shadows, who did whatever I asked without question. I could never have fought Jarryth, had Jimmy not been there to help me. We have a lot to thank him for."

Ryder said nothing for a long moment, then he nodded. "I understand," he said and that was it. He never again asked about Jimmy, nor spent time dwelling on the friendship.

*

They reached the outskirts of the village by mid-afternoon and even before they saw the earth lodges, a group of some twenty Omaha hunters came out of the trees to the south.

Among them were Te'tukhe, Wesa'shangke and Aishi-waahni'. Te'tukhe let out a great whoop of delight and pushed his horse into a gallop towards them, followed by Wesa'shangke and Aishi-waahni'.

"Go with your brothers, Ryder. I'll ride on alone," Madeleine said and reached out to take the rabbits from him before kicking her horse into a run, towards the two teepees standing on the far edge of the village.

The Bannock girls had wasted no time in raising the teepee traded with the Omaha. It was a good size, looming larger than the one Madeleine had traded with the Kansa.

Poongatse saw her first and waved before turning and calling for Harry.

The little boy came running from the teepee, screaming with delight as Madeleine rode towards him. When she dismounted and took the child in her arms, Harry scolded her for leaving him behind. Madeleine laughed then glanced back at Ryder. From the animated conversation between the men, he might be telling them about the Pawnee. No doubt Omaha scouts would be sent out within the hour.

Madeleine reached up to place Harry on the back of her horse, then walked alongside him as they headed towards the teepee, aware more than ever before that their days here were coming to an end. Soon they must head north, to the Mandan.

*

She was shocked to see that Poongatse and Wannge'e's belongings had all been moved into the other teepee, but even as she stood with the girls and admired the bigger space, she felt their tension.

For the first time since they'd left the Corrigan ranch, Madeleine thought both girls looked exhausted. But since Ryder and his brothers and the Comanche had arrived, the girls workload had more than doubled.

Now they must spend more time gathering wood for their fires, along with herbs and water.

They must set more snares to catch small game.

When the men brought in animals they'd hunted, Poongatse and Wannge'e were expected to help butcher them as well as cure the skins.

Although in truth, none of this bothered either girl because all this was seen as women's work. This was how they'd been raised, to work alongside their mothers.

Along with these chores came the raising of children and these girls had always taken care of Harry, never once complaining.

So when Wannge'e spoke, Madeleine was shocked and unprepared by her words. "*Haa*, we are well pleased with the teepee, Esa-mogo'ne'. But now Mi'wasa is back, will this be our home? Will you leave us here with the Omaha?" she asked, her voice brittle, almost accusatory.

Madeleine sat down on their furs, feeling exhausted herself, aware she had yet to butcher the rabbits and find wild vegetables to add to a stew to feed them all. She wondered briefly if the girls had baked any fresh bread. So as she wondered how best to answer Wannge'e's question, she felt a little wounded by it, that they would think she'd abandon them after all they'd been through.

"Of course not," she said, her voice soft with

dismay and bewilderment. "I've no intention of leaving you here. I'm taking you home to the Bannock, as I promised. I want my son to meet Paddake'e and Ese-ggwe'na'a and Mi'wasa knows this. Indeed, he has agreed to come with us."

The girls looked at her, then Poongatse began to cry. She sat down beside Madeleine as Harry crawled onto her lap, but Wannge'e stood back.

"What's this all about?" Madeleine asked, taken aback. "Why would you think this? Why would you doubt me?"

"Because we're not blind," Poongatse said softly. "We can see what you feel for him and now it won't be the same with him here."

Madeleine almost smiled. They were insecure about Ryder being here, yet had she not made it clear to them, even after all this time, just how much she loved them? They were her family! They had shared storms together, they had known freezing days and nights along with the heat, hunger, fatigue and fear as well as Harry's illness. They had fought against men who would have done them harm.

But they were right in one thing. It could never be the same now that Ryder was back.

It was no longer the four of them. The girls knew that Ryder would demand her attention and they knew Madeleine would give it freely.

"But my plans haven't changed," Madeleine said, embracing them both.

"You're still going to be a part of my life, along with Harry. And think on this, Mi'wasa will be able to help us hunt. He'll also head north to the Mandan, to help us find Deinde'-paggwe and her daughter. Then we head west to the Snake River

Plain, because we both want to go home, just as much as you do. As for Te'tukhe, Wesa'shangke and Aishi-waahni', well I'm sure they'll speak of their plans when they're ready," she paused, frowning.

"But we leave here as planned in the first week of spring."

Madeleine glanced at Wannge'e and understood with some shock that this wasn't only about Ryder.

It was also about Te'tukhe and she understood in that moment, that Wannge'e and Te'tukhe had become lovers.

*

They spent less than two weeks with the Omaha. During that time, Madeleine often felt like she was living in a dream. Wannge'e and Te'tukhe now lived openly together, sharing the bigger teepee with Poongatse, leaving Madeleine, Ryder and Harry in the smaller one, although some nights Poongatse crept into their teepee. Wesa'shangke and Aishi-waahni' continued to sleep within the lodge of one of the Chiefs.

Everyone was surprised by the relationship between Wannge'e and Te'tukhe, not only because of their age difference, but because they all knew Te'tukhe as an often cold, emotionally hard man. It didn't seem to bother Wannge'e that this was a fleeting thing, that Te'tukhe would leave soon and head back to the Wazhazhe with his brother and cousin.

Madeleine spoke with Wannge'e one day about the heartbreak which lay ahead if she continued to seek Te'tukhe's attention, yet the girl was unbothered by it.

"I don't care what his reasons are for being with me," she argued, her voice soft yet defiant. "I love him. I don't care how long I have with him, I'll take what he offers and be grateful for it."

"Wannge'e, be careful with your love," Madeleine said softly. "Because Te'tukhe isn't a man who will be careful with yours. You know full well how much I love him, but I also know him to be hard and ruthless and I've no wish to see you get hurt."

A shadow crossed over Wannge'e's lovely face at Madeleine's words, then she nodded. "I know you want me to be happy Esa-mogo'ne', but I know this about Te'tukhe already. When he lived with the Shoshone we all saw the kind of man he was, but I accept him for who he is and love him for it. I know he is hard, I know he is fiercely independent and I know full well he will kill without remorse if he must. But I also trust him, because his word is his truth and in his own way I believe he loves me."

Madeleine's heart lurched with pain on hearing those words even as Wannge'e reached out to take her hand in her own.

"I know you mean well Esa-mogo'ne', but I fell in love with him the moment I saw him, that day he rode into the Shoshone and Bannock village. I was a child no older than ten, yet I felt him here," she put her fist to her heart, her eyes deep pools of emotion, pleading with Madeleine to understand.

"He stole my heart with his tattoos and scalp lock and his arrogance. So you see, it is hopeless Esa-mogo'ne'. I know he'll never settle down, but if he were to ask me to travel the world with him, you know I would go. When he leaves for the Wazhazhe or Comanche lands without me, then I'll be grateful for the short time we've had together and I promise you, I'll have no regrets."

"But what if there's a babe?" Madeleine asked, desperate for Wannge'e to see this in all its truth.

The girl bowed her head. "Then so be it, Esa-mogo'ne'. I shall have a part of him with me always, until the end of my days and if that makes me weak, then so be it. But I'll be there for him no matter what he asks and if that is my fate, then I accept it willingly."

Madeleine closed her eyes, feeling hopeless, knowing that such a love was dangerous, because she'd felt the same way about Ryder. Hadn't she left everything and everyone she loved to be with him?

She spoke to Ryder one day of Wannge'e and Te'tukhe's burgeoning love affair and he surprised her by being as concerned about it as she was. "I have already spoken with my brother. I asked him to take care with Wannge'e and in reply, he said she's special, that he won't hurt her. So let it play out as it will, Madeleine," he said, then added softly. "Life isn't the same out here as it is in England. Life is hard, and men and women take what they can when they have it. Wannge'e might be considered a child in England, but she isn't a child out here. Age means nothing in the wild. So leave it be."

But if Te'tukhe consumed Wannge'e's life, Ryder was like a blazing torch moving through Madeleine's life. She found herself watching him, waiting for him, still unable to believe he was here. At night when he turned to her in the privacy of their own teepee, as Harry lay deep in sleep on the other side of the chamber, they came together in silence, desperate, the years lost between them forgotten.

Madeleine found pleasure in simple things, like cooking him meals after years of having their meals cooked by servants in their homes in England. Or watching Ryder take Harry for rides on his horse, the little boy held secure before him. Or when Ryder walked around the Omaha village with the child sitting on his shoulders, the boy's chubby hands holding tight within Ryder's thick dark hair.

During these times, Madeleine saw how alike they were, in the way they moved, the way they pushed their hair off their foreheads, the way they threw back their heads and laughed.

But Te'tukhe, Wesa'shangke and Aishi-waahni' also claimed the child's attention, although Madeleine was startled sometimes by Ryder's possessiveness as he watched the men with his son. It surprised her, because he wasn't someone to begrudge another man anything, much less his brothers spending time with the little boy.

She knew it was because of the years Ryder had lost with Harry, so she said nothing. Besides, the relationship between Harry and his uncles and Aishi-waahni' was destined to be short-lived.

Those few weeks together at the Omaha village became a time of hope and endings, of letting go the past and looking towards the future, even as Te'tukhe, Wesa'shangke and Aishi-waahni' began to make plans to leave.

*

One evening towards the end of February, as Madeleine sat outside with the girls and Harry, roasting four wild rabbits and three prairie chickens which the girls had caught in their snares, she looked up on hearing Ryder's laughter. He was in the company of his brothers and the Comanche, all of them having been out on the river for most of the afternoon fishing with the Omaha. Madeleine watched as he walked towards her and as he caught her gaze and held it, she saw the promise of their future laid bare before them.

She sat unmoving, taking in the strength of his well-muscled body, the easy stride of those long legs dressed in buckskin, the broad width of his shoulders, the day old growth of whiskers on that handsome face, the generous mouth that knew so well how to kiss and pleasure her, those eyes, dark lashed and blue, full of love and lust and the sheer joy of the day. She hoped he saw something similar in her, although as she stared at him, she was still in awe even now that he was here, almost two weeks after he'd arrived. After so many years of not knowing where he was or even if he was alive, it was a shock sometimes to see him there.

The men joined them by the fire, the eight of them sitting around the two firepits as the meat slowly roasted above the flames, as piñon nut bread baked near the hot ashes along with wild mushrooms and some chokeberry cakes Poongatse had made. When some Omaha women approached with several dozen strips of smoked venison, the men took it eagerly, as this meat was part of their share of the deer killed during their recent hunt with the Omaha.

But as night drew down and they ate their fill, listening to each other's stories of the day, the drums and chanting started over in the Omaha village. They would join the rest of the village later, as the celebrations for the end of winter took place around the Huthuga.

Ryder moved to add more wood to the two fires as the chill of the evening settled, when Harry suddenly left Poongatse's arms and for the first time went willingly to Ryder, snuggling into his warmth. When Ryder brought out a simple toy made of twigs and bound together by rawhide string, a toy he'd found months ago near a lake many miles south of here, Harry squealed with delight, recognizing it as something he'd played with when they stayed with the Kansa.

Madeleine also recognized the toy as something Mi'nanpanta might have made for his son. But surely it was a coincidence, nothing more. Until Ryder mentioned he'd found it near a lake, in the same place he'd met up with Wesa'shangke and Aishi-waahni'. If Ryder had indeed camped in the same place where she'd stayed with the Kansa, then Madeleine was sure it was the work of the ancient one.

As twilight settled and before they joined the Omaha, the men brought out their pipes. Madeleine joined them, packing her favorite pipe with tobacco, the one made by Dosa'huih all those years ago. She glanced over at Ryder, surprised to find him watching her and knew he was thinking of those other times when they'd sat together, smoking their pipes. She smiled and leaned into him, feeling her own contentment mirrored in Ryder's eyes.

When Te'tukhe asked when they planned to ride for the Mandan, Wesa'shangke and Aishi-waahni' leaned forward, eager to hear Ryder's answer.

Madeleine knew what he'd say, because they'd talked about this earlier.

"Less than a week, no more," he said. "The weather's starting to turn for the better and the sooner we make it to the Mandan and trade for Deinde'-paggwe and her daughter, the sooner we reach the Bannock. We hope to reach the Snake River Plain no later than November, as we've no desire to spend a winter camped out somewhere in the northern wilderness."

The men remained silent, as Ryder asked them of their own plans. It was Wesa'shangke who answered, his voice grim.

"We've decided not to return to the Wazhazhe, because if the pox is making its way upriver, we've no care to travel south or risk taking the disease back to the Comanche. So now we think we'll head north, to spend some time with Allard Lemoine's family at the Lakota. We don't know how long he planned to stay with the Wazhazhe, but we can stop over with the Hŭŋkpapha before we head south for the Comanche. If we head home that way, we avoid all European settlements."

He glanced over at Te'tukhe, who was watching Ryder and Madeleine.

"What my brother is saying," Te'tukhe said, "if you are agreeable to it and will have us, we shall accompany you north, for some of the way at least."

Madeleine turned to Ryder in astonishment, then looked back at Te'tukhe.

"I don't understand," she said softly, even as Te'tukhe smiled.

"I made a promise to you that I would accompany you north," he answered, watching her. "Although I had no definite plans to go as far north as the Mandan, I shall keep my promise to you. But there is another reason. Like Mi'wasa, I thought of Ese-ggwe'na'a as my brother and if he is unable to claim his daughter himself, then we shall do it for him," he paused to look at Ryder.

"The three of us spoke of this while you were away at that fort and we are all in agreement, although none of us can guarantee we'll get that girl back. But I know this northern country better than any of you, along with the people who live in it and I don't think you can rescue her without our help."

In the silence that followed, Te'tukhe turned to Wannge'e, acknowledging her publicly, proving his feelings for her in front of everyone. Very few men would have done that, or ask the opinion of any woman. "Tell my brothers and cousin of the attack on your village five years ago."

Wannge'e looked unsure for a moment, then she began to speak. She told of the viciousness of the attack, most of it taking place before dawn while the Bannock and Shoshone slept. She spoke of men, women and children falling under the strike of axes, lances and musket fire. She spoke of the women and girls taken as slaves, of their lives with the Hidatsa before being sold to the Mandan.

There was a moment of silence around the camp as the girl bowed her head and began to cry. Then Te'tukhe glanced at Madeleine.

"I understand now why you cannot leave Deinde'-paggwe at the Mandan," he said softly. "Because I must avenge her brother's death. Huu'aidi was my friend."

Madeleine nodded, wiping away her own tears,

even as Poongatse cried softly.

"Deinde'-paggwe was like my own child, I watched her grow from a babe. I cannot return to the Bannock and do nothing to help her," she glanced over at Poongatse and Wannge'e. "Mi'wasa and I thought the girls could take Harry on alone into the west, perhaps to the Ponca. They share the same familial and linguistic ties as the Wazhazhe, Ugákhpa and Omaha so they'll be safe enough while we ride north to the Mandan."

Te'tukhe shook his head. "You cannot do that. You cannot leave them to ride on alone, it's too dangerous. Along with the Mandan, Hidatsa and Pawnee you have the Cheyenne, Blackfeet and many other Sioux tribes living in those northern territories," he paused, frowning. "Besides, from the Mandan you'd be backtracking for weeks to get to the Ponca. Your plan doesn't make sense to me."

He glanced over at his brother and cousin before looking back at Ryder and Madeleine. "Let the girls and the boy go north with Wesa'shangke and Aishi-waahni' to Allard Lemoine and the Lakota. They will be safe there, until we can meet them. No-one need go to the Ponca and waste precious weeks backtracking."

Wesa'shangke and Aishi-waahni' nodded in agreement, as if they'd already discussed this. Madeleine turned to Ryder in bewilderment. She had expected to ride to the Mandan alone, leaving the girls and Harry in a safe place until she could join them later, with Deinde'-paggwe and her daughter.

Now it seemed a small army would ride alongside her, for part of the way at least.

She looked back at Te'tukhe. "You would come

to the Mandan with us?" she asked him, her voice brittle with emotion.

Te'tukhe almost smiled, softening that hard, handsome face. He shrugged then looked over at Ryder, Wesa'shangke and Aishi-waahni'.

"It's been many years since I saw my brothers and cousin Esa-mogo'ne', so I think it's important I spend time with them. One day I shall return to the Wazhazhe, but for now, I ride to the Mandan with you and Mi'wasa."

Madeleine felt Ryder tremble beside her with emotion and she leaned into him as he looked at the three men sitting opposite him, along with the two Bannock girls. Then he nodded.

"I agree your plan works, yet how do we thank you?" he said. "There's only a handful of people in the world I'd trust with my son's life and I'm looking at five of them. So! It is decided. You ride northwest to the Lakota and wait for us there," he said before turning to Madeleine and Te'tukhe. "While we ride north to the Mandan."

Snake River Plain: April 1805

Spring arrived in all its scented glory in the vast mountain range of the Pacific Northwest. The dense evergreen forests swept away across lower foothills while deciduous trees bore the color of spring growth.

Between the mountain ranges lay a wide, fertile valley, named by the Shoshone as the Snake River Plain. Its name was taken from the Snake River which made its way through the center of the valley, before threading its way between other forests and valleys to eventually meet up with the mighty Columbia River in the distant northwest.

Soaring high above the river was a massive bald eagle, a female of almost thirty years, the length of her body more than three feet, her wingspan close to seven. She drifted easily on the cold air currents, moving with grace and beauty despite her size and as she turned and drifted further west she uttered a high-pitched cry. The sound echoed out across the valley and although it seemed she was the only living creature here, she was not alone. The valleys and forests bore an abundance of life, from the fish that filled the river and its subsidiaries, to massive herds of deer numbering in their thousands that thrived within the forest, to the families of bears, moose and wolves.

The eagle turned suddenly and dived, taking a fish from the river in her claws, before flapping those giant wings and heading towards the great pine forests and her nest high in the trees.

On a northern ridge, a pack of thirty wolves stopped on hearing the eagle's cry, before continuing their climb up the mountain through deep snow which still lingered from the brutal winter. They were heading towards a distant rocky outcrop, where a huge white wolf lay deep in sleep.

The creature was oblivious to everything, including the approaching wolves, as he dreamed of a woman clad in buckskin, her fur lined moccasins silent in the snow, her voice soft and familiar as she called to him. In his sleep the great wolf trembled as she reached out to embrace him. He whined softly, then abruptly woke, blinking as he lifted his great head, his stunning yellow eyes looking out across the land.

Then he turned and saw the pack of wolves a few miles below his perch. He stood up, growling deep within his throat, then threw back his great head and howled, the sound drifting out across the plain and river below, echoing out across the mountains and forests and every creature that heard it, paused and looked up.

He was a beauty at nine years, yet his body showed his age along with the battles he'd fought over the past five years. He turned back to look at the wolves below him, then reluctantly left his quiet perch on the rocky outcrop and headed on down the mountain, to meet his pack.

On the following page is an excerpt from the next book in the series, *When the Wolf Breathes*. But because it's an excerpt, it might change.

Excerpt of When the Wolf Breathes

in the wild: April 1805

It was Harry who saw them first and there was a sense of urgency about my son as he stood up and pointed towards the forest.

"*Mama*," he cried.

We rose quickly from where we'd been resting and saw the group of riders on a hill way in the distance, beyond the tree line. They were at least two miles north of our temporary camp, but we'd been expecting these riders. We'd been waiting for them, although they couldn't see us because we were deep within the trees, having chosen this high spot as a look out, knowing they must pass this way to get to the ridge.

I'd seen them first, just before we left the ridge. They had been nothing more than a smudge on a distant rolling hill, many miles north of us but clearly heading our way. Which gave us a reason to move, to get off the ridge and seek shelter in the trees.

Te'tukhe and Wesa'shangke stood beside Ryder as he peered through his spyglass, twisting the canisters to get a clearer view of the men before they disappeared back under cover of the trees.

"Fur trappers, four of them with two packhorses apiece, loaded down with furs," he said, passing the spyglass to Wesa'shangke.

I reached for Harry as he made a move to sprint into the trees even as Wannge'e and Poongatse began to pack away the waterskins, smoked meat and chokeberry cakes we'd unpacked when we stopped here less than an hour ago. When Wesa'shangke offered me the spyglass I took it and saw for myself that the riders would be here soon enough. They had only to reach the valley below us and climb the hill, a short ride from where we now stood.

If you liked *When the Wolf Dreams*, check out *When the Wolf Breathes*, the next book in the series
https://www.amazon.com/gp/product/B0773MHBQ9/ref=dbs_a_def_rwt_hsch_vapi_tkin_p1_i6

And if you want more, you'll find everything you need to know about Sadie here www.sadieconall.com including free previews on all her books as well as excerpts. You can join up for her newsletter, find social media links, her Amazon page, Goodreads page and if you want to contact her personally by email, then go here, sadieconallauthor@gmail.com

Made in United States
North Haven, CT
23 August 2023

40670501R00205